MURDER IN CITY HALL

MARY JANE RUSSELL

MURDER IN CITY HALL
© 2010 BY MARY JANE RUSSELL

All rights reserved. No part of this book may be reproduced in printed or electronic form without permission. Please do not participate in or encourage piracy of copyrighted materials in violation of the author's rights. Purchase only authorized editions.

ISBN 10: 1-935216-13-9
ISBN 13: 978-1-935216-13-1

FIRST PRINTING: 2010

THIS TRADE PAPERBACK IS PUBLISHED BY
INTAGLIO PUBLICATIONS
WALKER, LA USA
WWW.INTAGLIOPUB.COM

This is a work of fiction. Names, characters, places, and incidents are the product of the author's imagination or are used fictitiously, and any resemblance to actual persons, living or dead, businesses, companies, events, or locales is entirely coincidental.

Credits

Executive Editor: Tara Young
Cover design by Tiger Graphics

Dedication

For the city of Lynchburg, Virginia—my hometown and former employer—and for the seldom recognized women who work behind the scenes in local government. Peggy, Melissa, Curly, Debbie, Stephanie, Annette, and Ricarda—you guys made it bearable

And for my beloved Dolly Louise—may her paws rest in peace—who purred me through half of my city hall years.

Acknowledgments

Many thanks to the men who helped me enter their world of engineering, local government, and economic development—Lee Cobb, Fred Armstrong, Charlie Evans, Jim Amos, Greg Poff, Tom Wilson, Bob Torian, and posthumously Charlie Parker, Ed Moyers, Harry Cumby, and Terry Reid.

Repeated thanks to Sheri Payton and Kate Sweeney at Intaglio Publications; and my editor, Tara Young.

And, as always, I'm indebted to Joyce M. Coleman for her unfailing encouragement of my attempt at writing and her door that was always open to me at city hall.

PROLOGUE

Molly Hamilton felt as though she was forcing one foot in front of the other. She tugged at the strap of the OD messenger bag across her body until comfortable. She had parked her Jeep on the top deck of the garage at exactly 8:23 a.m. This allowed her just enough time to walk to city hall and set foot inside the front door by the prerequisite 8:30. She would only do the work required of her; she would not put any extra effort into her job—if she still had a job. She had spent most of the night convincing herself that this strategy would work, at least temporarily.

Molly thought about Chris as she began the three-block walk up and over the hill sitting above the center of downtown; they would weather this. Molly would find another job as soon as possible. She couldn't stay on with the city after what had happened the day before. She had finally told Jack Sampson exactly what she thought of him as a man and a boss, and it hadn't been pretty. Molly couldn't recall the last time she had so completely lost her temper. She had been so angry that leaving city hall and walking to the garage the previous night was a blur.

Molly glanced down. She had also forgotten to change into her usual business casual clothes that morning—she missed her lightweight cotton sweater. She wore the faded jeans and polo shirt she had donned to take a quick walk around the neighborhood. She tugged at the sleeve of her shirt to hide the bruise on her upper right arm.

"I'm a frickin' mess." She sighed as she crossed the street, then grimaced as she forgot and jammed her hand into the pocket of her jeans. She glanced at the Band-Aid on the back of her right hand. Jack's nail had scraped her during their argument. She thought her hand would never stop bleeding. She had ruined a good pair of khakis, as well as her favorite blue sweater, by sticking her hand in her pocket before realizing what had happened.

Molly glanced down the sloping hillside that the buildings and streets were terraced into. The ornamental pear trees were beginning to show leaves underneath the white blooms; the cherry trees showed the last of their spring pink. She glimpsed the front of city hall as she started down the long flight of spalled concrete steps connecting two east-west streets. There was a crowd milling about city hall and bright yellow tape tied between the handrails of the main entrance steps. The double doors were closed. Police and fire vehicles lined the street. Molly walked a little faster. Something must have set off the fire alarm; they might need her help with the building's systems.

A uniformed police officer was making his way through the crowd gathered along the sidewalk adjacent to the steps into the building. He appeared so young that he looked as though in grownup costume—the single stripe on his sleeve confirmed his line officer status. He held a notepad and wrote down everyone's name, department, and time they left work the day before.

Molly spotted Angela, the city attorney's paralegal. This was one of the first times Molly didn't feel in the mood to flirt with the buff black woman.

Angela began talking while Molly was twenty feet away. "Windy is fit to be tied. The police have cordoned off the side streets. She can't get to the handicapped parking spaces. She's cruising downtown trying to get Colonel Evans on the phone to give his men permission to let her through." Windy, aka Wyndham Perrow, had been so nicknamed in law school for her ability to talk nonstop about any subject.

"I know she hates wasting gas in that van." Molly glanced along the sidewalk. "I don't see any executive staff members. We know about Windy. Where are Jack, Campbell, and Barbara?"

Susan joined them as Molly spoke. "Barbara's in a meeting with the school administration. We think we have budget problems." She rolled her eyes before hugging Molly. "Hey, sweetie, I heard you had a rough day yesterday. Don't let them get to you. We're all behind you."

"How do you manage cute and perky this early?" Molly asked. "It must be a blond thing."

Susan punched Molly in the shoulder.

Donna was on Susan's heels. She had dark smudges beneath her eyes and less bounce than usual in her short brown curls. "I couldn't sleep last night for thinking about you and how much I hate that damn Jack." Her eyes bored into Molly's.

Molly didn't envy Donna sitting outside Jack Sampson's door all day; that was partly why Molly had waited until after normal office hours to talk to Jack the night before. It was well known among staff that neither Molly nor Jack usually left the building before 7 p.m.—Molly to work, Jack to appear to work.

"Amen to that." Tamika put her arm around Molly. "He's a son of a bitch. Somebody ought to catch Jack in the parking lot and beat the crap out of him."

"Or worse," Donna said softly as she looked at the young black woman. "At least you can get away with hating him outright. He needs you to operate the GIS system."

Tamika flashed an uncharacteristically wide grin. She was one of a handful of employees who knew the city's geographic information system intimately.

Molly shrugged, feeling like a referee. "I'm okay. Don't worry about what happened. If they want to take some of this work off of me, they're welcome to it."

"Yeah, just wait until they see how Eric screws it up." Susan shook her head. "He only made it as Jack's deputy director because you helped him with every project. He and Jack are on the way out from what I hear."

"City council will be telling us to go out with you and keep you happy so the work gets done properly when they figure out that boy is as empty as those big suits he likes to wear." Angela chuckled.

"Does anyone know why we're out here?" Molly asked. It was way past time to change the subject.

"I heard it's a bomb scare," Susan offered.

"I'm hoping the files in the attic are on fire. Spontaneous combustion is much better than the purge Windy keeps nagging me to do." Angela raised crossed fingers.

"I heard it's so a certain police officer can kick a certain engineer's butt for not taking her telephone calls last night." Chris Miller walked up behind Molly and waited for her to turn around to continue. "I worried about you half the night until I was able to at least drive by your house and see your Jeep out front. I didn't have time to knock on your door."

The other women drifted back to give the couple privacy.

Molly and Chris complemented each other. Molly had shoulder-length chestnut hair to Chris's chopped blond bob, green eyes to Chris's blue, and both were fit and in their mid-thirties.

Chris grabbed Molly by the belt. "What's the deal with blowing off my phone calls all night? You know I had no choice about working."

"What's the deal inside?"

"Damn it, Molly."

"Aren't we in enough shit because of that photograph making the rounds without adding lesbian drama to it? Damn camping trip." Molly looked around uncomfortably, not used to being the center of attention.

"Who the hell cares what anyone else thinks? Tell anyone who gives you grief that it's none of their damn business who you're in a relationship with, and if they even think about mistreating you, they'll have a lawsuit filed against them." Chris followed Molly as she tried to turn away from her. "Hey." Chris touched Molly's arm. "Talk to me."

Molly cringed at Chris's touch to her bruised arm. She lowered her voice. "Yesterday was really bad. I lost it with Jack. I'm talking yelling and bitch slapping."

Chris blinked rapidly. "And you couldn't tell me that last night?"

"I should have. I'm sorry. I don't want to have our first fight in front of everyone." Molly looked as though she had lost her last friend.

"How about our first making up?" Chris hugged Molly. "I was crazy with worry about you."

Molly wanted to tell Chris that she was not thinking clearly the night before and that she loved her. She wanted to tell Chris that true crazy was the thoughts going through her head the previous day. Molly held her breath, trying to calm down. All she could manage was to think how good it would feel to be in Chris's arms.

Chris's cell phone rang. She answered it, holding her hand up to Molly to wait. Chris frowned as she ended the call. "The homicide team is activated." She made sure no one was close enough to overhear. "There's been a suspicious death in the building." She inclined her head toward city hall.

Molly gasped.

"I'm sorry I didn't have time to come over last night and talk through all of this. I know it's a bad situation. Just remember that I love you." Chris stared meaningfully into Molly's eyes before walking away. Chris waved at the baby-faced patrol officer.

Molly rejoined her co-workers.

"Tell me you didn't just break up with that woman." Angela put her hands on her hips.

"Just a fight," Molly said.

"Dumbass," Tamika said, offering no softening of the insult.

Susan smacked the back of Molly's head.

Molly's mind reeled. Who was dead inside the building? She knew who was missing from the sidewalk. "Thank God, you know where Windy is."

The others looked at her questioningly.

"Someone's dead in there."

Donna's face lost all color.

Molly dug in her messenger bag for her cell phone. "Answer, answer," she chanted.

"Hello?"

"Jeez. Where are you?" She looked at the others and shrugged. "Eric," she said.

"I'm at home. Erin and Robin are sick. I don't know if I'm nauseous from looking after them or coming down with the same crud they have. Damned stomach flu that the kids are passing around at the child care center. I really get my money's worth there so that Robin can have time for all her precious volunteer meetings. I left a message on Jack's voice mail and e-mail after I couldn't reach him at home this morning as usual. What's going on?"

Molly watched as Tom came to the doors of city hall. The city manager stepped out on the landing and motioned everyone closer.

"I'll call you back." Molly told Eric, ending the call without waiting for him to respond.

Tom cleared his throat. "You may go home for the day. Please stay close to your contact numbers that HR has on record. Tomorrow will be business as usual. I am saddened to announce that Jack Sampson, the director of community development, is dead. I can offer no further details because of the ongoing investigation."

"Well, you're likely the only one who's sad." Donna said it so only Molly heard her.

Chris appeared at Molly's side and pulled her away from the others. "Tell me that building maintenance is yanking my chain when they say there's no way to know who's been in this building overnight."

Molly felt as though in slow motion. "All they have is a list of who's been issued a dimple key for the deadbolt. Council has been too tight to approve funds for a card reader system. I tried a sign-in notebook that no one paid any attention to. God help risk management if there's a disaster and the building has to be evacuated." Molly spoke by rote.

"Or if accountability is needed." Chris studied Molly. "Are you all right?"

Molly shook her head. "I was in Jack's office last night."

Chris stared. "What?"

"The throwdown with Jack was *last night*. We had a hell of an argument. He came at me. I pushed him. He fell back and hit his head. I thought he was okay. He was still yelling and threatening me when I walked out." Molly spoke with flat effect, as though not believing the words tumbling out of her mouth.

Chris grabbed Molly's arm, noticing the bruise. "Don't say another word."

Molly shivered. "I must be one of the last people to see him alive."

Chris placed her hand over Molly's mouth. "Careful. Say only what you know for a fact. You left him alive, right?"

Molly nodded.

Chris pointed to the police officer. "Tell him what time you left Jack's office. Don't freak when he asks you to go to the station for questioning and a statement." Chris couldn't shake the bad feeling that came over her as she watched Molly approach the officer. It had taken only nine months for Molly to become an integral part of her life.

CHAPTER ONE

Molly stared at the mound of boxes that filled the kitchen. She felt eyes on her and looked about the room until she found the source. Dolly, her Maine Coon tabby and best friend for the past eight years, was perched on top of the stack nearest to her.

"I know. I haven't learned a damn thing about relationships, have I?"

Dolly stared down at her with what Molly thought of as the cat's Lauren Bacall look as though imperious that her human needed to ask the obvious.

"Why does a really good second date compel me to talk about renting a U-Haul and moving in together? I am such a dumbass."

Molly sighed. She thought she marked all the boxes with some idea of the contents. Standing in the doorway between kitchen and living room, she learned differently. Chances were she hadn't been thinking too clearly when she packed most of her possessions. Funny how a bad breakup and needing to move as quickly as possible out of someone else's house shot organizational skills to hell. Not to mention the distraction of the thirty-year debt she giddily committed herself to just to have someplace of her own to go.

"Don't worry. I think I know which of the boxes has the Science Diet in it." She waited for Dolly to cross the stacks with delicate leaps, finally selecting the highest box in the pile farthest from the front of the house to turn around twice and settle onto for a nap. "If not, I made sure to find out that the pet store three blocks away carries it and is open late tonight."

Dolly ignored her.

It was taking the movers two days to have Molly settled in. The three black men seemed far more concerned about her furniture than she was. She tried to tell them that *yes* the pieces were old but *no* the collection was not valuable. She had started out by searching for abandoned pieces to refinish while in her college apartment. While she lived with Sarah, she added a few more, again refinishing furniture set on the curb for refuse collection—a habit borne from her frugal upbringing that embarrassed Sarah. Lately, Molly watched craigslist for furniture or furnishings people wanted to be rid of for a fraction of the purchase price. Her greatest coup had been the acquisition of an oak rolltop desk sold by a lifelong railroad employee's widow.

Each piece of resurrected furniture was wrapped in plastic and separated with heavy blankets when loaded onto the moving truck. Consequently, the men unloaded the boxes last and filled the kitchen since no other furniture went into that room. They halfheartedly unloaded a few chairs before breaking the news that their shift was over; August had provided a brutal day for physical labor. For all their care with her furniture, they were unconcerned about leaving her without a bed to sleep in the first night in her new home. Molly was so tired, it didn't matter. She unrolled her requisite sleeping bag—bought for bonfire parties with no intention of camping—in the living room near the hearth with the street light as a nightlight and felt herself cozy as she settled on the soft layers still wearing shorts and a T-shirt. Thank goodness she was moving in when the nights cooled the house enough to make the days bearable without central air conditioning.

Molly almost didn't miss Sarah. At least that was what she tried to convince herself. The breakup had been as much her fault as Sarah's; it always was. Of course, Molly moved in too soon. In fact, her first hint of the mistake she was making happened on the day she moved. Molly made what she considered an innocent joke about her last girlfriend; Sarah responded by letting the screen door close on Molly's arm. Molly accepted it as her own fault for a bad joke.

What hurt beyond mending was that Sarah started seeing someone else before telling Molly she was fed up with her long hours at the office, her bringing more work home, and her need to swing by construction sites on the weekend. Molly couldn't help that she loved being a civil engineer. She thrived on working for a local municipality that was small enough to allow her to design a little of everything—roads, utility lines, site plans, and buildings. A typical firm would plug her into one specialty until she was bored out of her mind by her work. This way, work was a continuous challenge to prove that she could handle any project. She loved a challenge to her mind. A challenge to her emotions was altogether different. Emotions she would just as soon shove aside and not have to deal with. In all fairness to Sarah, Molly was surprised they lasted over three years. Typically, Molly wore out her welcome with women after two years when she began to lapse into indifference. "Well, at least I've never cheated on anyone."

Molly sighed as she walked through the long narrow living room and looked out the front storm door. She might as well watch for the return of the moving van as start something she would have to stop in the middle of. She waved at the woman across the street tiptoeing out in her housecoat for her newspaper. Most of her neighbors appeared to be retirees, which was good considering how little Molly would be home. They wouldn't mind keeping an eye out for her or the house.

She was almost at the end of the block. Her house faced a narrow street with a sidewalk on her side and a cul-de-sac just past her driveway. Her driveway went down at a forty-five degree angle from the street and ended with a concrete retaining wall anchored into the ground ten feet below. If Molly felt brave, she might park on the slope in good weather.

Her Realtor swore that the previous owner had been able to make the sharp turn at the bottom of the driveway and park his sports car in the small garage. Molly wouldn't attempt that maneuver with her Jeep on a bet. She glanced at the printout of the floor plan taped to the opened wooden door; the garage was barely eight feet wide. The movers teased her every time they came in, knowing she had already planned exactly where she wanted everything as it came off the truck. She didn't mind paying them for back-breaking work, but she wasn't wasteful of their time or her money. What amused the men was that everything fit perfectly. She managed to get room names on boxes if not a list of contents.

She made the circuit of the first floor of the 1,300-square-foot house, killing time by pacing. As sure as she left the house for a quick breakfast, the movers would show up. She paused in the kitchen and munched on a Pop Tart she had thought to pack in the box with the coffee maker—the first appliance she had unpacked the night before. She glanced up to see if the cat had moved. "You can wait for me." The only sound she heard was gentle snores from Dolly.

The living room was rectangular with a fireplace on the long exterior wall and steps to the second floor on the long interior wall. She loved the six big windows spaced around the room taking most of the exterior wall space but leaving perfect locations for two-shelf bookcases to line the two exterior walls except for a break for the fireplace. A swinging door led into the original kitchen. The appliances were old but working, and that was all that mattered to her—it was not as though she would spend much time cooking. The Realtor repeatedly apologized for the lack of dishwasher and couldn't understand that Molly didn't want or need one.

There was open space at the end of the counter for two stools in front of the radiator—perfect for dining. The door on the back wall of the house led from the kitchen to the deck that overlooked a tree-filled backyard with little grass to mow fifteen feet below. The other door in the kitchen led into what had been a dining room that Molly was going to use for her bedroom. She thought that a chandelier over her bed would make a good conversation piece even if a ceiling fan would be more practical.

A small square hall separated bedroom from den and opened into a bathroom and the living room.

The den on the front corner of the house had thin paneling covering plaster walls she didn't want to know the condition of. The front wall of the den was a double window surrounded by built-in bookcases.

Molly smiled. She knew she bought the house because of all of the bookcases. She had saved every book since she was a child—from her first Dr. Seuss books and paperbacks she bought from the Scholastic Book Club through the books she went to sales for now. Her mother taught her to read before she started kindergarten and Molly never lost her love of words on paper.

Words had been the bridge that connected Molly and her mother to the outside world after Molly's father walked out on them when she was eleven. Mother and daughter had lost themselves in school activities; Molly's mother had been a teacher. During college, Molly's reading was mainly textbooks—she kept all of them also.

Upstairs were a tiny bedroom and half bath that gave her claustrophobia with only gable end windows and sloped ceilings. It would do for a guest room on the rare occasions she had company. The basement was dank and smelled of dog, likely to be ventured into only to use the washer and dryer.

Molly also knew that she bought the house because it was small. She would not be able to have a "roommate." She looked at Dolly. "I know, for crying out loud, to just say no to girlfriends for a while."

Dolly opened one eye briefly.

Molly returned to the front door. She considered herself reasonably attractive—no great beauty but inheriting enough of the family's Irish blood to give her thick chestnut hair, green eyes, oval face, and medium build. She kept her hair cut in a long choppy bob just above her shoulders so she could pull it back in a ponytail when needed. She wasn't sure where the predilection for freckles came from, but she had just enough to be offered to play connect-a-dot in an entertaining fashion. She was five feet six inches tall, tried to keep her weight below 140 pounds, and turned thirty-five next month.

Her father and his second family, as well as assorted cousins, were in Michigan and did not understand why she stayed in Virginia after attending college in a small mountain community. Molly knew that her mother's grave in Michigan was why she remained in Virginia.

Molly first worked for a private engineering firm in the same town as the college until she passed her professional engineer's exam; it was the company's practice to work license-seeking engineers sixty or more hours a week while they honed their college studies. She then accepted a job in a city of 45,000 that was halfway between skiing in West Virginia and sunning on the North Carolina beaches—the best of all worlds as far as Molly was concerned. The only challenge was taking time off from work to actually do something on the weekend besides sneak into the office to catch up.

"At least I won't have as far to drive now. I can even catch a bus if I hike up the street." She was five minutes from downtown where she worked in city hall.

Molly returned to the kitchen and squeezed between the stacks of boxes so that she was able to stroke the black and tan cat affectionately. "You and me, Dolly. Enjoy the few days I've taken off. I know Jack has projects piling up and waiting for me when I go back next week. Busy is good. Busy will keep me out of trouble."

Dolly gave her what Molly referred to as her mother's over-the-glasses look, implying improbability.

Molly heard the hum of the truck motor and knew the guys were on the way with the last of her possessions. It was good to be home. She was fine. She didn't need Sarah or anyone else in her life. Molly was certain that Jack Sampson would keep her occupied.

CHAPTER TWO

Molly carefully balanced the project notebook, a legal pad, handouts, and cup of coffee as she left her office. She knew from bitter experience not to be late to Jack Sampson's Monday morning staff meeting. Why he couldn't wait until the middle of the week when most contractors weren't trying to catch up on phone calls to schedule work for the coming week was beyond her. Of course, it could always be worse; he could really show his disdain of them and have the meeting late on Friday. Likely the only reason he didn't was because he was the one notorious for ducking out at lunch for a long weekend. Molly often fretted that she knew Jack too well, having worked for him almost eight years.

She eased past the corner office and heard Jack on the telephone with his wife—the only woman he spoke to civilly. She didn't want to understand that relationship and suspected that Shirley ruled Jack at home and Jack took it out on them at work. She went to the opening in the five-foot-tall partition walls just outside of Jack's office. Donna Brooks rolled her eyes as she turned briefly from her computer screen when Molly whistled at her.

"Agenda?" Molly asked.

"He just gave it to me in longhand. I have ten whole minutes to make it look like he came in on time and ready for his own damn meeting." Donna returned to the keyboard. She shook the short frosted corkscrew curls that kept her hair off her neck. Her dark tan was a result of a tanning bed during the week and working in her yard or vegetable garden most of the weekend.

"We live to serve." Molly chuckled when Donna raised her hand with middle finger extended.

It was a well-known secret that the lowest-paid women in city hall were the very ones who kept the work flowing. Donna was ready for a promotion and Molly intended to help her despite Jack's dependence on Donna in an administrative job.

Molly continued along the short middle stretch of the U-shaped hallway. No one was in the staff kitchen. The small conference room beyond Donna was vacant; Jack held on to the space as a status symbol, preferring to hold private meetings away from his office. Molly glanced into the next office. Campbell Chamberlain was not at his desk. Molly worried about Campbell, knowing how he struggled with advanced rheumatoid arthritis and the drug experimentation by his doctor. She knew that the utilities director was trying to hold his work life together for two more years until he could take early Social Security retirement, as well as draw on his full city pension.

She tapped on the partition end walls and waved as she passed the row of three departmental administrative associates; they knew she would come back later to chat. Frankie Mahoney and Rusty Witt were deep in conversation; Molly heard utility rates mentioned several times and didn't interrupt the utilities accounts manager and the finance director.

"Hey." Molly stood in the doorway of Eric Blackstone's office.

His face brightened. "I won three sets of tennis yesterday. I love to pound my opponent into the court during the hottest time of day. My neighbor now hates me."

"Way to go?" Molly had given up trying to understand the way Eric thought. She inclined her head along the hallway—the large conference room was next door. "Come on."

"We have time." Eric opened his briefcase. "New baby pictures." He held up a thick envelope from the drugstore. "You were the one giving me grief last week for having none."

"You're killing me with your timing. I'll look at them later."

He waved the packet.

"Bring them with you then. I'm not setting all this stuff down until I'm in the conference room." She walked away, knowing he would follow.

Eric was true to form. He bounced out of his office, holding a legal pad with one remaining sheet of paper in his teeth as he juggled the photos and pulled free the back half of his shirt tail. He ran back for the soft drink that constituted his usual breakfast.

Molly looked him over as he entered the conference room. "Don't even try to get away with that. I refuse to listen to Jack rail for ten minutes about the dress code."

"Come on, it distracts him from all the boring crap he brings back to share with us from executive staff meetings. Got an extra pencil?"

Molly sighed. She glanced down at her outfit. Khaki suit with blue oxford shirt, low heel pumps—plain and comfortable, nothing to cause controversy. She carried a sharpened wooden pencil to back up her favorite mechanical one that matched the dark blue stripe in her shirt. She reluctantly surrendered the Black Warrior and made a mental note to bring two wooden pencils next week.

Eric's suits were at least one size too big for him; he preferred the longest jackets he could find. He looked like a boy playing dress-up in his father's suits, much less trying to experiment with his shirt tail. None of them believed he was twenty-nine. He laughingly told them about the multiple hair products he used for thirty minutes grooming every morning to achieve the slicked-back look and bragged about spending more on his long black hair than his wife did on the baby.

He kept the back and sides razor short with weekly salon trims but let the top grow below his ears so that it slicked back almost touching his collar. He was an inch shorter than Molly. He fit the mold of rising young white-collar executive with a wife who stayed at home with their six-month-old daughter. How they managed financially was beyond Molly. She persisted in the belief that he had a part-time job somewhere that he hadn't reported to HR. She hoped it didn't bite him later.

"Before you distract me with the most beautiful baby in central Virginia, take a look." Molly handed him a project checklist. "I worked on this at home last week when I was fed up with unpacking." Molly felt protective of Eric. She liked him instantly upon their introduction two years earlier and knew that as a business major he was in way over his head in managing federal grant-funded construction projects. She had cut her teeth on construction projects while working for a general contractor during high school—full time in summer and part time during the academic year.

"Damn, this steps us through everything needed for a construction project, from plan review to council approval, with a macro for cost estimating."

"One for each annual contract according to the way we take unit price bids from the road and pipe contractors." Molly held out her hand for the photographs.

He tossed the envelope in her direction. "I don't see any

difference in Erin's expression from one photo to the next, but Robin swears differently."

Molly juggled the catch, not wanting to play fifty-two-photograph pickup, and frowned at him.

He grinned. "You may have to help me stay awake during the meeting. The college kids are moving back into town. I hit all the bars last night." He jingled his pants pocket. "You wouldn't believe the money I make hustling pool games."

Molly flipped through the photographs. "Do you do anything at all at home to help with this darling child?"

Eric shrugged.

"I'm glad I brought more projects with me if this is all you two have to do on Monday morning. I can just imagine what you would be up to by the end of the week." Jack Sampson strode into the conference room with an armload of file folders and copies of the agenda still warm from the machine. "Molly, put those away until your own time at lunch."

"That she always works through," Eric said with a smile.

Molly knew better than to defend herself. It only made the meeting last longer and end with the same outcome. It was wise to choose battles carefully in local government.

Jack was one of those men who swore that his pants size had not changed in the last ten years. What he chose to ignore was the increased stomach bulge that overhung his belt. His body fat was out of control and his cholesterol levels barely within a safe range with medications. His diet was the only thing that hadn't changed in ten years. He was fifty-one years old and looked sixty, often debated dying his hair but was concerned it would make the thin spot on the back of his head more noticeable, and wore shirts that tested the thread strength holding the buttons on the front placket.

He glared at Molly. "About time you rejoined us. The GIS tech position is still empty. If you don't fill it, I will. I won't lose a position because we keep it vacant long enough to catch finance's attention."

Molly jotted a note to herself. "I'll have Ann pull the applications—internal first." She made another note to check that Donna had her résumé up to date and posted with HR. Donna would be perfect to learn the geographic information system from the ground up, then teach the rest of them in the community development department.

"Did you get moved in, Molly?" Eric smiled at her across the table. He knew her scheme to promote Donna and the need to distract Jack from personnel matters. He also knew that Molly had just been through a breakup with her partner of three years and that her partner was a woman. The key was that Jack knew none of this for sure. Jack believed he controlled the women in city hall with his male prowess. Most of the women who worked on the same floor with him learned quickly to allow Jack that fallacy, among others. It was all in knowing how to dance backward to his awkward lead and still make him look good—pathetic but a means of surviving poor management.

"I did, and I love being back in the city," Molly said.

"It looks better that way since the city pays your salary. Live here and contribute to the tax base that employs us all." Jack shuffled through the stack of folders and shoved one-third toward Eric and the rest to Molly.

Molly glanced at Donna's color-coded labels—three new residential subdivisions, two building renovations, and one industrial site. The previous week had been average in new project applications for early fall.

Jack tapped Eric's two folders. "I heard about a new round of recreational grants opening up after the first of next year. You need to research those and check if any apply to the bike trail or playing fields being discussed." He reached to the telephone in the center of the table and punched a frequently used extension. "Donna, join us in the conference room." He dialed again. "Rusty, we're ready."

Molly stared at Eric and raised her eyebrows. He shrugged.

Rusty Witt strolled into the conference room, glowing with the dark tan he managed by playing golf year-round. His skin tone was the only way he could pull off wearing the garish sport coats he marveled at finding at sale price. Today's jacket was school bus yellow. He grimaced at Molly when he took a seat at the table beside her. He leaned forward to brush off his trousers leg and whispered, "Sorry."

Donna entered the room. She relied on steno pads for all of her notes, even though she had given up using shorthand years ago. She was two years older than Molly with hair as curly as Molly's was straight. Donna was as straight as Molly was gay. "Yes, sir."

Jack nodded at Rusty.

Rusty cleared his throat and spoke as succinctly as he ran numbers through formulas. "We took the preliminary audit to the manager yesterday and found a discrepancy in line items between the summary and detail sheets in only one department."

Donna stiffened.

"It was ours." Jack hit the table with his fist. "It made me look as though I'm not capable of my job."

It was too early in the day and week for anyone to mention that the implied responsibility of a department head was accountability for everyone who worked for him no matter how work was delegated.

"I was to have checked the numbers and didn't get to it before my scheduled vacation to move. My bad." Molly looked about the room. "I have no problem telling Tom that."

"I have a problem with it. You don't initiate those types of conversations with the city manager. I'm the one who sat in front of the finance committee and looked like an idiot." He stared at Donna, as Rusty excused himself from the room. "This will be noted in your file. Don't count on a merit increase this year. That's all."

Donna left the room rapidly before she lost her temper and her job. They all heard her voice from the hallway. Jack chose to ignore the words that floated back at them. "Goddamned son of a bitch."

"Jack, that's not fair." Molly leaned forward in her chair. "Anyone can make a mistake. I should have come back in one afternoon and run the numbers with her."

Eric knew that Jack was not listening to either of them. "Or called me to do it. I didn't realize the figures were being submitted."

Jack waved his hand in dismissal. "Tom knew it wasn't my fault. I took care of it. It was just preliminary. Everyone had revisions to make."

Molly heard little else during the rest of the staff meeting. She had an e-mail waiting for her from Donna. The message's subject line was full of symbols, implying a lengthy string of curse words. The body was in all caps—"ONE OF THESE DAYS, HE IS GOING TO PUSH ME TOO DAMN FAR, AND I WON'T BE RESPONSIBLE FOR MY ACTIONS."

Molly knew that Donna would have to stand in a long line of employees in city hall who hated Jack Sampson.

CHAPTER THREE

Christine Miller didn't know what the sound was, but she resented it. She rolled over in bed and stared out of one eye at the collection of empty microwaveable food containers and imported beer bottles piled on the nightstand at the empty side of her bed. It didn't matter that she had slept alone for three years, she was most comfortable along the right edge of the queen-sized mattress.

"Who the fuck is it at nine thirty on Sunday morning?" She identified the sound as the knocker on the main door to her one-bedroom apartment.

Chris rolled out of bed and frowned at her reflection in the dresser mirror. Her blond hair looked as though someone had run an egg beater through it, her deep blue eyes were rimmed with dark shadows, and her cotton T-shirt and shorts had almost too many holes to go to the door in, but she didn't care.

"Wake me up and this is what you get, damn it." She had worked until two o'clock that morning on another fruitless stakeout. She stretched as she walked through the living room and flung open the door to the main hall. Curses died on her lips. "Julie!"

The redheaded seven-year-old stalked by Chris and went to the kitchen.

Julie's father, Spencer Davis, stood on the threshold and grinned, raising one eyebrow. "Did we wake you?"

"You piece of shit, why didn't you call first?"

Spencer whispered in Chris's ear as he passed her. "Check how many messages are on your cell phone that I'm guessing is turned off somewhere." He followed his daughter into the kitchen. "See, I told you she'd have cereal. We brought fresh milk." Spencer looked over his shoulder and held up the half-gallon of two percent. "No more lumpy cereal like last time."

Julie made a face. "Eww."

"How many times do I have to say I'm sorry? I apologize for

having spoiled milk. Okay?" Chris said.

"Okay." Julie poured corn flakes from the plastic container that kept the cereal fresh indefinitely.

Spencer poured the milk.

Chris found the bag of brown sugar in the cupboard and sprinkled the bowl.

Julie returned to the living room and focused on the large-screen plasma television Spencer had helped Chris pick out the previous winter.

"Disney is on twenty-four," Chris reminded Julie.

The television burst forth with giggles as the cartoons provided a mellow background to a typical Sunday morning.

"Big plans for today?" Spencer glanced around the apartment. "Want me to find a shovel?"

Chris mouthed a silent profanity. "There's a method to my mess. I have things sorted in boxes and like things in piles. I'll rent a storage unit eventually and move some of this out."

"This place is a damn cocoon. You could have shifted your equity into another house since you didn't want to keep Ruth's."

Chris made a face and raised her voice for Julie's sake. "Of course, I have plans—cereal and cartoons. I like your daughter's style."

Spencer stayed close to her. "How about going to the park with us? We'll hit the swings, then the bike trail. We can stop at the Cancer Awareness garden if you want."

Chris frowned. Spencer knew her too well—quiet thoughts at the garden had been her goal for the day.

Chris and Spencer had started on the police force at the same time and decided to become buddies rather than killing each other when their competitiveness surfaced in the academy; discovering they both enjoyed girl watching sealed their friendship. They still egged each other on but not maliciously. Chris continued with the police department, advancing to detective. Spencer commuted to law school and eventually passed the bar exam, finding the career he wanted with the commonwealth attorney's office. Along the way, he built his friendship with Chris and alienated his wife with the changes he was going through.

"I may just stay in today," Chris said.

"Aw, come on," Julie protested. "I brought my new kite that Pa bought me at the beach."

"Aw, come on," Spencer echoed. His hair was as red as his daughter's, casting no doubt who Julie's father was. He was four inches taller than Chris and trim, even though Chris teased him about the fifteen pounds he had gained due to a desk job and nearby vending machines. Chris used to be able to borrow his jeans when she wanted a slightly baggy look; now, his pants were big enough to slide over her hips. "Don't sit around here and brood. She wouldn't want you to."

Chris looked away. It had been three long years since Ruth lost her battle with pancreatic cancer. Chris was just beginning to soothe the sting of the memories of the last months of Ruth's life that had been a flurry of morphine IVs, emergency room visits, and hospice taking over their home.

"It's time for you to live again, honey." Spencer gave Chris a quick hug. There were no mixed signals between them—Spencer was straight and Chris gay and neither had any inclination to change. "You've mourned Ruth enough."

Enough, Chris thought ruefully. Ruth Wilson had been one of Chris's high school teachers. She had reached out to Chris when Chris's mother suffered the first of the strokes that would take her life in a year when Chris was fourteen. Ruth had made Chris wait until she was eighteen before taking her romantic overtures seriously. Ruth had been the first and only woman Chris had been in a relationship with; they had lasted thirteen years. Ruth had been a short, blond spitfire who had more use for Maker's Mark than doctors.

"You're a fine one to talk. How many dates have you been on since your divorce?" Chris kicked Spencer in the seat of his cargo shorts and continued toward the bedroom.

Spencer followed her. "That's different. At least I'm willing and looking. I've been out to dinner twice so far."

"And bombed," Julie said from the sofa.

"Hey!" Spencer looked at Julie as though insulted. "I've been single less than a year. I'm out of practice. Besides, I have a beautiful young lady who runs me ragged. You ought to try it," he said under his breath to Chris.

Chris pushed Spencer out of her bedroom. "Do you mind? I'm getting dressed."

"We'll be waiting."

Chris closed the door, shaking her head. She truly did love those two. It was just so hard to open up to anyone new who didn't know what Chris had been through. On more than one occasion, Spencer had balanced Julie on his hip and wrapped his other arm around Chris as he consoled her through Ruth's quick and devastating illness. Chris knew there were worse things than being alone.

CHAPTER FOUR

Molly was dressed for a long day in the field. She would spend the next six hours walking behind a self-propelled scraper and verifying the compaction of a site for an industrial building the size of a football field—just one of the ways the city coddled new businesses that relocated within its limits. It gave her the perfect excuse to dress as she preferred in neat blue jeans and lavender polo shirt with boys' work boots and her chestnut hair in a ponytail. She carried her hardhat and wore a messenger bag containing digital camera, personal cell phone, BlackBerry, pager, and project specifications.

She left her office, intending to head out of the building. It always amazed her to think about being allowed a year-and-a-half to construct city hall in 1932 and 1933. For its time, the Neoclassic building had been quite a production—locally designed but approved by the supervising architect of the Treasury since construction was federally funded. She would love to see the amount of paperwork such a project required then; that much probably hadn't changed in seventy-five years. It was truly a beautiful building, faced in rusticated granite with Ionic pilasters separating the façade's bays and capped with a smooth entablature and parapet surrounding the copper hip roof.

When Molly reached the main hallway, she went toward the elevator instead of the steps to the street. Just before the double elevator doors was a half glass door leading into a small office. The area previously used by a secretary was now occupied by a very attractive paralegal.

Molly tapped on the glass before entering the office. She smiled at the black woman who looked up and motioned her to come inside. Angela Bennett clearly worked out as evidenced by the rippling muscles of her bare arms. Her hair was straightened and cut in a thick pageboy just below her ears with sweeping bangs.

"Hey, girl. What gives with the casual outfit?" Angela leaned back in her chair and looked Molly up and down.

Molly held up her hands and did a circle. "I'm really working today instead of sitting at my desk shuffling papers and juggling telephone calls from irate citizens. What do you think—Village People's long lost first cousin?"

Angela waved off the joke. "More like construction worker poster girl. You better watch out for those big women the contractors like to hire."

"Now don't go stereotypical on me and give the girls a hard time. You'll be talking about short hair and clipped fingernails in a minute and I'll have to be defensive."

Angela leaned forward. "Well, honey, if I had known gay women looked like you, I wouldn't have married so soon."

Molly blew air between her lips. "Right, give me hope when I know I don't have a real chance with you. Tease."

"You two do know that I'm at my desk and not deaf as a post?" The voice carried from the adjoining office belonging to the city attorney. The door connecting the two offices remained open unless a meeting was taking place in the inner sanctum.

Molly lowered her voice. "I wondered how long it would take her to say something. We both know she's not going to stay out of a conversation but so long."

"I heard that, too. Get your butt in here before I leave for court. You can flirt with Angela later."

Molly kept her voice lowered as she entered the office. "I always do. You know my weakness for beautiful women." She said it knowing that Angela was close behind her.

"You're all talk," Angela said, giving Molly a push. "I'm going to the courthouse to do research." She left the office.

Molly watched the slim figure in the short dress negotiate the door.

"Shame on you, she's straight and happily married."

Molly sighed. "That doesn't mean I can't look."

"You mean lust."

"That too. It's not easy being single again."

"Let me find my CD of violin music."

Molly looked for something on the cluttered desk to throw at the woman giving her such a hard time. She settled on a small stuffed bear. The brown bear did a double flip before Windy caught him. Molly grinned at Wyndham Perrow, known as Windy. "Good catch."

Windy was in her mid-forties with Mia Farrow 1960s super chopped dark blond hair, brilliant blue eyes, and a few extra pounds. She had been in a wheelchair since a teenager involved in a diving accident that left her paralyzed from the waist down. Her shoulders had the breadth and strength of a girl who had spent her formative years training as a swimmer. She insisted on a chair with wide push rims and disdained suggestions of a motor propelling her. She was also an advocate for reasonable handicap parking in a parking-challenged downtown.

"Remind me to tell Angela that not all women with short hair are lesbians." Windy returned the bear to its usual place on the row of code books on the corner of her desk.

"Make sure I'm around when you two have that discussion." Molly dropped her bag and hardhat on the floor and took a seat on the end of the sofa closest to Windy's desk. "Angela hears you on the phone with Dave." Molly liked the bear of a man who had been Windy's husband since high school, encouraging her to attend college and law school while he built houses.

Windy actually blushed as she straightened a pile of papers. "I'll have to close that door more often."

"There's nothing wrong with enjoying sex." Molly looked beyond Windy and took comfort in the wall of bookcases even though the shelves were filled with legal tomes.

Windy stopped packing the bag that she carried on the hand grips of her chair. "Need to talk about something, dear?"

"Well, yes, now that you mention it." Molly's expression was dour. "It's another Jack story and it involves Project Night."

"Oh, Lord." Windy rolled closer to her desk and leaned forward. She looked at her watch. "I have twenty minutes. Will you have to kill me if you tell me about a state project?"

It was a running joke in the office any time they worked with the state's economic development division. Everything was top secret, few proper names were used, and code names were assigned to projects. It was so competitive among battling states that no one locally involved really wanted to know any more than necessary to respond to the state's request for information and decide when a prospect was right for the city to pursue.

"No, you're safe. This project is a done deal. We're under construction on the building—that's the problem." Molly looked toward the hall to make sure no one was listening. "This project is huge. Everyone became caught up in going after it. Promises were made. Twenty acres in our new industrial park and a half-million in cash given as the incentive for the company to invest twenty-five million in building and equipment. It's a manufacturer that produces portable substations."

Windy whistled. "I bet Homeland Security loves that."

"Exactly. Well, the problem is that we have temporary construction access through the adjoining farm in the county, but we have no viable road right-of-way to reach the site."

"Oh, boy," Windy said.

"Jack sent me out to the Reynolds property to evaluate the best route for a new road to the industrial park before we ever heard of Project Night. I met Mr. and Mrs. Reynolds a year ago when we went through the rezoning for the heavy industrial usage of what had been agricultural land on the parcel they sold us adjacent to their home. Jack sort of put the parcel into the state's database saying the road was in design and could be built while an industrial site was developed and building constructed."

Windy covered her face with her hands.

"I did my usual. I called last week and asked for an appointment. I was at their front door a few minutes early and thought we would just walk their three acres and determine what would have the least impact on their home. I was trying to do no more than clip a corner of their lot to keep the grading down on the road and give them better access to their property. The cheapest alignment goes through the center of their house. The city could buy them out if they wanted to sell their property and relocate, but the city does not have the right of eminent domain for something like this. I realize I'm singing to the choir. I just wanted you to know I do have a slight grasp of the law. Besides, who wants bad press for a project that should boost the business community?"

"Makes sense." Windy pulled a legal pad from a drawer, realizing she needed to make notes.

"I found out in no short order that Mr. Reynolds hates Jack with a passion. So much so that when I tried to talk to them about routes for the road on a map from our office, Mr. Reynolds went into irregular heartbeats and had to take medication and lie down. Mrs. Reynolds then proceeded to chew my ass for daring to bring the same map into their home that they had thrown Jack out their front door with, which by the way was the last time Mr. Reynolds's heart problems occurred. Jack started off by telling them he would do them the favor of putting them off of their property."

"Let me take a wild guess that Jack gave you no warning or background of his history with these people."

Molly touched her nose signaling that Windy was right on track with her guesses. "I offered to call 911."

Windy chuckled.

"Or drive them to the doctor." Molly stared at the floor dejectedly.

"And their response?"

"Mr. Reynolds was yelling from the far end of the house what I could do with Jack and the map. Mrs. Reynolds just held the door open until I slunk out."

Windy's chuckle became a hearty laugh.

"We are now left with the route through the wetlands on the city's property that will cost twice as much in money and time. I'm sure this will be all my fault by the time city council hears it reported." Molly looked at Windy. "I sent the Reynoldses flowers yesterday. The vase hasn't come hurdling through my window yet."

Windy actually guffawed. She reached into her jacket pocket for a tissue to wipe her eyes. "Remind me to lock my brakes the next time you tell me a story. I think I laughed so hard I banged my knee on my desk."

"It's a gift."

"More like the Sampson curse."

Molly hit her forehead with the heel of her palm.

Windy held her hand up for silence and jotted on her legal pad. "How about I draft a letter for you to send to Mr. and Mrs. Reynolds explaining the approximate amount of land we'll need to purchase with the current appraisal numbers for crossing the corner of their parcel? They can call me directly to negotiate, and I'll let them get me to the upper budget limit and justify it with legalese. I'll even hedge with buying them out. I'm guessing the difference in cost between road alignments would cover it. Can you redo the map so it doesn't look like the one they saw with Jack, showing how far away from the house the road will be and how much screening vegetation would be planted?"

"You bet. The drawing is always the easiest part of a project, and you're right about the cost."

Windy shook her head. "Don't you hate being used to this?"

Molly raised her eyebrows.

"Jack operates by keeping a certain amount of critical information to himself so that he can swoop in at the last minute and save a deal. That's how he maintains control of people smarter and more talented. Plus, he wants to keep friction going in the office. He can't have all of you operating too smoothly. It would look as though he wasn't needed."

"I learned that the hard way years ago," Molly said.

"One of these days, Jack is going to pull this shit too many times or on the wrong person, and his horrible business practices just might get him hurt."

"You think?" Molly sounded hopeful.

"I thought I heard voices." Tom Stafford walked into Windy's office from the short hallway that led to his front corner of the building. "Molly, you have to take a look at something for me. You're dressed for it."

Molly grabbed her bag and hat and followed Tom, looking back at Windy questioningly.

Windy shook her head. "Bless your heart," she mouthed silently.

Tom was Molly's height and a decade older than Windy. His thinning white hair was kept in a buzz cut. He stayed trim by walking his neighbor's dog every morning before venturing to city hall for the day. He made it a practice to keep a very low profile in the office, usually attending meetings only if a council member was to be present. He managed by delegating to his executive staff and waiting for them to report back to him, yet knowing their progress before hearing it from them directly.

Two walls of his office were lined with old casement windows fitted with interior storm windows with a wide marble sill below. He walked to the window directly behind his credenza and pointed.

Molly stopped beside him and followed the trajectory of his finger.

"How do we get those out?" He stared at three dead horseflies, lying on their backs with legs raised.

Molly looked at Tom, then back to the flies. She fought the impulse to glance about the office to see if anyone was in the background waiting to burst out with the joke. "I'll be glad to call the custodial supervisor for you."

Tom nodded. "They haven't changed position in four days. I'm sure it's the same ones and that they're dead."

Molly made herself count to five. "No doubt. They'll be gone by the time you come back from lunch." It was well known that Tom went home each day at noon, refusing to eat in a restaurant unless it was a working lunch he did not have to pay for personally. She dug in her bag for her BlackBerry. She didn't trust herself on the phone or anywhere near Windy.

"Things going okay with you?" Tom's gaze returned to the computer monitor and the homepage of *USA Today* that he checked at least once an hour for breaking news.

"Great. We're almost ready for footers on the first building in the industrial park. I'd really like to have Donna Brooks in our GIS position." Molly began an e-mail to building maintenance that she hoped she would not receive a callback on until she was in her car.

"Fine woman. I know her father-in-law. I'll keep an eye out for the paperwork from Jack."

Molly eased out of the office before Tom started reading news headlines to her.

CHAPTER FIVE

Chris circled the block around city hall for the third time. "Damn it, why do they make us come downtown for this if they don't have anywhere for us to park? Dumbasses." The public safety building that her cubicle was located in had purposely been built away from downtown to avoid the congestion caused by more workers than parking spaces and to address security concerns. The downtown traffic flow and turn radii had been designed in a time when most workers rode streetcars to the office.

She bounced her fist off the steering wheel and was glad to be in a nondescript pool car. It was beside the point that she should have done this the week before. She hadn't had the time then, either, to deal with the city hall bureaucrats who controlled the geographic information system. Why didn't the chief stand up to the city manager to have someone at their office trained and equipped on site to handle accessing the maps for courtroom exhibits when their arrests went to trial?

"No, that would be too damn logical. Instead, I waste an hour I don't have to spare." She glanced at her Mickey Mouse watch. "Shit, it's going to be lunch by the time I park and hike to the building. Who in the hell will help me then?" She had to be in court and fully prepared by 1:00 or the judge would chew her ass for wasting his time.

Chris had earned her gold badge two years earlier. Most of the crimes she dealt with as a detective were petty in nature, dealing with robbery and vice. Thankfully, their murder rate was two per year. Her specialty was sketching crime scenes. Today's case was a documented stakeout observation and raid of a store openly selling electronics stolen from area residences. What disturbed her most was that average citizens bought the equipment knowing it was likely fenced. She needed an enlarged aerial photograph to clearly explain their operation. She looked again at Mickey and had a bad feeling.

Finally, she gave up on the spaces along the sidewalk and drove toward the pay-by-the-hour lot at the end of Main Street just before the bridge crossing the river. She spotted a car pulling out of a parking space two blocks from city hall and cut off another car with the same intent. She neatly parallel parked while the driver was still blowing his horn at her. "Sorry." She flashed her badge as she climbed out of the sedan. She felt a silly pride in the dented Ford assigned to her when she made detective.

Chris entered city hall through the first-floor state offices. She hurried two senior citizens caught in the original bronze-framed revolving door with her and crossed the lobby for the elevator tucked in the center of the building. She glanced at the floor indicator and opened the door to the stairwell, taking the steps two at a time. She reached the top of the stairs, glanced at the women's restroom and decided she would wait to pee until she reached the courthouse, and went to the first office to the right of council chambers along the back wall of the building.

Below the stenciling reading map room was a "Gone to lunch" sign taped to the glass door. She looked inside and saw no one in a far back corner trying to hide from the public long enough to choke down a sandwich. Chris passed the men's restroom, debating whether to tap on the door to get someone's attention, and went through the employee-only door. She slowed at the first office on the left. A woman leaned over a drafting table, standing as she worked. "Excuse me."

The woman who looked up literally tore herself away from the topographic map stuck to her sleeve from leaning on the ink. A box filled with clear plastic curves balanced near the end of the drafting table. She smiled. "May I help you?"

"I hope so. I'm running late."

"Is that your Indian name? I'm Molly."

Chris rolled her eyes.

Molly chuckled. "Sorry. I'm a little punchy. I've worked on this all weekend and still can't get it right. I finally gave up trying to design this with the computer software and reverted to railroad curves and manual calculations. What do you need?" She clipped her pencil to her pocket; its barrel matched the pink stripe in her shirt.

"A large aerial photograph. I'm Chris Miller with the PD. I have to be in court in forty-five minutes."

Molly grimaced. "Okay, now I understand." She motioned Chris to follow her. "GIS office is next door. Let me see if Gary is here." The office was empty. Molly knelt on the floor in front of his keyboard and accessed the software that managed the GIS system. "Address?"

"Langhorne and Murrell, the old shopping center."

Molly nodded. She found the four-map quadrant and zoomed in, then centered the shopping center. "Is this to set on an easel?" Molly glanced at the woman.

Chris was Molly's height and slightly thinner. Her hair was cut in choppy layers forming a classic bob with angled bangs that suited her thin face. From her deep blue eyes, Molly guessed that Chris's hair was naturally light blond. The look worked for her. Chris was feminine, yet her look was not fussed about. At first glance, Chris bore a slight resemblance to Jodie Foster; Molly stopped herself from blurting that out.

Molly looked past Chris as Gary entered his office carrying a brown bag. "Hey, Molly, I picked up Chinese for us. There's plenty for three." He winked at Chris. "I have to make sure she doesn't go all day without eating." Gary grinned as he glanced at the monitor. "Need any help?"

"Why don't you take that to the kitchen? I'll meet you in a few minutes." Molly waved him out of the room as Chris watched him leave. Gary chuckled as he continued along the hallway.

"Cute." Chris turned to Molly. "He looks like the guy on *ER*— Noah Wyle."

Molly nodded. "He's one of those rare men who are gorgeous but with no ego, a real buddy."

"I heard that. The only use I have for men is friendship. At least they're not as hormonal as female friends."

Molly focused on the plotter settings. "For the most part."

Chris laughed and smiled as she took a closer look at Molly.

Molly pointed to the long machine against the wall. "Should start in just a moment."

The heads on the machine clattered into action as the image printed lineally.

Knuckles rapped on the door frame to draw their attention. "I need that road alignment by 8:30 tomorrow morning. What's on your board doesn't show much progress." Jack Sampson stepped into the

GIS room that was the last office before his own on the corner. He looked Chris up and down.

"I'll have it before I leave today, just needed a better estimate of the grading before committing to an alignment." Molly watched the plotter to make sure the paper fed off the roll correctly and that the roll didn't give out midway—her usual luck when in a hurry.

"Where the hell is Gary? I told you we needed to fill our tech position. If you'd hire someone, you wouldn't have to be the backup in here. Of course, I know you love being able to do everything yourself." Jack smoothed the hair he had just combed over the crown of his head.

"I'm sure the chief will send Molly an e-mail thanking her for this." Chris studied the map as it advanced into the plotter tray.

Jack nodded. "I thought I recognized you. You interned here before you applied for the police cadet program. You haven't changed much." He leered at her.

"That was twelve years ago. You haven't changed, either, just a little heavier and a lot grayer." Chris did not smile, picking up right where she left off with Jack Sampson.

"How's your father?" Jack barely smothered a belch and made no excuse.

"Deceased."

"Sorry." He gave her a mock salute and walked away.

"Prick," Chris said.

"Amen to that. You do know him." Molly laid the plot flat on a large table and reached for a long straight edge to square the border. She trimmed the paper to a standard size. "Hand me that foam board." She pointed to the stack Gary kept on the floor beneath the plotter stand.

"I don't know why I'm telling you this. I worked in community development the summer before I finished college. I was here long enough to figure out that I didn't want to become a small cog in local government. So I decided to try the police department. At least there was a structure in place so you could work your way up once you were in. Jack tried to stop me from leaving by telling the chief about my father's bankruptcy after my mother's death and how much college debt I carried, implying that I was a poor risk for staying around."

"That was none of his business."

"No shit. He was pissed because I didn't have sex with him during the summer I worked for him. I didn't realize when I accepted the job that when he chose interns it was for more than office work. He was too damn dense to comprehend that he had absolutely no appeal to me." Chris helped align the copy on the board.

Molly looked away. She had seen it happen. She had warned a few of the girls, but they didn't listen or hadn't wanted to believe her. Jack's success rate was not what it had once been. "I threatened him with the EEOC after I had been here a month—not that I would have had sex with him if he looked like Brad Pitt. Angelina Jolie would be a different story." Molly paused to grin at Chris. "He hasn't been able to find enough solid dirt in my personal life, so he loads me up with work just to see if he can find a reason to fire me. He doesn't seem to understand that I love working. So we've been in a long stalemate."

"Son of a bitch. How do men like that live with themselves? How do we let them live?" Chris covered her mouth with her hand. "I'm not supposed to think that way, am I?"

Molly tore a sheet of brown wrapping paper to cover the board.

"You saved my life. Lunch sometime when I'm not in such a hurry?" Chris eased the mechanical pencil from Molly's shirt pocket and jotted a number on the back of her business card. "My personal cell if you'd like me to repay the favor." She handed the card and pencil to Molly. Chris couldn't believe she was actually flirting. Spencer would be so proud of her.

"You bet." Molly followed Chris and held the door to the main hallway open for her. "Don't be a stranger."

"No stranger than I usually am, but I'd rather you get to know me first." Chris grinned at the other woman.

Molly would like that very much.

CHAPTER SIX

Molly blinked at the bright daylight coming through the blinds. She loved fall. She couldn't remember the last time she had allowed herself the luxury of lying in bed as sunrise gave way to morning. The sky was a brilliant deep blue—the color of Chris's eyes. What had gotten into her the past few days? She might as well admit that she had stopped beating herself up about Sarah ever since meeting Chris. "I will not rush into anything." Molly felt the slight shift in body weight against her legs.

"I could get used to this." Molly looked at the Maine Coon cat curled into the bend of her knees.

Dolly stood and stretched and looked back at her. She slowly walked up the side of the bed, sat on her haunches, and kneaded Molly's neck with her front paws sans claws.

"You do love me." Molly hugged the cat.

Dolly's throat rumbled with a loud purr. She leaned forward and bumped foreheads with Molly.

"I feel the same about you, girl." Molly hugged the animal again until the cat squirmed free and jumped off the bed.

"So much for affection." Molly sighed and stretched. She loved Saturdays even if her routine made no sense to her co-workers. She usually rose at 5:15, the same time as during the week, but dressed in old baggy clothes—faded Henley and jeans worn threadbare—pulling her hair back in a ponytail before going to the kitchen to make coffee and pancakes.

Her breakfast during the week was cold cereal during the local early morning news. She tossed a load of clothes in the washer, reminding herself to transfer the load to the dryer just before she left the house. Her mother would be horrified that Molly left the dryer running in an empty house, but Molly was engineer enough to clean out the hose connected to the vent as part of her monthly maintenance chores. While the clothes washed, she did a quick top dust and vacuum.

She went to the den and loaded the work papers on her drafting table into her messenger bag. She checked the side pocket for quarters for the vending machine. She added treats to Dolly's food bowl, even though the cat was hiding because she was miffed with Molly for leaving home so soon.

Molly detoured by the automated car wash and ran the Jeep through for a quick cleaning. She drove downtown, able to park on the street beside city hall since the businesses lining the sidewalks were closed for the weekend. Not quite enough people lived in the downtown lofts taking over the historic brick warehouses to keep the merchants in the black on weekends.

Molly used the dimpled deadbolt key to let herself in the side door of city hall. She took the stairs, never trusting the elevator on the weekend when none of the building maintenance guys was around to help. She was not about to call the duty man in because she was stranded by her own laziness. She stood in the second-floor lobby and felt strangely at home.

She had worked for the city for a little over eight years; that in itself was hard to believe. She loved Virginia. She had absolutely made the correct choice in college to study civil engineering, even though she appreciated architecture. She thought the granite building constructed with WPA funds had more character and beauty than anything any architect nowadays might come up with, and that was only partly accountable to the natural rivalry between engineers and architects. From the tall ceilings that abutted plaster walls that rested on terrazzo floors, the building exuded charm and grace.

It never bothered her to be in city hall alone. She was careful about locking doors behind her and keeping her iPod volume low so that she heard any disjoint sounds while using ear buds. She was able to get so much work done when she was alone in the building on Saturdays; she only worked half days on Sundays.

Was it awful that she totally zoned out when she was able to focus on work? She enjoyed the women she worked with, but some form of drama always went on—someone wasn't speaking to someone else, someone told something that was supposed to be kept in confidence, or someone was unhappy at home. It was always something. Molly teased the straight women she worked with by listening to their man problems to a certain point, then telling them they just hadn't met the right woman yet; it stopped their male-bashing in its tracks. Alone, Molly lost all thought to the task before her.

She had yet another rush project—Project Ring, an inbound call center. Molly wondered if Jack would ever realize that she thrived on deadlines. She loved playing the game with any work of how fast it could be accomplished. She had learned that trick when she worked part time while in high school. Among other piddly duties, she was paid to make copies and assemble bid packages for subcontractors on construction projects. On her own initiative, she experimented with how fast a packet could be done, then found ways to cut her time down even more to make the days of tedious assignments fly by. Bosses were always amazed that she didn't really care what she worked on as long as she had plenty of work to keep her mind challenged and engaged. How complex or how menial was not the point.

She needed to fine-tune numbers on rehabbing an abandoned tobacco warehouse on the riverfront to have the city in the running for a call center for insurance adjusters. The criterion was for a rented plug-and-play facility with its own parking deck.

It fell right into the Industrial Development Authority forming a limited partnership with her as the manager to go after state historic tax credits. It was a perfect time for a bond issuance. The city had purchased the block of buildings ten years earlier just before downtown started to bounce back.

The historic building with exposed interior brick and heart pine columns spaced in bays across the open maple floors was perfect for the trendy companies that recruited the young professionals every city was going after now. What worked best with wooing a potential prospect was to find out who on the site selection team really did the work and make a connection with that person.

There was nothing that a consultant seemed to like better than discovering a public servant in the office on Saturday, the same as he or she was. Molly knew which state project managers kept their BlackBerry on all weekend. Commiserating often led to tiny tidbits of information that when applied to a proposal made all the difference in the world.

The slant today was to show that the city understood structuring this type of deal so that the state would issue an incentive based on a building provided by the IDA. Again, a win-win, no-brainer for city council that would have the city owning the renovated building in twenty years.

Something was nagging at Molly as she ran the amortization numbers and factored rent and maintenance into a square-foot lease rate for the prospect. She had lost count of the number of times she had looked at Chris's business card and remembered the rush of Chris's simple act of taking a pencil from Molly's pocket. Molly dug through her messenger bag until she found her LG. She flipped open her cell phone and punched in the number from the back of the card. Chris's personal cell rang. Molly scaled the dimensions on the original blueprint drawing as she waited for the message to kick in. Instead, she was surprised by a man's voice.

"This is Spencer, answering Chris's phone."

Molly swallowed the knot rising in the back of her throat.

"Hello?" He tried again.

"Sorry to bother you. I'll call back later," Molly said.

"Hey, wait. I'll be happy to take a message. Chris stepped out and forgot her phone. I keep telling her she ought to wear it around her neck. I'm surprised it was charged and on." His tone was friendly and amused.

"I'll just call back."

"At least let me tell her who called," Spencer said.

"Molly," she punched end, "the supreme dumbass. Boy, did I misunderstand."

Molly tried to focus on the map. She caught herself staring out the window. The ringing of her phone startled her. She didn't answer. The tiny front display showed Chris's number. Of course, Molly's number was now in Chris's call register. "Damn cell phones." Molly opened and closed the phone to stop the ringing.

"Fool me once, shame on you. Fool me twice, shame on me," Molly whispered. She had been so sure that Chris was sending her all the right signals that she was a single lesbian.

Molly's desk phone rang. She glanced and saw Chris's name on the caller ID. "Damn, she's persistent enough to go to the trouble of looking up my office extension in the city directory. I should've left her alone and just been grateful for another friend."

Molly concentrated on the project. She converted the blueprint of the floor plan to an AutoCAD drawing. She experimented with tall and short cubicle spacing to keep an open layout but provide enough workstations. She would verify the rehab numbers with a local contractor once she had the finishes fleshed out. She wished she hadn't thought of flesh. Molly sighed and concentrated on data needed for the estimating program prompts.

By the end of the day, the strategy for the proposal was proving itself. Again, the numbers seemed to be coming together close to what she had guessed at; the city might actually have a shot at this one. She had to verify her seat-of-the-pants answers given when caught in demanding conference calls. Jack and Eric had thought it such a long shot that they handed off the request for information as a second thought to deleting the e-mail from the state's project manager.

Molly left the building, carefully engaging the lock and deadbolt of the side door. She debated which fast food restaurant to stop at for a take-out dinner as she approached her Jeep. She saw folded paper beneath the windshield wiper and couldn't believe she had been given a ticket on the weekend. There was no other vehicle parked on the side street. Why would any of the cops care that she was parked here?

Molly removed the paper and read a note instead of a fine.

"You were here all day on a Saturday and not answering your phone. I can explain about Spencer if you'll give me a chance. Give me a call. We can meet for a drink. C."

Molly read the note again before crumpling the paper and stuffing it into her pocket. She had a girl waiting at home for her, a girl who truly loved only her. Dolly was all the company she wanted.

When Molly entered the house, the first thing she noticed was the cushions pulled off the sofa and lying on the floor. The next thing she saw was the blinking light of her answering machine. She hit the play button.

"Okay, how'd I know you'd ignore my note and go home? For future reference, having just your initials and last name with 411 doesn't discourage callers. We're both hard-headed and stubborn. I missed your call because I'm terrible about remembering my personal cell phone. You don't answer while you're working. That makes us even. Spencer is my best friend, no parentheses or wink here. I walked out for a newspaper. Let's start over. Call me so we can set up the lunch or dinner that I feel I owe you."

Molly smiled. Talk about a real deal.

CHAPTER SEVEN

Molly and Donna commandeered the large conference room for the day. Everything had come together on the industrial park at the same time—the building's structural steel was being erected, so all the shop drawings for the interior finishes were coming in from subcontractors; the Reynoldses signed the sale agreement contingent on the city paying their moving costs, so bids were being received from local moving companies; and the road plans were done, so general contractors were picking up bid packages.

Molly had written herself a note to call Chris that was now buried somewhere deep in her office and subconscious. Work had to come first. Molly was determined not to rush into another relationship—and here she was, never having seen Chris but once and thinking long term. Molly knew she was an idiot when it came to women she found attractive.

"How in the hell did you manage to have all of this hit at the same time?" Donna brought in another stack of papers from Molly's office.

"I could lie and say it was through extreme project management." Molly grinned at the other woman.

"This is crazy," Eric said. His necktie was tucked inside his shirt to avoid snagging the silk on any of the binders. He set the stack of books on the table, then returned to the door frame. "Woot!" Without warning, he jumped straight up and smacked the metal header with the palm of his hand; not a strand of his hair moved. "Slam dunk! I needed to check if I got my gel right this morning."

Molly rolled her eyes, then looked about the room at the massive amount of paperwork. "Okay, as much as I like to hoard work, you two are now drafted. Eric, you're going to volunteer to handle the moving companies—review the bids, check their references, then run your recommendation past Rusty. You'll want to let the Reynoldses know as soon as the contract is awarded, then be with them on moving day, so keep that in sync with your calendar."

"Got it. I can handle all of that, except Rusty's bright pink sport coat." Eric grinned.

"And it's much appreciated. I'll call the newspaper and check if it warrants an article, may be able to have you interviewed." Molly sorted the stacks. How did she accumulate all of this in her office?

"Good add to my portfolio." Eric grinned and flipped his tie out. He mimicked swinging a bat to loosen up.

"Donna, honey, you are going to deal with the contractors who want road plans." Molly batted her eyes at her friend. "All you do is collect their deposit and keep a list of numbered plan sets with all their contact info in case we have to issue addendums."

"Understand. I talk to most of those guys when they call in for you anyway. It will be a trip to finally meet some of them." Donna pushed the box of project manuals across the room to the corner where the rolls of plans were stacked.

Molly lowered her voice. "Just be mindful of the ones who pay the deposit in cash. Give them a receipt and immediately take the money to Rusty—no matter what color jacket he's wearing—and make sure he initials the receipt as receiving public funds."

Donna nodded. "I know they'll hang us both out to dry if there's not a paper trail on every dollar bill."

Molly found her ink pad and began stamping covers so she could check the box for approved or disapproved on the shop drawings. "I'll sort the submittals and work through verifying against the specs. Those guys start calling a few days after bringing packets in if they don't hear something back. There's so much lead time on ordering everything, my guess is that we're already behind schedule. I'm so glad we volunteer to do this as part of recruiting the new companies. Aha!" She held up the log sheet where she recorded when each packet of information was received. She always reviewed product information in order of receipt to keep the guys from accusing her of favoritism.

Eric gathered the four envelopes to take to his office. He pumped them back and forth over his shoulder as though about to launch a pass. "Well, I'm sure it sounds good when Jack sweetens the deal with the city's record of fast tracking construction by doing most of it internally. You know how those contractors hate dealing with us on plan reviews."

Donna waited until Eric left the room. "*Us*? How much longer are you going to carry him?"

Molly didn't raise her head from the stack of papers she was sorting into piles covering the conference table.

"Don't ignore me." Donna tossed a paperclip at Molly.

Molly looked up. "He's a nice guy."

"I'm glad you think so. He's weird as hell." Donna cupped her hands and caught the paperclip tossed back at her. "All this sports shit he talks—either his high school only had enough boys to fill a roster or he's reminiscing about glory days in the pee-wee leagues."

"Give him a break he's still a kid." Molly studied her paper assembly line.

"Almost thirty is way past being a kid. Do I have to remind you again that you two are the same classification level, yet he does nowhere near the amount of *professional* work that you do? How often do you see him do something with an actual result?"

"I did just now." Molly grinned at Donna.

"With moving companies. Hell, that's so simple even Jack could do it." Donna's hands went to her hips for emphasis.

Molly laughed. "How do you really feel about the men we work with?"

"They're not as smart as my husband. Even Tim understands who manages our finances and keeps us out of debt on everything but the house." Donna eyed the six boxes of project manuals and rolled blueprints on end.

"Will you be able to swing fall classes at the community college?" Molly frowned at the set of binders held together by three rubber bands—the supplier had turned in two less than needed to distribute after reviewing.

"I've applied and paid my tuition." Donna tested the weight of one of the plan boxes. "I'll call building maintenance for a hand truck."

Molly made a thumbs-up sign. "Resourcefulness—that's one of the many things I like about working with you. I drafted the letter formally offering the GIS technician job to you. It's on Jack's desk to sign. You are my recommended candidate based on the interview ratings."

Donna held her arms up as though a touchdown had been scored. "I'll get to work with Gary and not be an admin—finally. The college classes look so interesting. I've already bought my books and started reading the materials."

"What in the hell do you think you're doing?" Jack stood in the doorway of the conference room with his hands behind his back.

Molly prepared to answer, but his gaze was on Donna.

Donna stared back.

"She's helping me. Everything for the industrial park hit at the same time." Molly stood and walked toward Jack.

He threw the four envelopes from the movers on the table.

"Eric works on special projects for me or the city manager. He's not on call to you."

"We're swamped. Do you want us to meet the deadlines set on the critical elements of the biggest project that the city has ever attempted? I need help." Molly hated making the admission.

"Bull. Why didn't I know that she," he pointed at Donna, "was in here with you? How do you think it sounds for all my calls to go to voice mail? You need to get back to your desk."

Donna looked at Molly and shrugged. Molly nodded toward the door.

Jack continued deliberately before Donna managed to leave the room. "I called Ann this afternoon and asked her to readvertise the tech position. I want to see who applies from outside. I wasn't satisfied with the internal candidates."

Donna froze.

"Jack, no, don't do that. You told me I had the call on that hire." Molly stared at her boss as though he had two heads.

"I changed my mind," Jack said.

Tears ran down Donna's face as her hands clenched into fists. "You'll regret this," she said as she passed Jack and left the conference room.

"Do you want her to quit?" Molly asked.

Jack actually smirked. "She won't. She needs the benefits. She carries her husband on her insurance so he can work as an independent drywall contractor, not to mention what the benefits mean when you have two young children."

Donna had told Molly about hitting thirty and panicking about waiting too long to have children. She now had a six-year-old and four-year-old at home who constantly visited the pediatrician.

Molly glared at Jack. "That's not the point. Donna has worked for the city for fifteen years and proven herself an excellent employee. She has earned the right to advance. Donna would be great with the GIS system."

"That's your opinion. I can get a kid with a college degree for less than I pay Donna. Donna knows my system, my contacts, and how things work around here. I don't want to train a new secretary." Jack left the room.

Molly walked out into the hallway. Eric hesitated in the doorway to his office. She looked at him. "You knew, didn't you?"

He shrugged and went into his office, closing the door behind him.

The admin bullpen across from Eric's office was silent. The three women waited for Molly to calm down and speak to any of them first.

"I hate him," Molly said, standing in the hallway.

"Jack or Eric?" Susan asked.

"What's the difference?" Molly returned to the conference room and closed the door behind her. She stared at the mounds of paper and wished for a match. She did not touch a single document for fifteen minutes.

Molly heard a slight tap on the door. "Yes."

Campbell Chamberlain limped into the room. "Nancy told me what happened. Are you okay?" Nancy was Campbell's admin assistant.

Molly hated the tears she felt well up in her eyes. She truly loved Campbell. The man had been through hell in Vietnam without receiving a single wound, only to return to the States and be diagnosed with rheumatoid arthritis. All his joints swelled until he was barely able to move.

The doctors experimented with everything from gold shots to powerful cancer drugs trying to slow the degeneration of his limbs. Molly also hated the RA commercials on television showing people living normal lives with the disease under control thanks to recent pharmaceutical miracles; she railed about the meds not being available in time for Campbell. By the time relief was found, Campbell's joints had little cartilage remaining and his fingers were misshapen and multidirectional. Campbell took it all in stride, continuing to work as his body failed. It was easy to be put off by his gruff expression and quiet nature.

He had finally allowed his hair to grow out of his trademark military cut after losing most of it to one of the drugs he tried. It had grown back a fine and soft dark blond that his barber kept in a neat shingle cut. He not so much walked as rolled with the stiff gait his limbs limited him to. At one time, he stood six feet tall; with the degenerative effect of RA, his posture lost three inches. The meds he took kept him puffy and overweight; exercise was limited. He resembled an aging brown bear.

"No, but I will be. I'm going to kill Jack," Molly said.

"Is that all?" Campbell closed the door behind him and sat across the table from Molly.

"No court would ever convict me."

"Probably not. Everyone around here would cover for you. There's likely a line forming in the hallway to help you do it."

"I just have to plan it well enough to fool the PD. They're actually smart enough to encourage and promote females into their investigator's jobs." Molly's mind drifted to Chris Miller as it tended to do with increasing frequency when she needed an escape.

Campbell nodded. "You know if any of us in utilities can help you, we will. I have time to take care of the moving company." He held up his hand. "Don't turn down help when the offer is genuine."

"But you're a director." Molly was able to smile.

"That means I'm supposed to be smart enough to recognize when an employee is overworked and do something about it."

"Let me rephrase that—you're a good director."

Campbell inclined his head in thanks.

Molly pushed the four envelopes across the table.

"Mark can keep the plans and specs for the road in the map room for the contractors to sign out. His is the first office everyone stops at for help anyway. He's used to handling money. He'll come over before he leaves today and move everything. I've already told Donna so she can direct the guys who call or come in asking for you."

"Thank you, Campbell."

"Chose your battles wisely, Molly. Jack is not worth ruining your career over. He's been operating his own way for too long. He's a much stronger adversary than you imagine. You're too good at what you do to become caught up in the tactics it would take to put Jack in his place. Okay?"

She nodded. "Okay."

Campbell hobbled out of the room like a wise old bear on the way back to his cave after breaking up a rowdy cub fight.

Molly knew she could survive as long as Campbell and Windy had her back.

CHAPTER EIGHT

"You watch. Want to bet a Diet Coke out of the machine tomorrow that the hostess takes one look at us and seats us at a table in the far corner?" Donna leaned over and spoke in Susan Neville's ear as they passed through the double doors from the lobby into the restaurant.

"Maybe we ought to come in separately instead of waiting for each other." Susan looked to Molly, the ringleader.

"But half the fun for me is being able to walk in with all of you—my harem." Molly tried to look serious.

Susan rolled her eyes and watched Frankie Mahoney smack Molly in the back of her head. "Yeah, right," Frankie said.

Susan linked arms with Molly as they were escorted all the way across the tabled section of the restaurant. "Oh, humor her. You know how she is about blondes. This probably is a cheap thrill for her. It will at least get the first round of drinks on her check."

The bar was across from the lobby separated by standing tables for two with a section of booths on the far left, tables for four or six to the right, and a separate banquet room on the far right. The ceiling was shiny fake antique tin, the walls painted black, and the floors bare wood. Dim lights dangled from the structural members of the ceiling. What made the choice of location easy for Molly was the long row of beer taps spaced along the end of the bar.

Molly made it a habit to start the round of e-mails near the first of each month to get the group together for dinner. It usually took at least a week to coordinate everyone's calendar because no one wanted to miss a gathering. They knew they would end up talking about work, but it also gave them a chance to catch up with one another while not looking over their shoulders at the office.

Donna had finally calmed down about Jack's latest with the GIS tech position. He had made her angry enough not to drop her enrollment at the community college. She casually talked with the consultants who came through the office about their computer systems. She was determined to move into a technical job with or without remaining on the city's payroll.

Susan was another member of the admin bullpen along with Sharon Rogers and Nancy Harris, who resided across from Eric's office. She was assigned to the deputy city manager but also did work for Tom or Windy as needed. Since she was quick about her work, it usually took more than the reports Barbara generated to keep Susan busy. Susan turned thirty the previous month, was divorced for over a year, and managed her five-year-old son with her mother's help. Her blond hair was razor cut just below her ears. She applied makeup with more skill than the department store experts.

Francine Mahoney was three years older than Molly. She started working immediately after high school and presently managed the city's utility accounts fairly but with a firm hand. She heard all the sob stories about turning water off to a home and possessed the innate ability to know which was genuine enough to pass along to social services for assistance. Heaven help anyone who pleaded financial hardship with a pack of cigarettes visible on them. Frankie had modeled herself after the Donna Krebbs character on *Dallas* in the 1980s and saw no reason to change her short in the front, long in the back puffy frosted blond hairstyle.

Molly pulled the chairs out on either side of her for Frankie and Susan.

"I know where this leaves me." Donna sighed as she seated herself opposite Molly. "I never thought of brown hair as a handicap until now." She dodged a kick from Molly under the table.

"You guys don't have to fight over me." Molly grinned.

"In your dreams." Susan winked at Frankie. "We ought to go on a date with her just once to find out if she's all talk."

Molly held up her BlackBerry. "Tell me when."

Susan shook her head. "Wouldn't that set off city hall? I bet Barbara would know all the details before we kissed good night. How does Barbara find out everything?"

Donna didn't miss a beat as she studied her menu. "She's devious. That's what makes her indispensable to the city manager. Jack is just plain mean."

"Look at us." Frankie gestured around the table. "We haven't been here five minutes and we're talking about Jack. That's just pitiful."

"Welcome to my nightmare," Molly said.

They ordered their first round of drinks—Donna and Susan chose white wine, Frankie a White Russian, and Molly a dark imported beer.

Molly raised her glass. "To you guys, the best friends I could hope to work with."

They all took long swallows.

"So, speaking of Jack." Donna's eyes glimmered wickedly. The others waited, knowing this was going to be good. "How would you kill him if you could get away with it scot-free?"

Molly almost choked.

Frankie patted the handbag in her lap. "That's easy. I'd shoot him without a moment's regret."

"Oh, God, you're not still carrying that handgun around?" Susan leaned back in her chair.

"Damn right I am. I went through the PD training class and have a permit. As late as I work and as badly as I piss people off about shutting their water off, I'm not about to walk to my car alone without it," Frankie said.

"Remind me not to sneak up behind her in the parking deck." Molly leaned close to Susan.

"You just stay with me in the dark," Susan whispered. "I'd poison him, so he would die slowly and suffer." She earned a stare from the next table.

Molly shrugged. "I can't top any of those."

They looked at Donna.

"STD that would make his dick and all his hair fall off," Donna said matter-of-factly. It was obvious she had put a lot of thought into her answer.

Everyone in the restaurant turned to look as hoots and howls of laughter erupted from the corner. Each of the women at the table high-fived Donna.

Molly wiped her eyes. "Okay, you win. Your drink is on me."

"I think mine is, too." Susan wiped her chin.

"That SOB backed me into a corner yesterday—figuratively." Frankie waved to their waiter for another round. "One of his rich bitch friends had the water connected to her new million-dollar house without setting foot in the office or filling out an application to start monthly billing. I only found out because Johnny forwarded the e-mail to me with Jack's work order for him attached. Campbell had a closed-door meeting with Jack. The bitch sauntered in this morning with a dog in her damn purse and tried to talk me out of full fees since she was already connected and couldn't understand why she had to pay something called an availability fee. Jack sent Eric in to take care of her and make sure I didn't add a penalty fee to her total." Frankie rolled her eyes.

"Those two are as thick as thieves." Donna watched Molly's reaction.

"Don't start on Eric again. He can't help the mentality of his generation," Molly said.

"Entitlement without earning it," Donna added.

"He hasn't given Jack any ammunition about my sexual preference," Molly said.

"Give him time." Donna shrugged when the others frowned at her.

They studied their menus, deciding on entrees to go with the alcohol.

Molly caught motion out of the corner of her eye. Chris stood across the restaurant at a tall table for two next to the bar with a redheaded man in a suit. She waved when Molly acknowledged her.

Molly smiled and waved back.

"Holding out on us?" Susan saw how Molly's expression lightened when she saw Chris.

"She's the police detective Gary told you about who came in for a map one day at lunch." Molly was deliberately neutral.

"You didn't say anything about how cute she is. Guess who has a crush?" Susan grinned, bumping shoulders with Molly.

"Don't start that." Molly's thoughts about Chris were way ahead of reality. She sighed.

"Bless your heart." Frankie leaned over and hugged Molly. "Maybe I can make her jealous."

Susan started a round of giggles.

"We almost had a moment." Frankie snapped her fingers at how quickly it had passed.

Chris started toward the front door; the man with her detoured toward the group of women. Chris caught up to him as he reached the table.

"Ladies," Chris spoke to the group. "Molly, it's good to see that you actually do take an evening off sometimes."

Molly nodded. "I'm betting the same could be said for you."

Chris nudged Spencer, trying to move him away from the table of women.

"Spencer Davis, her best friend, extremely heterosexual, and curious to know who might you be." He held out his hand to Susan.

"Smooth," Chris muttered.

Donna snickered. Molly rolled her eyes. Frankie finished her drink and signaled for another.

"I happen to like the direct approach. I'm Susan Neville." She shook Spencer's hand, inclining her head toward Molly. "Molly's friend and co-worker. We're all friends and co-workers, but not *family*."

"The Molly who called you last weekend when I answered the phone." Spencer grinned at Chris.

Chris smacked her palm against her forehead.

"Now we have to talk so we can fix the two of them up," Molly said to Chris.

"And yourselves." Susan smiled like the Cheshire cat.

Chris took Spencer's arm and tugged him into motion toward the front door.

The women at the table called goodbyes that turned Chris's face as red as Spencer's hair.

"What was that all about?" Spencer waited until he was at Chris's apartment to ask the question.

"What?" Chris concentrated on adding beans and water to the coffeemaker.

"You didn't introduce me in the restaurant. I didn't mean to embarrass you in front of *Molly*." He said the name as though they should be on a playground.

"It wasn't the right time."

Spencer walked up to Chris and put his arms around her. "Neither is waiting until you're in the retirement home to make your move."

"You'll make me lose count of scoops and have to start over." She pushed him away. "You certainly lost no time setting things up."

He went to the couch to channel surf. He idly ran his hands over his spiky red hair and smoothed his mustache. "And managed a date for myself. Susan's cute. Molly too. I want details."

Chris stared at the coffee beans and finished loading the built-in grinder. She walked into the living area. "I didn't know the rest of the women at the table and wouldn't have interrupted them if you hadn't started over to them without me."

"Like I don't know that? Christ, fearless when facing a gun and a wuss around a woman who obviously finds you attractive," Spencer said.

Chris tried to be aggravated with him but couldn't pull it off. She walked toward the bedroom. "I met Molly when I went to city hall for a map for court. She saved my ass. We were both dropping hints as subtle as cinderblocks about being lesbians. She works for that God-awful Jack Sampson. I told you about my brief internship when I graduated college."

Spencer grunted. "She must be into masochism. Kinky might be good for you."

Chris hit him with an aptly named throw pillow. "Go home. Julie has likely worn out herself and the babysitter by now."

"And you have a phone call to make," Spencer said as he ducked out the front door.

Chris actually checked the time.

CHAPTER NINE

Molly was supposed to spend the afternoon in training along with everyone else in her department. She knew when she blocked the time on her calendar that she likely would blow off the mandatory four-hour session on workplace violence. She carefully weighed the importance of a twenty million-dollar building under haul-ass construction versus listening to Ann Lawson drone on about remaining calm during conflict. It was a no-brainer. If she attended, all she would want to do was hurt Ann. If she stayed at her desk when no one expected her to be in her office, she might stand a chance of almost catching up on paperwork without having to stay in the office until midnight. "Sorry, Ann, no disrespect intended."

Molly looked forward to closing her door and not having it tapped on every fifteen minutes. She could ignore her telephone—she wasn't supposed to be in her office. Imagine the luxury of uninterrupted work time on a weekday.

"Come on, help a guy out. You know how I hate having to sit still that long. It's torture." Gary was trying to convince her that she needed his services once he figured out what she was doing.

"Can't do it. I'm going to be in enough trouble as it is when Ann turns me in to Jack." The wall that separated Molly's office from Gary's cube contained no soundproofing. They raised their voices and talked back and forth throughout the day.

He settled for flipping a note through the gap at the window.

"Turd face," Molly read aloud. "Love you too, Gar."

He thumbed his nose at her as he passed her door on his way to the makeshift training facilities set up in council chambers.

"Alone at last." She sighed contentedly and rolled sideways to the HVAC control on the unit attached to the wall below the window. It never ceased to amaze her that when the building had been renovated, the new interior walls had stopped at the deep windowsill, leaving a gap of three inches between wall and row of windowpanes. She normally ran the blower just to drown out Gary's telephone conversations with his wife. He claimed to get a kick out of listening to her soft-soap citizens and bully contractors all day long. She relied on text messaging with her personal cell phone and Hotmail to protect her privacy.

Molly decided she could take a moment to check her private e-mail one more time before settling in to work. Sure enough, Chris had answered her back.

"*Spencer is psyched about Susan. He's willing to try anything she's interested in, just asks for enough advance notice to line up a babysitter—me—and he's ready to go out with her. I agree about us. I'm interested but not sure I want to be involved right now because of work. Let's take it slow and try phone and e-mail for a while to give us time to get to know each other, keeping things open and low key. Thanks for understanding. I still owe you a meal. C*"

Molly was disappointed but knew it was for their own good. She opened a new Excel window and began a spreadsheet of bid quantities versus construction quantities. Someone entered the office next door. Molly almost yelled and caught herself. Gary would have done something obnoxious in passing if the training had been canceled. A second person entered and closed the door of Gary's office.

Molly smelled Jack's cologne before she heard his voice. What was it about middle-aged men that made them think they had to use twice as much of anything scented as they used to? Molly felt like a bloodhound, able to track her boss by sniffing the air when she was close enough in following him through a room. She had won lunch from Donna not long ago when her tracking ability was challenged.

"This position should have been filled by now. Even that damn Campbell has someone running GIS for his pipe work. We're the planners who wrote the grant for the stinking system, and only Molly has figured out how to use some of it." Jack rolled the chair out from the U-shaped work station that Gary occupied as utilities' GIS technician. A duplicate on the opposite side of the room was for community development's GIS station, sharing the wall with Jack's office. A chest-high partition divided the two stations.

"You know Donna has her heart set on the job." Eric paced about the common open area between cubicles and door in the hard wall. "Shouldn't we slip into the back row of the training?"

Jack blew a raspberry. "Donna will get over it. I've kept her back for years. She won't fight me. There's a lot to be said for management by intimidation."

"What do you have on her?" Eric asked.

Jack chuckled. "You don't need to know."

Molly didn't know whether to clamp her hands over her mouth or her ears.

"But I will tell you what I do as a test." Jack lowered his voice slightly. "I rig her performance evaluations."

"What?"

"I fill in one set to review with her as that damn bleeding-heart HR requires. Then I trade out the last page that Donna signs with front sheets loaded with negative comments. Every time she applies for another job, the department sees her evaluation on record with HR."

"Jack!"

Molly waited for Eric to protest further. Instead she heard a subdued laugh. "You are the master."

"She's an excellent worker, does most all of my routine work well enough that I don't even have to review it. Everything was fine until Molly started encouraging her about this GIS job." Jack slammed Gary's chair against his desk.

"Couldn't Donna accomplish just as much with GIS for you?"

"That's beside the point now," Jack tapped his fingers along the empty workstation, "thanks to you."

"I just happened to mention the vacancy to Barbara's niece. Tamika has computer training and is running a cash register at the grocery store. She could owe her career to me needing a case of beer. Ain't it cool?" Eric asked.

Molly heard the hum of the digitizer that was the size of a drafting table.

"What in the hell is this thing for anyway—a suntan?"

Molly shook her head; leave it to Jack to turn on equipment he had no concept about but issued purchase orders for.

Eric shut the equipment down. "Gary never runs the back light on that monster. He'll know someone was in here if the surface is warm from the bulbs."

"You worry about details too much."

"It's helped you so far." Eric hesitated. "I've another idea for you."

"Go ahead."

"Let the CD GIS tech report to me instead of Molly."

Jack didn't miss a beat. "But Molly's the engineer."

"I can be the computer expert." Eric lowered his voice. "I'll sit through some of the IT classes. You can tell Molly how overworked she is and that this will lighten her load a little."

"And you can hire Barbara's niece, helping me out, and leaving the deputy city manager owing me a favor."

"Exactly."

"Barbara's keeping a low profile on this one. I'm not supposed to know it's her niece. Barbara's posing as sponsoring a young black woman who's currently underemployed. Evidently, Tamika didn't tell her aunt about your nudge."

"It's a good thing I remembered Tamika's older sister from high school. Barbara forgets that I know the family and their connection to her." Eric sounded so smug that Molly felt herself gripping her pencil until her hand hurt.

"Barbara, nor any of the rest of them, realizes how much you pass along to me." Jack opened the door and the men left the GIS room.

Molly flashed back to the day early in her career that Jack approached her about spying on the others in the department for him. She had refused without hesitation, not caring about the consequences. Molly would choose an overloaded desk and clear conscience any day.

Molly's ideal afternoon was ruined. She alternated between staring out the window, at the computer monitor, and across her drafting table for three hours. She drank two Mountain Dews just to have the justification to walk to the vending machine.

A tap sounded on the door. Gary opened it wide enough to stick his head through sideways, using his necktie to mime a noose.

Molly did not laugh as usual.

"Damn, what did you get into this afternoon? You look as though you're way over budget instead of under." Gary frowned.

"What?" Molly said.

"What's wrong?" Gary walked into her office and closed the door.

She shook her head. "I can't talk about it. I've already had a good cry in the restroom. I'm trying to decide what to do next."

"You're scaring me." He pointed to the notebook in his hand. "I now know the physical, psychological, and behavioral signs and symptoms of stress."

"Spare me."

He counted off on his fingers. "Take care of yourself, manage your time, take time off, and choose your battles."

"Battle, hell. This is war, and I'm taking no prisoners nor showing any mercy." She grabbed his arm. "Don't say anything to anyone else on this floor."

He looked at the tight grip her hand had of him. "Are you going to explain these finger-shaped bruises to my girlfriend?"

"Tell her to sue me for sexual harassment. It'll help me fit in with the rest of the creeps around here." Molly grabbed her suede jacket and left the office before five o'clock for the first time that month.

CHAPTER TEN

Chris hoped she didn't look like she felt as she left work by the rear door of the public safety building. It would set her reputation back considerably if the guys knew how exhausted she was by ten hours of pulling files to prep for court cases coming up within the next week. How could working indoors, sitting at a desk at least half the time, make you so tired? How did people work in cubicles all day long? No wonder Molly loved being outside on construction projects. Chris wondered what else Molly loved.

Then she wondered why she was thinking of Molly so much after telling her she wanted to go slow. Her shoulders sagged and her back curved slightly more. Maybe she should stay at the office another hour and hope for exhaustion when she entered the empty apartment.

No such luck. She opened the door to the four-room apartment, looked at Spencer perched on the edge of the sofa emptying another bottle of beer to line up with two others, and remembered that they were to go out for a *nice* dinner to catch up. Spencer couldn't wait to tell her about his date.

"Oops." She couldn't think of anything else to say.

Spencer glanced at her. "It's okay, what I expected." He tapped the face of his watch. "I'm on the clock with a babysitter, though." His wardrobe had disintegrated as the evening wore on. His jacket was thrown on the floor near the front door. His shoes were kicked off toward the kitchen. His collar button loosened and necktie flung across the lamp shade. His shirt sleeves were shoved up his forearms rather than the precise three folds she liked to tease him about.

"I forgot." Chris tried a weak smile as she set her briefcase in the tall chair to the bar table near the door. "I can be ready in five minutes." She started toward the bathroom.

He drank the last of the beer and pretended as though he was going to throw the bottle somewhere in her vicinity. "We can stay in if you'd rather talk here. I just wanted to treat you to a nice dinner out to pay you back for your part in setting me up with Susan." His smile stretched his face to its limit.

"Aren't you hungry?"

"Well, yeah, but I can see that you're beat."

Chris stopped at the end of the sofa. She idly wondered if she would be able to stay awake if she went into the kitchen for a beer. "Let's go out. It would do me good."

Spencer held his hand up for a high-five. "I'm only going to bring this up once. It's your call, but that's what you should tell Molly." He shook his head. "Hell, I had so much fun with Susan that my lesbian chromosomes are kicking in. I want to move her in with me as our second date."

Chris groaned. "Come on." She motioned toward the front door and went around the room gathering his clothing. "Five minutes or less, I won't even change clothes. We'll go out and have a nice meal. We're both too tired and hungry to sit here and seriously discuss anything at this point." She nudged him into motion.

"Starving." He stuck out his lower lip in a mock pout before smiling.

They entered the restaurant at 7:45, late for them but still early enough for a good crowd in the renovated train station. Amtrak actually operated from the basement of the building on track level. Chris liked the restaurant because no one thought it odd to stop and start conversations as they waited for the passing freight trains to clear the area; it was like the game they played as children dropping into chairs when the music stopped.

Two-thirds of the building was the dining area. Booths constructed from salvaged church pews lined the walls. Tables made from abandoned telephone cable spools were spaced across the interior of the room with screens and potted plants breaking the open space into private dining areas. The remainder of the building was the kitchen. The exterior door leading into the kitchen accommodated carryout order pickup—previously it had been the segregated entrance for blacks when the building was constructed by Southern Railway in 1912. Chris often stopped by and picked up dinner on days when she ate neither breakfast nor lunch.

They settled into their booth, agreed to try the newest microbrew on tap, and ordered their food without having to consult the menu, choosing the blackened tilapia that was one of the night's specials.

Chris finally felt herself relaxing as Spencer smiled with his discovery of a new beer that he liked. She thought the brew master a little carried away with spices but did not care as the alcohol content loosened her lower back.

"Don't look behind you." Spencer leaned across the table as he stared over her shoulder.

Chris raised her eyebrows as she took another drink from the tall pilsner glass. She whispered. "Why not?"

He grinned at her. "It's Molly, and she's on a hot date."

Chris felt her back tighten up.

"Damn." He couldn't stop staring across the room.

"Scoot over." Chris slid to the end of her seat and pivoted onto the bench beside him without standing. She followed his line of sight and had no problem locating the couple diagonally across from them. She felt like a Peeping Tom as she peered between the plants and screens.

Molly wore a pale pink cowl neck sweater that made her dark chestnut hair and tan skin glow provocatively. The slightest trace of dark mauve lipstick remained on her lips. Her green eyes sparkled. She sat as close to her date as their chairs allowed. The woman with her was older, blond, and wore a low-cut black sweater that Molly was unable to raise her eyes from.

"I feel like I should have rented this on video." Spencer's mustache tickled Chris's ear as he whispered to her. "Damn, that could be you."

Chris elbowed him in the ribs. He was annoying her and knew it. She felt her temper flare. "What is it about seeing two women together that turns men on so? If that were two men, you'd be calling the office for a warrant and having me radio a patrol car." She signaled the waiter and pushed the half full pilsner to the edge of the table. "Too damn fruity. May I have a Yuengling, please?"

Chris saw only one of Molly's hands. She watched the blonde guide Molly under the table. "What the hell is Molly thinking, seducing this woman in a public restaurant?"

"That at least two people are going to get lucky tonight." Spencer signaled for a refill. "I would have drunk yours." He held up his glass when Chris glanced at him. "No sense wasting expensive beer. You might have at least asked before you sent yours back." His gaze remained on Chris. He waited a few moments and snapped his fingers. "Remember me? Damn it, Chris, you're the one who stressed platonic and open to Molly. Sheesh, I should have kept my mouth shut about seeing her."

"I cannot believe she is carrying on like this in the middle of a crowded restaurant. Something is wrong with this picture."

"Who cares anymore? From what you've said, Molly's reputation is gold because of her work. I see her name in the newspaper at least once a week now that you've brought her onto my radar screen." He leaned back as their food was served. He held up his fresh glass of beer. "To relationships based on not being able to keep your hands off of each other. Please let Susan and me be that way for a few decades." He looked upward.

Chris tried to return her attention to him as she toasted. She no longer had an appetite for anything at the table.

"Come on, babe. Lighten up and enjoy the evening out. I'm not going to say 'I told you so,' but women like Molly don't sit around lonely for long. You had your chance." Spencer motioned to her plate as he scooped a large forkful of fish into his mouth. "This is absolutely delicious."

Chris sighed and picked at the food with her fork. She had made her bed. Chris looked up on eye level with two very filled-out sweaters.

"Hey, I almost didn't see you." Molly's arm was around her date's waist, as much to keep herself upright as to show affection.

"I'm not surprised," Chris said flatly.

"Because of the crap scattered across the floor." Spencer nodded to Molly.

Molly fumbled with her words. "This is Bev. We met on Match.com a few weeks ago. Before you came to city hall. I had promised her dinner."

"I promised to help Molly recover from her breakup with what's-her-name. Best $19.99 I ever spent." Bev shook Spencer's hand firmly.

"I told her I'd give her a refund if she was disappointed." Molly looked sheepishly at Chris.

"I told her I owed Match at least twice the usual membership for all the fun I've had with our e-mails. She steams up my laptop."

"I knew it was time to do something when I almost wrecked the city car when I saw the slinky blonde on the David Yurman summer billboard." Molly whistled appreciatively and ducked a punch from Bev. She looked at Chris. "You understand, right?"

Spencer spoke first. "She's just a little tired."

"A lot tired of too many things," Chris said. "It's you I'm worried about being okay." She stared at Molly.

Bev pulled Molly toward the door. "We *need* to go."

Molly nodded. "Oh, yeah. See you guys." She hesitated. "How about lunch next week, Chris?"

"I'll call you in case you don't remember much about tonight." Chris's expression was as sour as her stomach.

Bev kissed Molly's cheek and pulled her toward the exit. "I might have to do some serious butt kicking if you two decide to be more than pen pals."

"I'd like to see you try." Molly's voice carried across the restaurant. "Did you mean mine or hers?"

"Come find out." Bev was out the door with Molly in pursuit.

"Jeez, she's going to regret this in the morning." Chris shook her head and slid her untouched plate of food over to Spencer.

"But I bet she has a hell of a good time tonight. I can remember when you did things like that." Spencer set Chris's full plate on top of his empty one.

Chris watched him eat. She hated when he was right.

CHAPTER ELEVEN

"Just where were you last Thursday? Your name is on none of the sign-in sheets for the training that was *mandatory*. That means everyone, including you, no matter how busy you think you are. We are all overloaded, that's why the training is required." Ann frowned across her desk.

Molly had expected no less when she entered Ann's office and closed the door behind her. She tried to keep at bay the first thought that always entered her mind in Ann's domain—how could Ann expect anyone to take her seriously when the end of her desk provided background for a collection of motivational magnets and her windowsill displayed the kitchenware she sold on the side?

Molly freely admitted to uncharitable thoughts about Ann. After all, the woman's job was about everyone else's jobs—where was the real work in that? It did not help that Ann was only an inch taller than Molly, sixty pounds heavier, and went to a hair stylist who specialized in frosted peaks mixing blond, brown, and gray so that no one was sure of Ann's hair color. The fact that Ann's taste in clothes often ran to big plaids or floral prints did little to help her image.

"Do you have a minute?" Molly knew the next two hours were empty; Susan had checked Ann's calendar for Molly earlier.

Ann sighed. "Yes." She sat straight in her chair and folded her hands on her desk blotter. This conversation was to be strictly business.

Molly pulled the side chair as close to Ann's desk as possible and lowered her voice. "The GIS technician position for community development."

Ann raised her eyebrows. Molly knew it was a bad sign that Ann was volunteering nothing.

"Is it still assigned to me?"

Ann reached across her desk to the bottom-most basket of the inbox on the corner. She opened a file folder and pretended to refresh her memory. "It's been reassigned to Eric. Jack was to have discussed this with you."

"I heard about it by accident. I just wanted to check how far along this scheme was."

Ann's back and face tightened.

"That's not all I heard." Molly leaned forward.

Silence.

Molly continued. "I need to see Donna's performance evaluations."

Ann shook her head. "You're not her supervisor nor do you have a position to be considering her for. You have no need to know what's in her record."

Molly took a deep breath. "Come on, Ann. The door is closed. What's said in this office stays in this office. I need to see Donna's evaluations."

"No, that's privileged information." Ann closed the file and returned it to the bottom basket. "Make a request to the city manager and bring his approval to me in writing."

"I'm not ready to do that yet."

"Then I can't help you."

"You mean you won't help me."

"That too."

Molly nodded. "I heard Jack tell Eric how he handles Donna's performance evaluations—good ones to review with her, bad ones in her file to discourage another department from hiring her. I'm trying to help you out by giving you the benefit of the doubt that you don't realize that personnel records have been falsified. I will go to Donna with this. I'm trying to help her advance so that she won't quit her job and sue the city. It's your call. Donna is willing to take classes at the community college. I'll make time to work with her and help her. Eric is welcome to being her supervisor—I never wanted to cross the us/them line and move into management anyway. Eric does. He will do anything that Jack tells him to. I won't. It's that simple."

Ann studied her hands—her stylist was better with nails than hair. "Jack warned me that you were upset after I readvertised the position. I didn't think you would take it to this extreme." She hesitated. "I tried to talk with Donna when I saw that her evaluations didn't match my perception of her work."

Molly waited for the rest.

Ann shrugged. "She wouldn't discuss her review with me other than to verify her signature on the form."

Molly felt her chin drop.

"Tamika Travers is an extremely good candidate. She already has the college education without the city having to participate in tuition reimbursement. We can hire her at the lowest pay band because it's so much more than she currently makes at minimum wage."

Molly stared.

"You said this conversation is off the record," Ann reminded Molly.

Molly's voice was flat. "You know who Tamika's aunt is?"

Ann nodded. "Jack told me, not Barbara. Barbara knows her boundaries and has stayed out of this other than introducing me to Tamika when she filled in an application for a vacant city position and advising Tom of the relationship. Barbara has handled this correctly."

"And I haven't?" Molly finished the thought for the pompous, overbearing skunk-haired woman—not that Molly would describe Ann in that fashion.

"The tech job and Donna's job are none of your concern." Ann tried to dismiss Molly.

Molly took the hint. She stood, moved the side chair away from the desk, and placed her hand on the doorknob. "You haven't heard the last of this." She looked over her shoulder at Ann.

"I have if you want to keep your job, Molly, and I say that as someone who respects you and has enjoyed what you have allowed me to know of you in the office. I know your opinion of me and what I do. That's okay, it's the way your brain works. Your thoughts must produce a physical result of blueprints or a building or a pipe line. You're an excellent engineer, but you're not a team player. You're too introverted and idealistic for your own good in an office setting and much too task orientated. You can't be an individual in what must be a team atmosphere." Ann straightened the papers in her top basket.

"You tell me who else cares more about their work or takes more responsibility for their own actions? We're not exactly manufacturing widgets here on an assembly line. We're public servants with accountability to the taxpayers to be good stewards of public funds. We damn well better look out for each other or the Jacks will take over and do any damn thing that suits them. I thought being the moral compass in the broad sense of employees' welfare was part of your job. Team means being able to point a finger at someone else when there's blame involved. Flattening management just means the finger doesn't point upward as easily. Don't think that we don't realize that whatever jargon comes out of your mouth is just one more style of screwing lower paid employees until the next management bestseller comes out and you decide to goosestep in a different direction. What flavor Kool-Aid do you serve these days?"

Ann's face was pale.

Molly was past the point of caring what she said. "Am I not politically correct? I'm sure there's mandatory training for that, too, or an employee referral session. Just be sure that you quote me correctly when you go to Jack with this."

Molly closed the door behind her and was shocked to see Tom Stafford in his corner office when she followed the short hallway to exit the suite. He was to have been out until mid-afternoon.

"Shit." Molly walked faster.

Tom didn't speak until Molly was just past his door. "Thanks for looking out for me."

Molly returned to his doorway.

"My windows have been cleaned—no more bugs. My concentration is much better now that I don't feel as though I'm being stared at by empty carcasses."

Molly walked away and wished she could say the same.

CHAPTER TWELVE

"Miller going off-call during construction monitoring." Chris glanced at her Mickey Mouse watch. She was early, but the gravel parking area was already full of pickup trucks. She eased off of the paved street onto the very corner of the staging area and looked for oncoming cars before opening her door. She unclipped her radio and cell phone from her belt, making sure both were turned off, and tossed them on the seat. She locked the unmarked car and made sure the single key was deep in her pants pocket. She went to the trunk and exchanged black Rockports for boots—no sense ruining another pair of shoes.

Chris glanced across the street at the retirement condominiums. The flat roof was lined with folding chairs and spectators. The facility's activity director must be a brave soul to make an event of the demolition scheduled for mid-morning. The residents definitely had the best seats with a clear line of sight from the rooftop, over the woods, to the creek bottom below.

The street dipped thirty feet to connect to an old concrete bridge at least sixty feet higher than the stream below the structure. The bridge was the second built on the street; the first had been made of wood and burned after World War I.

The annual inspection report on the concrete structure completed in 1920 had finally scared city council badly enough that funds were appropriated to replace the bridge with a triple box culvert and compacted fill to the road elevation.

The fire marshal's office handled the demolition permitting and requested a police officer on site as a precaution. Chris was assigned to the project since the other detectives had already rotated through construction projects involving blasting. She complained of the extra duty as was expected but found herself looking forward to observing the process. She had talked with the subcontractor at length the previous week. Jeff educated her on his method and convinced her that he did know what he was doing. He relied on a relatively simple combination of explosives, blasting agent, and detonators in conjunction with an intricate pattern of drill holes to collapse the structure into rubble that would be used in the bottom fringes of the fill material as riprap to protect the compacted layers of dirt.

Chris waved, catching the attention of the general contractor's superintendent. He walked across the area cleared for staging, equipment parking, and access road down to the creek. Chris had made it a point to stop and introduce herself to him the week before also.

"Ma'am." He scratched the stubble on his cheeks.

"Trying for a beard by hunting season, Charlie?" Chris asked.

The slight man nodded as they shook hands. "If I can get through the first few days of itching." He wore a heavy flannel shirt suited to the woods.

Chris adjusted the band on her hardhat and set it on her head again, this time snugly. "On schedule?"

"Just about." Charlie glanced about at his crew. The earthmoving equipment that usually operated scattered about both slopes leading to the creek was gathered at the far end of the job site. The men were warned that anyone violating the cones set out at the safe distance from the bridge to avoid airborne debris would be fined. "They're like kids. They all want a front row seat to see the big bang."

"Just like them." She pointed over her shoulder at the rooftop gray hairs. "You've drawn quite a crowd for something you were trying to keep quiet."

"Have you ever heard worse gossips than a group of men?" He grinned, sending the ends of his mustache curling upward. "Don't answer that."

"I work with some of the best. They put little old women to shame."

"I heard that."

Chris stared across the crowd. She spied a woman who looked familiar, engaged with the contractor performing the final wiring on the charges.

Charlie followed her gaze. He shook his head. "She was here as soon as the blast crew rolled in this morning. You ought to have heard her discussing thermodynamics with the blaster-in-charge. Molly doesn't leave anything to chance on her jobs, and you don't want to piss her off."

Chris looked at Charlie and raised her eyebrows.

"Molly Hamilton, the city engineer, is a pistol. I've only seen her lose it once on a project, and the crew leader didn't sit down for a week after the ass chewing she gave him. She caught him sending men to lay pipe without a trench box where the soil was loose and the men deep." Charlie waved to flag down the last bulldozer. "You're on standby up here with me in case they need you for something. Go on down there about twenty feet behind the blast station and keep your eyes on Jeff."

Chris followed the D-8 as it rumbled along. She waited until Molly stepped back from the demolition team before speaking. "Looks as though you have these guys under control."

Molly glanced at Chris, her concentration never leaving what the men were doing. "I wouldn't go so far as to claim that. They're just like little boys with firecrackers, but Jeff is good. I've worked with him before."

The man looked over his shoulder and nodded. He caught the reflection off of Chris's badge in his tinted glasses. "You must be Inspector Miller. We spoke on the telephone." He held out his hand.

"I am. I'm just here to observe, not interfere. The uniform guys have traffic control in place and are manning the barricades with the city guys to make sure no one comes through once you're in countdown mode."

Jeff nodded. "Good deal. We're on time. They're to button up traffic in five minutes." He glanced at his wristwatch. Despite the nature of his work, Jeff's khakis were immaculate.

Chris nodded and caught a whiff of aftershave; there was no sense of nervousness about the demolition expert. Chris found herself more interested in observing Molly than the demolition crew. Molly was dressed in crisp jeans and a navy cotton sweater. She wore a digital camera on a strap around her neck and her hardhat was as scuffed as those worn by the construction crew. Chris felt foolishly self-conscious of her shiny white hardhat purchased just for that day.

Molly moved in synchronization with the contractor, never in his way but close enough to see everything he did. She nodded occasionally and seemed satisfied with procedure and execution. Chris followed her lead.

Jeff stood and signaled the men on the opposite side of the bridge. No one remained within the demarked area. He looked at Molly. "Ready?"

"You bet." Molly grinned for the first time that morning. "I feel like Gomez Addams with his train sets."

The guys closest to her laughed.

Jeff nodded and talked them through what he was doing with the blasting machine while connecting the master cable and setting the timing of the charges. Jeff depressed and held the button on the left to charge, waited thirty seconds as the button on the right lit up, and depressed the fire button.

Chris felt a chill go down her back. She watched all eyes but Jeff's and Molly's stare at the bridge; they focused on the row of small lights glowing in succession on the lunchbox-size blasting machine.

Jeff finally released both buttons. He looked at Molly. "Electrical charge to all circuits."

Molly nodded. "Woo-hoo."

A series of puffs of air in a zigzag pattern popped into view after each boom. The noise was surprisingly muffled. The puffs ceased. The bridge remained standing.

"Damn it." Jeff depressed the buttons in sequence again. Nothing visible happened on the bridge. He motioned for the D-8 and disconnected the master cable.

"Whoa. It's too soon to leave the control area. Give it a few more minutes." Molly grabbed the man's sleeve.

"I need to check the drill holes. We must have misfires. That damn bridge should be in the gully by now."

"Hell, no. Wait. You haven't given enough time for the stress fractures."

"Then I'll help the cracks spread with the weight of the D-8." Jeff motioned the driver off of the D-8 and climbed into the cab.

Molly followed him. "If it's safe enough for you, I'm going along." She stared the man into compliance. She glanced at Chris. "Don't even think about it."

"Suit yourself." Jeff started the bulldozer.

Before he drove twenty feet inside of the cone line, the center section of the bridge collapsed, pulling the ends after it, leaving a huge cloud of thick dust in its wake.

Everyone in the crowd fanned their hands in front of their faces and coughed. A cheer went up from the group gathered on the rooftop.

The bulldozer stopped. Molly and Jeff climbed down, coughing and covered in a layer of fine particles.

Molly grinned and gave Charlie a thumbs-up. She hit Jeff on the back to help clear his lungs. "We'll talk about this at next week's project meeting."

"All clear!" Jeff called. The two words were repeated by others across the site as though an echo.

Molly walked uphill toward the staging area. Chris fell into step with her.

"Is anyone else with us?" Molly took off her sunglasses and pulled her sweater up to get to the shirt tail tucked inside her pants. It was the only part of her clothing clean enough to wipe her glasses.

Chris glimpsed firm, tan abs and looked over her shoulder. "No. They're still patting each other on the back."

"Men are so stupid. I guess they do need to be able to pee standing up." Molly let out a deep breath as Chris chuckled. "He could have been badly injured."

"How about you?"

Molly shrugged. "They're my responsibility. Jack sits in the office, handling projects by telephone, and would blame me first and find out if I was dead second."

Chris stared at Molly. "And you put up with this why?"

"Because it's my job and I love it. I have no contract stating that my work will be fair or easy." She smiled at Chris. "How about you?"

"Hell, no. We have to do it as well and backward."

"While in high heels." Molly knew the supposed Faith Whittlesey quote by heart.

Chris leaned close and whispered to Molly. "Secretly, I think some of the guys I work with would like to try the high heels."

Molly laughed and bumped shoulders with Chris, leaving a dusty spot on Chris's jacket. "Is Spencer as insufferable as Susan? You'd think they were the first two people to fall in love for crying out loud."

Chris chuckled. "Even their kids like each other. I keep holding my breath, waiting for that first glitch."

Molly shook her head. "I don't think it's going to happen. They've both been through enough with early marriages and ugly divorces to genuinely appreciate each other."

Chris nodded. She hesitated before speaking. "How about us? Have we each been through enough to appreciate the other? It worries me the way you seem to go through women."

Molly sighed. "Bev was a mistake. I've apologized to her and you. I think I was trying to get your attention."

"Well, it worked. I haven't felt that jealous in a long time."

Molly was silent as she thought about what Chris had said. "I always seem to rush in, then feel the need to pull away. I don't know why. I do know that I felt instantly comfortable and relaxed with you."

"Should we give dating a try?" Chris pulled her key out of her pocket and unlocked the car.

"Yes, please." Molly opened the door for her.

Chris stared deep into Molly's eyes. "I'm talking monogamy."

Molly nodded and squeezed Chris's hand. She would do her best.

CHAPTER THIRTEEN

Molly stared at her computer keyboard. She was drafting an update briefing on the industrial park—Project Night, sans Mr. and Mrs. Reynolds. It was all good information, but the report just would not come together even if the actual work was progressing beautifully. The first portable substations would emerge from the plant in little more than a year.

Molly missed Donna. When Tamika's hiring was announced, Donna waited until she knew the black woman's start date and requested two weeks of vacation. Being a firm believer in avoiding direct confrontation whenever possible, Jack approved it. He reasoned to Molly that this would give Donna time to cool off and Tamika a chance to meet everyone without Donna glaring in the background. Eric offered no comment on any of it, wisely choosing to avoid Molly as much as possible. Jack tiptoed around Molly also, much to Molly's amusement. Molly was still debating what to do.

"I'm going to copy the design guidelines you loaned me." Tamika stopped in the doorway of Molly's office. She held up the notebook. Tamika Travers was an attractive young woman in her mid-twenties with an air of calm assurance about her. That attitude plus the fact that she made it plain she would be pleasant but not take crap from anyone made it easy to be around her. She was slightly shorter and heavier than Molly, carefully skirting the fine line between voluptuous and overweight. Molly liked her immediately. Tamika had already learned all that Molly remembered from her rudimentary GIS training.

"Good idea. If you have any questions…"

"I'll ask you when Eric isn't around." Tamika grinned at Molly.

Molly waved her off. She liked the fact that Tamika was quick to catch on to everything in city hall.

The minimized e-mail window on her task bar highlighted. She had mail. The message was from Windy. There was no text other than the subject line—MEETING ROOM IN TEN MINUTES.

Molly grabbed change from her desk drawer. She might as well grab a drink while she was away from her desk. She left her office and went through the employee-only door into the main hallway. She glanced in the map room as she passed the double doors and waved to Mark. What was it about a bald man with a neat beard that was so attractive? If she were straight, she would spend time away from work with Mark. He was long over being embarrassed at asking her out before he realized she was a lesbian; he still held out hope that Molly would change her mind.

The door to the women's restroom was across the hall from council chambers. Molly pushed through and waited. She didn't need to pee. "Come on, Windy, I have a deadline," Molly said to herself, checking the time on her BlackBerry.

The next woman to enter was Windy, ably maneuvering her chair through the two doors of the vestibule that afforded the restroom privacy. From her vantage point, Windy glanced toward the stalls lining the long wall to check for shoes. They were the only ones in the restroom.

Molly made sure the surface was dry and leaned against the sink.

Windy stared at her. "I can't believe anyone would throw away their reputation over another woman's performance."

Molly rolled her eyes. "Jesus, how does gossip circulate so fast?"

"You might have at least given me a heads-up so I would've been prepared for the questions. Two of those idiot council members called me at home last night."

Molly grimaced. "Sorry, it didn't occur to me. I honestly didn't think anyone else would be that interested." She hopped on the edge of the sink, sensing Windy was about to launch into one of her filibuster rantings.

"Not interested." Windy rolled her chair back and forth slightly, her equivalent of pacing. "Who would not be interested?"

"In my sex life?"

Windy was momentarily speechless, something she rarely experienced. "What are you talking about?"

"What are you talking about?" Molly jumped off the sink.

"Tamika and her *Aunt* Barbara."

Molly blew a puff of air between her lips. "I thought it was out about me at The Station."

"So you did know about the relationship between Barbara and Tamika and didn't tell me." Windy rolled within an inch of Molly's toes. "Who were you with at The Station?"

Molly placed her hands on the armrests of the wheelchair. "Tamika was recruited and hired by Eric at Jack's bidding. That's why Jack reassigned the tech position to Eric. Jack knew that Barbara would try to keep it quiet that Tamika is her niece and wanted Barbara owing him a favor—screw Donna. I went to the person I thought I was supposed to discuss personnel matters with, Ann—screw me."

"Oh, boy." Windy closed her eyes.

"Oh, yeah. It made me want to shoot myself. Tamika looks great on paper and is a good hire from what I've seen so far. Donna is finally taking some time off. Jack has everyone else in his pocket. I didn't want to make you feel obligated to do something by telling you any of this. Who in the hell can do anything about this mess we call local government? So I went on Match and found another stalker to go out with since my life wasn't complicated enough." Molly straightened up. "Bev was almost worth it," she fanned her collar suggestively, "since Chris saw us out together."

Windy placed her hands over her ears. "Don't give me details. I don't want to know about anyone else's sex life, gay or straight, and, yes, I still enjoy sex."

It was Molly's turn to put her hands over her ears, but she was smiling.

"How bad a stalker?" Windy asked. "What about Chris?"

Molly folded her arms together. "Bev's into phone calls and e-mails on the hour but not camped out on my doorstep yet. I don't think she's following me during the day. Her job as a drug rep keeps her fairly occupied during the week. I'm hoping she meets a cute nurse and forgets me." Molly waited until she had Windy's full attention. "Chris and I are ready to give it a try."

Windy placed her fingers in the corners of her mouth and whistled. The sound echoed off the tile walls. Molly covered her ears for real. "Sorry," Windy said. "It's about damn time. You two are perfect for each other. I first met Chris when she was with Ruth. You do know about Ruth?"

"Some. Chris will tell me in her own time." Molly hesitated. "It sounds so damn corny, but it just feels right to think about years with Chris."

"That's a good start. You know I want this to work for you." Windy had been the first of Molly's friends to sing Chris's praises when Molly finally told Windy of the good chemistry of their meeting.

Molly raised crossed fingers. "I'm going to try."

Windy frowned at her. "Don't hyperventilate. You can maintain a relationship when it's the right person." Windy waited for Molly to nod in agreement. Her expression hardened. "How did you find out about Jack and Eric and Tamika?"

"Eavesdropping, of course. You don't actually think any of the men around here who stir the pot have balls enough to do or say anything to someone's face?"

Windy shook her head. "Are you okay?"

"No, but I feel worse for Donna. I led her down the path of thinking she had a promotion. She says she's not angry or disappointed in me, but how can she not be? There's something festering between her and Jack that she allows. How in the hell do I fix this?"

"Tom is the only one who can do anything at this point."

Molly blew air again. "Yeah, right. How much Internet news do I have to read or bugs do I have to remove from his office for him to realize I have a problem I actually need his help with?" She held up her hand. "Rhetorical questions."

"I thought Barbara was smarter."

Molly shook her head. "I thought Jack would wait longer to spill this. He must be afraid Tamika will do the job well so he's thrown out the nepotism accusation early to see if it sticks with anyone."

"Or he tried to hold it over Barbara and she didn't take him seriously. How do any of us get actual work done around here for juggling the dance card tracking schemes?" Windy rotated her chair toward the door.

"I actually feel badly for Tamika. I like her, and she seems very competent," Molly said.

"As opposed to Barbara?"

Molly chuckled. "Yeah." She rattled the change in her pocket. "Buy you a drink, you sexy thing?"

"Only if you promise not to give my e-mail address to any of your rejected lust bunnies." Windy made a second run at the door to align her wheels correctly—there was little margin for error. "I better not catch you doing anything stupid like Internet cruising as long as you're seeing Chris."

"Yes, ma'am."

"Or I'll prop myself up and figure out how to kick you in the ass."

"You would, too." Molly laughed loudly enough to glance about the hall to see who else was close as she held open the doors for Windy to exit the restroom.

Neither of them heard the soft click of the bolt on the corner stall after Barbara eased her feet to the floor.

CHAPTER FOURTEEN

Chris stared at the pieces remaining to finish the jigsaw puzzle—this had been Julie's idea. Julie was now fast asleep on the sofa as Chris struggled with the solid blue sky pieces that all looked alike. Why couldn't it be next Friday night when Chris had a date? Chris smiled at the prospect. Spencer had been unable to find a substitute sitter that night, so she and Molly waited yet another week for their first evening out.

The door opened, and Spencer walked in. Chris held her index finger to her lips, then pointed to the L-shaped sofa.

Spencer nodded. He looked at the puzzle and rolled his eyes. "I warned you not to let her talk you into that."

Chris studied her friend. "Oh, my—afterglow." She batted her eyelids.

Spencer shrugged and grinned. "We're still not sure about spending all night together. The kids sort of know and are okay so far, but we don't want to push our luck. Smith is two years younger than Julie, and they act as though separated at birth." He sat at the bar-height table opposite her and pushed puzzle pieces around, fitting two that she had been staring at.

Chris smacked his hand away from the jigsaw. "You make it look too easy, just like with Susan. No fair."

Spencer crossed his arms and leaned on the table. "It's supposed to be easy when it's the right person. Isn't that what finally dawned on you and Molly?"

Chris looked at him. "You know, for a man, you're surprisingly intuitive."

Spencer cupped his face in his hands. "I'll take that as a compliment."

Chris laughed. "As was intended."

Spencer reached for another puzzle piece, handed it to Chris, and pointed to the location it fit.

"Jeez, that's even worse, you don't have to hold it close and rotate it to fit."

"There are so many responses I could make to that." Spencer batted his eyes.

She threw the piece at him and waited for him to pick it up off the floor.

"I debated talking to you about this as I drove over. It truly is none of my business. But…" He stopped, gauging her receptiveness.

"Go ahead."

"Have you really told Molly about Ruth so that she'll understand what she is walking into here?"

"I've told her bits and pieces as we've e-mailed and talked on the telephone. She's done the same about her past, even though I can't pin her down on an exact count of the number of women she's slept with." Chris set the puzzle box aside.

Spencer puffed out his cheeks as he thought. "Because of that—and I'm not implying promiscuity—shouldn't you make sure she understands where you're coming from before you become emotionally invested and discover she's just out for one more fling?"

Chris stared.

"I say this as a friend who loves you and would leave my child to you," Spencer finished.

"You make it sound like I'm damaged goods."

Spencer leaned across the table and kissed her forehead. "More like precious cargo." He picked up Julie without waking her and left the apartment.

Chris tossed and turned most of the night. The next day, she nested in sweats on the sofa and covered herself with an afghan while enjoying old movies on a rainy day. As darkness fell, she decided to call Molly.

"Hello?"

Chris took a deep breath. "I just wanted to hear your voice."

"I'm flattered and mildly aroused."

Chris heard the smile in Molly's voice. "How can those few words from you make me feel so much better?"

"It's a gift." Molly chuckled low in her throat. "Seriously, are you okay?"

"I haven't done a damn thing all day but think of you."

"Bless your heart." Molly tried for a proper Southern drawl.

"Did you work today?"

"Of course," Molly said. "I'm hoping next Saturday I'll be too tired to think of the office."

Chris was silent.

"Hey, that was just a joke. Sorry if it was poorly timed."

Chris pulled the afghan tighter around her. "No, it's okay, it's me, just the mood I'm in."

"What's going on in that head of yours?" Molly asked gently.

"We need to talk," Chris said.

"Uh-oh. Usually, I hear that after I've lived with someone for a year or two." Molly still had not picked up on how serious Chris needed the conversation to be.

"Molly, you're not making this any easier."

"I'm sorry, sweetie. Just talk to me."

"I've told you about Ruth."

"Yes—she was your first long-term relationship and she passed away while you two were together." Molly summarized what Chris had told her in previous conversations.

"Ruth was much more. She was my mentor in high school. I made an awkward pass at her while in my junior year and she held back until I graduated."

"Wow, talk about protracted foreplay."

"Molly!"

"Sorry. I tend to joke when I'm nervous."

"And I'm making you nervous just talking about real commitment. Maybe this was a bad idea." Chris sighed.

"Don't start huffing. I've wondered about you and Ruth. I know I'm stepping into shoes I will never fill and that's pretty daunting." Molly was finally serious.

"Please don't think of it that way. Ruth seems another lifetime ago. I'm no longer who I was when I was with her. I was always just a kid with her because of our age difference." Chris hesitated. "She's the only woman I've ever been with."

"Say again?"

"You heard me."

"Wow. She was ten years older than you?"

"Yes. She was always the teacher and mother substitute. Ruth helped me grow up and embrace being a lesbian."

"I can appreciate that," Molly said quietly.

"Ruth was so much a part of my life. When she died, I had spent almost half of my life with her. I've grieved for the past three years. That heavy, dark feeling has become habit. When I met you, I felt that darkness begin to lift." Chris took a drink of water. "Sheesh, my life sounds like a really bad lesbian movie."

"Tell me all of it. You haven't changed my mind so far."

"I'll never forget the day Ruth was diagnosed. She had gone to the doctor because her eyes were jaundiced. She thought the drinking had finally taken its toll. She was facing tests to confirm pancreatic cancer, yet she was so calm and detached. She was processing all she had been told and the finality of it just hadn't sunk in yet."

"Who wants to think about death? The prospect scares the hell out of me."

"I watched her change from the vibrant partner I always counted on to a dependent patient. It was my mother all over again—she went through a series of devastating strokes when I was in high school. It was too soon for me to go through losing someone again—the doctor's appointments, the injections, the exploratory surgeries, the glimmers of hope that crashed with blood analysis, and hospice taking over my home. The county teachers mobilized and set up a car pool to help her make all the appointments so I didn't have to quit work. I didn't let her see me cry when I took her to the stylist to have her head shaved when her hair started coming out. Through it all, she denied that she was dying. I was amazed that she had a will and accounts set up jointly to help me settle things."

"And you managed all of this with only transportation help?"

"Neither of us had any family. Spencer was my rock, but he had just begun practicing law and had a toddler and unhappy wife at home. The guys I worked with knew and covered for me when I needed time off but never really talked about it."

Molly let out a long breath. "No wonder you're reluctant to get involved with me."

Chris shook her head, not thinking about Molly having no visual of her. "That's not the reason for this at all. I'm afraid I won't be enough fun for you."

Molly laughed. "Girl, you're a piece of work. All you've been through and you're thinking about me. Look, we both have pasts, yours just happens to be much more honorable than mine. I say we give this a try, we keep talking, and we let the past settle itself as we try for a future together."

"That's not all," Chris said. "I very much believe in my job. Being a police detective is twenty-four-hour duty. I can be called onto a case at any time. An investigation usually takes weeks, if not months, of tedious observation. I have to be an example to the community. I take my oath very seriously."

"I don't believe I'm hearing this instead of saying it," Molly said. "I'm as bad in my own way. I'm a steward of the city's funds and welfare. I have to put in long hours on important projects."

"Pact to understand each other's obsession about work?"

"Absolutely."

"What about your ghosts, Molly?" Chris waited and thought Molly was not going to answer her.

"I had a father who walked out on my mom and me when I was eleven. I had a mom who put up a good front but died from a broken heart. I'll always believe suppressed stress exacerbated her illness—lung cancer when she never smoked, but my father did. I learned to work hard for whatever I wanted. I have a difficult time talking about feelings or letting anyone get too close. I tend to bolt. Have I scared you off?"

Chris didn't hesitate to answer. "No. I'd say we're starting out even."

"I'd say I'd just like a chance with you." Molly's voice lowered. "Let's look our ghosts in the face, say 'boo,' and run like hell."

"Sounds like a plan. Good night, Molly."

"Sleep well, darling."

"No bad dreams." Chris thought she heard Molly say "amen" as she hung up.

CHAPTER FIFTEEN

Molly knew that Jack was somewhere in the building. His jacket and car keys were tossed on the coffee table as when he arrived that morning. Donna usually hung up his jacket before any scheduled meetings in his office.

Donna had stepped away from her cubicle just outside of Jack's office long enough to miss his departure. Her corkscrew curls continued to move after she stopped shaking her head to answer Molly. "Not a clue where his sorry ass is. He knows I hate it when he does that."

"Damn," Molly said to herself. She made the circuit of the U-shaped hallway, avoiding checking insects in Tom's office and finding Windy and Angela gone to court. If she had learned nothing else in eight years, it was that when a deal felt right for all involved, act on it quickly before something fouled it up. She needed Jack's signature on a report recommending action for the city manager to present to council.

Molly stood in Angela's office and took a deep breath. "She smells good even when she's not here. Damn, am I not supposed to think things like that now?"

Molly stepped out into the public hallway and thought about where else Jack would slip off to. He didn't care for the downtown restaurants since it was too easy to be spotted. There was no meeting on the daily calendar printout Donna left on his desk each morning. "Son of a bitch." Maybe he had fallen off the wagon and started smoking again. She would check the sidewalk.

As Molly started up the steps to the main doors of city hall, she heard voices. Someone was in the council anteroom that opened off of the stair landing. She went to the unlabeled door that most thought went to a maintenance room. In actuality, it was a break room for city council members before they took their formal places at the council dais in chambers.

Molly eased across the break room and listened before just barging in on someone. Her stomach growled with the sight of the snack baskets ready for the next day's council meeting. She idly wondered if anyone would miss a granola bar.

Jack Sampson was engaged in an intense conversation with Barbara Ross, the deputy city manager. Molly rolled her eyes; if there was anyone she tried to avoid in upper management, it was Barbara.

Barbara was in her early forties and would be lucky to make retirement. She barely weighed a hundred pounds and was two inches shorter than Molly. Her hair was closely cropped and curled tightly against her head. Barbara, derisively called Diana Ross as in The Supremes behind her back, was a chain smoker and wondered why each winter's bout of pneumonia was worse than the last.

She had begun as a public information officer for the school system when she graduated from high school and rode the wave of being an outspoken black woman to advance to Tom's number two. Barbara never missed an opportunity to remind everyone how hard she worked for the job she had and how everything was stacked against her.

She had struggled through commuting evenings and weekends to take the college classes she needed. Molly's theory was that Barbara had been treated the same as a white-collar male who was promoted rather than anyone tackling the documentation for a dismissal. Barbara thrived on reverse discrimination and used Tom's fear of her to undermine other employees. What Molly found most interesting through casual remarks by Angela was that the black community did not like Barbara, either.

Molly hesitated, knowing she was damned either way, and decided to eavesdrop to have some idea of what she was walking in on. She eased the door open a quarter of an inch.

"Did you really think it would be that easy?" Barbara's question had an underlying bite to it.

"I don't know what you mean," Jack said.

Molly knew that tone—Jack was busted.

"Tamika is my husband's niece. I went to Tom and the council members individually when the job was advertised externally. Tamika told me she finished college and that she wanted to apply for a job with the city. Eric didn't tell her anything she wasn't already aware of," Barbara said.

"So?"

Barbara huffed. "So you don't have some sort of leverage over me in your back pocket just because you hired her. Her credentials substantiate her hire, and I learned long ago to cover my ass."

"I actually owe you. I didn't want Donna in the tech job, and Eric thinks he has accomplished something on his own." Jack chuckled.

Molly felt nauseated.

"We have more important matters to think about," Barbara said.

"We keep things flowing in spite of Tom. He has no idea about day-to-day operations." Jack leaned against the front of the long desk anchored to the edge of the raised platform.

Barbara sat on the first pew in the gallery. "He has no idea what his staff does. He'll sign anything. Council will never admit to a bad hire."

"You know if we work together, we can hang him out to dry and be rid of him." Jack sounded too casual.

Barbara didn't hesitate. "Oh, am I considered a player now that you fell flat on your face with that stunt you thought you pulled about Tamika?" Barbara didn't wait for an answer. "I document everything, including how long Tom is in his office and what he does. I have a buddy in IT tracking his computer usage."

Jack whistled softly. "I guess I need to be more careful."

Barbara began a laugh that ended in a long, rumbling cough. "How are we going to decide which one of us gets his job?"

Jack was silent.

Molly was as dismayed with herself for listening as she was by what she had heard. There was a long enough lull in the conversation for her to make an entrance. She tiptoed to the hall door and opened it, then banged it closed as though she had just entered the small room in a hurry. "Jack!" She stomped her feet across the floor as though running and pushed open the door to the larger room. "Crap. Sorry, I didn't mean to interrupt, just looking for you, boss." She smiled weakly. She knew she was the mouse staring at a cobra and a tiger, either of which would take her down in a heartbeat when it served their purposes.

Molly held up an envelope. "We need funding to close the deal I discussed with you last week. I drafted a council report for you. It has to be turned in before 1:00 to make the next scheduled meeting. May I go over the numbers with you? Sorry, Barbara."

Jack nodded. "Is it within the limit we discussed yesterday?"

"Yes. The city's incentive is returned in less than five years, according to policy. We have to match state funding. It will guarantee keeping the expansion at a local plant."

"Sounds like you came up with a win-win again, Molly." Barbara watched her manipulate Jack.

"It was Rusty's doing with Jack's guidance. I just assemble it all and plug in the numbers."

Barbara's look said she knew better even if Jack didn't.

Jack motioned for the packet. Molly handed him her pen. He signed the document without reviewing any of the information.

"Thanks, boss. I'll get this to Sharon for Tom's review. I'll close the doors on my way out." She turned to leave the room.

"We're done here, aren't we, Jack?" Barbara pushed off the back of the bench to stand and follow Molly.

Molly made herself slow down; it wouldn't go unnoticed to ignore the deputy city manager.

Barbara was already out of breath by the time they reached the hallway. "I'll walk with you." She glanced at her watch. "Tom has gone home for lunch. Sharon will be covering his phone."

Molly held the staff door open for Barbara. Barbara caught Molly's arm and pulled her toward her office next to Tom's and away from their administrative associate.

"You heard part of that conversation, didn't you?"

"I need to catch Sharon before the agenda is set with me at the bottom of a long meeting." Tom made it clear in executive meetings that the agenda was set by the order of the submittals.

"I know you work Jack just as I do Tom. Would you support me for Tom's job?" Barbara's grip of Molly's arm tightened.

"That's not my call, Barbara. I hear things all the time that are never repeated." Molly fought the urge to run.

"I could help you go after Jack's job. Besides the fact that I loathe the man, Jack has no business being a director."

Molly sighed and waited until the hand on her arm relaxed its grip. "I love being an engineer. I have no desire to be any more of an administrator than I have to be now. You're talking to the wrong person. I just want to work on construction projects that make the city look good."

"While Jack takes most of the credit for what you do."

"I learned a long time ago that I'm a work horse and not a show dog. I like being in the background."

Molly glimpsed Sharon leaning across her desk to watch the confrontation. Molly held up the handful of papers and raised her voice. "Hope the council agenda hasn't been finalized yet. The higher up you put me, Sharon, the less time I have to spend at the meeting."

Sharon smiled. "I can always bump someone else if it's an important item. No one knows the order in which I receive the draft reports except Barbara." Sharon waved Molly over.

And very few realize how much editing you do to make us all look semi-intelligent, Molly thought to herself.

Sharon had not changed her lank hairstyle—pulling it back from her face with clips—since high school, refusing to color the gray that mixed in with a mousy brown, and wore the plainest clothes she found on the rack at discount department stores.

Barbara nodded. Sharon ducked out of Barbara's sight, achieving her goal to be invisible.

Molly wouldn't trade being a part of the female underground that did all of the real work for any promotion. The last thing she wanted was to become a manager anything like Jack Sampson.

CHAPTER SIXTEEN

It was as though Chris read Molly's mind; to Molly, that was a scary prospect. Chris called Molly on Friday morning to remind her of their dinner plans just in case she had forgotten. Molly appreciated the humor in that gesture and was both thrilled and hesitant. She hoped she wasn't making a fool of herself yet again; chances were that it wouldn't be the last time she would be off the deep end over Chris.

They agreed to meet at a neighborhood restaurant a few blocks from Molly's house. It had been displaced as part of a shopping center sold to make room for a new Walgreens. The western section of the city rallied to support the owner and a local developer stepped forward to build a new location two blocks from its original. The new restaurant had been open for two months and Molly had not taken the time to check it out.

Molly felt silly driving the five blocks to the restaurant, but she wanted this to feel like a date. She also didn't know if Chris would want to go somewhere else after they ate. She purposely arrived early and parked the Jeep so she was able to watch the front door. Chris eased in five minutes before their scheduled meeting time driving a green Subaru Forester in need of a good cleaning.

Molly opened her door and slid out of the Jeep. The horn beeped once as she locked the spotless Liberty. Chris looked her way and smiled.

Chris waved. "I should have known the engineer would arrive early enough to have the layout analyzed."

Molly grinned. "I can't help myself." She walked over to Chris.

Chris gave her a quick hug. "It's good to see you."

Molly nodded. "Can you believe we're finally doing this?"

"I just hope we haven't built this up so much that it falls flat." Chris locked arms with Molly as they walked across the parking lot. "I think you escaped just in time today."

Molly glanced at Chris and raised her eyebrows. "How so?"

"I ran into one of your co-workers at the courthouse late this afternoon. Windy seemed more wrought up than usual. She wouldn't talk about what was bothering her but mentioned several times that city hall is a snake pit."

"SOP," Molly said. "Standard operating procedure."

Chris punched her arm. "I know that. Don't tell me you're into TLAs—three-letter abbreviations."

"More like T and A, which means…"

Chris placed her hand over Molly's mouth as they pushed open the double doors.

They entered the restaurant and were overwhelmed by the smell of spices and herbs mixed with a rich tomato fragrance.

Molly's mouth watered. "Damn, I didn't realize how hungry I am. You're going to think I'm a pig."

Chris looked Molly up and down. "Hardly. I feel a few cravings myself."

Molly blushed and was embarrassed by being so transparent.

Chris chuckled. "Italian food is my favorite. It tastes so good and the calories will motivate me to exercise."

They were led through the dimly lit restaurant to a table for two along the side wall. A fountain gurgled in the center of the room. Their waiter was in black and instantly at their table lighting the votive and filling their water glasses as they removed their jackets. He hung their coats on the backs of their chairs as he pulled each chair out to seat them. He gave them a quick appraisal. "Ladies, may I recommend beginning with a bottle of Pinot Noir?"

Chris looked to Molly and received a nod. "Wonderful."

He explained the nightly specials, bowed slightly, and left them with their menus.

"How did it go with the guys at work finding out you had a date tonight?" Molly tried to sound casual.

Chris looked over the top of the menu at her. "Surprisingly well. I could have kicked Spencer in the nuts for blurting it out when he dropped by yesterday, but the guys were so sweet stopping at my desk, trying to find out more details and giving me advice."

"Now there's a scary thought."

"The thought that kept going through my mind was why it had taken me so long to do something everyone else thinks is so great for me." Chris shook her head.

"Bad case of dumbassitis." Molly kept her eyes on the food choices and her voice nonchalant.

Chris kicked her under the table.

"Ouch!" Molly rubbed her shin.

"Want me to massage that for you?" Chris grinned.

"Ladies, have you decided?" The waiter returned unnoticed.

They had—salads and baked pastas. The women stared at each other across the table. Molly took a long, cool drink of water—the way she thought of Chris.

"Have you always been out at work?" Chris asked.

Molly wiped her mouth with her napkin. "Only to the people I discuss my personal life with. I don't wear a rainbow sticker or introduce myself as a practicing lesbian…"

The waiter returned with the wine and poured two glasses.

"…to people who just happen to walk up on a conversation at the right time." Molly blushed.

"It's that dumbassitis thing again."

Molly giggled. "I deserved that." She leaned across the table. "Believe it or not, I'm very low key."

"Oh, I believe it. I bet you're still on speaking terms with your exes, however many that is."

Molly nodded. "When you break up over work, it's easier to let go of the sense of betrayal." She held up fingers as she mentally counted names. "Four that I've lived with."

"How do you meet women?"

"Started out on the party circuit, but it began to feel incestuous. Too many of us were just trading dates around and overstepping friendships to be involved with someone. Then I tried the weekend beer parties until the novelty wore off. Knowing who was going to take their shirt off and no longer being interested in what they looked like told me I was over that phase. Then it was the bonfire and camping scene, but I'm too allergic to weeds and insects to go often enough."

"I love to camp. My God, don't tell me I've hooked up with the one lesbian who doesn't like to pee in the bushes."

The waiter returned to refresh their glasses.

Molly and Chris burst out laughing as he walked away shaking his head.

"He's going to leave us a tip tonight for having the least boring conversation to interrupt." Chris glanced at the adjoining table. The middle-aged hetero couples were paying them no mind.

"You think?" Molly raised her glass in a toast. "To new beginnings."

"I'll certainly drink to that."

Molly continued. "As far as the women I work with, I love that they seem to enjoy hearing dating misadventures and don't mind me flirting with them—harmlessly, I swear. They look at the Internet sites and screen the profiles for me."

"I should have known you'd be into cyber sex." Chris's eyes twinkled.

"Cyber flirting, please." Molly tried to act mildly offended and failed.

"I stand corrected." Chris leaned back as plates of food filled the table.

"Sheesh, this is at least three meals." Molly rotated the plate, studying the amount of chicken and pasta piled on.

"You can't handle two breasts?" Chris calmly stabbed her fork into her vegetarian pasta and twirled.

Molly choked, as did their waiter serving the next table.

Molly wiped tears from her eyes. "No fair. I'm still trying to figure out if this is a real first date or a survey."

"I thought it was foreplay."

Molly pulled at the collar of her turtleneck. "You're killing me. Is it really warm in here?"

Chris leaned across the table and started to speak.

"Don't do it." Molly held her hand up. "I can't trade anymore. I'm about ready to drag you to the restroom as it is."

Chris grinned and pushed her chair back from the table.

Molly held her hand up again. "Don't go there."

Chris batted her eyes. "I'll behave, or you can punish me."

"Oh, God." Molly sighed. She stared at the food she no longer had interest in.

"Seriously, I'll behave. Enjoy your dinner. I had forgotten how much fun it is to talk trash, I haven't lost my touch." Chris finished another breadstick, licking garlic butter from her fingertip.

Molly leaned forward and covered her face with her hands.

They moved as much food about on their plates as they put in their mouths. They waited while the table was cleared and leftovers boxed.

Molly looked at Chris. "I need to ask you a serious question."

"Go for it."

"Would you be upset with me if I said I don't think we should have sex on the first date? Not that I'm presuming anything. I think we should wait one month." Molly couldn't believe she was able to pose this as she stared into gorgeous blue eyes.

"I'd be amazed and flattered in an extended foreplay kind of way." Chris was no longer joking.

Styrofoam boxes were set gently on the table with the check. "Ladies, believe me when I say it has been my pleasure to serve you tonight."

Chris inclined her head slightly.

Molly looked at him and smiled weakly. "An excellent meal. The wine was perfect. Thank you."

They watched him walk away, then reached for the check at the same time.

"I believe that I asked you first, therefore this is on me." Chris didn't let go of the folder.

"I'm not accustomed to being paid for." Molly finally surrendered.

"Then you had best get used to the idea." Chris pulled a credit card from her trousers pocket. She leaned forward. "He didn't charge us for the wine."

They walked out of the restaurant to Chris's Subaru.

"So we survived our first date?" Molly waited as Chris set the leftovers on the back floorboard, then leaned against the driver's door.

"Yes." Chris grabbed the open lapels of Molly's suede jacket and gently pulled her forward until their bodies touched.

They kissed until there was no doubt that either of them was serious.

Molly's hand ran over the front of Chris's sweater. "Best breasts I've encountered all evening."

Chris pushed her away and laughed. "What are you doing next weekend?"

"Big date with a hot blonde, if I'm lucky."

"Call me?"

"You can count on it." Molly closed the door for Chris and waited until Chris rolled the window down. "One more." She leaned into the car and kissed her again. "Sweet dreams."

Chris made a face. "More like sweaty dreams. Call me, no excuses acceptable."

"Yes, ma'am." Molly watched Chris drive away and felt very lonely. "This is for you, Ruth, to let her be absolutely sure."

CHAPTER SEVENTEEN

Individually, Molly genuinely liked and respected all of the city council members, particularly the women since she knew what crap they endured to be elected. Collectively, she hated going before city council as a body. As a pack, it was difficult for the individuals to resist posturing and one-upping one another with sometimes irrelevant questions. Heaven help any city employee presenting a concept that triggered the watchdog response. It never ceased to amaze Molly that the members would beat to death a five-figure request for funding and blithely support seven-figure expenditures based on the charisma of the presenter.

Molly sat beside Jack in the front row of short staff benches perpendicular to the council dais. Molly kept looking out the corner of her eye at her boss. He was being extremely benevolent, inviting her to attend the meeting with him. She usually waited until he left his office for a scheduled item, then slipped into chambers hoping for an open spot on the rear bench or standing against the back wall if other minions had already filled the choice anonymous seats.

Campbell sat in the front row of the long spectator bench facing council. He mimicked lifting folders on his lap and winked. He never failed to tease Molly that she always carried several inches of files into meetings to keep anyone from asking her a question that might require her digging through all the information on a project. He leaned across the aisle as council took a five-minute break to replenish snacks. "Does all of that have anything to do with the agenda item you're here for?"

Molly grinned. "Actually, it does. You never know what they'll ask, and I didn't want to leave my boss stranded in mid-question."

Campbell nodded.

"I appreciate that. I can always count on you, can't I?" Jack smiled at Molly and placed his hand on her knee. His hand remained on her until several of the male council members took notice with subtle double takes.

Molly felt her face turning red and hated that she embarrassed so easily, and Jack knew it. Jack also knew that she worked circles around him and Eric but struggled with presentations. They were next on the agenda.

Jack leaned close as though a co-conspirator in something. His grip of her knee tightened. "I think it's time for the work horse to take center stage."

Molly felt her mouth go dry—that damn Barbara. Surely, Molly was misunderstanding Jack.

He inclined his head toward the podium. "You're the one who wants to be involved in matters over your head. Go for it." Jack made no effort to move.

The item was the first of its kind and it was big—code name Project Cover—involving an expansion of a local printing company. Of course, Molly crunched all the numbers, wrote the report, and sold the concept to the state officials who would be partnering with the city on this. It was essential that the expansion take place in Virginia and not Georgia or South Carolina; Virginia had lost too many projects to the Deep South lately. It would take upfront funds of $1.5 million, the full amount of the city's annual cash reserve for such projects allowed by the current bond issue.

The tricky part of the entire deal was that all the paperwork was in place and ready to be signed after confidential negotiations through the city's Industrial Development Authority, which Molly served as staff. The local plant manager had issued letters of intent to local contractors for $4 million of renovations to the building based on handshakes. It was only now that the project could be discussed in public. If council was not properly briefed and in agreement with its own authority, the entire negotiation might well be jeopardized by stumbling over what should be a routine, no-brainer consent vote.

"Don't do this, Jack. This is way too important." Molly slid forward in her seat. Someone had to stand at the podium.

"Don't worry, you'll do fine. If not, I'll bail you out." Jack's grin as he gave her a nudge told her he was counting on just that. He momentarily forgot that he was supposed to look as though a supportive mentor, fully aware of all the intricate negotiations.

Molly stood and walked the half-dozen steps to the podium. Campbell caught her eye and nodded slightly.

The city was fortunate to have a local printing company within its limits that thrived on their European buyout several years earlier. So much so that several name brand clothing companies had executed multi-year contracts for the printing of their catalogs.

The contracts were sizeable enough that a higher capacity press was required. If Molly enjoyed one aspect of her job, it was touring the industrial plants and helping companies by formulating incentive proposals so that the companies grew locally. Regardless of the increase to the tax base and the number of jobs added, the bottom line was always upfront money.

This time, the stakes were high enough that the state had agreed to participate with matching funds—the governor himself had made the announcement of the pending deal. Several states had been in a bidding war with similar plants that the parent company would choose from to expand. The catch was compounded by the fact that not only was all of this agreed to and memorandums in place, but local funds would be awarded upfront, state funds after the investment was made. The company promised to spend $30 million on building and equipment upgrades, all of which would add nicely to the city's tax base.

Molly crunched numbers through every scenario she could imagine. The money had to be justifiable and recoverable. Jack and Eric had laughed at her. Jack's policy had always been to simply dangle the total capital investment amount before council on behalf of an unnamed company and ask for a flat percentage to offer the company in a deal bound by grins and winks that would be difficult to track. What Molly came up with could be easily documented.

She ran the increase to the real estate taxes and the machinery taxes and structured a return in less than five years without looking at soft costs of payroll that would be pumped into the local economy or the trickle-down effect of home sales and local sales taxes. She sealed the deal with a claw-back clause if the taxes were not increased as projected by the end of six years, allowing a grace period but holding corporate feet to the fire nonetheless.

Molly's presentation walked city council through the calculations without their eyes glazing over. She spoke slowly and paused for questions. She looked each member in the eyes as it dawned on them that this was a win-win deal.

Jack had no reason to leave his seat.

Near the end of the presentation, the local plant manager approached Molly. Molly yielded the floor to him.

"My name is Alfred Cross. I've been the plant manager since the buyout three years ago. Molly told me that this would be presented to council today. I just wanted to reassure you that we are completely serious about this expansion. In fact—and Molly, please don't faint—we started some of the work to the building prior to the state's approval to have a jump on our deadlines. I have no doubt that our payroll will double, more than the current expansion agreement shows projected. The jobs are computer-based with above-median salaries that will attract young couples to move here for work. Molly and I have spent many hours strategizing this so that corporate was duly impressed and state officials sponsored our appeal to the governor for his discretionary funds that he announced just yesterday. When this happens, it's Molly's doing." He backed away and jokingly genuflected to her.

Molly didn't hesitate to give him a mock curtsy. Council members chuckled. The motion was made and seconded to fund the incentive package; the vote was seven ayes.

Alfred held out his arm to Molly and escorted her from council chambers—their plan was an obvious partnership and success.

No one paid any attention to Jack Sampson as he stroked the bald spot on the back of his head and glowered from his seat in the staff section.

CHAPTER EIGHTEEN

Chris always dreaded hurricane season in central Virginia. Thankfully, they were too far inland for a direct hit but instead were often lashed with days of heavy rain trailing a major category storm. Creeks and storm sewers overflowed and caused the river to rise past flood stage until everything was saturated. Trees fell; power poles snapped, downing overhead lines. The track of the current hurricane was amazingly similar to Camille in 1969 and struck terror in the hearts of all law enforcement officers who experienced or had read about her. The mountain communities along the Blue Ridge were hardest hit again with continuous heavy rain and flash flooding of streams in the valleys between the rounded peaks of the worn summits.

Twenty deaths had been reported so far with less than half the bodies accounted for. The James River passed through the city on its way to Richmond and the coast.

Chris had volunteered for the eight hours of training that would enable her to operate the department's ATV as needed. She enjoyed her rotations patrolling the bike trails when the guys were short-handed. She had to admit that the department's boxy four-wheel Suzuki was dependable but a clunker compared to the ATVs she had careened about on as a teenager. What really set her off was anyone teasing her about the black storage box or the tall triangular flag usually seen on a kid's bike on the back bumper. It was all part of being safe. She was the only detective in the department who knew the trail system and was certified for ATV duty. Her assignment during weather emergencies was a no-brainer.

She popped in her ear buds and used the speed dial on her cell phone as she dug through the bottom of her closet for her insulated jumpsuit and heavy boots. She planned on wearing her personal gloves and helmet instead of the department issue. Her job was to patrol the river banks and be on the lookout for floaters. "Hey, just checking in. Are you okay?"

Molly sounded out of breath. "We're heading into a briefing now. Hopefully, the weather service the city subscribes to will give us fairly accurate flood-level predictions."

"Stay in touch, okay?" Chris asked. "I'm on patrol today."

"Will do. Let's just hope cell service doesn't drop out."

"Later." Chris made sure her phone was securely snapped into a chest pocket. She headed out and couldn't help feeling excited—it was that inherent cop rush at being on the front line during an emergency that kept most of them on the force.

It never ceased to amaze Chris that she could follow the river and feel as though in the midst of a wilderness, yet be only three blocks north of downtown. Granted it was three blocks suited to nothing but railroad tracks, briars, kudzu, and snakes, but it still seemed strange that civilization was so close yet so far.

She drove slowly, stopping often to walk away from the idling motor and listen as she made sure she was alone along the river. She stood on the footrests and scanned both banks. The trails were blocked by downed trees so she rode along the crossties, straddling one steel rail of the train tracks. Norfolk Southern kept its right-of-way clear enough to avoid most of the downed trees from the surrounding ravines.

The early economy of the city had been based on four different railroad lines sending trains through the downtown station. The proximity to the James River also enabled early commerce to move by bateaus along the canal channel that paralleled the river. Public sewer happened along about the time the canals were being phased out and provided open trenches to lay the huge joints of cast iron pipe. The rail lines were later rebuilt above flood elevation and rose in ballasted mounds running parallel with the sewer and river.

The usual freight train traffic was on hold once the flooding commenced. This was the first day of overcast skies that allowed crews out to assess damage as the trailing end of the system moved out, leaving heavy clouds in its wake. The railroad crews were quick to flag her down and tell her of any suspicious landfalls spotted as they cruised the track in their work trucks with drop-down steel rims to ride the rails.

Chris stopped the ATV as she approached the remains of what had been a hundred-year-old wooden bridge spanning the tracks, creek, sewer, and river to reach a small island that had been a favorite vacation site in the early 1900s boasting its own luxury hotel. She faced a mound of debris that started at the foot of the steep slope from the residential neighborhood high above all the way to the edge of the swollen river. She heard a noise other than wildlife. Someone was calling for help on the other side of the fallen timbers.

Chris slowly guided the ATV around the upper side of the debris, having to stop several times and hack an opening with a bush ax, then walk the ATV on the steep slope. It took thirty minutes to return to the rail bed.

"Hey!"

Chris followed the sound of the woman's voice and saw a young black woman waving frantically in the distance. She waved back. The woman ran toward her. Chris gunned the Suzuki and stopped just short of the approaching woman. She was off of the seat and checking the storage box when the woman slid to a stop on the loose stone surface.

"She's stuck." The woman pointed ahead and halfway down the railroad embankment.

A figure struggled, trapped in soft mud to mid-thighs.

"Oh, jeez." Chris clicked her radio. No reception this far below the tower. She glanced at her cell phone. No bars. "Shit."

The black woman held up a branch. "I've been trying to pull her out for the last hour." She struggled to catch her breath. "I'm Tamika Travers. We work for the city. They sent us out as one of the teams to check the sewer main, make sure the watertight tops are on, and locate any exposed pipe that's been washed out of creek crossings."

Chris slowly approached the city worker, not wanting the ATV to loosen a landslide of gravel. She climbed off again and looked down. The water from the creek between the tracks and the sewer had crested and fallen, leaving a layer of red mud on the bottom half of the ballast stone and burying all but the raised tops of the sewer manholes. She stood fifteen feet above original ground. The worker had made the first few steps on the mud before sinking.

"Fuck!" This from the trapped worker.

Chris recognized the voice. "Molly, what in the hell?"

"I don't believe this." Molly leaned back on the slope to rest. "I have tried every way possible to twist and pull and get myself out of this. It's like quicksand. Dumbass me wanted to take a look into the manhole when I saw the cover missing from the tracks. Tamika tried to tell me to just log it and call it in once we went back to the truck. But, no, I knew the first question from the crew dispatched would be whether the line was clear or blocked. So I decided just to walk over and take a quick look. I didn't think about all the mud and sludge that has washed downstream collecting against the embankment. It didn't look deep. What a dumbass I am."

"Are you waiting for an argument?" Chris asked.

Tamika caught herself before she smacked Chris. "She's pulled a muscle in her leg trying to get herself out. She won't let me climb down to help her for fear we'd both get stuck. We thought for sure a rail crew would come in to start removing the old bridge."

"Maybe in a day or two. They're still spread thin like everyone else." Chris shook her head. "Where's your boy toy Eric?"

Tamika shook her head frantically.

Molly glared over her shoulder. "He and Jack are back in the office, waiting for the team reports and preparing to be creative with the numbers for the FEMA estimates."

"How pissed are you?"

"Evidently not quite enough to get myself loose."

Tamika looked from one woman to the other. "I take it you two know each other."

Chris grinned at her. "Oh, yeah. She's as hardheaded as hell, isn't she?"

"You think?" Tamika put her hands on her hips.

Chris attached the rope to the winch on the front axle of the ATV and made a loop she threw down to Molly. "Can you put that under your arms or do I need to climb down and help you?"

"I think I can manage." Molly struggled to get the rope over her head while wearing a bulky jacket.

"Hang on." Chris started the winch. She and Tamika jumped on the ATV when it started to move with the effort of freeing Molly. Molly finally popped loose. Chris dragged her until she was clear of the mud. She followed the rope down the embankment to Molly. "If you wanted me to pick you up or tie you up, all you had to do was call, not go through all of this." She spoke quietly so only Molly would hear.

Molly laughed tiredly. "My hero. Thank you."

"It's okay to say you're exhausted." Chris ran her hands down

Molly's legs and spoke over her shoulder to Tamika. "No sign of cuts or tears, just plenty of mud," Chris sniffed her glove, "mixed with raw sewage." She untied Molly. "I didn't know you guys took the hep series. We have to since we're first responders."

Tamika gasped.

Chris looked from one woman to the other.

"Jack told us to stop by the doc's today, said it would protect us to take the shot before or after going out in the field." The words died on Molly's lips as she saw Chris's expression. She sat up, wincing when her leg shifted.

"Honey, it's a series of three shots taken months apart to be fully effective." Chris let the "honey" slip.

Molly stared up at Tamika. "Is that what you understood?"

Tamika slowly shook her head.

Molly looked at Chris. "Help me up."

Chris put her arm around Molly's waist and grabbed the hand on her shoulder. Tamika came down the slope and held on to Molly from the other side. They walked in tandem up the slope and sat down together when they reached the rail.

"Well, you're clean from the waist up. Nothing on your face near your eyes." Tamika looked at Molly closely.

"There doesn't appear to be any punctures in your shoes or clothes." Chris looked again and saw no sign of anything but mud on Molly's lower body. "I'm obligated to file an exposure incident report. You both will need to follow up with medical testing and complete the vaccination."

"I'll go hose off at the maintenance yard," Molly's face was tight, "and alert the other teams not to make contact with the silt near the sewers."

"And you'll have the doc check your leg." Chris wanted an assurance that Molly would not stay in the field all day.

"Yes." Molly nodded.

"I'll take her myself," Tamika said firmly.

"Jack really looks out for you guys, doesn't he?" Chris asked.

"He damn well will after this," Molly said quietly.

Molly angled her head and listened. Sure enough, someone was tapping on her front door. Dolly raised her head, then jumped down and crawled under the bed.

Molly limped to the front door with flashlight in hand. Electricity was out and would be for several days due to all the uprooted trees and flooded substations. These were the times Molly was grateful to live in the city and pay for service from the water and natural gas mains—she could flush the toilet and take a hot shower.

Molly gaped at the sight of Chris on her front stoop. "Wait here just a second." Molly pointed to the rug at the front door, then hurried to the bathroom for towels—one for Chris to stand on, another to dry off with.

"That's okay. After all the effort it took me to get here, I don't mind being left to drip dry," Chris called.

"Hang on." Molly handed her towels in exchange for a plastic bag filled with take-out cartons.

"I figured neither of us would be able to cook at home tonight so I might as well bring dinner over. That also lets me get a look at you so I don't worry that you were hurt worse than you let on this morning." Chris kicked off her boots and peeled off the jumpsuit and left it on the rug at the door. She dried her hair with the towel. "What?"

"Is that thermal underwear?" Molly's voice was strained.

Chris looked down. "Give me a break. All the store had in women's sizes had the pink flowers on it."

"That's not what I'm staring at. It's sort of see-through."

Chris grinned. "You like?"

"You're trying to kill me." Molly hobbled toward her bedroom. "Come on, the candles and the portable heater are in here."

Chris stepped into the former dining room and whistled. "Nice touch." She looked up at the chandelier.

"It came with the house. I wanted a bedroom on the first floor. Thank God for no steps tonight."

Dolly peeped out from under the bed.

Chris knelt down and held out her hand. "Hi, beautiful."

Molly watched the cat ease closer to Chris, sniff, and rub her head against the offered hand. "You've passed my first screening test. If Dolly doesn't like you, you're out of here."

Chris chuckled. "Thanks, Dolly, you're a lifesaver."

Molly looked at Chris intently as she stood. "No, you are. I was done. I didn't have any strength left and Tamika was freaking out. Did I thank you enough this morning?"

Chris shrugged. "I'm just glad I was there. What in the hell was Jack thinking, sending just you and Tamika to the riverfront?"

"Revenge. He hates me and the feeling is mutual. Good thing I'm not the only one in the department who feels that way about him or I'd be worried about my mental state." Molly settled in the bed and patted the empty side for Chris.

Chris faced her. "Hungry?"

"Starving."

They shared the Chinese food, saving the best pieces of chicken for Dolly.

"Better?" Chris asked.

Molly nodded. "I soaked in the tub. It's just pulled muscles in my leg and back. No big deal, but you've now seen how I'll get around when I'm in my eighties."

"Or sooner." Chris laughed.

"Hey!" Molly punched her in the arm. "You're welcome to stay the night."

"I sense a but with one t."

"I'm too damn sore to do anything but sleep." Molly made it sound like an apology.

"It would be nice to sleep with someone again," Chris said. "I wouldn't be crowding you and Dolly?"

"Not at all." Molly watched Chris blow all the candles out and turn the heater off. Molly held up the covers.

Chris slid between the sheets and held her arm out so that Molly could lie against her. They talked about everything and nothing until dozing off.

Molly awoke first the next morning and looked at the blond head on the other pillow. She was amazed that she felt so satisfied without having sex. She felt complete for the first time in a long while.

The moment lasted until their cell phones rang simultaneously. Chris scrambled out of bed to retrieve hers from her jumpsuit; Molly reached to the bedside. Work called both of them.

CHAPTER NINETEEN

Molly reported the hepatitis snafu to Tom, copying Windy. The result rumbled across the second floor of city hall like a tidal wave. Jack was taken to task by Tom with Windy and Ann present. Both women were stunned by the ferocity of the normally laconic city manager. Tom was justifiably incensed at the liability Jack had exposed the city to if any employee became ill from their flood duty. Council backed Tom when he placed Jack on notice with warning of dismissal if another such incident occurred. Of course, Jack blamed Molly.

A sense of serenity settled over Molly after the night Chris spent with her. Molly didn't know how to rationalize the deep connection she felt with Chris. As she hobbled about at work, Molly resolved not to allow anything or anyone to ruin her peace of mind. She hadn't felt anything like this since losing her mom.

What Molly decided on was completing each project assigned to her the best she knew how. Her other strategy was to work with Donna on the side, teaching her engineering basics while learning the intricacies of the GIS system along with her until Donna was ready to apply to one of the engineering firms that Molly routinely worked with and would coerce an interview from. Molly had a strong suspicion that Tamika would help them. It hadn't taken Tamika any time to catch on to the undercurrent of gossip about her and let it be known that she was related to Barbara by her uncle's marriage, not direct blood ties. Molly was used to keeping Jack at bay, and she could count on Windy and Campbell. She was okay.

Molly found enough loose change in her desk drawer for a Mountain Dew—a habit she knew she needed to break but continued anyway. She left her office for the restroom and vending machines in the main hall. She made it as far as the map room.

Frankie leaned against the flat drafting table in the center of the room. Molly fought a grin as she looked at Frankie and heard the theme to *Dallas* in her head—the eighties look worked for Frankie. Frankie's back was to the double doors. She gestured and bobbed her head as she talked to Mark, frequently pointing to a sheet of paper on the table's surface. Mark nodded occasionally but was unable to get a word in edgewise. The fluorescent lighting made Mark's bald head glow.

Molly slowed to wave and was about to continue when Mark looked up. An expression of guilt quickly passed across his face. He motioned her to join them.

Molly chided herself—do not get involved, listen and walk away. Her peace of mind was too precious to her to lose this quickly as difficult as it had been to achieve. "You two are going to have the rumors flying."

Frankie looked over her shoulder at Molly. The air between the two women became frigid.

Molly stopped abruptly. "What the hell is that for?"

Frankie slid the job listing printed on yellow paper to denote internal advertisement across the table. "I hate seeing someone sell out so easily." The insult hung in the air.

Molly looked at Mark and raised her eyebrows. His face was blank. He was clearly walking a tightrope between two women he enjoyed working with. He could have handled them individually by agreeing with both; now he was trapped in having to choose sides.

Molly glanced at the sheet. It had been posted online the day before. She didn't bother to look at the HR listings, freshly determined not to interfere in a career path ever again.

Frankie jabbed her finger midway down the sheet. "Your idea or Jack's to help you forget about Donna being cheated out of a job?"

Molly felt her temper rising to the occasion but first she wanted to know why Frankie was so pissed before she jumped on her with both hiking boots.

The bold type of the job title jumped out at Molly—deputy director of community development. It was a new position describing everything she currently did with the exception of supervision duties of an engineer and technician. "This is the first I've seen of this."

Molly looked at Frankie and Mark. She felt as though she was being sucked out of the room without moving her feet.

Frankie's demeanor changed immediately as she read the complete surprise on Molly's face.

Mark looked at her as he always did; they were all friends who cared about one another. "You don't know anything about this job?"

Molly shook her head. She made herself read the description again, including the fact that the pay grade was four above hers.

"It's an internal listing, to be closed a week from posting. It has to be a hand-picked job for someone already here. Who else does the same as Molly?" Mark froze as soon as the words were out of his mouth.

"No one, but who is on the same grade and has been cutting deals with Jack lately?" Frankie asked.

"Eric," Molly said in a whisper. She backed slowly toward the corner of the room, sitting on an old drafting stool next to the row of plat cabinets.

Frankie slammed her fist on the green board cover. "Sons of bitches. I've been fighting with HR for almost a year to reclassify me as Campbell's deputy. Ann won't start the process even with Campbell's official written request on file for the past three months. Whose ass was this pulled out of?"

Mark cleared his throat deliberately loud and long.

"Speak of the devil." Frankie raised her hand slightly, motioning Molly to stay put.

Eric exited the elevator cab and walked toward the map room. He smiled broadly and came to the doorway. He pointed to the paper on the table. "You've seen it?"

"What's the deal, man?" Mark jumped ahead of Frankie.

Eric was so puffed up, he almost appeared tall. "I've been helping Jack with more administrative duties. He decided to make it official and went to Tom a month ago with a special request on my behalf. They found the money in the personnel budget for reclassifications that haven't been approved. It goes into effect as soon as they close the listing. Council is insisting the position be filled since Jack's trouble with the hepatitis shots. Pretty cool, huh?"

"How long have you worked for the city, Eric?" Frankie spoke with her jaw clenched.

"Almost two years, but this was part of the deal when Jack hired me. I was to work with the staff engineer, pick up on the technical side, then take it off of Jack." Eric bounced with excitement. He straightened his tie and ran his hands over his thickly gelled hair.

"And where does that leave me?" Molly spoke from the corner

of the room.

Eric froze. He slowly turned to look at Molly. "This is a discussion you should have behind closed doors with Jack."

Molly shook her head. "I'm asking you face to face."

Eric did his best imitation of his mentor, Jack. "It leaves you reporting to me and taking over the projects I've been handling. We may not fill my old job. I'll recommend a five percent increase for you since you'll be taking on more work."

Molly refused to look at the young man she had considered a friend. She stared at the far wall of the building as she spoke. "Just how in the hell am I to manage any more work than I'm already doing?"

"You have to delegate, Molly. You'll never move up thinking you must do all the work yourself. Train Tamika and Donna to do most of what you do. That's what works for Jack and me." Eric eased toward the hallway, clearly wanting to escape without giving the appearance of retreat.

Molly nodded to herself. "If they're already doing their own jobs, as well as the majority of yours and Jack's, how are they supposed to do mine?"

"Time management." Eric was clearly annoyed by the questions taking away from his promotion buzz. "We'll have this discussion later with Jack to clarify duties and priorities." He glanced at his watch. "I have to run. Tom is presenting me at the council work session, to let them know first about my imminent promotion and who to go to if they can't find Jack. You know how important it is to have a department in council's good graces. We're still doing damage control from the flood fiasco, thanks to you, Molly."

"Excuse me, that's Jack's own doing." Molly almost didn't say anything else. "Eric, watch your back. You know Jack will eventually turn on you just as he has everyone else. He treats all of us like shit."

Eric studied Molly. "I've been handling Jack ever since he hired me. Don't worry, your secrets are safe with me. I may need to blackmail you someday so I haven't told all to Jack." He tried to soften his rationalization with a cocky grin. "This is all part of my plan to be a department director before I'm thirty-five. You've been working Jack totally the wrong way."

Molly felt as chilled as the outside November temperature.

Frankie made a sucking noise as Eric left the room. "Un-fucking-real. Damn Ann for not giving you a heads-up." Frankie was still focused on her original question. "You really didn't know anything about any of this? Eric never gave any indication that he had a deal in place?"

Molly walked out of the map room without answering Frankie and returned to her office. She sat before her drafting table and used a red pen to mark up her own drawing to complete the design of a sewer line. There were five families in an older subdivision whose septic system had failed. The city had to extend sanitary sewer service as quickly as possible. Someone had to look out for the real work that needed to be done, and Molly knew too well who wouldn't do that job.

Molly thought about it and e-mailed Chris. Communication was part of their arrangement. Molly's personal cell phone beeped with a text message.

"Bless your heart," Chris had written, sending it the fastest way for Molly to receive her comfort.

A brief smile passed across Molly's face; so this was what a true relationship was all about.

CHAPTER TWENTY

Chris eased her battered black Ford sedan along with the slow-moving downtown traffic. It was good that the cold rain forced her to have her window up. Otherwise, a citizen might hear the curses yelled at the incompetence of civilian drivers. Spencer hated riding with her and usually slumped down in his seat. She glanced at her Mickey Mouse watch—six o'clock—and was surprised that she was right on time. She would have thought the downtown office crowd emptied out earlier. Things must be tight to force this many to work an extra hour. She was too used to swinging through the abandoned central business district as her middle-of-the-night shortcut.

Chris squinted at the figure on the street corner hunched against the November rain with only a thin jacket and no umbrella. Molly struggled to keep her bulging briefcase dry with the lower half of her coat as she stood poised to hobble to the wagon.

Chris ignored the cars behind her and drifted over to the curb, coasting into the bus stop. She lowered the passenger window. "I thought I told you to wait at the steps where you'd be out of the rain."

Molly bent down and looked at her. The dull expression on her face brightened. "I'm perfectly capable of crossing the street so you don't have to go around the block in this traffic."

Chris hoped Molly didn't feel as bad as she looked. "Humph. I can see how easy it is for you to walk. Taking work home? What am I going to do with you?"

Molly frowned.

"Just humor me and get in the damn car, will you? Don't make me get out and put you in as though arresting you."

"I might enjoy that." Molly finally smiled as she reached for the door handle.

Chris watched her struggle into the car with a stiff leg and sore back. Molly appeared as though she had lost weight. Chris tried not to obsess about her. "So how did the rest of your day go after you found out about Eric?"

"Fine." Molly's lips barely parted.

Chris nodded. "Did you talk to Eric or Jack any further?" Her voice sounded too casual to her own ears.

Molly appeared not to have noticed. "Of course not. They avoided me. All the others stopped to tell me how unfair Eric's promotion is, even Barbara, and I think she actually meant it."

Chris pulled into traffic and changed lanes as soon as she was able. "Are you in the public deck?"

"Oh, yeah. I'm too cheap to rent a space close to the building."

The city provided parking for its employees three blocks uphill from the Main Street building.

Chris waited for the traffic signal at the corner to change. "Can you approach the city manager or council?"

Molly looked embarrassed. She shook her head. "If I know anything, it's that Jack has fabricated all the paperwork to make Eric appear the ideal candidate. He likely has council endorsements in hand."

"Apply for it yourself."

Molly shook her head again. "I don't want to be Jack's minion."

Chris thought for a moment. "I can see your point. So what do you want?"

Molly stared out the window. "I want life to be fair. I want to be paid for the work I do. I want others to receive promotions they've earned. I want people like Jack to disappear off the face of the earth."

"Is that all?" Chris asked softly. She placed her hand on Molly's thigh.

"My God, it's nice to have someone to talk to about all of this. I don't know which was better—dinner at the restaurant or dinner in bed the other night."

"I know which I'd choose to repeat."

"Oh, my, aren't you smooth?" Molly was finally able to tease as her mood lifted.

"I have to make a confession. I didn't realize how much I'd missed the banter and innuendo."

"There's that foreplay thing again," Molly said. "Seriously, it's wonderful to talk to someone who understands enough so that I don't have to explain every nuance of local government. I'm not such a tough old broad after all."

Chris glanced at Molly as the traffic light finally allowed them to turn. "Work crap can ruin your life if you let it and what do you have to show for it?"

"I know." Molly sighed. "I know you guys have the same kind of stuff going on. Don't you hate it when it gets overwhelming?"

"That's when we go out drinking. So many of the guys wind up sleeping with the wrong people just to get their minds off of their jobs—abstinence is no solution, either."

"I heard that. The women I work with are straight, some happy with husbands and boyfriends, some living with men they don't even like. I suspect several of them are tempted to experiment."

"Not that you would take advantage of them."

"Not unless I'd given my notice first." Molly chuckled. "One or two of them would actually be worth it if I was single."

"I sense fantasies." Chris baited Molly as she turned onto the street with the parking deck entrance.

"Like you wouldn't believe."

"How about me?" Chris cut her eyes at Molly.

Molly did a double take. "Excuse me?"

"Do you fantasize about me?" Chris knew one sure way to distract Molly while she concentrated on driving up the ramp of the parking deck.

Molly slowly released a deep breath.

The rain pelted down as Chris pulled onto the top open deck of the parking structure. She put the gear stick in park. "You might want to wait a few minutes until this lets up. You'll be soaked to the skin." Chris felt her face flush.

"That might be a good thing." Molly shifted her briefcase in her lap.

"You didn't answer my question. Do you fantasize about me?" Her voice lowered suggestively.

"Chris, do you know what you're doing?" Molly turned sideways in her seat. "We're in a damn government car in a public place."

As if to emphasize Molly's point, a patrol car made the circuit of the parking deck. The uniformed officer hesitated until Chris flashed her badge. He waved and continued.

"You'll be the talk of the station tomorrow. We agreed to take our time. Do you know what you're playing with here?"

Chris placed both hands on the steering wheel. "I only know that I find you incredibly attractive, and I find myself thinking about you entirely too much. You and I have crossed paths for a reason."

Molly looked out at the rain. "Maybe we're supposed to be very good friends. I hear you talking the talk, but I'm not so sure you're ready to walk, at least not with someone like me."

"Now you're just trying to pay me back."

Molly shook her head. "You've just played out one of my fantasies about you." Molly leaned across the seat, took a deep breath of Chris's scent, and kissed her softly on the cheek. "I would say that I'm going to get wet now, but that would be so tacky."

"Not exactly tacky." Chris pushed Molly's briefcase to the floorboard. She ran her hand over Molly's breasts, then slid her hand into Molly's pants. She nuzzled her lips against Molly's neck.

Molly gasped. "Keep that up and we're crawling into the backseat."

Chris rubbed her fingers clockwise. Molly moved slightly with her, then gasped. Molly put one hand on Chris's and increased the pressure, the other she used to pull Chris to her for a real kiss.

Chris's mind blanked for a split second. "Get your sweet ass out of my car before we're booked for indecencies on public property. You'd better be glad I'm on surveillance tonight."

"It would almost be worth it. Thanks for the ride. It was good for me." Molly winked. "Sure you don't want to show me your big gun?"

"Stop it!" Chris clamped her hands around the steering wheel. "What I carry in my trunk is how I make my living."

"Woot!" Molly laughed and hopped stiff-legged to her Jeep.

Chris waited until Molly started the engine before driving away. She hadn't felt such a sense of anticipation since a teenager—a very sex-crazed teenager.

CHAPTER TWENTY-ONE

Molly glanced at the time on the bottom taskbar on her computer monitor. She was ready to have this next meeting over with. She took a deep breath and decided against carrying any form of pencil or paper with her. She took a left out of her office and walked deliberately to the end of the hall. Donna was silent behind her partition outside of Jack's office.

Molly tapped her knuckles against the open door to Jack's office and walked inside. "Boss."

Jack Sampson made her stand beside the coffee table while he stared down at the papers on his desk. He glanced at the telephone when it rang and dismissed the name showing on caller ID. "Close the door."

Molly turned and looked across the hallway into Eric's new office as she swung the door. Eric had arranged his furniture so that his desk faced his door, enabling him to keep tabs on Jack and Donna. How convenient, Molly thought.

Jack motioned to the chairs before his desk. "Sit." It wasn't an invitation.

Molly slid all the way into the cushions and placed her arms on those of the chair; this should be interesting.

Jack stood and walked around his desk, taking the chair beside hers. He leaned forward, their knees inches apart. "What in the hell has gotten into you lately?"

Molly idly wondered which of his management books he had pulled this approach from. She raised her eyebrows.

"You are questioning every decision I make, to my face and behind my back. Thank you so much for the memo about the hep shots instead of coming directly to me. You're not supporting Eric in his new position. How many times have I asked you for a report on the progress of the grant research for the new bike trail?"

Molly shrugged.

Jack clapped his hands together. "That's it exactly. You're working only on your own projects and none of the ones Eric handed off to you. We all have to make sacrifices in an organization. I've given up my small conference room to have Eric in an office close to me and Donna. Why are you blowing off the deadlines he gives you?"

"Because he's only testing me with worthless work. I'm too old to be jumping through imaginary hoops." Molly looked at Jack evenly. "I decided completing infrastructure projects that add to the city's fixed assets was more important than a snipe hunt for trail funding when we've bled that grant dry the past three years. No locality has ever been successful with a fourth application, or does Eric not know that?"

"You're not being a team player."

Molly stared at him. "Ooh rah."

Jack's face tightened. He moved his chair closer to her. "Ann can come up with all the training crap she wants to justify her own job. I'll make sure we all attend the sessions, even if we take paperwork along with us to pass the time. I can also spout the catch phrases back in executive staff meetings to keep the rest of them off of my back. But you and I both know what it comes down to, what local government will always come down to."

"Who the most underhanded son of a bitch is?"

Jack lunged at her and caught himself. "I won't forget being given a warning by that imbecilic city manager. If I'm on notice, so are you. Everything will be documented—projects assigned to you, expected deadlines, daily hours on a time sheet with a line for each project. One more stunt like confronting Eric in the map room about his job in front of other employees and you're out of here."

Molly blinked. She had been prepared to be fired but didn't think Jack had enough negative data about her to justify it yet. "I'll polish my résumé as soon as I have a few free minutes. I'll find another job providing I'm able to match an acceptable location with job duties. I just want to wrap up the big projects that have real deadlines. Catch my drift?" She stood up to leave.

He matched her stance and pushed her back into the chair. "I can have you transferred into a position that no one else will hire you from. They always need good workers at the waste treatment plant. How does that fit into your career development plan? I hear you're good at those."

Molly froze. He knew what she and Donna were doing at lunch and after everyone else left the building.

Jack smiled. "Donna turned in her resignation this morning. She's accepted a line position at the circuit board factory. How important is it to you to stay in a white-collar job, here or elsewhere?" He paused. "I briefed council in closed session about Project Cut. They're very impressed that *we* are on the site visit list. The state rep was very apologetic that I wasn't copied on all their e-mails with you. That won't happen again."

Molly swallowed. She felt herself slipping into mind-numbing shock. "My abilities mean nothing. My long hours mean nothing. All that matters is that I make you and Eric look good. Do I understand my place correctly?"

Jack nodded. "None of the damn women on this floor are indispensable, and I can shame any of them into submission. It pays to have friends on the inside of banks and doctor's offices."

Molly was numb. Surely, she wasn't really hearing this.

"I will grant you a draw, though. Focus on the big projects. Make me look good. I'll leave you alone about the rest. You're extremely talented, Molly. I can't argue that. Eric is a small dog occasionally nipping at your heels. I'm the junkyard dog about to break the weak link in his chain and tear you to pieces. Got it?" Jack stood and offered her his hand. He held on to her and pulled her close. "You want to be careful what you unleash, and you really want to be careful about who you accept a ride from. What's this I hear about you and Christine Miller steaming up her car in the parking deck?" He pointed the remote at the small television/DVD player on top of the bookcase. "My source at the PD was only too happy to make a copy for me."

Molly stared as she saw the car stop, Chris roll down the window to flash her badge with Molly visible in the passenger seat, and the time elapse before Molly left the vehicle. "What I do or don't do once I leave this building is none of your damn business." Molly's voice was calm; she could tell that he was bluffing, yet again throwing out an accusation to see if it stuck. Invading her space was an old ploy of

Jack's. She forced herself to hold her emotions in check.

Jack gave Molly a push toward the door when he was unable to get a rise out of her. "Not a word to Donna. She's finishing out the day, very emotional and upset, actually tried to threaten me." He waved her out of his office. She was dismissed.

Molly heard soft steps behind her as she stumbled toward her office. Hands against her back guided her through the door and to the stool at her drafting table.

Tamika closed the door. "Shall I call one of the others for you?" Her voice was low.

Molly shook her head. "I don't want anyone to know what was said in that office. I feel dirty."

Tamika studied Molly. "I can't help what I overhear, my ears are good. Gary was away from his desk."

Molly finally focused on Tamika. "Is it true about Donna?"

"He put a hurt on her about using the city computer for her personal advancement, threatened to write both of you up, and take disciplinary action that would go on your records. She quit."

Molly spread her hands over face. "I should just walk out of here."

Tamika sighed. "Who would ever believe what we've heard?" She hesitated. "You have to outsmart him, catch him in his own game. You're the only one who can do it, and I'll help you." She walked to Molly and put her arm around her.

"Are you making a pass at me?" Molly relaxed against Tamika.

"Lord, woman, how can you joke after what you just went through?" Tamika squeezed Molly before releasing her.

"Humor and lust are the only shreds of sanity I hold on to."

"I better get back to my desk before Eric does his usual walk-by. Keep the door closed for a while. Play a computer game. Find a hot lesbian site to surf. What's he going to do—fire you?" Tamika eased out of the room with a wink at Molly.

Molly stared at the site plan proposal for Project Cut—the state people were so original—a high-tech machine shop that specialized in working with titanium. The state's economic development office was soliciting sites to tour. Molly had actually thought herself capable of hustling a new company behind Jack's back as a means to win favor with city council. When was she ever going to learn about handling Jack?

Molly made a fist and pounded on the door of the apartment. It only took a moment for Chris to open the door and stare at Molly.

"There was a camera covering the parking deck. You didn't know about it?" Molly pushed Chris backward into the living room.

"How would I know the location of security cameras? I'm a detective, not a meter maid." Chris leaned against the arm of the sofa.

"Come on. You knew, and you didn't care." Molly stabbed her finger against Chris's chest.

"Well, I didn't park in front of it on purpose." A smile crept onto Chris's face. "Wonder if I can get a copy of the tape."

"Very funny. Jack already has one." Molly pushed Chris so that she fell back on the sofa cushions.

Chris rose up on her elbows. "What are you so upset about? Nothing could be seen through the windows."

Molly threw her coat down behind her. "But now Jack has ammunition and a strong suspicion. Do you know how hard I've worked to protect my personal life?"

"You were the one flaunting Bev in a restaurant not too long ago."

Molly glared at Chris. "That was a momentary weakness."

"Oh, and what am I?"

"A lifelong passion." Molly approached the sofa and lowered herself onto Chris. "Hell, if I'm going to be outed, I might as well enjoy the benefits."

They didn't miss a beat of finding their rhythm. Hands, mouths, bodies arched and explored. They traded positions and brought each other to climax separately and together. They finally lay still, breathing deeply.

"I had forgotten that sex could be that much fun and that good," Chris finally said.

"Everything happened perfectly." Molly looked up at Chris.

"You were a little fired up when you walked in." Chris brushed the hair from Molly's face. "I like that side of you. Want to see what we can manage in a big bed?"

Molly nodded. "Sorry. I've just had it with Jack. He finally drove Donna to quit and now he's coming after me if I don't make Eric look good. I'm going to have to change jobs. The funny thing is that I like being a public servant."

"I'll show you servant." Chris pulled Molly into the bedroom. Neither of them slept and neither was tired the next morning.

"Crap," Molly said as she blinked at the sunlight coming in the window.

"That's a fine way to greet the day." Chris rolled over and smiled at Molly.

"Has it been a month? I so want this to be right for you."

"Three weeks and five days, but who's counting, it was close enough. And if it was any 'righter,' I wouldn't be able to stand it. Relax. We're fine." Chris moved gently on top of her.

"What's better than fine?" Molly asked.

"I don't know a word for it, but I can show you." And Chris did.

CHAPTER TWENTY-TWO

Molly's hands gripped the steering wheel of her Jeep Liberty as tightly as she clenched her jaw. She stayed so angry lately when she wasn't around Chris. She left the office early on the pretense of a doctor's appointment; Molly was still limping from the damage to her leg from being stuck in the mud. She could not tolerate the looks and whispering as everyone expected her to be vindictive.

Eric slowly understood what it meant to be Jack's chosen. He was subtly ostracized by the rest of the department. Molly accepted Jack's halfhearted compromise/threat for the sake of the projects she wanted to complete. Eric was livid that Molly had bypassed him and made her own deal with Jack. He spoke to no one else on the floor. His boyishness turned into surliness overnight. Eric came to work and was totally disengaged from the rest of them. Molly believed that Jack would manipulate his protégé to take any fall that posed a threat to Jack. She held her breath about the flood damage numbers submitted to FEMA.

Molly juggled her cell phone and found the number saved in her contact list. "Hey," she said when the private cell phone was answered. "I'm worried about you. I miss my buddy."

"Don't be, you just miss mothering me."

She heard the tightness in Eric's voice. "Don't let a job do this to you, Eric, it's not worth it."

"Go ahead and say 'I told you so.' I've been expecting it." He sounded twice his age. "I deserve it. After all, I outsmarted all the rest of you."

"That's not why I called."

He waited. "Okay."

"We have to hang tough and together against Jack." She needed to know if there was a shred of decency remaining in Eric, if it was ever there to start with.

Silence.

"Eric…"

"I'm not interested in continuing this conversation."

"Eric, don't turn on all of us."

"You don't get it. I was never *with* any of you, and they've already turned on me. To hell with all of you." He disconnected.

Molly stared at the compact phone in her palm. She tossed it over the console into the passenger's seat. "Well, at least I tried."

She just wanted to drive, to do something relatively mindless. She followed Route 29 north away from downtown and toward the communities of Amherst, Lovingston, and Charlottesville. She really did need to make a fresh start somewhere else. It had been crazy to buy a house five months earlier. Oh, well. Maybe she could stick it out until spring. Winter was a horrible time to list real estate; the market was slow enough anyway. She wondered if Chris preferred relocating or a distance relationship.

Molly turned onto Route 130 at the outskirts of Madison Heights. The two-lane road was one of her favorites, weaving and climbing to the west toward the Blue Ridge Parkway and Natural Bridge. If she had a change of heart, there was a narrow county road that followed the river back to downtown. Why did she always need options?

She had the road to herself and slowed below the posted speed limit. What was it about driving that was so calming? Even in December, the evergreens retained their leaves and the houses made up for lack of color in the landscaping with Christmas decorations. She was amazed at the large inflatable characters that had not yet drawn a prankster's knife blade or, heaven forbid, bullet.

Molly glanced in her rearview mirror and was startled by the proximity of another vehicle. "Where did you come from?" A dark blue sedan was so close on her bumper that she could not identify the make of the automobile. "Great." She sped up to the posted limit. "Sorry, my bad for relaxing for a few moments."

The car stayed within several feet of her bumper. They drove through a curvy section of road marked with a double yellow centerline. Molly tried to remember where the next passing zone was. She thought it several miles ahead before the road took a long straight dip down and back up near an abandoned church site marked only by its cemetery. She increased her speed. The driveways were gravel and too narrow for a quick turnoff without substantially slowing.

Molly raised her hands and looked in the rearview mirror. "Give me a break and back the fuck off."

The car held its minimal separation from her rear end.

She concentrated on the road. The lanes were narrow and the shoulders graveled. One slip too far to the side and she would spin out of control into a deep ravine.

She stared into the mirror again. "Asshole."

The car behind her waggled in the lane. The guy was getting off on riding her. He appeared to be in his late fifties, heavyset, and wearing a suit.

"You're crazy as hell." Molly spied broken lines on her side of center just ahead. She slowed slightly to make passing easier.

The sedan stayed on her bumper.

"I don't fucking believe this." The line became solid again.

Molly sped up. She would outdistance the car behind her to have a safe cushion separating them so she could take the next side road. The car stayed tight to her. Molly debated slamming on her brakes. They had entered the stretch of road passing through densely wooded land owned either by a major paper company or the government as national forest. There was no house to seek help from even if she could spin out in someone's yard, only tall, ancient trees to wrap their vehicles around.

Molly spied the next passing zone. She slowed again, almost coming to a stop in the lane. The car sped around her and returned to the westbound lane. Molly would have let the driver go if he hadn't held down on his horn the entire time he was passing her.

All reason left Molly. It was just another middle-aged man used to having his own way with everything, used to being catered to, used to having no regard for anything done by a woman. She stomped the accelerator and closed to within a few feet of the dark blue Ford. "How do you like having someone up your ass?" she screamed.

Molly matched the Ford as it sped up and slowed down. She no longer cared if they wrecked. She no longer cared about anything. All she felt was the primal rage that had been building in her for months.

They reached the next passing zone and Molly blew into the oncoming lane. She stared at the large truck approaching in the eastbound lane. It was one of the stake body trucks that routinely worked the area hauling huge loads of pulpwood off the land owned by the paper conglomerate.

Molly stared at the grille on the tractor-trailer as it loomed closer. A large red bow was tied to the top of the radiator. She absolutely did not care if she slammed into the front of the truck head first at sixty-five miles per hour.

The blue Ford slammed on the brakes and stopped in its lane behind her. Molly reluctantly cut over and continued west. The tractor-trailer driver held down his air horn as he cleared the two idiots dueling on the highway.

Molly couldn't move her hands from their white-knuckled grip of the steering wheel. She sat slightly forward in her seat, unable to relax her back. She glanced into the rearview mirror. The blue Ford had pulled off the road, waiting for her to drive out of sight.

Molly's hand was shaking as she reached for the cell phone. She found the saved number and punched "send."

"Hello?"

Molly sounded strange even to herself. "Hey, I just wanted to hear your voice."

"Are you okay?" Chris asked.

Molly was silent for a moment. "I've been better."

"Bless your heart." Chris used the phrase good for most any situation.

Molly actually chuckled. "You say the sweetest things."

"Just wait until you experience all I can do, it only gets better."

Molly felt herself blush. What was going on with her hormones? "Tease."

"Absolutely."

"Got to go, I'm driving. I'm heading home to pack for my trip."

"Home for the holidays." Chris turned down the volume on the radio.

"Yeah, with my fingers crossed that it doesn't turn into the usual horrendous holidays filled with bad memories and awkward moments."

"Don't take this the wrong way, but it's good that you're going. I need time alone, yet all I really want to do is be with you."

"It would be overwhelming to change holiday rituals this year?"

"Yes." Chris sighed.

It was Molly's turn to laugh. "Now that's just pitiful. It's okay for you to need time with Spencer and Julie. Spencer needs your help as he and Susan try to have time for each other and placate families. I'll be back on the third of January. I'd rather you meet Syd and Jimmy when they visit next summer. There's no sense in you burning up all your vacation time to go to Michigan with me."

"I'll pick you up at the airport."

Molly didn't hesitate. "Deal."

"No hot dates with busty blondes while you're home."

"I'll try to restrain myself."

"Oh, I can restrain you."

"I'm hanging up now before I forget where it is I'm supposed to be going."

"Be safe." Chris didn't want to let Molly go.

"You too. Don't be so hard on yourself—have good thoughts of Ruth," Molly said softly.

"I will and good thoughts of you, too."

"There's only one blonde I'm interested in and she packs a gun, she really bangs."

"Cool."

"Ain't it?" Molly disconnected. She stared at her phone and felt better. She could deal with going home to Michigan. She could also deal with Jack and Eric. She was okay; at least that's what she'd keep telling herself until she actually believed it.

CHAPTER TWENTY-THREE

Molly approached the side door of the brick ranch house and took a deep breath. She never knew quite what to expect or how she would react to *home* when in Michigan. This wasn't the tiny frame house she had grown up in. This wasn't her mother living with her father. This was the closest thing to a family she had. She glanced at the old single-wide mobile home that had been set on cinder blocks in the back corner of the yard. Her father had written her about her half brother Jimmy wanting a place of his own.

It was funny. Her father would write her long letters with details of what was going on in Michigan, but when she saw him or managed to call when he answered the telephone, she couldn't get five words in a row out of him. She made him feel guilty, and he deserved to feel that way. Molly had finally grown out of her anger and disappointment toward him. She had reconciled as best as she was able to the simple fact that he had never seen fit to marry her mother. He had changed for the better in the years after he left them.

Vernon Hamilton, always called Ham, had transformed overnight from the deep voice who read her stories to the man who had left her mother when Molly was eleven. He was an extremely skilled welder, always able to find a high-paying job when he decided to change cities. He continued now in retirement to do piece work in his shop behind the house. He had grown tired of Molly and her mother after her mother put down roots and refused to move again. Molly had gone fifteen years without speaking to him. She made herself call him on his sixtieth birthday. In that interim, he married a woman ten years older than Molly and started another family. Molly's mother suffered through it all in silence and died from lung cancer at fifty-five, but Helen had forgiven Ham, allowing Molly to also.

Molly made herself visit her father and his new family when she turned thirty. Molly used her milestone birthday to make the conscious choice to no longer be angry with Ham. She met a half brother who was sixteen and a stepmother who looked the right age to be her sister. Even at forty, Molly could see why her father had been attracted to Sydney. Hell, Molly had been attracted to Syd; that was what freaked Molly out so. Syd had the look of Marilyn Monroe near the end of her life—a little heavier than fashionable but filled out in just the right places, a few wrinkles to evidence a life well spent, and blond hair she kept in a light shade and trimmed just below her ears. Syd didn't hesitate to tell her that she went to the gym each day and the salon every other week. Sydney knew she was toned, tan, and a knockout. Syd was why Molly could tolerate her father.

Molly raised her hand to knock, and the door was opened before her knuckles made contact with the trim.

Syd beamed at her and held the storm door open. Molly was no sooner inside the mud room than Syd embraced her.

"We're so glad you decided to come home for Christmas. Your father has been beside himself watching the clock and calling the airport to check that your plane landed safely and on time," she lowered her voice, "and peeking out the blinds to watch for the cab. He won't admit that he was worried about your arrival this late in the day." Syd turned her cheek to Molly for a kiss.

Molly bussed the proffered face. "I can't believe how nice the weather is. It's warmer here than in Virginia."

"Unreal, isn't it? I just had to pull these out to wear while I was cleaning and cooking." Syd looked down and patted the cut-off blue jeans.

Molly's eyes traveled down her stepmother's legs. She looked back up and directly into Syd's eyes.

Syd grinned. "Shame on you."

"And who's egging me on and loving every minute of it?"

"I am." Syd linked arms with Molly. "I admit it. I get a kick out of teasing you."

"Slut."

"Shh. Your father doesn't approve of me carrying on with you."

"That makes it all the more fun," Molly whispered in Syd's ear. "He's an old fart."

"Well, yeah, and I love him."

"He's a lucky man." Molly walked through the dining area of the kitchen and into the living room. She stared at her father. The brightness from the television screen reflected off his bald head. He looked as though he had aged ten years in the one since she had seen him. He must have his hands full, Molly thought, keeping a forty-five-year-old wife happy when he's one year shy of seventy. He, too, exercised with daily walks and was mindful enough of his diet not to gain weight since his retirement. He no longer smoked or drank. "Hey, Pop, how are you?"

He motioned to the television screen. "Damn good bowl game on." He patted the sofa cushion beside him.

Syd patted Molly's bottom as she started forward to sit with her father. "How about a beer, cutie?"

Molly rolled her eyes. "You're a goddess."

"That's what the men usually tell me."

"Women, too, if you give them a chance." Molly glanced at her father. He pretended not to hear as he also pretended not to understand that she was a lesbian.

The side door slammed open. "Hey, Ma, is she here?"

Jimmy entered the living room. He was as cute as his mother was sexy. Jimmy wore his thick brown hair almost to his collar, caught behind his ears and held in place by a baseball cap. He was no taller than Molly but stocky, looking like the wrestler he had been in high school. He dashed across the room to hug Molly, picking her up as she stood to meet him and grinning as he spun her around. He squeezed her.

Molly grunted. "Damn, boy, we're not on the mat for a takedown."

He laughed and set Molly on her feet. "Come on."

"She just got here." Syd came into the room with a Coors longneck.

Jimmy took the bottle and chugged it down

"Now that's just plain rude." Molly placed her hands on her hips.

"Go change. I'm meeting my friends at Hooper's and told them my lesbo sister would be with me." Jimmy handed the empty bottle to his mother.

"Jimmy!" Syd frowned at her son. She was back from the kitchen with a beer for Molly and a Diet Coke for Ham.

"She's yours the rest of the week, Ma. You can let her go out with me tonight. Pa will be sleep before halftime anyway." Jimmy tugged at Molly.

Molly looked at Syd and shrugged. To Jimmy, she said, "Give me ten minutes."

"Cool, I'll go shower and put on cleaner clothes."

"Romeo," Molly called to Jimmy as he ran out.

Syd followed Molly to the guest room on the end of the house across from her bedroom. She had moved Ham into Jimmy's room next to the mud room when the trailer was ready. "You don't have to go with him."

"I want to. He's grown up. I'm glad he wants to hang out." She set her bag on the bed and opened it to look for her black jeans and shirt.

"Need some help changing?"

Molly pushed Syd out of the room. "I can manage."

Molly thought about Syd as she changed. The thing she liked about the woman was that when Molly told her she preferred women, Syd didn't miss a beat in wanting to know who Molly was dating. She had waited a day to ask the usual questions—how long had Molly known, had Molly ever liked boys, how many women had Molly been with. At thirty, Molly had been out for fifteen years. She had never dated a boy other than as a group of friends going to the movies. She had slept with six women. Syd was fascinated.

Molly glanced in the living room as she passed through to the kitchen. Her father was sound asleep. Syd worked at the counter preparing dinner.

"Don't stay out too late, make him bring you home by midnight. I know you must be tired from traveling."

Jimmy honked the horn of his truck parked in the driveway.

"No wonder he doesn't have a date tonight."

Syd blew air between her lips. "He has the same girlfriend as when he was in high school. He just alternates between going out with her and his buddies. That boy never has any money."

"I'll keep an eye on him."

"Fox watching the hen house," Syd called as Molly went through the mud room.

Molly did watch her little brother for the next three-and-a-half hours. She was flattered that Jimmy and his friends were so interested

127

in what she did as an engineer after discovering that most of them worked as laborers on construction projects.

The highlight of the evening was when one of the boys asked her to dance. He waited until they were alone on the floor to talk to her.

"I remember your mom."

"Really?" Molly had almost forgotten what it was like to live where she had grown up, with people identifying her by her parents. Again, that was one of the things she preferred about Virginia.

"Yeah. I was a stutterer. Can't tell it now, can you?" He spun her around as the song neared its end.

Molly felt her age as she tried to keep up with a partner ten years younger. She shook her head and concentrated on moving her feet.

"I stuttered and everyone made fun of me. Your mom took the time to find out what to do and work with me during lunch. It took her the entire damn year I was in her fourth-grade class, but she taught me to slow down, visualize the words, and say things at my own pace. I'll never forget how kind she was." He led her back to the table and winked as he guided her to her seat by placing his hand on the small of her back.

Molly was amazed by her acceptance. Jimmy had put the word out that she was a lesbian. Of course, the idea of women having sex with each other didn't affect them the same as the prospect of men having sex together. Molly was overwhelmed by the twenty- to thirty-year-old women in the bar who wanted to meet a practicing lesbian. It had been a long time since she had phone numbers jotted on napkins and forced into her pockets. The guys loved it and kept buying rounds so she would continue to be their chick magnet. Strangest of all was that Molly enjoyed herself but was not tempted. She kept seeing Chris's face and hearing Chris's voice. Molly actually felt a pang of homesickness for Virginia when a woman walked through the bar wearing the same perfume as Chris.

At 11:45, Molly leaned over to Jimmy. "Okay, sport, take me home."

The group around the table groaned.

"I can't keep my eyes open, no offense to you guys. I was up early to make it to the airport on time, sat around while changing planes twice, and gained an hour with the different time zone. Give an old broad a break," Molly said.

"One last round for the old broad." Jimmy's best friend held a twenty up for the waitress.

Molly downed one last black and tan and stood. "Home, James."

The guys cackled and mimicked her in falsetto as Molly and Jimmy walked out of the bar.

Jimmy nudged her gently when they reached the house. "Are you okay going in by yourself? I'm going back. That Tania you tossed aside was cute and still sitting alone at the bar when we left."

"I'm fine, and shame on you."

Jimmy waved as he did a donut in the driveway their father would have him raking out the next morning.

Molly tiptoed into the house.

Syd was stretched out on the sofa watching the premier movie of the week on HBO. She motioned Molly to join her.

Molly sank into the soft cushions and began rubbing Syd's feet in her lap.

Syd moaned.

"Sorry, sweetie, a foot rub is all I'm up to tonight. I'm beat. You may have to help me up," Molly said.

"I'd be delighted to put you to bed." Syd pushed against Molly's crotch with her heel.

Molly waved her off. "You're all talk."

Syd chuckled. "Yeah, but don't we have fun trading trash?"

Molly smiled. "That we do." She studied her stepmother. "I need to ask you a serious question, and I'm tired enough now to do it without being self-conscious."

Syd raised her eyebrows.

"Did he really never mistreat you?" Molly held Syd's feet.

Syd blinked. "It bothers you, after all these years?" Syd would never forget the conversation she and Molly had when Molly first reconciled with Ham, partly because of her and Jimmy.

Molly nodded.

Syd took a deep breath. "His violence was tied to his drinking, Molly. Some people are like that. I'm guessing that he was mistreated as a child, though he'll never admit it. That type of behavior usually runs generation to generation. He has a good heart." She paused. "He came at me only once, before Jimmy, and I used a cast iron frying pan to put Ham in the hospital. I made him promise me that he would never drink again before I let him come back to me. We were apart almost six months as he proved himself. He still goes to AA meetings every week, calls them his church service. I wouldn't have brought Jimmy into that kind of situation." It was Syd's turn to study Molly. "Honey, you have to believe this. He is sorry. My heart breaks for what you and your mother went through."

Molly shrugged. "It was for the best that he didn't marry Mom and did walk out."

"Violence like that runs deep, changing the lives of the ones who were powerless." Syd made it sound like a question.

"There are other things in life that make up for it." Molly finally relaxed.

Syd turned her head sideways as she looked at her stepdaughter. "She must be pretty special."

Molly looked at Syd questioningly.

"I didn't expect you home tonight. Jimmy has talked about you all week. Weren't they lined up to meet you—male and female?"

"That turkey, he probably raffled time slots with me."

Syd nodded. "Is there someone special?"

Molly blinked. "Yes. She's different from the others. She's paid her dues like I have, but she's not in the midst of some huge drama. She's only had one partner—lost her to cancer—and is willing to take a chance on me."

Syd placed her hand over Molly's. "I'm glad to hear that. You know even with the age difference showing up so much now, I wouldn't want anyone but your father. There's something special that you recognize when you finally meet the right one. It was a few years after your dad walked out on you and your mother when we met. I'd change the way he left you two if I could."

"I know. It worked out like it was meant to. Mom and I were fine. I turned out okay."

Syd hugged her. "Yes, you did. Do I get to help you to bed now?"

Molly held out her hand and Syd stood and pulled her up. "This new girlfriend is lucky to have you."

The week passed quickly, and part of Molly was sorry to see her time in Michigan end. She ate too much, laughed more than she thought possible, and felt closer to her family than ever before. It was as though she was finally content enough with herself to accept all of them.

Jimmy volunteered to take her to the airport on his way to work. Ham never told Molly goodbye, disappearing into his shop when it was time for her to leave. Syd always made sure she rubbed enough of her perfume on Molly to last for the duration of the flight. Molly and Jimmy rehashed the holiday during the thirty-minute drive. He parked in the boarding lane in front of the terminal and carried her bag inside.

Molly stared at the young man who bore a striking resemblance to old photographs of her father with a dash of Syd mixed in. "You turned out okay, kiddo."

"You too, sis."

Molly liked that he called her that.

He grinned at her. "So when are you going to tell me about who's waiting for you in Virginia? Will I meet her when I come to see you this summer?"

Molly blushed. "I hope so." She hugged him tighter and longer than ever before.

He threw his cap in the air as she went through the first boarding gate.

Molly couldn't wait to get back to Virginia. She had barely thought of work during the entire holiday and hadn't stopped thinking of Chris. She finally had her priorities right.

CHAPTER TWENTY-FOUR

Molly was amazed. She actually enjoyed the holidays with her family. Her little brother, now legal at twenty-one and not so little, was fun to be around instead of a pain-in-the-ass smart aleck harassing her. She thought it a hoot that she and Jimmy went out drinking and trading comments about the women at the local bars for New Year's Eve, then hugged and kissed each other when the ball dropped.

Syd was Syd; Molly shook her head, feeling slightly guilty. Ham had been as detached as ever, but Molly was used to it. Through all of her time away, Molly kept thinking about Chris. Molly flung herself at Chris at the airport and didn't care who saw them. She also listened to all of Chris's reasons for not stopping at the office as she talked Chris into dropping her off anyway.

Of course, Jack was hovering around her door awaiting her return after she made the mistake of calling and saying she was on her way in. He shoved a folder at her. "This is urgent. I can't believe you took an entire week off. Don't do that again any time soon." He strode off as though extremely busy, ignoring the fact that he approved her leave time, seemingly glad to have her out of the office for a while.

Molly sighed. It was her own damn fault for coming in a day early; she hated when Chris was right. Molly smiled with any thought of Chris.

There were notes all over her desk and an unreal deadline on a report to Jack and Eric and city council. Eric had sent or forwarded fifteen e-mails to her. "Well, at least they missed me." She stared about her office trying to decide what to start on first—telephone or e-mail messages. She decided on telephone, usually the most urgent. The balance of the afternoon should be just enough time to clear messages and allow her to hit the ground running the next morning.

Molly glanced toward the hallway as Windy passed by on her way to the back corner office.

"What are you doing back?" Windy did not slow the rhythm of her hands pushing the wheel rims.

Molly went to her doorway and watched the woman roll determinedly past Donna's empty cubicle. Jack's strategy was to use temps until the new batch of college grads began job hunting. Ann wanted to make use of the vacancy to upgrade the job classification.

Tamika came to her doorway, looked at Molly, and raised her eyebrows. "She always stops to speak and ask how I am."

Molly shrugged. "Something's up."

Tamika motioned Molly to her office. They sat before the large monitor and pulled up a topographic file as though actually working on a project.

Tamika leaned over to Molly. "If she didn't want us to hear, she would have called him to meet her in the conference room. We have to look out for each other. Right?"

"Absolutely." Molly was pleased that Tamika possessed such a good sense of character judgment regarding her co-workers.

"How dare you!" Windy launched in on Jack without preamble.

"Close the door."

Windy slammed the door against its casing.

"Did you forget your meds this morning?" Jack asked knowingly. "How long have you been on the new antidepressant?"

"Screw you. That's privileged information. I will find out how you know about my prescriptions, but that's for another day. You know damn well what I'm talking about."

Molly whispered in Tamika's ear. "I've never heard Windy this angry, not even in court when a case is slipping away from her."

Tamika nodded. "I wouldn't want to be Jack."

Molly leaned back and looked down her nose at Tamika. "Hell, that goes without saying any time."

Tamika snickered and smacked Molly on the arm. "Stop it."

Windy started again. "I expect an apology from you. How dare you interfere with a case that I'm settling on behalf of the city? You have no right to enter into ongoing negotiations and certainly not to argue the issue of liability."

Jack sounded bored. "I know it's not the city's fault that some dumbass parent let a retarded child climb to the top of a set of wooden bleachers alongside a softball field."

"The parent is not at issue."

"He damn well is."

Windy's voice rose. "The bleachers had not been properly maintained. Parks and rec freely admits that. It is only right that the city pay hospitalization from its self-insurance fund."

Jack's voice lowered. "Yes, and if the city pays hospitalization, it admits wrongful doing and will be wide open for a lawsuit."

"They are not interested in suing. They are broke and need help paying bills so they don't go bankrupt and lose their home. We don't pay the hospital bill and you can damn well count on a lawsuit. Goddamn it, the child's health is what matters here."

"All that matters is that you never admit guilt when it comes to the city's best interest," Jack said.

"But the city is at fault and it's my call to make!"

Tamika looked at Molly. "Why does he do this?"

"Ego and idiocy—he's a master of both," Molly said.

Tamika shook her head.

Windy was not done. "We can do this all day long. You should have come to me to talk about it, but, no, you had to go to each council member one at a time and make me look like an incompetent weakling who can't handle a simple negotiation."

"Well, if the high heel fits."

Molly flinched, waiting for Windy to explode.

Windy's chair squeaked as she rolled slightly back and forth. "I'm going to hold a hard line now that council has called me on the carpet behind closed doors and reprimanded me. I'm also going to write a memo to the file explaining exactly what happened. When this blows up and the city is trying to figure out how to come up with a six- or seven-figure settlement, you will be held accountable for your part in this. Maybe this incident will finally get your ass out of city hall for good."

Jack drummed a pencil on his desk blotter. "The family's not going to do a damn thing. I've had his employer threaten to fire him if he doesn't let this drop, and all it cost me was a little incentive money for jobs that may or may not be created. You know how difficult it is for our companies to come up with definite employment numbers with the way temps come and go."

Molly had never heard Windy speechless before. She and Tamika visibly strained to hear the next as Jack's tone became threatening.

"If you want to play with the boys, you damn well better be ready to play like one. Even Tom conceded that it's a mistake to have women on executive staff. He may shift you and Barbara to different positions on the organizational chart. You know what my suggestion is for a position?"

Molly shot out of the chair and was down the hallway as Windy opened her mouth to speak.

"There you are." Molly dashed into Jack's office. "Angela asked me to look this way while she went to Campbell's office. Emergency phone call—Angela needs you back in the office ASAP. Sorry, boss." Molly grabbed Windy's chair knowing how much the woman hated being rolled and pulled her backward out of the office. She pushed Windy down the hallway, jerking her head at Tamika to cover their backs.

Windy sputtered as she tried to get her hands on the wheel rims to stop the chair.

"Don't do that unless you want burns on your palms." Molly didn't slow her pace. She spun around and pushed the door to the main hallway open with her butt. She crossed the wide area outside of council chambers and held her breath that none of the members was in their break room. She careened into Angela's office. "Close the door. This isn't going to be pretty!"

Angela was around her desk and shutting them in as Molly braced herself for the earful she was sure to receive.

Angela looked from Windy to Molly. "I knew she was pissed. How bad was it?"

Molly shuddered. "Jack now has an EEOC suit on his hands. Tamika and I overheard what he said to Windy."

Molly and Angela looked to the figure in the wheelchair. Windy appeared as though turned to stone.

"Ma'am?" Angela leaned toward the chair.

Molly chastised herself for enjoying her vantage point.

"If you can manage not to leer while looking down her blouse," Windy said as she looked at Molly and pushed away from Angela, "I need you to promise me something."

Angela looked at Molly reproachfully. Molly shrugged. "Sorry, can't help myself."

"But you could barge in on a private conversation." Windy made a half turn of the wheels toward her office. "I know you thought you were doing me a favor, but I very much resent what you just did." She turned away and spoke to the two women over her shoulder. "I need you to promise me that you'll talk to Tamika. I don't want a word of what was spoken in that office being repeated."

"Windy!" Molly said.

"Not a word." Windy's entire body shook. "He's right about one thing. I have to play on their turf. I will take care of Jack and Tom on their own terms." She finally turned slightly and looked at them. "It's my call. I *will* handle it my own way." She sighed. "I'd simply throttle Jack if it didn't involve physical contact."

Molly started to speak. She felt Angela's hand on her arm and reconsidered further arguing. "Whatever you say, Windy. This is your dog. Just know that I'll have your back whether you agree with my method or not."

Molly left the two women to salvage Windy's schedule for the rest of the day. Molly felt in need of a drink. She also felt very much in need of Chris.

CHAPTER TWENTY-FIVE

Molly paid no mind to the snow that began falling early that morning other than to think how beautiful it was and how she would love to be snuggled before the fireplace at home with Chris as the flakes accumulated. It continued snowing steadily during the day, closing schools after the children were served lunch so that the day didn't have to be made up later.

Most of city hall emptied out early due to workers nervous about driving in the deepening snow or parents suddenly thrown off schedule by having children home early. Eric had been among the first to slink out the back door with no explanation to anyone. Even Gary was leaving early to drive his girlfriend home since this was her first snowfall; being a native of Florida had not prepared her for winter driving. Gary loved it; it would give him a chance to prove why he needed a full-size, four-wheel-drive pickup.

"Are you sure you don't mind if I leave?" Gary stopped in the hall outside Molly's door as he put his jacket and gloves on. "Tamika is out today. It leaves no one to pull data for you."

Molly waved him on. "I've done all my map work before. I can do it again. We're only talking about a few hours here. I actually enjoy playing with the GIS datasets when you guys aren't watching my every move."

He grinned. "Promise you won't crash the system? I haven't done backup tapes since the first of the week."

"I will try my best not to corrupt the data. Who am I kidding? I probably won't budge all afternoon unless it's to go to the side of the building and watch the cars slide down the steep slope of the street."

"You're okay to get home?" Gary asked.

Molly rolled her eyes. "What do I drive?"

"A Jeep."

"Where was I raised?"

Gary grinned. "Okay, Ms. Michigan, I get your point. Call me if you need me whether you're stranded with GIS or snow, and I know who to call if I need help with driving."

"Or your girlfriend." She smirked appropriately. "Just go."

He threw the long end of his scarf over his shoulder with an exaggerated flip as he walked away.

Molly smiled—nice guys were few and far between. She settled in with the set of plans she was reviewing for compliance with city design standards. It never failed to amaze her that consultants charged their clients thousands of dollars for relatively simple engineering or architectural drawings and usually made the same damn mistakes every time.

Molly heard the hall door and glanced to see who was coming back for something. She couldn't believe her eyes when she saw Donna Brooks quickly walk past her door without stopping to speak.

Molly counted back. It had been two months since Donna resigned. None of them had any response from phone or e-mail messages sent to her. Molly had taken that to be a bad indication of how the new job was going.

Molly listened. Donna went into Jack's office and closed the door. Molly knew better, but she went to the GIS office and soundlessly closed the door behind her. She pretended to work on a map she pulled up on Tamika's computer.

"Thank you for seeing me." Donna's voice was flat.

"Have a seat." Jack's tone was as loaded as a venomous snake's fangs.

"I guess you know why I'm here."

"Tell me anyway."

Donna let a sigh escape. "Sorry." She cleared her throat. It sounded as though she was barely holding herself together. "I need my job back," she finally said.

"And why should I help you after you walked out on me?"

"I'm sorry, Jack." Molly heard the thickening of Donna's voice—she was fighting tears. "Production is being cut back because last quarter's sales were off. I'm not going to be making enough hours to carry us now that Tim's work has slowed down for the winter. We won't have any benefits if I get laid off. I haven't been with the company long enough to be vested in any of their programs."

Jack considered his options. "I'll take you back, but I'm cutting your pay one step and you start over with years of service and earned leave. I don't want to hear any more about you and Molly scheming to have you promoted. I want you to work only for me and let me know what else is going on in the office."

"Spy?"

"That's a harsh term for it. I want you to gather information for my ears only. Take it or leave it. I have a dozen good applicants to evaluate. You're fortunate that Ann dragged her feet on the new job description she wanted to put in place for all admin hires."

"I'll take it," Donna said, needing no time to think it over or check with Tim.

"Good enough. I'll talk to Ann. She'll call you about the paperwork and start date." Jack paused. "I won't tolerate this again."

"I understand."

"Good, I'm going home before the roads ice over. There's a report marked up on your old desk for the temp who didn't show up this morning. How about knocking that out for me before you leave?"

"Yes, sir," Donna said.

"I'll call in a day or two, or Ann will. Welcome back."

"Thank you."

Molly cringed at hearing what sounded like a slap to Donna's butt. Molly didn't budge as Jack left the office. She heard Donna blowing her nose as she settled in at her former cubicle.

Molly eased the door open and walked to Donna's desk. "What in the hell was that about?"

Donna stared blankly at Molly.

"I want you back here, but what in the hell was that about?" Molly repeated, hands on her hips.

"The new job didn't pan out. I'm the steady paycheck in our family. What choice did I have?" Donna spoke, trying to allow no emotion in her voice.

Molly dropped to her knees so that Donna wasn't looking up at her. She stared into Donna's eyes. "That didn't sound like the Donna I know and love."

Tears seeped from the corners of Donna's eyes. "You don't know me or you wouldn't love me."

"I can argue with that."

Donna looked up at the ceiling until the tears stopped. "When I first came to work here, I was warned about Jack, that he chased anything in a skirt. I handled him, not a big deal. I tended bar after high school until I married and decided it was time for a *career*. I know how to play men."

Molly nodded and handed Donna a tissue.

"The city began freezing positions. There was talk of consolidating admin workers. I went to Jack and propositioned him to keep my job."

"You what?"

"I slept with him to keep my job and my benefits for the sake of my marriage. He didn't force me, I offered. Ever since, he has held it over me, threatening to tell HR or my husband or both."

"Have you had sex with him since?"

"Just a few times over the years. I'm no conquest for him." Donna stared at her desk. "Now I'm trapped. I have only a high school education and lousy grades while in school. He won't give me a reference. I tried to get away from him and look where I ended up—one step from unemployment and food stamps. I need the steady paycheck and the benefits. You make twice what I do and can find a job anywhere. You can't possibly understand."

The sad thing was that Molly did. Molly flashed back to her mother and the way Helen must have felt burdened by a child and no marriage license, the shame Helen had lived with after Ham walked away, the secret Helen had spent her life protecting.

Molly stood and placed her hand briefly on Donna's shoulder. "It's not for me to understand or judge or anything else. It's what you have to live with, isn't it?"

Donna's voice was barely audible. "As much as I hate Jack Sampson—and I do—I hate myself more."

Molly had to walk away. Who else would understand that the fault was not in what Donna thought she was forced to do to survive but in the man who accepted her proposition and used it on her day in and day out?

Molly felt sickened for all of them, for all the women trapped in lives of misery by men. She walked slowly back to her office, feeling as though the weight of the world was on her shoulders alone. She automatically reached for her phone and dialed Chris's cell number. "Hey," she said quietly.

"Hey, yourself. Where are you?" Chris asked.

"Where I always am this time of day—the office." Molly couldn't keep the sadness out of her voice.

"Jeez, what's happened?"

"Donna's back. Jack has won again. I'll tell you about it another time." Molly was on the verge of tears; she knew this meant she was exhausted.

"I'm so sorry, sweetie. What do Windy and I keep advising you?"

"Document, document, document. I hate that my life has come down to observing someone like Jack Sampson so closely."

"It's called self-preservation. You shouldn't have to leave your job unless you truly want to."

Molly rubbed her eyes. "Once you wallow in shit, how do you ever completely rid yourself of the smell? I feel as though he has already won, no matter what I do, or the outcome."

"Go home and hug Dolly. You don't need to be at the office with those thoughts."

"I will, as soon as Donna is ready to leave. I won't walk out on her," Molly said.

"I know and that's one of the reasons I love you. See you later."

"You would do the same." Molly hung up the phone and stared out of the window with a silly grin on her face. Had Chris just slipped and said the *l* word?

Molly was better after she went home and took a hot shower, changing into favorite pajamas. She stood in the kitchen waiting for the microwave to heat water for cocoa. She looked down at Dolly. "I must be getting old, Miss Dolly. I came in here to get a beer out of the fridge and changed my mind after thinking how much better cocoa would taste."

Dolly started across the kitchen floor, reached the center of the room, and jumped straight up in the air before continuing to her bowl of dry food by the radiator.

"You too? That's kind of what I did." Molly laughed. How she loved that cat. She'd been thinking a lot about the things she loved lately."

She glanced at the clock on the microwave as she removed the measuring cup of bubbling water. "Chris should have been here by now."

It had become their routine on Wednesday night for Chris to stop and pick up a six-pack of Japanese beer and take-out sushi or Chinese food. Molly would pay for dinner out Friday or Saturday night. It saved arguing over checks.

Dolly lifted her head at the sound of the front door opening, then went back to crunching.

Molly walked into the living room.

"I hope that's hot and for me." Chris nodded at the cup. "I think my feet are frozen." She set down her bags. "You may have to hold the cup for me. My fingers won't uncurl."

Chris was covered in a heavy powdering of snow, her black boots turned white.

"Where's your wagon?" Molly looked out the front window. Nothing was parked on the street—her Jeep was at the top of her steep driveway.

"Your dumbass neighbors have blocked the frickin' street. Someone slid their BMW into two parked cars. I had to walk in from the avenue."

"Crap, you should have just gone on home." Molly held the cup for Chris to sip. She didn't mind sharing.

"And miss a night with you, I don't think so." Chris shrugged off her coat. Molly hung it on the shower rod in the bathroom. She motioned Chris to sit on the toilet and pulled her boots off for her.

"Want me to take the rest of it off while I'm at it? The gas logs are on high. I could put a blanket on the floor in front of the fireplace and warm you up." Molly smiled as she ran her hand along Chris's shirt front.

"I'm glad to see your mood is better," Chris said.

Molly held her hand up. "I don't want to talk about work."

Chris nodded. "I heard that. Can we take the food with us? I'm starving. I didn't stop for lunch."

Molly pushed the trunk that served as coffee table aside and spread out the afghan. She tossed down several pillows and sat cross-legged as Chris joined her. They leaned back against the sofa and watched the gas flames as they ate.

It wasn't long before Chris sighed contentedly. "I could get used to evenings like this."

"Me too," Molly said. "Did you mean what you said on the phone? That you love me?"

Chris smiled. "I wondered if you caught it or not. Yeah, I mean it. I love you."

Molly gulped. "I love you, too. Wow, it felt great saying that."

"We're still going to wait a year before moving in together?" Chris asked the question casually; it had been a mutually set time frame.

Molly blew air between her lips. "Yes."

Chris nodded. "I agree, just checking. It's so tempting."

"No rushing this time. We're going to do this right." Molly opened another beer and handed it to Chris. "Six months?"

Chris chuckled. "I would have been disappointed if you hadn't said that." She held out her bottle. They tapped glass to seal the deal. "It should be a momentous April."

"I'll show you momentous." Molly waited no longer to help Chris off with the rest of her clothes.

CHAPTER TWENTY-SIX

"You what?" Molly felt bile rise in the back of her throat.

Jack stared at her as though she was an idiot for not understanding what he said the first time. "I told the mayor and council not to worry about the budget shortfall with the state cutbacks that are coming down. Our manufacturing taxes will make up for it due to the crackerjack job you've done with industrial expansions."

Molly knew she was just having a bad dream. She shook her head and closed her eyes hoping for a different scene when she looked about the next time.

"I told council that if anyone could work magic with numbers and find unaccounted-for revenue, it would be you." Eric smiled at her with eyes as dead as the last of the leaves hanging on the oak trees outside the window.

Molly stared at the two men. "Rusty extrapolated all the projections, taking into account the industrial numbers, when we started on the budget. There is no revenue to be *found*."

Eric and Jack looked at each other. Jack nodded at Eric to run with the answer. "You still don't understand what we're saying. We told council that you'll be able to find source funds to fill the gap so that they look good in the press."

"In other words, call enough of the manufacturers to goad them into projections that we both know are exaggerated yet if plugged into the tax rate, our revenue works out just right?" Molly asked.

Jack and Eric nodded at her.

Jack leaned forward over the table. "You know those guys well enough that they will confide in you what they think corporate is almost ready to push down to them."

Yeah, like layoffs and production line closings, Molly thought to herself. Jack never heard half of what the men told her in confidence. Molly gathered her pad and pencil and left the conference room. She had to decide what if anything of their commitment she could do and live with.

It was all a numbers game with their major employers; the companies danced to the strings that corporate pulled from remote northern headquarters. It was always a crap shoot. Rivalry amongst plant locations was horrendous; not a manager she knew wasn't aware enough of in-house competition to base every projection on the output of their sister locations, just slightly better. What none of them wanted to recognize was that their competition generated false numbers at a fast and furious pace to look good with headquarters. It all came down to intermingled falsifications encouraged by upper management. Here the city was, the tiniest cog in the wheel, preparing to do the same.

Molly muttered to herself as she walked toward her office. "Every damn bit of it is a green pea and walnut half-shell hand jive." She listened as Jack and Eric followed her at a safe distance to return to their offices. Molly dropped her pad on her drafting table and stuck the mechanical pencil that matched her blue corduroys into her pocket. She stalked into Jack's office. "I won't do it!"

Jack glanced up at her and rolled his eyes at Eric.

"I will not fabricate numbers!" Molly crossed her arms over her chest.

Jack placed his hands on his desk and rested his weight on his arms. "You will generate the numbers that council expects to see. I don't care how you come up with them."

"Just do it, Molly." Eric dropped on the sofa in Jack's office as though he had nothing in particular to do for the rest of the day. "Work your magic. Council members think you walk on water. They know Jack and I are snakes in the grass."

Molly's chin dropped. "My God, Eric, you did sell your soul for this promotion. I hope it's worth it to you."

"I'm buying a bigger house and newer car and can pay for more day care hours. Robin has to have her *volunteer* time so that she can rub elbows with all the *right* people." He smiled at her with dead eyes. "No complaints here." Eric looked at Jack and shrugged.

Jack raised his eyebrows.

Eric went to the windowsill and picked up the shiny trophy

awarded the city for downtown revitalization.

"Perfect example." Jack nodded.

Molly fought the urge to cover her ears with her hands and close her eyes.

"Isn't this special? City council gets off on having their photograph in the newspaper with awards. I really didn't do anything on the application incorrectly. I just didn't do it exactly right, either." Eric smiled and struck a pose with the gleaming, silver-coated chalice. "I just used the few numbers I had on the city's downtown investment—mainly water main repairs—and did a little creative math with the downtown events to come up with volunteer hours no one can actually disprove. Then I claimed credit for private investment that was already programmed that we really had not a damn thing to do with except showing up for the ribbon cutting."

"Add a few color photographs, trade dinners, and drinks for letters of recommendation, and have the printer slap it all into a good binder. Look at the result." Jack held up his hands. Eric tossed the trophy to him. Jack neatly caught the large tapered cup. He feigned Eric going long, then passed the trophy back.

Eric held the trophy by the base and swung it like a bat. "Home run for all of us. We'll receive more grant dollars because of the recognition. It's all part of the game."

"Get with the program, Molly. You're the only one with a problem." Jack sat and flipped through his pocket calendar. "You better get started. The numbers need to be on my desk first thing Monday morning so Eric and I will be ready for council. Otherwise, staff is light at the sewage treatment plant. Donna can apply for unemployment and food stamps."

"You son of a bitch." Molly sensed someone behind her before she felt the hand on her arm.

Wordlessly, Tamika pulled Molly out of the office and through the building. They rode down the elevator in silence to the ground floor and took the side door out of city hall into the short alley from the loading dock. The smokers looked at them questioningly.

Molly coughed and followed the alley to the side street. She stood on the sidewalk, shivering and looking at the canyon of buildings looming around them. "You heard?"

"Oh, yeah." Tamika pulled Molly closer to Main Street to be out of view from the city hall windows.

"I'll do what they want." Molly thought aloud at a furious pace. "But I'll only call the plant managers who will give me their expansion projections actually being used for next year's work. Then I'll dig through the machinery and tool tax rates in the commissioner of revenue's files and look for any old-boy handshake deals that should have been cleared from the books by now."

Tamika looked at her questioningly.

"Everyone—*everyone*—plays the damn numbers games." Molly closed her eyes to try to slow her mind. "Past leadership for the city has done the grin-and-wink to defer tax collection by loosely interpreting state code. How many companies do you think we have kept in the city when they threatened to move to the counties for the lower rates and inferior services by leading them into answering questions so that the code structure would benefit them? The current commissioner has just begun a program of sending his auditors into the plants to work through the machinery listings with the company's accountant and verify what actually exists, what has been added or pulled from production lines, and the real age of the equipment."

Tamika held on to Molly's arm. "I still don't understand."

"You don't want to." Molly sighed. "We do business visits and encourage the plant managers to tell us how good everything is so that we award incentives for them to add more equipment and employees."

"Right, that I understand. Eric took me with him on his last one of those." Tamika pulled her cardigan together.

"Then we roll that into our charts and pat ourselves on the back about what a good job we're doing. Council loves it. Jack preens when he makes that presentation." The image repulsed Molly.

"And?" Tamika asked.

"Then the commissioner of revenue goes out, explains the loopholes in the codes to help keep the few manufacturers we have, and nowhere near the increase in revenue that we used as a basis for our incentive is generated," Molly said.

"But I read your last council report—" Tamika began.

Molly cut her off. "I've started council down the path of performance contracts between the city and the company with specific claw-back options with memorandums of understanding in place where we all spell out exactly what we're agreeing to. The plant managers hated it at first but soon realized it's doing them a favor so someone won't do exactly what I'm about to do—audit the interview notes and actual collection and make them pay the taxes they should have been charged or return incentives they shouldn't have accepted." Molly took a breath and looked at city hall looming over the bank building on the corner of the block. "It's all there in the archives and on record in the numbers the commissioner has to certify and submit to the commonwealth."

Tamika grimaced.

"I can come up with the revenue to balance the budget, but no one is going to like me, and it's going to take all damn weekend." The only "no one" Molly was concerned about was Chris; there would be no time that weekend for a leisurely date.

CHAPTER TWENTY-SEVEN

Molly was aware of a slight tapping noise, but it took her a few moments to look up from her desk. Susan stood in the doorway of her office and raised an unopened can of Mountain Dew.

"I thought you might need a break." Susan walked in and sat in the side chair next to Molly's desk. She crossed her legs and held out the can. "May I tempt you?"

Molly smiled. She tossed her highlighter down and leaned back. "I would say it'd be damn near impossible for you *not* to tempt me."

Susan burst out laughing. "You're so full of shit."

Molly tried to look offended. "Well, you're the irresistible one."

"At this point, any woman holding sugar and caffeine would look good to you," Susan said, holding out the soft drink.

"Maybe," Molly reached for the can, "but some look much better than others."

"So what's the deal with you and Donna?"

Molly sighed. "Nothing, absolutely nothing."

Susan tried again. "You two aren't talking. Is it because she came back to Jack?"

Molly shook her head.

"Meaning you aren't ready to talk to me about it?"

Molly nodded.

"She isn't the same with any of us." Susan looked at the printouts scattered across Molly's desk. "How's that going—wine from water yet?"

"That would be easy. I'm finding pretty much what I expected."

"I can see that on your face. When was the last time you took a break?"

Molly glanced at her watch. "When I came in this morning."

"This job and this city are not worth killing yourself over. You know that, right?"

"Yeah. It's just that now that I've gotten into this, I can't stop digging. The city is damn lucky none of this has hit the press." Molly ruffled the pages.

"Keep that in your back pocket in case you need to protect yourself." Susan lowered her voice.

"I know. I'm documenting the entire process in case Jack tries to make it come back and bite me."

"It's not Jack that concerns me."

"The dark prince?" Molly rubbed her eyes as she asked.

"Exactly."

"I know." Molly drained the can. "Great, now I'll have to pee."

"Well, at least that will be some exercise." Susan stood. "I'm not leaving you here again tonight. We're going to gang up on you about going home. Spencer's stopping by to pick me up for dinner. His mom's keeping both kids tonight."

"You guys are turning into the Brady Bunch."

"If we're lucky." Susan waved off Molly's misdirection. "I mean it, Molly. I'm not the only one worried about you. You know Chris is, but she's trying not to say anything."

"So she talks to Spencer, who talks to you, so you can check on me." Molly nodded. "I hear what you're saying, and I appreciate the concern. You're right. I need to spend some time with Chris and Dolly, too. I've been leaving Dolly home alone too much. I've lost two lampshades to her claws this week. Who knows what Chris might do, but I can think of so many possibilities."

Susan rolled her eyes. "Pay attention to the girls who love you. I know you care about your cat if not the rest of us."

"Just leave." Molly picked up the highlighter. "Hey, thank you."

Susan closed the door behind her.

Sure enough, a half hour later, Molly could avoid stopping for a restroom break no longer. It was one of the rare instances of having the restroom to herself. She hesitated at the prospect of returning to her office and resuming her witch hunt; she continued along the hall to the GIS room. There was a note on the door that Gary and Tamika had gone to lunch together and would return at 1:00. Molly took a deep breath and went to the back corner of the building; Donna and Jack were gone. Eric was at his desk. He looked up at her and waited for her to start the conversation.

"I miss us being friends," Molly said simply. "How's Erin?" She leaned against the door frame.

"She's fine, growing longer and heavier, and into everything—particularly taking things apart. I keep reassuring my wife that she's not raising a little butch." Eric almost sounded like his former self.

"Nothing wrong with that. A little tomboy in a girl helps her in the long run."

"I know, bad joke." He rolled back from his desk. "You look tired."

"I'm surprised you would notice."

Eric looked down at his hands. "I saw one path for advancement. I don't have your mind or training. I have to make do with being innocuous and fitting old white men's profiles for their successors."

"That's so sad."

"Maybe, but it's true. It's also just work."

Molly shook her head. "There's no dividing line. What you are in your professional life carries over into your personal life. Does Robin know all that you're into for this promotion?"

"Know, hell, she's the one nagging me about more money and a better title. She spends so much time nagging, I'm surprised when she notices Erin."

"Listen to yourself. You're on your way to becoming a divorce statistic."

He nodded. "How about you? What are you jeopardizing?" He studied her carefully.

"Nothing yet."

"I was afraid of that. You found a way to screw us over, didn't you, while you do what we asked?"

Molly nodded.

Eric ran his hands over his hair, smoothing strands already held snugly in place. "You're committing professional suicide. You know Jack is not going to allow you to show him up before council again."

"I know that. I'm hoping he'll be fed up enough with me to want me gone so he won't submarine reference calls," Molly said.

"Good luck with that."

Molly stared at him. "Okay, what should I do?"

"Come up with a number and have a reasonable excuse ready for why it doesn't pan out six months from now. The city has contingency funds. No one wants to surrender them just yet." Eric lowered his voice. "Hell, Molly, no one expects you to be able to do this." He watched her reaction. "You didn't understand that?"

She shook her head, feeling numbness taking over her body.

Eric leaned forward. "You really have no business dabbling in management. You still care about what you do too much. Don't you get it? You need some piece of shit like me to work for and run interference for you and allow you to be the intellectual everyone respects. If you do as I ask, I'll look out for you."

Molly turned and walked back to her office. She continued digging through numbers just as she had been.

At ten minutes before everyone else's quitting time, Tamika tapped on Molly's door and wiggled her finger for her to follow. Tamika placed her finger over her lips, indicating Molly should remain silent.

They walked along the hall to the kitchen.

Tamika flipped her personal cell phone open. "Is he doing his usual?" She held the phone so that Molly could see that Tamika was talking to Angela.

"Fool has his briefcase in his hand and is standing just inside his office watching the clock on the wall. Doesn't have the balls to just leave early, and he's the damn city manager," Angela said.

Tamika looked at Molly and pointed to the wall phone in the kitchen. "Intercom, then 22." She held up her hand. "When it's 4:59." She did a countdown of three, two, and one with her fingers. "Now." She snapped her wrist, pointing at the phone.

Molly punched the number, heard Tom's sharp answer, and hung up.

"Run." Tamika shot out of the door and crossed the hall to her office.

Molly hesitated, then scurried up the hallway to her door. She heard Tom stomp around the corner and into the kitchen.

"Who did that? Who called me from in here?" Tom went to the GIS room. "Did you two see anyone across the hall?"

Molly laughed into her sleeve as Gary and Tamika acted surprised by the interruption as they tried to finish their work and go home.

Molly hunched over her drafting table.

"How about you?" Tom stood in the doorway, face red with anger at his routine being interrupted. "This is going to make me miss my usual window of driving home while everyone else is still going to their cars." He stomped off, muttering to himself.

Molly heard the door to the public hallway open and close.

Tamika and Gary eased into her office and looked at her bug-eyed.

Angela walked in from the front hallway, avoiding the elevator and main lobby, just as they burst out laughing. Angela stomped her feet and pretended to busy about with a briefcase.

Molly laughed until her back hurt and she couldn't breathe. She bent over, trying to ease the stitch in her side.

"Are you all right, baby?" Angela walked over and rubbed Molly's back.

"You guys are killing me."

"He falls for it every damn time," Tamika said. "Tell me he's not the whitest white man you know."

"He's so afraid that one of the council members will call in to check how late he stays in his office." Gary held up his hand for a high-five from Tamika.

Molly leaned on Angela.

"Molly," Tamika tried to get her attention.

Molly turned to look at Tamika and saw Chris.

Chris stood in the doorway, carrying a brown bag from a popular gourmet sandwich shop. "I thought you'd be working late, but I didn't mean to break up the party."

Angela shooed the other two out of the office. "You had to be here. We just played a joke on someone. We knew Molly was tired and punchy enough to be the instigator before she realized what she was doing."

"Hey." Molly wiped tears from her eyes as she stared at Chris. Chris was a knockout in a black suit and shirt.

Angela stomped along the hallway as Tamika did her imitation of Tom mumbling about the telephone.

"I ran into Windy this afternoon, and she gave me an earful. She said you were shut away in your office with a mound of paperwork."

Chris looked around. "Not that I didn't believe her, but you better hope no one strikes a match in here."

"Jack dumped a huge project on me." She gestured about the office. "One that council has a close eye on. I don't have any choice but to work."

"How long is this project going to take?" The smile was fading from Chris's face.

"I only have until Monday morning." Molly had a bad feeling where this conversation was going.

"Meaning it will be done by the time you leave tomorrow so you have Saturday and Sunday to relax?" Chris asked.

Molly shook her head.

"Meaning that you are going to work all weekend and be too tired at night to do anything but crawl into bed?"

Molly nodded.

Chris set the bag of food on the drafting table. "You warned me about this, didn't you? You've always broken up with women over work. Well, I understand all too well, missy."

"Don't call me missy." Molly made the automatic response.

Chris moved so that she was within inches of Molly. "I do understand, missy, but I'm still going to worry about you. You need someone to take care of you."

"We'll have the nights this weekend." Molly felt her breath quicken.

Chris motioned toward the sandwiches. "Then you best keep up your strength."

Molly wondered how she was so fortunate with the women she knew, and one in particular she wanted to know better, and so cursed by the men. The thought recurred often during the next week.

Molly did it. No one—not Angela, Susan, or Tamika—thought she would. Jack was stunned at the amount of revenue she salvaged, furious that she hadn't done exactly what he told her, and ecstatic to take it to council. It made them all appear as though public servants on a crusade to clean up past loopholes; no one was mentioning any prior awareness of the loopholes.

Molly spent the week on damage control, calling on each company affected and explaining precisely why it was needed to let go of old favors. None of the plant managers congratulated her on her diligence, but there was tacit understanding that they would have done the same in her situation. Molly's presence in their offices reinforced that it was tough love and the city valued them—it was the only way Molly knew to do business.

CHAPTER TWENTY-EIGHT

It never failed to amaze Molly. She glanced about the apartment and felt herself relaxing. As much as she loved her house, there was such a sense of security and intimacy in Chris's apartment. Molly knew this wonderful woman loved her and the feeling was mutual.

Chris slipped Molly's cardigan off for her and handed her an icy bottle of beer. "Don't think I'm going to make a habit of waiting on you even if you do look as though you need someone fattening you up a bit. Are you trying to lose weight? You're looking too thin and your clothes are beginning to bag." Chris pulled at the loose seat of Molly's jeans.

Molly turned to face her and glanced about the living room. "I could have sworn I came over for dinner with an incredibly sexy woman, not someone's overbearing mother."

"Kiss my ass." Chris pushed her toward the sofa. "Sit down. Channel surf. I don't care what we watch. I'll serve dinner."

"You don't mind the local news?"

Chris huffed. "I was hoping you would take the hint of the movies on the shelf below the television."

Molly scanned the titles, all the prerequisite classic lesbian movies and series. "That's subtle."

"Don't laugh. I like to watch old movies from the forties and fifties, but I'll take a bad lesbian movie over today's hetero films any time."

Molly tasted the beer—a heifenweiser from a brewery she had not heard of. "I can't argue with that logic."

"We could videotape ourselves instead of being caught by a parking deck camera with all the good stuff blocked by steamy windows." Chris peeked around the cased opening into the kitchen.

Molly choked. At least the beer had gone down enough that it didn't shoot through her nose—talk about romantic. "I don't think so. I'm not into exhibitionism. Nice television, very masculine."

"Screw you. I bought the damn thing because Spencer complained so much about the one I've had since college. I've got the monstrosity posted on craigslist. Silly me, I'd rather have a CD in the bank than a plasma television on the wall. My college set works just fine in the bedroom, which is where I usually end up watching television anyway." Chris flashed her breasts at Molly, then returned to the counter.

Molly blinked. "So you're actually cooking food, not just thawing in the microwave like I do. I'm impressed." She stood at the end of the sofa where she could look from television to kitchen counter.

"A Crock-Pot is a wonderful invention. Throw ingredients inside early in the morning, and by evening, it's all blended together and tastes great, especially if I toss in a little wine—just like me." Chris came to the open doorway of the kitchen, wiping her hands on a towel. "Feel free to use my office if you just can't stay away from your e-mail." She grinned at Molly's hesitation.

"I'm good." Molly took another swallow of beer. "I like this." She held up the bottle.

"Spencer bought a case at the beach last year. I'm doing my best to drink it up before he remembers that he left it here."

"I'm glad to help." Molly drained the bottle. "Do you recycle?"

"Absolutely. Just rinse it and add it to the container." Chris pointed to the far corner of the kitchen and waited for Molly to walk past her.

Molly did as told.

Chris blocked her way to return to the living room. "You do realize that we're both upright, close to each other, and have nothing to prevent us from kissing?"

Molly closed the distance between them. "I was trying to be interested in the food."

"The Crock-Pot cooks indefinitely." Chris kissed Molly, short bursts followed by a long and lingering exploration. Her hands moved across Molly's body. "Damn, why does this feel so right?"

"I'm guessing you don't expect an answer to that." Molly leaned slightly back.

"No."

"Good." Molly wrapped her arms around Chris and thought of nothing except how full Chris's lips were and how soft the skin on her back was as she ran her hands under Chris's shirt.

Chris backed out of the kitchen and turned Molly. Molly leaned back when they were close enough to the sofa and held Chris to her as she tumbled backward.

"I'll never forget our first time on this sofa." Chris looked down at Molly.

"I happen to like holding you this way." Molly stretched on the cushions as Chris's body settled against hers.

"I'm not too heavy to be on top of you?"

"God, no."

Chris laughed and relaxed.

Molly reached to the coffee table for the remote control. "I bet you have music channels, R&B would be great."

"914." Chris ran her hands through Molly's hair. "Isn't that a ridiculous number of channels?"

They barely noticed which of the cable channels was playing. Molly ate dinner, marveled at Chris's culinary skills, and fell fast asleep. She barely remembered Chris putting her to bed.

Molly eased into the kitchen as soon as she heard the timer jumpstart the coffeemaker. She glanced at the clock and reached for the remote to catch the first local news broadcast. A familiar voice froze her arm in mid-reach for mugs. The program was close to its half hour break, wrapping up weekend sports with a feature on the annual pro-am polar bear golf tournament held each February at the city's lone country club.

Molly looked at the screen. Jack and Eric stood side by side in matching golf caps and pastel jackets. Eric wore yellow, Jack orange and mint green. "Rusty must have dressed them."

Chris walked out of the bedroom pulling on a T-shirt. She followed Molly's gaze. "What a wardrobe nightmare."

Jack smiled into the camera. "We should have a big announcement for you this week or next."

Eric's eyes were wide open as though he played on crack.

Jack pointed to the national trademark on his cap and winked. "Sports drinks are selling like crazy everywhere these days, meaning more distribution facilities."

Eric actually leered.

"Oh, shit." Molly moved closer to the screen.

Chris stared at Molly's face, then at the television screen. "What is it?"

"Those imbeciles. We're dead. We're fucking dead." Molly forgot all about coffee and went to her messenger bag dropped beside the front door. "Project Hugger."

"What?"

Molly dug to the bottom of the bag. She glanced at Chris. "Those two have just done a grin-and-wink announcement of an extremely confidential deal that is in the works. We are on the short list for a huge distribution facility, but it's tied in with state funding that may only be announced by the governor. I've been working my ass off for months as new deadlines for information were issued. We are so close but no one—*no one*—is supposed to say anything publicly."

Deep in Molly's bag, an old-fashioned telephone ringer sounded. She pulled out her work cell phone. "Yes, Tom, I have the news on. No, that was not supposed to happen. Yes, the final incentive package is still being reviewed by corporate. We were hoping for a decision by the end of the quarter. No, I haven't talked to the state people yet. I'm sorry. I don't know what else to say." Molly stared at the phone as Tom disconnected. "The city manager is pissed. He's part of the project because of the revenue stream we'll need approved. He's actually been doing a great job briefing council members in closed sessions."

Molly's bag now vibrated with the theme from *I Love Lucy*. She pulled out her personal cell phone. "Christ, Joan, I don't know what they were thinking. They are major dumbasses, what else can I say? I had everything locked in my files. I didn't think they had seen enough to know how close we are. No, I didn't prompt them to do this to try to manipulate a decision from corporate. I know you guys are the official liaisons. I just supply you with what the company wants to see. How many times have we done this drill with not a peep to anyone, including the press? Jack Sampson told me to run with the project just like he always does because he thought it a long shot and didn't have time to waste on it, for Christ's sake." Molly's face paled. "You can't pull the state's part of the incentive. We don't have the funds to compete with the other locations if you do that. I know only the governor makes these kinds of announcements. It wasn't an announcement, it was my jerk-off bosses trying to be coy with a local reporter when they don't have anything significant of their own to talk about. Chalk it up to too much fresh air and beer. Joan...Joan..." Molly threw her phone against the wall.

Chris eased off the sofa and picked up the pieces. She snapped the battery in and the back on, then flipped the cover and turned the cell phone on. "Still works."

Molly gathered her clothes from the sofa and quickly dressed. "They've ruined months of work and endangered a huge investment in the city."

"What are you going to do?"

"Kill both of them."

Chris pointed to her shoulder holster on the hall tree. "Don't say something like that even as a joke."

"Who's joking?" Molly repacked her messenger bag. "I've got to go. You don't want to hear all the phone calls that are going to be made in the next few hours."

"But it's too early, no one is in yet."

"This can't wait. I've got to call the Industrial Development Authority's chairman at home and gauge if that board had any additional funds for the project. I may go over to Tom's so we can call together. He's the only city official making any sense at this point, and he's usually crazy as hell on good days." Molly stared at Chris. "I'm so sorry. I'm rattling on like the crazy person." She crossed the room, took her cell phone, and hugged Chris. "Rain check on breakfast?"

"You aren't losing me over work." Chris stated a fact.

Molly kissed Chris. "No way. I'll make it up to you. I just don't know when. You're the best deal I've ever worked on." She grinned at Chris.

Chris held her for one more kiss and grope. "Go ahead. I know your mind is on nothing but work."

"Not quite." Molly put her finger to her temple and pretended to pull a trigger. "I should be shot for walking away from you when we could go back in there." She nodded toward the bedroom.

"Go." Chris held the door open.

Molly started to apologize again.

Chris put her finger on Molly's lips. "Just go, but you owe me big-time for being understanding, and I intend to collect."

"That's a deal I'll definitely close." Both of Molly's phones rang at the same time as she left the apartment.

CHAPTER TWENTY-NINE

Molly stared at her desk; if only she had a match. There was no way to salvage Project Hugger. Math was math, and the numbers didn't add up. She flipped her wooden pencil up in the air and let it fall as it may into the mess that had been a viable project. She refused to think about the hours she had worked on the proposals. She also didn't want to think about how Jack and Eric could have information on the project. Donna was the only one who knew the file system. Donna had put the system in place before Molly took over all of Jack's work on state prospects. Donna had fed the information to Jack. Molly had been foolish enough to hope that the info stream would be slow enough and select enough not to jeopardize the deal.

It was almost eight o'clock. Molly had gone to Tom's house from Chris's, exchanged pleasantries with Tom's country club clueless wife, then encamped in the den making telephone calls. The IDA had no secret pot of money to dip into; its funds were committed for the next two years. Tom knew that council had stretched its contingency reserve funds to balance the upcoming budget even with what she found from the industries.

Molly stared at her stapler and slammed her fist on the handle, even though no papers were between the jaws. "Shit!"

"It must be Monday."

Molly jumped in her chair as she turned to look at the doorway to her office.

Campbell grinned at her. He wore his trench coat over his suit, having come directly to her office upon entering the building. He hunched his left shoulder to keep his briefcase strap close to his neck. He held two paper cups of coffee from 7-Eleven. "How did I know you would already be at your desk? I don't want to know how long you've been here." He held out a cup.

Molly rolled her eyes and accepted the steaming drink. "Thank you. The coffee out of the vending machine is beyond description other than to say it's hot. I take it you saw the news this morning."

He nodded. "I was at home this morning to read my newspaper." He held up the local daily. Jack and Eric grinned foolishly from the front page. The headline promised imminent prosperity.

"Great. I give up," Molly said.

"Don't say that yet."

Molly studied the man. He definitely had an idea rolling around in his head; he looked as though the proverbial cat with one tiny feather sticking out of its mouth. She pointed to her side chair. "Take your coat off and stay a while."

He set his briefcase down, bending awkwardly to reach the floor. He shrugged the coat off, unable to raise his arms and neither expecting nor wanting help. He limped slightly as he stepped to the chair and flopped down unable to slow his descent once he started. He shifted to have his weight off his right hip. "Don't mind if I do."

"You've figured it out, haven't you?" She felt the positive energy radiating from the man as she always did. It just made her calmer being around him; maybe there was a way.

Campbell began. "Each year, city council approves a budget with millions of dollars for the utility projects called for in our master plan to replace undersized water mains, eliminate overflows from the older sewer pipes, and phase out pipelines that are past their useful life."

Molly nodded. She knew this from sitting through the budget hearings. Five-figure amenity projects were always challenged and discussed with the stronger department personalities winning out; seven-figure water and sewer maintenance projects were passed through with little or no discussion. Even the diverse egos of city management recognized the need to be proactive about infrastructure, knowing that the key to the city's long-term growth was in its core services. No expansions were possible without ample water and sewer capacities.

Campbell sipped the coffee. "We're a small department. We struggle to implement the phased work of the master plan. We use way too many consultant hours and still barely keep up."

Molly remained silent, following his line of thought.

Campbell continued. "Understand that I need to run this by the financial consultants who manage our bond rating each year. I've already discussed this with Rusty. He's on board and will set up a meeting as soon as the consultants are in."

Molly nodded again. Every year, the city's financial health was carefully scrutinized. The consultant compiled a report that had the appearance of a marketing plan for the city and contained an independent audit. Molly frequently used the report when courting new companies to move to the city. The report was intended to solicit bond issuance and insure excellent ratings. Molly didn't begin to understand anything but the rudimentary concept; she was an engineer, and accounting practices made her head swim.

Campbell finished his pitch. "What if we defer the heavy maintenance projects for the rest of this year and shift that funding to public infrastructure for this project? Every water and sewer main constructed on site built in a dedicated public easement with city funds so the lines add value to our fixed assets. I can even dip into our repair funds, recouping it after the plant is up and running from the additional utility revenue, provided council approves the fund transfers. No one is actually out of pocket for additional funds, and we close the gap the state has left us in."

Molly felt as though she would explode out of the chair. "That's the beauty of this project. It's not just an enormous distribution facility. It's that plus a bottling line, which means buying and processing huge amounts of city water but discharging a minimal amount into the sewer system. We won't need to upgrade any downstream sewer mains, and we already have unused capacity in the water treatment plant."

It was Campbell's turn to nod. "I remembered that from your initial briefing when you started working on this last summer."

Molly stared at the man and wondered for the umpteenth time if he had always been this way or had the battle with RA made him more aware and sensitive. She suspected the former influenced by the latter. There were actually some people born with a genuinely good soul and heart; she believed Campbell was one of them.

"If we need to come back with another counteroffer, we can go to council to modify the fee structure for the water usage and defer our recovery a bit longer. It all works out in the long run when the projections are calculated." He finished his coffee.

"And we write an agreement that politely spells out that if the company is exaggerating their usage projections we are basing our offers on, we renegotiate the rate reduction so that our recovery is guaranteed, by a cash payment from the company years out, if necessary."

Campbell whistled appreciatively.

"We're covering our butts on a deal this big." Molly held out her hand to Campbell. They shook on the deal. "Let's call the state and see what their project manager thinks before we go to Tom and council."

Molly closed the door so that the conference call would be somewhat contained even if heard easily enough in the GIS office next door. She trusted Gary and Tamika implicitly. She called Joan and explained sweetening the deal even without the state's contribution. Joan called the company's site selection consultant and was still amazed when she called Molly back and told her that the reaction to creative financing was favorable and the leak to the press negligible. The deal sounded as though it was coming back together. By the time it made the rounds in the state offices, funds other than those announced by the governor were *found* to be used. No one wanted to miss out on a deal that suddenly seemed to be building momentum toward closing.

Throughout the conversations, Campbell deferred to Molly. Molly constantly credited Campbell during the explanations, and he turned it back to her original work. Tom joined them, jotting notes to them while the conference calls played out, as they called the city's financial wizards and individual council members. By mid-morning, the deal was back on the table with Virginia suddenly pulling away from the other states in competition.

All went smoothly until Jack learned of the clandestine conference calls. He barged into Molly's office and only hesitated when he heard the state's top negotiator, as well as the CEO of the company on the line. After thirty-five minutes of intense calculations and counteroffers, Molly disconnected. "That's it, that's the best the city can do."

Tom and Campbell nodded in agreement. They were all exhausted yet exhilarated.

Jack stared from one to the other. He finally addressed Campbell. "Why in the hell didn't you come to me with your plan?"

Tom watched his executive staff members closely.

Campbell's eyes hooded. "Because I knew who in community development was doing the actual work on the project."

Molly thought she caught a glimpse of a blonde pausing in her doorway before moving on along the hall. Was it Chris or were Molly's eyes playing tricks on her?

Jack took a step closer to Campbell. "You know damn well that I should have been in on all of this."

Molly jumped out of her chair. "I know damn well that you're the idiot who tipped our hand and made us restructure the whole damn deal in a few hours when we had spent months setting it up and positioning the city favorably. Campbell might have just saved your sorry ass and your sorry career." Molly closed in on Jack and made him back toward the door.

Jack's face turned a brilliant red. He raised his hand as though to strike Molly and thought better of it. "You will answer to disciplinary action for that outburst." He dared Tom to argue with him.

Tom spoke deliberately. "Everyone needs to separate. Emotions are running too high at this point. Jack, you and Eric are to be at a closed-door meeting with Ann and me late this afternoon to discuss what was said before the media."

The color drained from Jack's face as Tom left the office.

Campbell cleared his throat. "Molly, are you all right? I should check in with Nancy and find out what else has been going on this morning." He stood and stopped beside Jack. "Tread lightly. You're in enough trouble. She was entitled to one shot at you."

Molly stared at Jack. His eyes narrowed.

"I will pay you back for this." Jack shook his fist at her. "Eric and I know you've been intercepting e-mails and taking the high-profile projects."

Molly shook her head in disbelief. "I what?"

"Barbara told me to watch out for you, that you were after my job." Jack stormed out of Molly's office.

Molly sat down, her knees suddenly weak.

Chris and Tamika came to the door of Molly's office. Molly looked at them bleakly.

"Jesus Christ. This is what you deal with every day?" Chris walked over to Molly and placed her hand on Molly's shoulder.

Tamika answered for Molly. "Oh, yeah."

"Honey, you are going to kill yourself with stress. I knew it was a snake pit, but I had no idea." Chris knelt beside Molly.

Tamika kept a watchful eye along the hallway.

"The project will be saved, and Campbell and I will wind up in trouble for something minor that we missed checking or someone's delicate ego we forgot to massage." Molly rubbed her face.

Windy rolled to a stop in the hallway. "Come on, girls. We're leaving the building for a late lunch that is going to run into the evening. You can all pile into my van. There will be alcohol involved. I dare anyone to say anything to any of us."

Molly was too numb to do anything but nod.

CHAPTER THIRTY

Molly felt the burden of Jack's disciplining heavier than she would have imagined. While no one seemed upset that Jack was temporarily displaced from authority, they did need someone to go to for issues he normally dealt with. To no one's surprise except Molly's, the go-to person was Molly. The day after Project Hugger was officially disclosed, Tom announced Eric's appointment as the acting director. Callers quickly discovered that Eric asked Molly for the answers and learned to ask her directly.

During the first days of this arrangement, Molly felt increasingly overwhelmed but tried hard not to show it. Donna worked with a frantic energy that was barely masking the glee she felt with her temporary reprieve from a tyrant. Eric sulked, pleased with the "acting" duty but furious that no one took it seriously. Molly was grateful for the figurehead; at least she didn't have to sit through the director-level meetings. They all carefully avoided Jack's office; he was known to be on premises intermittently.

Campbell and Barbara kept asking Molly if she was handling everything okay—Campbell because he genuinely cared, Barbara because she sensed a new contender. Windy sent Molly risqué e-mails, usually involving blond women. Tom was a figure in the shadows as always.

Molly thought herself able to juggle the flow of work on a temporary basis. What she was not prepared for was the way Jack appeared in the building on no set time schedule. It became more of a contest than March Madness to buy slots in the Jack-sighting pool.

"Don't know Jack," Tamika whispered as she passed Molly's door.

"Great." Molly jotted notes from her last telephone conversation as she waited for the other shoe to drop.

"What's up?" Jack stopped in the doorway of her office. He covered his eyes with his hands. "Don't let me see anything *confidential*."

Molly sighed. "Have you thought about a hobby or vacation? Think of this as a preview of retirement."

"Oh, that makes me feel better. Shirley ran me out of the house. Everyone I play golf or tennis with is working. It's too early in the day for a drink." He eased into Molly's office and sat in the side chair beside her desk.

"What in the hell were you thinking, Jack? First, to breach confidence on a major project, then to fly off at me in front of others for saving it?" Molly leaned back in her chair.

"That I was damn tired of you stealing all my thunder. Still am. But I'll be back, better than ever." He rested his arm on the edge of Molly's desk and motioned her closer.

Molly leaned forward and waited.

"You could make all of this easier on yourself." He reached over and touched her forearm.

Molly jerked away.

Jack chuckled. "It's as though you don't *like* men, Molly."

"Some men."

Jack nodded slightly. "So Tom is probably at the top of your list these days."

"He's in the top ten."

"I can't believe that son of a bitch got the better of me over employee inoculations and casual remarks to the press." Jack shook his head.

"Council jumped right on the bandwagon, didn't they?"

Jack cut his eyes at her.

"And your faithful companion has the reins," Molly said.

Jack blew air between his lips. "Eric's appointment to my job is meaningless unless Tom is trying to get rid of an empty suit. That boy calls me every night to keep me up with what's going on and ask my advice. I'm not really out of control."

"I'm sure he misses you." Molly said the words as though speaking of a lingering rash.

"At least he's not a Judas." Jack stood and turned the blower on the window unit to high. He closed the door to her office and returned to her desk.

Molly stared as she rotated in her chair to face him standing over her.

"How dare you question me and talk to me as though an equal? I'm your boss. I don't give a shit about this kinder, gentler management technique being shoved down our throats as the latest HR fad." Jack placed his hands on the arms of her chair. "Don't ever speak to me in that tone of voice again, you ungrateful bitch."

Molly was stunned, unable to move.

Jack leaned closer. "I know all about you. You ought to thank me for ever hiring you in the first place. Isn't it amazing what can be read in newspaper archives and confirmed by a few official-sounding telephone calls?" He smiled at Molly as he dropped to one knee to be on eye level with her. "Your mother and father were never married. You're a bastard. That must have really been difficult for your mother. Single mothers were still looked down on when I was growing up here in the sixties." He chuckled. "Your father has a police record for the assault of your mother. Your mother has hospital records for the injuries she suffered over the years. Your upbringing is actually quite pathetic when looked at in the context of public information."

Molly felt as though she couldn't breathe. Her worst nightmare was playing out before her eyes. "How dare you!"

"Oh, don't sound so offended. A lesbian in Virginia doesn't have the same rights as a decent woman. I know what you do with your free time. I just can't prove it—yet. I know how you play everyone in this office, male and female. No one seems to mind because you do excellent, nonstop work—my work horse. If you ever do an end around on me again, I'll see to it that you never work in local government in this state. Think about how you would feel if everyone knew that your parents weren't married and your dad just walked out on your mom and started another family. I bet your hometown newspaper would be very interested in a follow-up story on you."

Molly felt like a hapless animal caught in a sudden blinding light.

Jack lowered his voice to a whisper. "If I want to do this," he brushed the hair back from Molly's collar and straightened the fronts of Molly's shirt, "I will. If I want to touch you in a meeting so that everyone understands you are mine, I will." Jack rested his hand on Molly's thigh. "If I want to touch these in private," he roughly ran his hand over the contours of Molly's breasts, "I most certainly will. When I decide I want some of this," Jack's hand shoved its way roughly between the inseam of Molly's corduroy trousers, "I'll have it."

Molly literally saw red. She jumped to her feet, causing Jack to sit back on the floor. Her body shook with rage. "Never, ever go there with me again. Do you understand?" She leaned over him and stared into his eyes. "I will kill you, Jack, if you discuss my parents with anyone else. That's not a threat, it's a promise."

Jack stared at her appreciatively. He clapped his hands. "Congratulations. I believe you." Jack struggled to his feet and faced her, short of breath. "Then you back the fuck off. I tried asking you nicely to do the work Eric and I give you. Now I'm telling you to do exactly as we direct or I will share the documentation to support all I've found out about your parents."

Molly clenched her fists, ready to pummel the man.

Jack waited, taunting her to strike. "Excellent. We understand each other. Welcome to my way of doing things—threats that create a standoff. Bravo, Molly, your parents would be so proud of you."

Molly blinked back the tears she hated feeling in her eyes.

"Six weeks will pass like nothing." Jack tipped an imaginary hat and left her office. "I'll be back."

CHAPTER THIRTY-ONE

Molly stared at the total on the bottom of the estimate form. This was crazy. She usually did a quick check with her calculator of the Excel spreadsheet just to make sure the extensions of quantity versus unit price had carried through as set up, knowing it was a belt and suspenders habit that she couldn't break herself of. She had run the numbers twice and been unable to get the calculator and spreadsheet to come out the same. Project Ring—the call center—was not that complicated. She liked to think of it as her tax credit scam. How could it be legal for the city to qualify for so much money back from the state—$80,000 on a $2 million project? The numbers on a project should make it stand on its own; why bring another government entity into play to complicate matters? The paperwork and auditing were unreal. She definitely was better at being a small cog in a big wheel.

"Argh!" She growled as she pushed her chair back from her desk.

"Been spending too much time with your cat?" Tamika stopped in the doorway.

Molly frowned at her.

"Okay, excuse me, just checking when I hear strange noises. Do you want anything from the vending machine? My treat. I have a pocketful of change." She shook the waist of her skirt to demonstrate.

Molly shook her head.

Tamika started to say more and stopped herself.

Molly heard coins jingling all the way down the hallway.

A new e-mail arrived. Molly switched screens. It was sent from Windy's BlackBerry.

"I waited until 12:20, then had to order. You owe me an

explanation for being stood up for lunch again. I'm in court until late."

"Shit." Molly had a vision of Windy furiously pecking away at the tiny keyboard on the handheld device. Molly hit delete. She looked at her calendar. There it was, plain as the date and day—lunch with Windy at noon. Molly turned and stared out the window. It didn't matter that she looked at the brick front of the camera store across the street. She idly wondered how a store that charged high prices for expensive cameras survived the competition of online and big box store sales.

Molly caught herself dozing in her chair. "What in the hell is the matter with me?" she whispered. When she went home, she couldn't be still. When she was at the office, she couldn't concentrate to work. In between, she couldn't remember a damn thing. She paced at home and office trying to think of what had been on her mind five minutes earlier.

Molly gave herself a mental shake. She had a growing pile of project submittals to check. The contractors were being patient with her, but they would also track any delays that might make them run over the allowed days on a project and subject to a penalty.

"Okay. I'm going to do half that stack before I leave here tonight." Molly did not notice that Tamika tiptoed into her office and left a cold Mountain Dew on her drafting table until the can had left a ring on her worksheet. Molly picked up the drink and popped the top. She raised her voice when she spoke. "Thank you."

"You're welcome. You know you need to drink something besides soft drinks," Tamika said.

"They'd write me up for drinking a beer." Molly sighed.

"But you can carry a gun as long as you have a permit," Gary reminded them.

"Go figure." Molly would rather have the Mountain Dew anyway.

It was their running joke about one of the city's many inane employee policies. Molly concentrated and managed to hold her thoughts together. She didn't notice her co-workers leaving shortly after five o'clock. She didn't look up when Eric stood in her doorway, staring at her for several minutes. She began to feel almost like her old self by the time she was two-thirds through the pile of papers.

"I knew you would still be here." Windy rolled through the door opening and stopped just short of Molly's desk.

"I'm so sorry about lunch."

"Lunch, hell. I've been in court most of the day and met friends for dinner. When was the last time you went out with the all-girl posse?"

Molly thought back to what seemed a very long time ago. "Last fall, about the time I met Chris, before Donna quit."

Windy studied her friend. "You never told me the deal about Donna coming back, yet there has been a significant change between the two of you, between all of you."

Molly closed her eyes briefly. "Donna slept with Jack years ago to keep her job. She initiated it and he never let her forget it. Donna finally told me about it the night she begged for her job back."

"And dropped considerably in your standing?"

Molly shook her head. "No. She made me finally realize how bad it is here and how awful Jack is. How we are at fault for putting up with him and what hideous things we do associated with careers."

"Is that all that's been on your mind lately?" Windy puffed her cheeks out. "I thought I was the one struggling when I went to the trouble of fighting that damn deadbolt after I saw your light on. Come on, you're going home."

Molly shook her head. "I'm almost finished. I've finally been able to get some real work done. Everything's been chaos since Jack's shunning."

"What, for all the celebrating going on?" Windy's patience was wearing thin.

"Windy!"

"Well, if you expect me to fake sorrow for him, I refuse. I'm just sorry there's only three weeks of it left. He should have been fired. You or I would have been." Windy's eyes narrowed. "Is that how you came to work today?"

Molly looked down at her comfortable jeans with just a few paint stains and her polo shirt. "Yeah."

"Are you on a busman's holiday? Do you no longer care about that *professional* look we all strive for with these frumpy suits?" Windy adjusted her lapels.

"I guess I don't, now that you mention it. What I wear just doesn't seem that important. I don't really care what anyone else thinks anymore."

"My, my, what a rebel." Windy rolled slightly back and forth. "How much weight have you lost?"

"I don't know that I've lost any. I haven't weighed lately." Molly leaned back in her chair. "Am I being cross-examined? Who put you up to checking on me—Chris?"

Windy didn't react, which told Molly she had caught her dead to rights. Molly stared.

"Okay, I'm busted." Windy shrugged and stopped rocking.

"If Chris wants to know how I am, she can ask me. We talk." Windy rolled her eyes.

Molly frowned at her friend.

"You hold too much inside, Molly. Those of us who love you can see that there's more, that there's something just beneath the surface. It's maddening to your friends much less your lovers."

"It's not that simple." Molly rubbed her eyes.

Windy nodded. "Yes, it is. Don't you dare push this woman away. It's too late to make a run for it."

Molly controlled her reaction. She felt as though on the verge of a panic attack. "What do you mean?"

"Chris took you by surprise, didn't she? You love her and her, you?"

Molly finally bobbed her head.

"Then don't act like a couple of contrary dumbasses. Just be a couple." Windy looked at her watch. "You have to go home now because I want to go home and I'm not leaving without you."

Molly sighed.

"I thought you had decided to ease up on work. I thought that Eric being appointed acting director while Jack's on administrative leave had taken away your motivation to overachieve." Windy baited Molly. "Eric works eight hours a day, if that, and goes home on time each day."

Molly smiled. "Damn, you're good. You know exactly how I feel about Chris and you hit the nail on the head with Eric." Molly shivered. "I guess you have me all figured out."

"Molly," Windy took a deep breath, "there are a few of us who know what hell work has been for you lately. We're concerned. Chris would be here if she wasn't as caught up in her work as you are in yours. Maybe I should just sit you two side by side and knock your heads together. She cares about you, and, yes, I did agree to be her proxy."

"We always want what we can't have." Molly looked at her diploma and her engineering license framed on the wall. Life had been so simple when those were the only two things she truly desired.

"You're slammed. Tell Tom. He can hire someone temporarily to help. If Tom doesn't know what dead weight Eric is, he can't do anything about him. Campbell will back you up as he always has."

Molly's face hardened. "It will always come down to white-collar men protecting each other, and I'm not going there."

"Hard head."

"One of my many endearing qualities." Molly batted her eyes.

"That's part of it. Someone has to love you." Windy shook her keys. "Come on, kiddo. I can't manage that damn heavy door by myself again. Help an old crippled woman out, will you?"

Molly finally laughed. "You must be desperate to pull that line."

"Wait until I work in the one about being in a butt-kicking contest."

"Pul-lease. I will call Chris to come arrest you for something."

"Whatever it takes to get you two spending more time together." Windy smacked the arms of her wheelchair.

Molly packed her messenger bag and walked beside Windy to her van parked on the street directly before the entrance to city hall.

"I love being downtown at night, it's the only time I don't have to curse at people about parking in handicap spaces illegally." Windy hit the control to lower the lift to get her into the van.

Molly marveled at what Windy did as part of her routine to be self-sufficient. "Good night."

"Night, sweetie. Drive carefully. Do you want a ride to your Jeep?"

Molly shook her head. "The walk will do me good. I keep forgetting it's early spring."

"Don't you love this time of year?" Windy waved as she started the van. "Outdoors, what a concept."

Molly enjoyed the walk. It was still light enough to feel safe going into the parking deck. She thought back to the day Chris had picked her up in the rain; thoughts of Chris carried her all the way home.

Molly made it as far as the refrigerator for a beer and the living room sofa to stretch out with the television on and Dolly lying on her lap. She loved the cat dearly. Molly glanced at her clothes—clean enough for the next day. She'd be ready to return to the office when she woke up.

She felt her phone vibrate with a text message from Chris. "Good night, baby. Sorry I have to work. Love you."

"Ditto," Molly texted back.

Molly clutched the cell phone as though it was the ripcord on a parachute. She slept until 3 a.m. before the recurring dream of her lifetime began to play—Molly was ten years old and frozen in place watching Ham strike her mother.

Molly awoke and would have sworn that she had just been pummeled. She checked that Dolly's food and water bowls were full and gathered the contents of her messenger bag so she could return to the office. That was enough sleep—she didn't want to chance dreaming again.

CHAPTER THIRTY-TWO

Molly stared at the paper in her hand and not for the first time. She crossed the kitchen and used a magnet from the Outer Banks to stick the memo to the refrigerator door. She glanced down at Dolly. "Do you believe that?" Strangest of all, Molly smiled.

She received the memorandum from the city manager late the previous day, delivered by Sharon. Sharon said nothing, simply handing Molly the envelope and offering a sympathetic shrug. Molly opened the envelope as though in slow motion, managing to slice her index finger with the glued edge. She unfolded the single piece of paper and stared, reading and rereading what Sharon had typed. It bore the fountain pen stroked, full signature of Thomas Stafford.

"Windy." Molly was too tired to be angry with the friend she knew to be the instigator.

The memo stated very succinctly that Molly was granted immediate paid leave, not to count against sick days or vacation. She was to take one week off. She was not to set foot in city hall. Her week off just happened to coincide with Jack's first week back.

Tom added a handwritten note at the bottom of the sheet. *"I greatly appreciate your efforts sans Jack. I will check the building during the weekend to make sure your office is empty. Humor me on this, Molly."*

And Molly had. She made a copy of the memo, taped it to her office door, then packed her bag and left the building. She took no work files home with her. She had not set her alarm before climbing into bed. She actually watched an entire episode of *Friends* before sleeping a solid ten hours.

She stood in the kitchen in sweatpants and T-shirt, no bra, and sock feet. She felt wonderful. She wanted nothing more than to spend the day with her sweet Dolly. She carried her third cup of coffee into the den and looked at her desk. She loved the antique rolltop from the tambour of the top to the cavernous side drawers of the bottom. It had been her indulgence after passing her licensing exam. There was nothing on the glowing oak surface from the office. She idly pushed envelopes around. Of course, her blotter was oversized quad-ruled sheets. Utility bills needed to be paid—a few were overdue, yet there was plenty of money in her checking account. When did she ever take time to shop anymore? Never. She booted her laptop and went to her bank site to pay her bills online. She couldn't remember the last time she had bought a stamp other than metered postage for sending packages to Michigan.

Her cell phone rang from the nightstand beside her bed where the charger stayed plugged into the wall socket. She logged out of the secure site and jogged across the square hall to the bedroom.

"Hello?"

"I love it when you're slightly out of breath," Chris teased.

Molly tried to slow her breathing. "Why? Because it means I'm getting old and fat?"

"Yeah, right, that's it exactly. Whatcha doing?"

"Watching soaps and popping bonbons."

"Soaps aren't on yet, knucklehead, and I bet you don't have anything sweet in your house."

"Just Dolly."

Chris made a gagging noise. "God, you and that cat. No wonder you barely have time for a girlfriend."

"Dolly is not listening. You're the one who works nights."

Chris chuckled, sending shivers down Molly's back. "See, I could have worked the word *pussy* into that line, and I refrained myself."

"Wouldn't it be more fun if I refrained you?"

"Those were the days," Chris said wistfully. "Did you sleep all night or what?"

"I did, as a matter of fact, and ate breakfast."

"Damn. I don't know why I was worried about you."

Molly hesitated. "I do feel better than I have for a while," she finally admitted.

Chris's voice became serious. "I know. I just wanted to find out how you were doing with being exiled, and I'm pleasantly surprised."

"Me too."

"How about if I bring lunch over? Just kick me under the table if we start talking about work. Let me at least share a meal with you."

Molly didn't hesitate. "Okay."

"Okay?" Chris whistled. "I'm running a little behind—"

"And it's a mighty cute little behind," Molly interrupted.

"Jeez, is that what I'm going to have to put up with all through lunch? Never mind. I'm running late, so it will be 1:00 or so before I'm on your doorstep."

"That's fine."

"See you, cutie." Chris hung up.

Molly returned to the den. Chris would be pushing her schedule to have an hour free. They needed a little time together. Molly would try Windy's suggestion; she would try to open up more to Chris. She had to talk to someone about Jack.

Molly opened the Mahjongg game that had been dormant for months and beat one of her top ten times for clearing the tiles. "Cool."

The cell phone rang again. Molly paused the second game and hurried to the bedroom. Next time she'd remember to put the phone in the pocket of her sweats.

"Hello?"

"So how mad at me are you?" Windy asked.

Molly laughed. "Are you kidding? How often can I get you to do this for me?"

"For real?"

"Yeah." Molly took a deep breath. "I know I was over the edge. This is okay. I had forgotten how much I enjoyed my home."

"Sweetie, I'm proud of you. How about dinner tomorrow night? I'll swing by and pick you up. We'll try a new restaurant I've wanted to go to but can't budge Dave out of the house to experiment."

"It's a date."

"Now don't get carried away, I'm spoken for."

"That's what all straight women like to think."

"Oh, Lord, I'm hanging up. Maybe I can persuade Angela to go with us."

"Woo-hoo, that sounds even better—a threesome."

"Go Google mood swings."

"I love you, too." Molly disconnected. She slid the phone into her pocket.

She was determined to be upbeat. She knew they all had to see this during the week off before she would be allowed back at work. Besides, if she pretended long enough, maybe it would actually start feeling genuine. How had Jack managed to find out so much about her parents? Did she really have him in a stalemate? How could she possibly *trust* him not to reveal what he knew about her parents? Sooner or later, the temptation would be too great for him.

Again, Molly returned to the den. She opened the middle drawer on the right side of the desk and pulled out her résumé. She scanned the text, remembering each of the projects she had listed under significant work. She marked in red a technical misspelling not caught last time by spell check in the word-processing software. She added the latest touchy-feely training that Ann had put them all through. The revisions were done and she printed three copies.

Dolly strolled into the room and jumped on the window seat built to enclose the steam radiator. The cat stretched in the sun, paying no attention to Molly.

"Let's see if the job offers that some of those guys joked about were real," Molly said. "That way, we wouldn't have to move."

She suspected Windy was right. Molly came into contact with enough of the business owners that she wouldn't have to rely on knowing someone personally within several of the local companies to apply for a job. She'd follow up with a phone call later next week. This time, she really meant to leave being a public servant. She would not continue to work for Jack, and she was no longer able to tolerate Eric.

Molly jumped when the knocker on the front door was tapped. She glanced at the clock. "Shit." She had not changed clothes. Where had the past ninety minutes gone? She was still seated at her desk, the blotter sheet full of doodles. Molly couldn't remember what she had been thinking about. She stretched as she walked to the front door.

Chris smiled at her. "I'm glad you didn't get all dressed up on my account."

Molly shook her head. "Sorry, I lost track of time. Come on in." She leaned into the screen door and held it open as Chris passed through the doorway.

Chris made the most of the opportunity and gave Molly a

quick kiss. "It's good to see you. Mmm, those lips are as sweet as I remember."

"I didn't promise anything in return for lunch," she reminded Chris as she pushed her toward the kitchen.

"I know, but I'm an eternal optimist." Chris walked through the living room and into the kitchen.

"Keep going. The deck is in full sun now, unless you mind being outside."

"Fresh air, what a concept." Chris glanced into the woods off the backyard. "It doesn't even feel like we're still in the city."

Molly brushed a few leaves off the chair cushions surrounding the round glass-topped table.

Chris unpacked containers from a nearby Chinese restaurant.

"You're going to make me take a nap this afternoon with all of that."

"How about some company?" Chris waggled her eyebrows.

Molly laughed. "Like you don't have to get right back to work as soon as we can eat part of this."

Chris sighed. "Sad but true."

They divided the food, Molly preferring rice and Chris noodles. Chris was very adept with chopsticks. "How are you really?"

Molly looked at her fork. She hadn't wanted to risk the frustration of the wooden sticks setting her off. "I concede that I need to be at home for a few days."

Chris nodded. "That's a good start."

Molly's jaw tightened.

Chris took a sip of hot tea. "It's more than taking on Jack's workload, isn't it?"

Molly set her fork on the table. Her appetite was gone. "I've been carrying him for eight years, so it's nothing new."

"Which is all the more reason I'd think you'd be glad to be rid of him for a few weeks," Chris said evenly.

"But we weren't rid of him. He kept showing up, and now he's on a witch hunt about you and me." Molly knew her voice was too loud.

"What?" Chris stopped midway to putting food in her mouth.

Molly stared at the rough wood planking of the deck. The warmth of the wood felt good on the soles of her feet. "We're going to have to be very careful until I can find another job. He wants to out me."

Chris let her chopsticks drop on her plate. "Do it yourself so he can't hold it over you. You cannot possibly allow him to dictate our relationship. What else is going on here, Molly? Who are you protecting?"

"I think you need to leave." Molly pushed her chair back from the table.

Chris reached for her and froze when Molly recoiled from her touch.

Chris wiped her mouth with the napkin on her lap and stood from the table. "I didn't come here to upset you. I honestly don't understand what's going on with you. Why can't we talk through this? What do you not trust me enough to tell me?"

"Just leave. It takes more than a quick lunch hour or an abbreviated text message to maintain a relationship." Molly had a flashback to her last partner; it felt weird to say the words instead of hear them.

Chris walked rapidly through the house. Dolly lay stretched on the back of the sofa—distance chaperoning. Chris rubbed the Maine Coon's exposed belly. "Keep an eye on her, Miss Dolly. She needs your comfort. She won't accept mine." Chris left the house.

Molly sat on the deck until the warming rays of the March sun moved on and left her chilled. She went inside and back to bed. She stared at the old chandelier above her and allowed her eyes to lose focus on the dangling cut glass as she reached for her cell phone.

"Hello?" Syd answered the phone on the second ring.

"Hey," Molly said.

"What's wrong?" Syd turned the television's volume down.

"Everything."

"He's back at work, isn't he?"

"He's threatened me about Mom and Dad. Chris doesn't have a clue."

"You haven't told Chris about the violence?"

"Nope. Can't." Molly choked up.

"Come home, sweetie. You don't sound so good." Syd hesitated. "It's the dream again, isn't it?" Syd was the only one Molly had ever told.

Molly couldn't answer.

"You don't have to stay here with us. I can find an empty lake cottage for you. Take a break." Syd's tone was pleading.

"I can't."

"Talk to me then." Syd calmed herself down.

"I can't do that, either. I shouldn't have bothered you. This was a mistake."

"Molly…"

Molly disconnected and powered her phone down. Chris was the only mistake she hadn't made lately, and she was losing her.

CHAPTER THIRTY-THREE

Molly stood in the hallway in front of the row of file cabinets, repeatedly chiding herself not to act like a five-year-old. She faced Jack Sampson and couldn't stop herself from doing a mental la-la-la to avoid listening to what he was saying. She wanted to smack Eric for the intense look on his face as he pretended to hang on Jack's every word. At least the la-la-la was by choice in her head; she guessed it was by rote in Eric's. Eric would no more be able to do what Jack was talking about than Dolly, and she didn't mean to insult her beloved cat.

Jack droned on. "What we need to do is bring the company rep in from the airport so that he sees exactly the things we profiled about him without making it obvious what we're doing. Let him see the community college, the minor league baseball team, the Virginia Employment Commission office, the Civil War sites—he's a history buff—but steer clear of the nuclear designers and the armament manufacturer."

Molly finally engaged in the conversation. "It's okay for him to see competitors since he needs to be aware of the availability of trained employees. It lets him know the employees he needs are in the area and available to jump. Just make sure to mention how long the other companies have been in business. I'll pump their HR people for wage rates. Coming in from upstate New York, he'll think labor is a steal compared to what he's paying now."

Eric's head resembled that of a bobble doll in the back of a classic car. "I could show him the restaurants with bars that the employees like to hang at. They're a little too loud to take him in and hear what he says, though."

Molly looked at Jack to see which of them was going to respond to this. Jack rolled his eyes and sighed. He placed his hand on Eric's shoulder. "You want to take him to the money end of town for dinner.

He's a cruiser for the site selection team. Buy him a nice wine with his meal. Do not take him to a packed bar and down pitchers of draft."

Eric nodded and clearly didn't quite understand.

Molly held her hands up. "It's my night to go home at 5:00. I'm not exactly dressed for the snobby end of town anyway." She had been inspired to go with black cargo pants and an untucked gray pinstripe oxford shirt.

Windy rolled up to them. "Now that wasn't so difficult to say, was it?"

Molly smiled. "Actually, not at all."

Windy nodded. "Eric can handle it, can't he?" She pointedly looked at Jack as Tom came to the doorway of his corner office.

Jack's voice said one thing, his body English the opposite. "Yes."

"Windy," Tom said.

Windy looked over her shoulder. "See, Molly's week off made all the difference in the world, shame we can't say the same about Jack." Windy smiled like the Cheshire cat.

Tom joined them, studying the group and the wallpaper of the hallway.

"She's even gained a little weight back, not that any of you would notice," Windy said.

Tom coughed. "Now, Windy, you know a woman's weight or age is something no gentleman discusses."

They all laughed.

Tom tapped his watch. "I only have an hour open, Windy, if you want to go over the matter you called me about." He started to walk away, speaking over his shoulder. "Eric, call about the wallpaper. That seam is pulling apart."

Windy covered a chuckle with a cough. She mimed holding a phone to her ear. She gripped the rims on the wheels and rolled the chair after Tom. "Call me later," she said in Molly's direction.

Molly nodded. She looked at the confusion on Eric's face. "He means for you to call building maintenance. Ask for Bobby, he's been there the longest and is used to strange requests from city hall."

Eric made a note on his BlackBerry as he walked away. He had so much to do that he would likely do nothing.

Jack looked at Molly. "Enjoying yourself?"

Molly couldn't believe how much she had allowed Jack to

worry her. He was, after all, only a man. "Immensely. How come the honeymoon's over between you and your boy toy?"

Jack looked to make sure Tom and Windy were out of sight. "Tom is encouraging me to hand off more to Eric and back off from you. Any ideas why?"

Molly shrugged. "Eric's the anointed one with the suits. I haven't repeated our *conversation* to anyone."

"You're enjoying being a loose cannon, aren't you?" Jack asked disgustedly. "But don't forget I'm the fodder who knows about your mother."

Molly groaned. "Kind of falls into that be-careful-what-you-wish-for category, don't you think?" she asked as they reached Jack's office. "You're blackmailing me. Tom is on to something about or with Eric. I need a damn scorecard to keep up with who's screwing over whom." Molly snapped her fingers. "Damn, I forgot I wanted to ask Ann about HR people she knows through her professional organization." Molly retraced her steps to the front offices.

Tamika stood in Ann's office.

"Excuse me." Molly stopped in the doorway.

"That's all right. Come in. We were just talking about you," Ann said, motioning to the other empty chair in front of her desk.

Tamika looked as though she had been ratting out a list of Underground Railroad stations to the bounty hunters.

Molly didn't move. "I don't mean to interrupt. I'll come back later."

"You *need* to come in." Ann approached the door and closed it after Molly stepped inside the office.

Molly looked sideways as she sat in the chair next to Tamika's. "You didn't."

"I did." Tamika's lower lip jutted out slightly.

"I could have saved you the trouble," Molly said under her breath. She had meant to order Ann a Demotivator poster—the one with the elephant advising to find the biggest ass and kiss it for success at work.

"I want to schedule an intervention between you and Jack." Ann leaned forward, elbows on her desk, as she engaged with Molly.

"I bet you do. I don't think so." Molly slouched in the chair in what she thought of as her Eric posture—an old dog could too learn new tricks. She glanced at the kitchenware on the windowsill; HR handouts were piled on top of the inventory. Ann must be busy for a change.

Ann was on a roll since Jack's fall from grace, conducting workplace stress sessions to help employees deal with unexpected events. "I'll go to Tom if necessary."

Molly pondered her situation. "I remember the first time I met you. You were in the new employee orientation. Isn't that an oxymoron by the way? You were the greeter at the door and the flip chart manager during the training."

Ann's face blanched. "That was eight years ago."

"I remember you telling me that you were planning on going back to college, that the personnel job was temporary."

"Life has a way of changing things, doesn't it?" Ann squirmed in her seat.

"But look what it says for our city—no specialized college degree, yet you can be director of human relations," Molly said with wonder to Tamika.

"What's your point, Molly?" Ann was clearly pissed because she was losing control of her emotions in a situation she taught the training to deal with.

"I'm glad you asked that. Riddle me this, Ann. You know damn well that doors close every day because someone is or isn't married, is or isn't gay, isn't young enough or old enough. Who do you suppose Tom will defer to in any type of controversy—his HR manager who was promoted from the ranks and hangs on to her job because she can't have one like it anywhere else without a college degree, or a middle-aged white man with all the correct friends, family, home, and pets?"

Molly smoothed a wrinkle from the shirt tail that was purposely not tucked into her pants. "Tamika, it's not your fault that you don't know the system here quite well enough yet, but, Ann, you've overstepped. Feeling cocky because of all the counseling lately? Don't kid yourself. They'd drop either one of us before Tamika because she's a promising young black woman, before Eric because he's a promising young white manager, and before Jack because he knows too much to challenge. Jack is vindictive enough to take all of us out the next time he feels threatened." Molly sat up straight in the chair. She liked this role very much. "Low profile is a wonderful thing. Why anyone wants to be a manager of any description is beyond me.

Let the men handle things while we know damn well we could do it better. Working behind the scenes is much more challenging, so Machiavellian. I love it." Molly slapped her thighs, making both of the other women jump. She grinned at them.

Ann looked at Tamika. Tamika stared at Molly.

"Before I forget," Molly said, "I need to borrow your list of local HR managers. I need to steal some wage rates, but it means I can go home on time."

Ann opened her drawer and found the folder. She handed the list to Molly. "Keep it. I have it on my computer. I'll print another later."

"Thank you so much." Molly jumped up and left the women in stunned silence.

Molly was shaking by the time she returned to her office. She opened her Hotmail account and drafted an e-mail to Chris.

"Silly argument. I miss you and need you. I love you. I feel as though my world is coming apart without you. I have things to tell you. There, I've admitted it."

In less than fifteen minutes, Molly had an answer.

"I'm trying. I forget how different city hall is from the PD. I'm so sorry about lunch. I did exactly what I promised myself I wouldn't. I'll think of some way to make it up to you, seriously. I love you, too."

Molly wondered why she didn't feel any better.

CHAPTER THIRTY-FOUR

Molly could not shake the feeling of having lost all touch with reality. How much longer could she continue to juggle her emotions? Rumors were flying about reorganization and resignations. The atmosphere was not conducive to any productive work. She was suddenly aware of someone standing in her doorway.

"Do you know how many times I've done this without you noticing me?" Eric asked. His jacket was off. His oversized shirt was sagging out of his trousers. His sleeves were rolled up into thick bands around his forearms. It was not yet mid-morning break.

Molly shook her head. She did not have the energy for a conversation with anyone, especially Eric.

"Dozens. Dozens," he repeated. "How can you be that intense about work?"

Molly frowned. "It keeps my mind off other things."

"How many times were you just pretending not to notice me so that you didn't have to be *bothered* with me?" Eric made no attempt to keep the bitterness out of his voice.

"What are you talking about?"

"You've won." Eric acted as though talking about basketball brackets, one of the few things he did have a genuine talent with. "You've won it all."

Molly raised her hands, palms up.

"Come on. I know what's being talked about. As much of a dumbass as I am, I can figure some things out." He crossed his arms over his chest. "I'm here for you to brag about your upcoming promotion. Payback is hell. Give me hell."

Molly stared at him. If she suspected she was over the edge, she knew he was. "Take the afternoon off, Eric."

"No can do. I use my leave time as I earn it, just another way I'm clearly not like you. I don't have hundreds of hours on the books that the HR people worry about me using and wrecking their budget. No one would miss me around here, just like Jack. I'm truly his protégé. I could be gone like that and who would notice or care?" He snapped his fingers. "Tom is setting Jack and me up for a fall."

"I'm the last one who should say this, but have you considered a self-referral appointment with the Employee Assistance Program?"

"Go talk to a shrink for an hour or so?" He did an imaginary jump shot. "I can do that like a slam dunk. I can fool anybody for an hour. It's after that they realize I'm—what's the phrase floating around—an empty suit." He challenged her.

Molly's shoulders slumped. "Look, I can't help you. I can't help me. I don't have it in me anymore."

"But they still want you to take over the department." He looked as though ready to spring in the air again. "Do you have any idea what this will do to my career? I might as well apply for a commercial driver's license and transfer to refuse collection."

"I honestly don't know what you're talking about. I've sent résumés out to find a job in the private sector."

Eric slammed his fist into the door. "I knew it. Nobody would tell me outright, but I knew something triggered this. Tom will offer you the department to keep you. Damn, you are conniving. I sold my soul to move up. I planned it all out. I gave up my days and nights. Oh, yeah, I'm the city hall ghost, coming in at night to go through everyone's desk and feed information to Jack, as well as Barbara and Tom. It's all turning against me. That's been the plan all along, hasn't it? I'm so fucking naïve. I never saw what you are capable of."

"How about I call Tom and we'll sit down and talk through all of this?" Molly reached for her land line.

"Hell, no."

"I don't know what else to do for you. You've got it all wrong. Jack is going to disgrace me out of my job."

"Right." It was clear that he hated her. "Will I be your deputy?"

Molly shook her head. "I'm not taking any other job here. I don't know what you're talking about."

"Lower? Will I be demoted back to special projects manager?"

"Eric."

"Lower? What—your assistant?"

Tamika came within two feet of Eric. Gary was at her side.

Molly waved them away.

Eric turned as though to punch whoever was behind him and looked up at Gary with his hand formed into a fist.

"Are you okay?" Gary asked, clearly ready to force Eric wherever Molly wanted.

"Molly?" Tamika said.

Tears ran from the corner of Molly's eyes. "Damn hormones."

"Molly?" Gary said, keeping a close watch on Eric.

"I'm okay. Tamika, will you ask Tom to join us? Gary, will you sit tight next door?" She pleaded with her eyes for them not to push Eric any further over the edge.

They both nodded.

"See how well you handle all of us. You'll be perfect in upper management." Eric was only slightly subdued.

"I don't know any other way to say what I've been saying. I'm neither seeking nor accepting Jack's job." Molly's voice was firm. "I know nothing about Tom terminating Jack or you. You've fabricated all of this."

"Jack warned me. He told me that you were the one to watch out for—the quiet force in the office who couldn't be manipulated like the other women. But, hell, I played you after he hired me. I didn't tell Jack about your personal life. You fell in line when I was promoted. We could have been a good team."

"Me doing the work and you taking the credit?"

"Jack and I splitting the credit." Eric flashed a familiar grin. "It could have worked. I even handled Jack, old goat thought he was so damn slick hanging all blame on me. I documented everything and fed it to Barbara so she could go after Jack and to Tom since I knew he was keeping closer tabs than anyone gave him credit for. None of you ever gave me credit for doing any of that. You think work only matters if it shows up in bricks and mortar, but it takes much more than that to keep this place going."

"Yeah, a whip and a chair." Windy rolled up beside Eric. "Young man, you need to leave the building. Tom is not in his office, and Barbara deferred this situation to me." Windy looked at the antique pendant watch pinned to her jacket lapel. "I have a call in to Ann to put this in place with HR. You have fifteen minutes to wrap up e-mail and telephone calls and clear out for the rest of the day."

Eric stared down at Windy.

Donna walked up behind Eric. He spun on his heel and gave her a quick push, sending her reeling backward as she lost her balance. She sat abruptly on the carpeted concrete.

"Did you really think you could manage an entire department?" Windy asked him quietly.

Eric stared from one woman to the other. "I don't know what you're talking about. I thought it was Gary behind me. I thought you guys were going to throw me out." He seemed to deflate as he held his hand out to Donna.

Gary helped Donna to her feet, then closed on Eric. "I'll walk you to your office and escort you out of the building."

"Or we can call the police," Windy said.

Eric stuffed his hands in his pants pockets. "I surrender. I just lost it. All I think about anymore is this damn job."

Tamika returned with Sharon. Sharon handed Eric an EAP referral form. "Tom gave me instructions over the phone. He expects you to keep the appointment this afternoon. He'll call the counselor to make sure you're there and to follow up on their recommendations."

"This is mandatory or you're fired as of this moment," Windy said.

"Eric, please go. This can be salvaged for you. Think of Robin and Erin. Promise me that you'll keep the appointment," Molly said.

Eric stared at the paper in his hand. "I'll give you this much, Molly. You do care. You've always cared about me." He looked up, his eyes brimming with rage.

"I'm so sorry," Molly whispered, knowing it was too late for both of them.

"Hey," Molly managed to say when Chris answered her cell phone. Tears streamed down her face.

"Is it that bad?"

"Yeah." Molly fought to calm herself down.

"Talk to me so I can help."

"Can't right now," Molly said.

"Yes, you can. I'm not going to lose you. You're stuck with me no matter what's going on. Tell me," Chris pleaded.

Molly stared at the telephone; if only it was that simple.

CHAPTER THIRTY-FIVE

"Move your butt." Tamika stood in the doorway of Molly's office.

"I'm going." Molly jotted one last note on the construction drawing.

"You said the same thing five minutes ago." Tamika glanced at her watch. "You're already late. Do you want me to call Sharon and say you were called out on an emergency at a project? It doesn't look good to be late with Tom and you know it."

"And the more you nag at me, the later I'll be." Molly set her red marker aside. She liked not giving a damn about work anymore.

"Don't you want to freshen up?" Tamika sounded hopeful.

"I'm about as fresh as I get these days." Molly walked past her. The mood had struck her to wear overalls, but she dressed them up with a crisp white cotton shirt with the sleeves rolled halfway up her forearms.

Molly took the long way to Tom's office so she could have the full effect of walking along the interior corridor past everyone else's offices. She hummed quietly, not sure of the tune. She was certain that she was on her way to being fired and she was surprisingly okay with that. She felt as though taking a stroll along death row—at least she was about to be released.

Eric was in his office struggling to read through the three-inch-thick capital improvement projects manual. Molly would wager that he still had not a clue which projects were programmed into this fiscal year's budget. Campbell was on the telephone. The brief snippet of conversation sounded like Project Hugger had hit a bump in the road—too bad. Rusty was off. Molly smiled; she would guess he was playing golf where his love of bright colors was right at home.

Frankie was struggling to tell a customer that an overdue water bill meant service would be cut off, no matter income or number of children. Eric's old office had quickly been raided of decent furniture and now served as a storeroom.

"Psssst!" Susan hissed as Molly passed the row of admin cubicles.

Molly stopped.

"Are you on your way to the corner?" Susan teased.

"Yep." Molly stuck her hands in her front pockets.

"To discuss crop rotation?" Susan frowned. "Am I going to have to start dressing you?"

"Mebbe." Molly grinned. "That's the best offer I've had in a while."

"Idiot." Susan walked to Molly and straightened her shirt collar.

"Mmm, you smell so good."

Susan smacked the seat of Molly's overalls.

"Thank you." Molly slid her thumbs under the suspenders.

"You worry me."

"Sorry." Molly continued along the hall.

"He's ready for you, said to go right in," Sharon directed as Molly passed.

"Thank you."

"Good luck." Sharon didn't break the rhythm of her typing.

Ann didn't look up as Molly went by. Barbara stood in the doorway of her office and watched Molly saunter into Tom's, closing the door behind her. Molly heard Barbara trying to find out what the meeting was about from Sharon. Sharon was used to avoiding direct answers.

"My apologies. I lost track of time," Molly said as she stood before Tom.

Tom sat perpendicular to his desk, staring at the computer monitor on his credenza. He waved his hand in dismissal. "I do that all the time, that's why I have Sharon."

Tom pointed to the computer screen as he looked at Molly over his shoulder. "Have you seen this?"

Molly walked around the end of the desk and leaned down slightly to catch the angle of the monitor to be able to read the page of text—the local newspaper's home page. It was the story about

Jack's retirement announcement.

"No, I haven't read the press release. Jack e-mailed us that his effective date is September 1. It should make for an interesting summer as he winds his career down. I'm trying to stay neutral." And holding my breath, Molly thought.

"Advice from Windy?"

"I always check with her."

Tom nodded. "Molly, that's what I can always count on from you—logic tempered by common sense. Council is very impressed with how you handled the past several months."

"That's good, I guess. I try to look out for the city's best interests."

"I know." Tom swiveled to face his desk.

Molly took a seat in the chair angled at the corner of Tom's desk.

Tom brought his hands together and touched fingertips to his lips. "I hear you're job shopping."

"I am. No offers yet or I would have come to you."

He nodded. "I've had three phone calls that tell me you'll soon have as many job offers."

"Wow." Molly was surprised with the possibility of offers and by the old boys' network asking permission of Tom first.

"I knew Eric wouldn't work out, but several of the council members were determined to give him a try. Our council members are good people and well intentioned, but oftentimes fooled by first impressions."

Molly nodded. She knew what he meant. The elected council members performed a thankless job that consumed countless hours of time, but if they had those hours to dabble in local politics, it meant they weren't well grounded in day-to-day living. Every one of them had a spouse with a hefty six-figure income or substantial trust funds from inherited family money, or both.

"But they do eventually figure most things out." His eyes wandered to the ceiling.

Molly had fallen for this too many times before. She kept her gaze on Tom. "Really?"

"The majority want you to apply for Jack's job."

"I'm not so sure Jack is leaving. I have the feeling he is gathering ammunition on all of us, including council." Molly adjusted the pencil in her bib pocket.

"It's too late. Council wanted a trial period of his absence. They saw the difference while you were in charge in lieu of Eric. They saw exactly how inept Jack and Eric are. Jack was strongly encouraged to enact early retirement by a unanimous closed-door vote of city council. He's being allowed to stay on the payroll long enough to fulfill his thirty years in the system so he'll have full benefits. He could just as easily have been summarily dismissed. He knows how much he has riding on easing out quietly."

"What?" Molly sat up straight in the chair.

"I'll need you to go back to the way you used to dress, and I would appreciate no more prank calls at 4:59." He smiled. "They knew you were carrying Jack and finally realized that Eric is an empty suit. They suggested trying Eric as an executive assistant if he wants to stay on. That's why I gave you the week off—you kept bailing Eric out just in time. He had to melt down. I finally started floating the rumors."

"But…" Molly could not sort out the thoughts racing through her mind.

"Council is finally disgusted enough with Jack's tactics to do something about him. Donna explained her situation to them in great detail," Tom said matter-of-factly.

Molly stared at Tom, frankly amazed.

To his credit, he waited a few moments while she processed what he had said.

Molly felt detached from reality. "He's really leaving without a fight?"

Tom nodded patiently.

"Whose conscience finally bothered them enough to lead the pack in doing the right thing?" Molly asked quietly.

"I won't tell names and tales at the same time."

Molly had a flashback to her mother using the same expression. "Why didn't someone step up to the plate sooner?" she asked wistfully.

"None of them wanted to take on Jack. Council knew how dirty a fight that would be. They had given me a year to be rid of him." Tom explained their strategy.

"Jack abused everyone in the administration in some way, shape, or form. All of us put up with it to a certain degree rather than risk confrontation. It had gone on so long it was ingrained in our daily routine," Molly said.

"I can't argue with that."

"All his peers closed ranks and covered for him the few times anyone dared to challenge him. Of course, they received the least of his treatment or had motives of their own."

Tom nodded.

"Now you all expect me to step into a miserable job that takes eighty hours a week to do well and be appreciative of the promotion. Let me take a guess, because of my lack of management experience, you'll pay me substantially less than Jack at the same time knowing I'll do a better job." Molly waited for some form of denial.

Tom dipped his chin once.

Molly looked down and closed her eyes. When she raised her head moments later, she said slowly, "Have I got a deal for you?"

Tom watched her closely.

She used another of the old standbys. "You'd do that for me?"

"Molly," Tom said.

She stood. "It's too late."

"You just told me you haven't received an offer yet."

Molly shook her head slowly. "That's not it at all. It's too late. I cannot in good conscience accept the job." She turned to leave.

"Just think about it. Sleep on it. Come back and talk to me again tomorrow."

Molly stopped halfway to the door and looked at Tom. "It's all an act, isn't it—an affectation? You're as sharp as anyone who's ever served as our city manager."

Tom looked at her innocently. "I may need a few ceiling tiles replaced. I see cracked corners that I don't like the looks of."

"I'll make the call for you. I like dealing with the building maintenance guys. They're real people."

"That's what I've always admired about you." Tom focused on her. "You simply take care of things and move on."

Molly felt as though he was reading her mind. Whatever he was doing made her break a sweat.

Tom was detached as he continued. "I knew that Jack and Barbara were after my job. I also knew they'd end up stabbing each other in the back. Barbara will never be a city manager."

Molly gasped. She left the office quickly—too much information.

Tom was a freak who fancied himself smarter than all the rest of them put together. It didn't matter. It *was* too late. She would never accept a corner office, and Jack Sampson was not defeated that easily or cleanly. She finally just wanted out.

CHAPTER THIRTY-SIX

"I hate April," Chris grumbled to herself. "Decent weather brings all the crazies out who have been shut indoors too long." She reversed the direction of the unmarked car she was driving. She had just escaped downtown and was responding to a call that took her close to where she had just left—the old armory building.

The dark brick building had seen better days, but it was one of her favorites downtown because of the medieval effect of the design and the use of local greenstone. It was a monument to the craftsmen of the 1930s who constructed the building that served as a training site for local boys deployed during World War II, Korea, and Vietnam before it gave way to hosting professional wrestling.

The National Guard had long since abandoned downtown for an industrial park site and a sterile new metal building with acres of paved parking. The old building sat empty for several years, its upper floors crumbling from roof leaks and vandalism and its main floor gym ravaged by inner-city basketball leagues; it was truly an abandoned fortress.

Each corner of the building was marked by a projecting three-story entrance pavilion set out from the two-story central mass of the building. The end pavilions were behemoths constructed by gifted masons as twin piers of brick separated by a column of greenstone. Each pavilion had a corner street-level sentry box of greenstone to match the center insert.

Grant money had recently been awarded to renovate the building for a new criminal justice academy—it was a faux pas to say police academy these days. There was no telling how many cars would roll on this call since the police had a vested interest in the condition of the building and the quality of the construction.

Chris wasn't sure exactly what she was responding to. If her brain transcribed the code correctly, debris was being thrown from the roof.

"Oh, boy." She passed a row of cars parked on the street in front of the building—two-thirds had broken windshields or dented roof and hood, or all three. Bricks and terra cotta tiles lay scattered on the sidewalk and street. Luckily, no pedestrians had been hit so far. Several people crammed into each of the corner sentry boxes rather than risk a dash to clear the debris field.

Chris parked past the area of damage, no sense in having to file paperwork on her car, as well. She saw other officers approaching the front doors. She turned ninety degrees and ran down the alley to the basement service entrance. She had been part of an audit of the basement when she first worked for the city out of college. She entered what felt too much like a dungeon and glanced about at the abandoned city equipment parked in neat rows for storage until auctioned—police cruisers, firetrucks, ambulances, tractors, and garbage trucks filled the rows she could make out in the dark. She spotted movement. Her hand instinctively went for her sidearm. "Who's there?"

"Clive," a voice whispered. A slight black man in city maintenance blues stepped from behind a battered pickup truck.

"Jeez, you startled me." Chris relaxed and lowered her hand to her side.

"You scared the crap out of me." He laughed nervously.

"This building yours to clean and maintain?" Chris asked.

"Yes, ma'am. I come down to check the boilers and heard the racket up top, decided to lay low."

"You heard it?"

"Yes, ma'am. There's a shaft that runs beside the service elevator. Sound carries real good. We're always yelling in it to scare each other." He grinned.

"Service elevator takes you all the way to the roof?"

"As far as the top floor, ladder beside the elevator shaft takes you to the hatch to the roof."

"Let's go"

"I was afraid you was going to say that." He sighed.

"Come on, Clive. I'll look out for you. You can brag to your buddies later about helping the police."

"I ain't worried about that."

She patted his shoulder. "You know who's up there?"

"Oh, yeah. Rainey Lorton's crazy as hell and everybody knows it."

"Why's he here?" Chris waited as Clive opened the cage on the service elevator.

He motioned her onto the platform. "He's the best tile man around. He just drinks and messes with that bad shit the kids are selling. He's always a little bit out of his head. If everybody leaves him alone, he's okay. He'll lay tile ten, twelve hours when he shows up. They was picking with him this morning."

Chris raised her eyebrows.

"One of the older guys dared a kid to start asking Rainey questions about what he was doing, set that crazy bastard off like a match to a firecracker."

The elevator groaned and moved slowly, gears creaking with each story. They stopped on the second floor from the basement.

Chris looked out at dust- and dirt-covered storage boxes. She bet no one in city hall had a clue what was actually here or had set foot on the rough concrete floors in a decade.

Clive tiptoed along the hall and pointed into the small room to the right of the elevator.

Chris looked at the ladder attached to the wall. "At least I wore slacks today." She stood in the hallway and radioed that she was going onto the roof.

Chris thought she was in decent shape, but climbing the vertical ladder fifteen feet to the roof hatch left her winded. She slowly brought her head up just enough to see over the cast iron frame of the opening. "I hate heights," Chris said.

"Yes, ma'am," Clive whispered. "I'll wait here to show the others the way." He stood in the hallway.

The roof was built-up asphalt and gravel with a series of walkways laid out to access the condensers scattered over the surface. Small plastic pipes directed the condensation from the units to the perimeter of gutters that ran into scuppers at the downspouts. A parapet wall two feet tall enclosed the surface of the roof.

On the far end of the building, a row of chimney flues rose above the parapet. A man sat on scaffold erected around the bank of chimneys.

Molly stood at his feet.

Chris gasped. "Oh, shit." Of course, this was one of Molly's renovation projects.

Molly tried to reason with the man. "Come on, Rainey. You're in deep shit. Climb down before the cops get up here. You're running out of time."

"I'm the rainmaker—get it?" He plucked another brick loose from the crumbling chimney.

"I get it," Molly said.

"That dumbass sack of shit kid gets me in trouble and what does the super do—sends me up here to repoint chimneys. I'm trying to get all the bathrooms done while the tile layout is clear in my head, and that dumb shit sends me up here to work with fucking brick—fucking old brick. I hate brick!" Rainey threw the brick over the side and selected another.

Molly ducked when he threw the brick over her shoulder. "I'll explain it to them. You only work with tile. Everybody knows that. You're the best there is with ceramic. You do beautiful work with patterns and colors."

"Damn right. Shitty bricks." He cackled and threw another toward the street. Glass shattered and a car alarm sounded. "Leave me the fuck alone," he yelled to no one in particular. He held another brick, poised to toss, as he focused on Molly again.

"Go ahead."

The man blinked. "What?"

"Go ahead. I don't give a damn anymore, either."

Chris gasped as she eased through the opening. What in the hell was wrong with Molly? Chris kept her hands down as she walked slowly toward the other two.

Rainey looked at the brick in his hand.

"I'd rather you hit me up here than somebody down there." She motioned to the street below.

He tested the weight of the brick and looked at the woman. "You're okay, you know that? Not like those others from the city that always want to show you how stupid you are and tell you how wrong everything you do is."

Molly held out her hand. "Come down. I'll buy you a cup of coffee."

Rainey dropped the brick and grabbed Molly's hand.

Chris froze. How easy it would be for the man to swing Molly over the wall and drop her two stories. Chris fought a wave of panic like she had never experienced before.

Rainey looked up and Molly glanced over her shoulder. Chris nodded at the man.

"She's a friend of mine." Molly's voice was calm.

"I'm Chris. I came to escort both of you down."

"You a cop?" Rainey showed no intention of releasing Molly.

"I'm her girlfriend," Chris said quickly.

"No shit?" Rainey stared from one woman to the other.

"No shit," Molly said.

Chris forced herself to smile.

"Good for you." Rainey jumped down beside Molly, still holding her hand. "They all told me you were frigid, didn't like anybody." He chuckled. "Girl power."

"That's right," Molly said.

Chris eased closer. "I'm also a cop."

"I knew it." Rainey shook his head. "Go ahead." He held out his wrists.

Chris pulled a heavy plastic band from her pocket and secured the man.

"Fuck, I stayed on the street two weeks longer than the last time." He nodded to himself.

Chris radioed in that the suspect was in custody.

They started toward the roof hatch. Rainey led the way with Chris holding his arm; Molly was on Chris's hip.

"What in the hell were you thinking?" Chris hissed the words at Molly.

"What?"

"He could have thrown you over."

"No, I wouldn't," Rainey said.

"No, he wouldn't," Molly repeated.

"You didn't know that," Chris said.

Molly shrugged. "These guys see me every day. I treat them right, they do the same back. It's not like city hall." She went down the ladder and disappeared into the cluster of uniforms below.

Chris didn't understand Molly at all. If she didn't know better, Chris would swear that Molly was disappointed not to be seriously hurt. What was going on?

CHAPTER THIRTY-SEVEN

Chris took Molly's mental well-being seriously. She spent two weeks insisting that Molly take a much-needed long weekend.

"But we could have a project heat up again at any minute." Molly protested as she stared at the telephone on her desk as Chris propositioned her again. "Council trusts Campbell and me to manage all the prospects now that Jack and Eric are on the shit list."

"Then give Campbell all of the files and a good briefing. He'll handle it. You know you can count on him. We're only talking about taking Friday off—one day." Chris paused. "You owe me a decent weekend."

Molly swallowed. "I know I do."

"Haven't I been extremely patient with you for weeks now?"

Molly nodded, then spoke. "Yes, you have. I know I shouldn't say it out loud, but I'm actually beginning to believe that Jack is easing out quietly. It's been a month since he announced his retirement and there's been no car bomb or missing elevator car so far."

"Then take Friday off. I have it all planned. You don't have to do a thing but show up. You're going to love it." Chris sounded excited already.

"Oh, God, what do you want to do?" Molly started jotting a list of all that needed to be done over the next three days to take one off. It was doable but hectic.

"Trust me. Just pack *very* casually. I'll take care of the rest."

Molly sighed. "Like for outdoors?"

Chris giggled. My, you do catch on quickly."

Molly stared at Chris's Subaru. The entire rear end of the Forester wagon was packed solid. "You've got to be kidding. How could we possibly need all of that for three days? Where are we going—California?"

Chris hopped out and opened the passenger's door, beckoning Molly to climb in. "Mind your head. The rack extends over the side of the roof just a bit."

Molly bumped her head anyway. "Camping and canoeing—that's your idea of an intimate *fun* weekend?"

Chris stared until Molly stopped complaining and climbed in. She tossed Molly's one backpack on the pile covering the backseat. "I've called and reserved a spot in my favorite campground. They'll only guarantee it until 4:00, then we're on our own to find something else if they have someone on the waiting list."

"Camping?" Molly asked again as Chris backed the car out of the driveway.

"Are you going to whine all weekend?" Chris stopped halfway out into the street.

"Probably."

Chris patted Molly's thigh. "Well, just get over it, will you? Trust me, we're going to have a blast. Ruth loved camping. The more primitive the conditions, the better. I haven't been able to use all of this gear in years."

"Great, camping outside and everything is going to be musty."

"Not everything, darling." Chris spun the wheel and headed out of the neighborhood of cozy homes.

Molly looked longingly at the cat's face in the window of her bungalow. It was as though she could hear Dolly's predominant thought—"Dumbass."

They reached the campground in plenty of time to claim the reserved site. Molly stared around the clearing. It was a flat spot of packed dirt surrounded by trees with other sites at a discreet distance. Chris had insisted on paying the park fee while Molly made only a token argument. Molly was holding out to pay for the motel room in the middle of the night when they abandoned the *great* outdoors.

Molly attempted to help Chris snap the tent framing in place and only got in the way. She bent down and looked at the opening they would crawl in and out of. "We could just unload the wagon and sleep in the back of it. At least that way we'd be off the ground and avoid a few of the no-see-ums and crawly things."

Chris stopped setting up and put her hands on her hips. "You really are going to whine all weekend, aren't you?"

"Pretty much. I don't like camping. I thought I told you that Mom was a nut for it and made me go with her. I just wanted to stay at home with the cozy sofa and television."

"A lot of people say that, but they don't mean it once they're outside." Chris leaned closer. "Hell, you're a lifelong lesbian, you're supposed to love this. I thought this would be a really romantic weekend."

Molly stared.

"I also thought this would be really relaxing for you—completely out of touch with work." Chris began breaking the tent down.

"Well, since you put it that way, I'll stop complaining. I promise." Molly smiled at Chris and went to the wagon for the camp stove and cookware. "See, I'll help."

Chris smacked Molly's butt in passing.

"Now that's what I'm talking about." Molly gave an exaggerated wiggle as she walked.

The Subaru was soon unloaded except for the canoe on top.

Molly looked at the dark green aluminum craft and gauged its weight. "Where do you want to set this?"

Chris glanced at her Mickey Mouse watch and looked at the sky. "About three miles due south. We have time to go out before dark."

"We what?"

Chris looked at Molly.

Molly held her hands up in surrender. "We have time to take the canoe out." That was as far as positive reinforcement got her. "On the river?"

Chris nodded. "There's a new boat ramp I want to try. One of the guys at work told me how easy it is to get out in a good deep section of the river where you don't have to worry about scraping bottom on rocks."

Molly looked around. "Pardon me. I'm going over there to pee while I have a chance." She pointed to the community bath house six hundred feet away in the center of the campsites.

Chris sighed.

"You're not allergic to poison oak, are you?" Molly asked over her shoulder. "Trust me, you don't want it there."

Chris shook her head.

"I promise, I'm coming right back."

They drove slowly along the hard surface road. Chris leaned slightly forward in the driver's seat. This was their second pass. "Watch for a sign. It has to be right around here. We're between the landmarks of the falling-down barn and the abandoned country store."

"We could wait to go out on the water tomorrow." Molly tried to sound upbeat.

"It's beautiful on the river at sunset. Trust me."

Molly watched the road shoulder on her side. She glanced straight out of her window and saw railroad tracks parallel to the county road and a dense tree line beyond that had to border the river.

Chris pulled off on the shoulder. "I give up." She held up her hand and silenced Molly's response. "We just carry the canoe across the tracks and slide it down the bank into the water. See, there's a creek feeding into the river. It'll make it easy to find our way out and back to the car."

Molly doubted that but knew she had pressed her point enough as it was.

"Come on. We'll portage."

"Excuse me?"

"Carry the damn canoe." Chris loosened the bungee cords securing the canoe to the bumper.

"Oh, boy."

"Molly, I'm starting not to like you very much."

"Oh, boy." She said it with enthusiasm this time.

"Okay, that's better. Try to remember that we're having fun. You do remember *fun*?"

"Oh, boy." Molly repeated and would have added elbow action if not struggling to get the canoe over her head.

"Keep on. I'll dunk you in the river yet," Chris warned.

"If I go in, I won't be alone."

Chris chuckled. "That would make it almost worth trying just to see what you would do."

"Come on." Molly started toward the railroad bed.

By the time they covered the three hundred feet between road and river, they were out of breath and covered with beggar's lice.

"Have you ever considered kayaking? You know, those nice little plastic one-seaters that are easy to carry alone?" Molly asked.

"Molly, you're trying my patience. I'm not letting you ruin this weekend."

"You just gave me a flashback of Mom." Molly giggled. "It's fun pushing your buttons. I love canoeing."

Chris gave the canoe a push, sending Molly scrambling down the bank. They were launched.

Molly laughed so hard she had to hold on to the side of the canoe to keep from falling into the water.

Chris tossed Molly a paddle and a life preserver. "I don't want to hear it, just put it on." She shrugged her shoulders until the bright yellow vest was comfortable.

"Yes, ma'am." Molly saluted. She climbed into the front end of the canoe; Chris took the stern.

The sun had already dipped behind the surrounding hillsides as they headed toward the middle of the river. Molly tried to find a landmark, but it was all trees along the shoreline. She couldn't see far enough to spot utility poles along the road. They soon approached a pasture and a small white house that would have to do.

They paddled in silence, absorbing the silence of all but nature. Peepers sounded in the distance. Night birds called. Molly thought she saw a bat glide between the trees. Molly's oar entered the water about half the times that Chris's did. Chris steered and propelled them from the back.

"This is gorgeous," Molly finally said.

"Aren't you glad we came?"

"I'll always be glad when we come at the same time and place."

Chris groaned. "Let's go closer to shore. It's a little deep out here."

Molly chuckled.

They approached another stream emptying into the river and began to rotate.

"Hang on. I'll get us out of this. We just caught an eddy. Paddle when I tell you, okay?"

"You got it."

They paddled and spun faster.

"Shit," Chris said.

"You're the expert at this, right?"

"I told you it's been a while. We always went in groups before," she finally admitted.

"What?"

"Paddle."

By now, full darkness had taken the river. They turned so many times that Molly was completely disorientated. They finally fell into a rhythm of drifting and paddling and worked their way out of the undercurrent. They drifted to shore as a freight train rumbled by.

"Well, at least we know we're on the same side of the river as the wagon." Molly sounded hopeful.

"Hold on to that thought."

They reached the bank and used overhanging limbs to pull in as close as possible.

Molly looked up. "You do realize that's about a five-foot climb."

"That's why I have a rope tied to the bow." Chris tied the other end of the rope around her waist, carefully stood and stepped up on the bank. She turned and held out her hand to Molly.

Molly followed. They searched for hand and toe holds and pulled themselves up the bank. They collapsed into an overgrown field.

Chris patted her pockets. "Aha." She turned on her penlight.

Molly shielded her face. "Save that for the road. My eyes are adjusted to the dark enough to see okay."

"I also have my cell phone. We're good. Ready to haul boat?" Chris rested her hands on her thighs.

"Very funny."

"Payback is hell." Chris leaned over, caught the fronts of Molly's life vest, and pulled her close enough for a kiss. "I'll make it worth your while."

"You better or I'm telling all the guys in your unit that you got us lost on the river." Molly stood and held her hand down to Chris, pulling her to her feet.

They grabbed the rope and dragged the canoe up the bank.

Chris looked around and tied the rope off to the closest tree. "I'm thinking we leave the canoe, mark the road where we come out, and walk back in for the canoe once we drive the wagon here."

"Okay by me, it's your canoe." Molly tossed her life vest in with the paddle.

Chris smacked Molly on the back of the head.

They started across the field with Chris in the lead. They were halfway across the open space when Chris stopped abruptly enough that Molly ran into her. Chris didn't turn when she asked, "Did you hear that?"

Molly listened. She started to make a joke about horror movies when she heard the noise. The hair on her neck bristled.

"That's a cow, right?" Chris asked.

"In this field, I don't think so. Shh." Molly concentrated on separating sounds. Something else was in the field with them. It was close to the ground, not panting like a dog nor lumbering like a cow or horse. They heard a low growl like a baby's cry. In a split second, Chris jumped behind Molly.

"Give me the light," Molly whispered, holding out her hand. Molly panned the penlight across the field in front of them. She glimpsed a dark brown creature the size of a medium dog. "Goddamn." Molly felt the grin spreading across her face. "Did you see that?"

"What the hell was it?" Chris hung on to Molly's back and peered around her.

Molly started laughing and couldn't stop. Minutes later, she was finally able to talk. "Believe me, we scared it worse than it did us. It had to be a bobcat. I heard they were in this area. I used to see them when I hiked the national forest around college. That is too cool."

"It's gone, right?"

"Oh, yeah. We won't see it again. We were lucky to see it at all. Wait until I e-mail my old roommate." Molly started toward the road. She went back to Chris. "Are you okay?"

"Yes." Chris quickly resumed the lead.

Molly couldn't help herself. She mooed. "It's a cow, right?"

Chris stalked ahead of her. "I'm never going to live this down. If you tell anyone…"

"What happens in the woods stays in the woods." Molly scratched her leg and felt a lump. "Crap. Mosquitoes are out."

They reached the pavement and turned back toward the direction they had parked. Chris placed the penlight on the shoulder and turned it on. They walked in silence for forty-five minutes.

"Thank God, there's the Subaru." Chris dug in her pocket for the keys.

They drove until they saw the small light, then crossed the tracks and the field using the last of the light to locate the canoe. Chris looked anxiously to either side as the light died.

"Portage?"

"There's cold beer in the cooler in the tent."

"Portage." Molly picked up one end and waited for Chris.

They loaded up and returned to the campsite. It was after midnight when they crawled inside the tent.

Molly looked at Chris as she opened the cooler and handed her a Heineken. "Chris, I always enjoy sex with you, but right now…"

"…we just feel sweaty and buggy."

Molly nodded.

Chris stretched out on the sleeping bag. "How about a good snuggle tonight? We have tomorrow and Sunday to look forward to." She winked.

Molly stretched out beside her and was almost embarrassed at how quickly she fell asleep.

Molly awoke first the next morning. It took her a moment to realize where she was. She stared at Chris until she began to freak herself out with the sense of attachment she felt. Molly eased out of the tent and went to the bath house for a pee and shower. The water felt wonderful. She was almost done when Chris came in.

"Don't leave yet."

Molly watched Chris lather up and rinse off. She had never felt so many emotions raging within her at once. The fact that other women were in and out of the shower room didn't distract Molly or the show that Chris was staging for her.

They walked quickly back to the tent. Chris went in first and pulled Molly on top of her. Molly never thought the inside of a tent could be so appealing. So what if they went on an afternoon hike rather than morning. Molly stretched contentedly and rubbed her legs together.

"Are you starting again without me?" Chris rose up on her elbow and looked down the length of Molly's body. She idly rubbed at her own calf. "Uh-oh." She stared at Molly's legs. "Is that what I think it is?"

Molly looked down. "Chigger bites."

Their legs were covered with tiny red dots.

Molly rubbed her forearm and looked at the skin forming tiny blisters. "Poison oak."

"Oh, no."

"Oh, yes. Does it make you break out?"

"No, it's never bothered me."

Molly scratched her side.

Chris smacked Molly's hand.

"I'm starting to itch all over." Molly sounded like an eight-year-old.

Chris pinned Molly's arms down and placed her leg over Molly's. "So is this like torture, not letting you scratch?"

Molly wiggled. "You better have packed Calamine lotion."

"What's that and Benadryl worth to you?" She kissed Molly as she reached across her for the first aid kit. "I can see I'm going to have my hands full taking care of you."

"Just scratch my damn back if you want to hear me really moan." Molly rubbed against the sleeping bag.

"I'll find something else to rub to take your mind off of it." Chris hesitated. "Do you realize that we made it?"

Molly looked at her questioningly.

"We survived our first trip together. We resisted renting a U-Haul once our April deadline came and went. I think we're ready to move in together the next time we both have a weekend off." Chris waited for a reaction.

"C-c-c-c-commitment?" Molly asked and grinned.

Chris made her moan.

It was a beautiful spring weekend that Molly and Chris would always remember and laugh about.

Sunday night, Chris gave Molly an oatmeal bath to calm her skin, then kept her awake all night as they shared a real bed together. Dolly maintained a safe distance. For once, Molly dreaded Monday morning—work just didn't seem all that important anymore. After three days with Chris, Molly truly believed that Jack would fade away, no one would care if she was a lesbian, and the truth about her parents would never come out.

CHAPTER THIRTY-EIGHT

Molly was still smiling and scratching when she returned to work on Monday. She delayed the inevitable by stopping at several construction projects on the way downtown so that she wouldn't set foot in the building until almost eleven o'clock.

Molly hit the speed dial for 5 as soon as she parked on the public deck.

"Hello?" Syd was out of breath.

"Did I interrupt something?" Molly teased.

"I wish. I just finished thirty minutes on the stair stepper. What's up, kiddo?"

"Everything." Molly felt the silly grin that wouldn't leave her face spreading into her voice.

"Bitch, you're moving in another one, aren't you?"

Molly laughed. "Only because you're spoken for, and not yet, but soon."

"Yeah, yeah, yeah. You're in love. I hear it in your voice." Syd shrieked.

Molly held the phone away from her ear until her stepmother calmed down.

"I'm so happy for you, sweetie. You sound so much better."

"I'm happier than I've been in a long time. I just called to share." Molly dashed across the street between cars instead of waiting for the light to change. We made it past our move-in moratorium, so we're both sure."

"Ha, Jimmy owes me $20. We had a bet on how long before you made another conquest. He thought you'd wait until summer. I knew you wouldn't hold out that long."

Molly chuckled. "You know me too well. The weekend was

worth a lot more than $20. I'll send Jimmy a check to make up his loss."

"You'll do no such thing. A bet is a bet and he lost."

"Got to go. Love to all of you," Molly said as she approached the front of city hall.

"As though there's any left." Syd huffed.

"I have more than enough to go around. Hey, happy belated Mother's Day." Molly disconnected as she entered the building.

She couldn't believe she had actually gone three entire days without physically being in her office. The building still stood and the city still functioned. From her stops on the way in, she knew that work had gone smoothly on her projects on Friday. The superintendents were gearing up and planning their week's work with no dangling questions awaiting her immediate action.

"Cool," Molly said as she entered the second floor of the building. Council chambers were quiet; no meetings were scheduled until Tuesday.

Angela walked out of her office juggling her briefcase and shoulder bag. She took one look at Molly and began shaking her head. "We thought you were still on your *romantic getaway*." She tapped the face of her watch. "My goodness."

Molly grinned. "Go ahead and say I told you so. It was a wonderful weekend and wonderful to get away."

"Was Chris *wonderful*, too?" Angela stretched out the adjective.

Molly actually blushed.

"Girl," Angela shrieked, then remembered where she was. "Got some!" She tagged Molly on the arm as they passed. "About damn time you had a little fun. I'm proud of you. I can't wait to tell the others." She glanced at her watch again. "Damn, I'm going to be late if I don't hustle my butt. Later." She jogged up the steps and out the door to the street.

The grin stayed on Molly's face as she turned the corner to her office. She waved at Mark in the map room; maybe he would finally give up hope of them dating now that he could see how she was with Chris. "Not my problem." She hummed as she approached her office.

Molly glanced across the drafting table and desk surfaces. Not bad, a new set of plans on her drafting table with a review request and several pink phone message slips from people reluctant to trust voice mail. She booted her computer and glanced at the panel of her phone—only five messages. She might just become used to three-day weekends. "Good, good, good." Only eight e-mails and two of those were from Angela and Susan that morning checking on her about the weekend. She couldn't wait to tell them all about Chris and camping. Well, almost all.

Molly double-checked her calendar. She knew there was a 1:30 meeting with Campbell to go over projects. She just wanted to make sure there were no other invitations lurking on Lotus.

There was a tapping on her door frame. Molly turned and saw Tamika. Molly was about to launch into a canoe story when Tamika put her finger to her lips. She looked entirely too serious for midday Monday.

Molly raised her eyebrows. Tamika motioned her to follow. They went into the GIS office. Gary closed the door. He was silent also.

Molly looked from one of them to the other and was about to speak when she heard voices from Jack's office. Gary squeezed her hand.

Molly suddenly had a very bad feeling as she listened to Jack trying to take Campbell into his confidence.

"I'm not interested in Molly's personal life. How many times do I have to tell you that?" Campbell said. The frustration was clear in his voice.

"Well, you damn well better be. This new project that you have saved the day on," Jack's voice dripped with sarcasm, "is located in a very anti-gay-anything fundamentalist area. Do you want to be responsible for losing this deal just because you don't want to know about Molly? Tom won't listen to anything from me now that I'm on the way out. Jesus H. Christ, I'm fifty-two years old and being forced out of my job. I'll end up working for someone like Eric if I go to another city. I hate public service. What the fuck else am I supposed to do? They have to let me stay on."

"Jack, this is getting us nowhere." Campbell sighed. "You brought this on yourself."

Molly heard Campbell drop into a chair just as Jack's desk chair did its usual squeak.

"I know I'm going to regret asking this." Campbell sounded as though he would as soon take a beating. "What do you think you know about Molly?"

"I don't just think it, I know it for a fact now. She's a dyke, a damn butch, a friggin' lesbian! One of my buddies saw her this past weekend, camping with another woman. He sent me a photo with his cell phone of them kissing. They were all over each other for three days from what he saw. She was with that blonde who worked for me years ago and is a cop now." Jack's voice became louder with each sentence. "I knew there was something between those two months ago, but Molly denied it."

Molly looked at Gary and Tamika. "I guess I've been officially outed."

Gary started to speak. Tamika touched his arm and silenced him.

"It doesn't matter," Campbell said. But the deliberate tone of his voice said the opposite. He chose his words too carefully.

"Ha! Hell, yes, it does. It matters to you. I saw the look that just crossed your face, and you know and like Molly." Jack seized the weakness as always.

"Are you done?" Campbell asked.

"I haven't even started. I sent the photograph to all the council members. Having a lezzy in charge has to be worse than my cheating and lying. They won't allow me to retire now." Jack sounded pleased with himself.

Molly gasped.

"Jack, what Molly does on her own time is her business. She is entitled to a personal life. Surely, you aren't that surprised." Campbell struggled as he said all the right things.

"I've never seen her out in public with a man, if that's what you mean. I just thought she worked all the time. Oh, wait a minute, I get it. You're ex-military—don't ask, don't tell and everything is copacetic," Jack said.

"What else have you done?" Campbell sounded weary.

"I e-mailed the state project director. Molly's probably screwing the female project manager for leads. How can anything she's done be trusted?"

Molly started for the door. Tamika grabbed Molly's arm. "Hear all of it first," Tamika hissed.

The silence between the two men was broken by the ringing of a cell phone. Campbell answered.

"I'm in Jack's office now. Yes, he has told me. It doesn't change anything." Campbell's voice faltered. He listened to a long speech, then sighed. "I hear what you're saying. I don't like it, but I have to agree. No, I'll do it. I'll take her off the project. No, I'm not going to tell her why. I'll find something else for her to work on. Because I don't want the city sued. I'll take care of Molly. Eric can handle the day-to-day. I'll be the lead contact. I'll talk Molly into staying in the background." The cell phone closed with a snap.

"Not another word," Campbell said.

"Is she fired?" Jack asked.

"Of course not."

"But she's gone from the project?"

"You heard what I said." Campbell sounded worn out.

"Eric will do a good job for you on this. He can bring the wife and baby to any lunches or dinners with the company. The old corporate farts love that. I was right to take that boy under my wing!" Jack sounded extremely pleased.

Campbell grunted as he stood. "Jack, I'm warning you. You are not to discuss this anywhere, and you damn well better delete that photograph. You'll have all the women who work for the city up in arms if they find out what you've done to Molly."

"I owed her," Jack said softly. "It's her doing. Wait until this hits the police station this morning." He whistled. "And that's not all. Her father…"

Gary flinched when he heard the breaking of hard plastic.

"That was uncalled for. I just bought that iPhone," Jack protested.

"Damn you, Jack. You make me feel as worthless as I know you are. No more!" Campbell left the office.

Molly was stunned. For one of the few times in her life, she couldn't think. She had to get out of the building or she would scream. She might scream anyway to see if it would make her feel any better. Jack knew about Chris, and it was a matter of time before he found an audience for the Ham and Helen saga.

Molly looked at Tamika's hand on her arm. She stared into Gary's eyes.

"It doesn't matter who you love," Gary said. "You have the best heart of anyone I know. People don't care. Most everyone knows. It's not that big of a deal anymore."

Molly shook her head. "He sold me out."

"You knew Jack was after you. You knew he would play dirty," Tamika said.

Molly shook her head again. "Campbell sold me out. He's taking me off a major project. That's a professional death warrant."

"There will be other projects." Gary tried to reassure her.

"That's not the point," Tamika said quietly. "Hell, I've a mind to take them on myself. If they mistreat a lesbian, they'll do just as bad or worse to me because I'm black."

Gary lowered his head.

Molly was numb as she returned to her office. All was ruined. She grabbed her messenger bag only because she needed her Jeep keys. Her personal cell phone rang.

Chris sounded as she had when Molly left her earlier. "Hey, sweetie. I know you can't talk. Just wanted to give you a heads-up. Some asshole took our picture this weekend. Most of the guys here have enjoyed it way too much. We've been offered several threesomes. Just didn't want it to catch you cold. I have to work tonight. How's your day going?"

Molly stared at nothing. "Not so good. I'll call you back later."

Tamika followed her. "Go. I'll shut down your computer. I'll keep an ear out today and let you know what else happens. Go for a drive or a walk. Get your mind off of this. Do you want me to call Windy?"

Molly shook her head. "I'm going for a very long lunch. I need to think. I may be back…or not." She headed toward the stairs, unable to remember how wonderful she had felt such a short time ago.

Donna waved Tamika to her cubicle when she left Molly's office. Donna pointed to her steno pad and whispered. "I took notes of the conversation. They can't get away with this. Too many of us heard. Enough is enough. They're all as bad as Jack or worse. My job isn't worth this."

"What are you going to do?" Tamika kept her voice low. She heard Jack in his office talking on the telephone. Eric had left just before Molly.

"I haven't decided yet. It's bad enough when they push me around, but I got myself into a bad situation with Jack years ago. Molly put months into recruiting that company and now they're going to cut her out of it because she likes women. Hell, I'd rather sleep with her than any of the men around here. They better think again. I never should have allowed Jack to see that file. I was so proud of Campbell and Molly, I let down my guard. Jack can't stand how good Molly is with projects. I thought it was too late for Jack to hurt Molly anymore. Tom never should have allowed Jack to stay on payroll for six months without banning him from the building."

Tamika looked over her shoulder as Windy rolled toward Jack's door. Windy motioned Tamika and Donna to leave. "You two don't want to be witnesses."

Tamika walked toward the map room. "I'll talk to you later," she said over her shoulder to Donna.

Donna went the opposite way around the hallway toward upper management's offices.

There was hell to pay in city hall.

CHAPTER THIRTY-NINE

Chris stared in disbelief as she watched Molly escorted toward the unmarked car by another of the department's detectives. Molly's words echoed in Chris's head—"I was in Jack's office last night." Molly had readily admitted to arguing with Jack after hours, causing him to fall backward and leaving him with a head injury; it wouldn't occur to Molly not to tell the truth.

Chris had silenced and advised Molly as quickly as she was able. It all had the unreal feeling of being a very strange dream—if only they would wake up and laugh about this. Chris returned to her department-issue sedan as the number she was calling rang. She opened the trunk while juggling her cell phone and tucked her tackle box under her arm and grabbed her briefcase.

"Molly Hamilton may need to hire you as her attorney," Chris said as soon as the telephone was answered. "She's on her way to the police station to answer questions. I didn't make this phone call."

Gibson Frost, the best criminal attorney in the city, didn't miss a beat. "I'll meet her there."

Chris calmed herself with the knowledge that Molly was in good hands. She envisioned the baby-boomer attorney with curly hair and colorful bow tie and knew she had done all she could for Molly at the moment. Molly had no idea what she was blithely walking into, thinking all she needed on her side was the truth.

Chris slid her phone into her jacket pocket and glanced over the crowd lingering about the entrance to the building, even though the city manager had closed city hall for the day. She waved over the boyish uniform officer. "Hey, Adam."

"Ma'am." The young man was over six feet tall and wore a twenty-nine-inch waist. His hair was in a short, neat trim that went with his exercise routine of morning swim at the Y. He looked over his shoulder and slid his notebook into his shirt pocket. "I've been released from the scene now that your unit is on site, just helping with security. I'm going to be late clocking out." He frowned.

"Were you the responding officer?" Chris was familiar with his meticulous work and ability to notice obtuse details from the robbery cases they had worked on together. She thought him an old soul rewarded with a cute body.

Adam nodded, looking a decade older than his usual baby-faced twenty-three.

"What's bothering you?" Chris asked.

"No way Molly did what I saw upstairs. I've seen you guys out together." He blushed.

"She says she caused him to fall and hit his head on the coffee table." Chris baited the young officer.

"Call me after you work the scene." He took a deep breath and stretched. "Do me a favor and release the cleaning crew."

Chris raised her eyebrows.

"I secured the scene after the dispatch from 911, called the duty officer so you guys would be brought in, and taped off the office and building entrance. I've been down here taking names and employee exit times from yesterday as soon as workers began showing up. I put the cleaning guys in separate offices at 4:30 this morning so they wouldn't influence each other's statements. I haven't logged them out of the building. Those two guys are scared shitless and will be forgotten about when the hot dogs see the scene that needs to be processed. Those black dudes were pale." He looked at Chris.

"What else, Adam?"

"You get it, don't you?" He nodded in answer to his own question. "Those guys told me that they are always creeped out cleaning community development, that it feels like someone else is there even though they've never see anyone. Now they've found a murder victim and are in bad shape. It's an ugly crime scene."

"I'll make sure they're questioned and released ASAP. I'll call the city's HR department about counseling for them. Are you okay?" Chris asked, touching Adam's arm.

He shrugged. "I knew I'd see something like this sooner or later. Thank God, they drilled procedure into me at the academy." He looked around. "I've already walked the building and the stairs checking for a discarded murder weapon. I'll keep on around the block and widen the search perimeter."

Chris glimpsed her supervisor entering the building. "I've got to go. I'll call you later." She took the steps into the building two at a time.

Chris stood on the landing inside the double doors and took a deep breath. How many times had she been in and out of this building over the years, yet today it felt totally different? Today it was the scene of a homicide.

She listened as the wooden steps creaked and groaned with her weight as she descended to the second-floor level. She caught herself wanting to whistle as she followed the wide main corridor, halfway expecting the elevator doors to open with Molly and her work friends. Chris glanced through the narrow glass doors to the map room and thought of the first time she met Molly. She heard her own breathing as she turned to the employee corridor leading to Molly's office and Jack's.

The back corner of the building buzzed with low voices and glowed with overhead lights accentuated with camera flashes.

Ray Oulds stood at Donna's workstation, already taking over her phone and desk space for a field office. His head and shoulders towered above the cloth-covered partition. He was 6'6" tall and carried close to three hundred pounds of solid, hard body. His mind was as able as his body. He had quickly risen through the ranks to make investigations captain, one of three captains directly under the police chief, by the time he was thirty based on nonstop, faultless work. There was already a pool on when he would make chief somewhere. He turned and saw Chris approaching and motioned her to join him.

"No one's been in yet except the responding officer, the ME, and Jackson to take photographs. I want you to do the sketch and observation notation. I've taken the lead on this myself since it's city hall," Ray explained. "Wait until Reichard gets here to start on the blood-pattern evidence so you two can work the scene in grids together. Reichard stopped on his way in to inform the family since they're neighbors of his. It's textbook blood pattern—passive and projected. Hope you haven't just eaten a big breakfast."

"I came prepared." Chris held up her briefcase. She actually enjoyed using the small drafting board with attached parallel bars.

"Thank goodness for a cast iron stomach." She stared into Jack's office.

The body was completely stiff and facedown on the terrazzo floor near the long exterior wall with windows. The medical examiner had already tied paper bags on Jack's hands. Blood pooled around the head and shoulders—lividity was present in the facial discoloration. The coffee table and side chairs normally in the center of the room were cast aside. The conference table and chairs were shoved all the way into the corner of the room. The surface of Jack's desk was cleared except for secondary spatter—every item, including the computer, had been swept to the floor. From the pattern and amount of blood on the floor and furniture, Chris could tell there had been a major struggle as Jack was hit repeatedly, causing what even she could see from twelve feet had been a fatal blunt force trauma to the head. Jack's office was nothing close to the way Molly described leaving it with Jack sitting on the floor nursing a goose egg from the corner of the coffee table.

Ray leaned closer to Chris. "I heard about Molly. Sorry, Chris. The ME's already determined that death took place eight to twelve hours ago."

Chris controlled her reaction. "I'm just here to gather evidence by the book. Suspects will come later after all of this has been processed."

Jackson spoke from within the office as he snapped the shutter of the camera. "This damage wasn't done by the coffee table unless someone picked the damn thing up and smashed him with it."

Ray studied Chris. "No one in their right mind walked away from this thinking Jack Sampson would live."

CHAPTER FORTY

"The best you can do now is let me take you to the police station and surrender yourself, instead of them picking you up." Gibson Frost leaned back in the chair at the conference table to Molly's immediate right. She had taken the seat at the end of the long table nearest the door.

Gibson couldn't help that he sounded like an intelligent snob. He was extremely intelligent, often past the point of recognizing that most others couldn't keep up with him. He wasn't a snob; he talked to the woman who cleaned his office in the same tone as he talked to his wife. He was partners with an extremely successful group of attorneys. Their offices were located in the second-tallest building downtown, on the second-highest floor. Each attorney had an office with a window that looked out over the old industrial section of town bordering the river, some actually saw the river. They were on the nineteenth floor of what had been a local bank's corporate offices. The entire floor had been renovated to accommodate nine thousand square feet of offices for lawyers and associated services.

Molly stared out the wall of windows. "It's been just over two weeks. How in the hell did my life turn into shit in two weeks?" It was a beautiful day in late May as evidenced by the leaves and blooms covering the trees and shrubs.

Molly had answered questions at the police station the rest of the day that Jack was discovered. She was released with instructions not to leave the city limits without notifying the police since she was a person of interest in the investigation. She had allowed her home searched since she had nothing to hide, even though the concept of strangers handling her possessions appalled her. She knew she was being watched. She made it easy on all of them by using leave time and staying at home with Dolly. She tried not to bother Chris, knowing how the investigation compromised their relationship. She had made a tearful plea to Chris to look after Dolly, but surely it wouldn't come to that. "I know damn well that evidence was in that office to show who came in after me," Molly said.

Gibson's words were measured. "The grand jury determined probable cause to indict you."

"On the basis of my pencil left in Jack's office," Molly said disgustedly. Everyone knew her trademark baby blue Pentel that matched her favorite spring sweater.

"That and fibers from your sweater, latent fingerprints, and DNA matches. I'm not surprised that the police are ready to arrest you. I told you from the onset to be prepared to be booked and charged with voluntary manslaughter." Gibson tapped the dull tip of the wooden pencil against the legal pad half used with written-on sheets rolled over the top binding. "They aren't going to let you go this time."

"I did not kill Jack Sampson," Molly said quietly.

Gibson pushed his glasses up his nose. "I believe you, but the prosecution's evidence is building against you. We should be able to get a reasonable bail amount given your standing in the community. It shouldn't take but a week or so for the arraignment to be scheduled for charges to be formally read. Will your family help with the bail amount?"

Molly nodded. "I've spoken with my father. He's prepared to post a property bond based on his home equity, and he'll draw against his life insurance as needed. No offense, Gibson, but you don't come cheap." Molly hated asking Ham, but she had no choice. She had also made him promise to keep the family in Michigan.

Gibson studied her. "Tell me again about that night."

Molly closed her eyes. "I waited for everyone else to leave the building, usually they all cleared out by 7:00, except for Jack and me. I think Jack avoided going home until it looked as though he had an extremely busy day. I used the only quiet time of the afternoon to get caught up on work." Molly smiled at the thought of the neat piles of paperwork for each project and how she had enjoyed methodically making the calculations and running investment scenarios.

"Jack and I had an ongoing argument about the latest project that had come in from the state—Project Ring, a call center for insurance underwriters. Campbell had the lead since Jack was a lame duck.

I was being pulled because of the ultra-conservative nature of the company. Jack had recently outed me at the office."

Molly lowered her eyes. She never knew what the reaction would be to her sexual orientation. She liked to think that most people who truly knew her wouldn't care. It was usually the least expected person who had a negative knee-jerk reaction to her being gay. She had tried so long to keep her private life private—a lesson drilled into Molly by her mother.

"Jack was simply awful," Gibson said.

Molly looked up, tears in her eyes. "He was that. He abused everyone in the office just in varying degrees and manifestations. He manipulated any information he could find out about an employee so that the slightest weakness was of benefit to him."

"And he had found your *weakness* in your sexuality." Gibson studied his long tapered fingers.

"We argued. He struck me. He grabbed me. We struggled. I pushed him away." Molly felt the silence in the room making her ears ring.

Gibson opened his file and spread out the photographs taken of Molly after her questioning by the police. "He caused the bruising to your arm and neck?"

"Yes," Molly said, "and I caused him to fall backward and hit the back of his head on the corner of the coffee table. He was yelling threats and insults at me as I left his office."

"Did you go back to his office?"

Molly shook her head. "I did not."

"And once home?" Gibson fingered his bow tie.

"I discovered my hand had bled all over my pants, as well as on my sweater. The blood was already drying by the time I changed clothes. That's why I put both pieces in the trash." She pointed to the photograph of her hand. "His nail nicked a vein on the back of my hand when we struggled. It wouldn't stop bleeding. My clothes were easily found by the police. I haven't concealed anything. I haven't done anything wrong!" Molly slammed her fist on the table, causing Gibson to jump. "Sorry."

"If you weren't upset, I wouldn't believe your innocence," Gibson said. "Molly, a glancing blow to the coffee table did not cause the blunt force trauma to Jack's head that killed him. The crime scene is horrific. There was one hell of a blow delivered to Jack's skull. What you describe is a simple contusion. What killed him is a skull fracture with enough bleeding to force brain matter into the spinal cord."

Molly shivered. "I can still hear his voice as I left his office." She gathered her thoughts. "Yes, I hated him. I know there were many times I wanted to harm him. I honestly believe that he deserved to die for the way he treated all of us, but I did not kill Jack Sampson. Who in the hell went into that office after me? Why is there no evidence of the real killer?"

CHAPTER FORTY-ONE

Chris raised her head from the back of the sofa and listened. It annoyed her that she dozed off every time she sat down and attempted to watch television in the living room; that was why she usually crawled in bed no matter the time of night or day when she finally took a break from work. Someone was knocking on her door. She frowned at the time on the corner of CNN—8:45. She glanced toward the window to make sure it was night. Her days were a blur ever since Molly was arraigned, even if she was released on bail. Chris looked through the peephole and braced herself as she opened the door.

"Hey." Spencer stood in the hallway, hands in the pockets of his cargo shorts. His shirt was from last year's Habitat Labor Day Weekend Building Blitz—one of the best weekends they had spent together.

"Hey, yourself." Chris stood back and gestured for him to come in.

"I can't stay long. Julie is playing at the neighbors." He walked to the center of the living room and sat on the back of the sofa.

"Okay." Chris folded her arms across her chest as she stopped several feet short of him.

Spencer blew out a long breath and pursed his lips. "Molly's preliminary hearing is tomorrow."

"I know the schedule."

"I have to take Molly's case to trial," Spencer said. "Gibson's motion to dismiss didn't stand a chance."

Chris remained silent.

"All the evidence leads us to Molly. You know it as well as me." Spencer was clearly miserable.

"Her and that damn anal habit of carrying a pencil to match her clothes," Chris said.

Spencer rolled his eyes. "You have to love her."

"No argument there," Chris said. "Molly is not capable of killing anyone."

"You and I have always disagreed on that concept. Given the right circumstances, anyone is capable of anything." He held up his hand, forestalling Chris's rebuttal. "I know I'm singing to the choir. I keep waiting for the lab to give me something I *want* to use," Spencer said. "As it is now, fibers from her sweater—found in the trash—were in his office. His DNA is on her sweater. Her DNA was under his fingernails and on him. She has bruises that match his grip. It's too much to be circumstantial, Chris." Spencer looked away. "I had to tell you this in person."

"And we won't talk again while the trial is taking place," Chris finished for him. "I know. I give you my word, Spencer, that I have done nothing untoward during this investigation. I've been so careful with processing the crime scene, documenting every item, and only working on tasks assigned to me. I will not compromise the process. I believe in the chain of evidence and due process. I've turned into the department's nightmare as I hound everyone to be thorough."

A slight smile passed across Spencer's face. "I heard. I wouldn't have expected anything less of you."

"Damn code of ethics."

"At all times and in all circumstances, we have to be more than ordinary, decent human beings." Spencer stood. "We wouldn't have taken the oath of office if we didn't believe in it."

"Our private lives have to be without fault. We have to be perfect. We can never discredit ourselves, our department, or our community." Chris hugged herself.

"I won't see you alone again until after the trial is over with. If you still want me for a friend, give me a call." Spencer stopped beside her.

"Molly did not kill Jack Sampson," Chris whispered.

Spencer pulled Chris to him. "I love you, sweetie. I know you believe in Molly with everything in your being. You're the best friend I've ever had. Susan's having a hell of a time with this also. I hope I don't lose either or both of you to this case. I have no choice other than to do my job."

"Being a paragon to the community sucks, don't you think?" Chris walked Spencer to the door.

"Oh, yeah." Spencer stopped in the hallway and looked back at her. "Later."

Chris held her hand up in a wave and closed the door. She leaned against the solid wood and looked about her home. All the people she loved were in limbo, and she couldn't do a damn thing to change it. She knew the trial had to take its course.

CHAPTER FORTY-TWO

"We must stop meeting like this." Windy coasted up to Chris on the stone patio out from the side door of the courthouse. It was a gathering place for those involved with the proceedings inside who had time to kill and would rather do so in July's heat. There were enough dogwood trees around the perimeter of the masonry to keep the patio shaded most of the day. Stone benches were spaced around the border, metal chairs and tables in the middle.

Chris turned at the sound of the familiar voice. As usual these days, she stood alone with her mind racing, preoccupied with her own thoughts. "Hey, lady, how are you?" Chris smiled at the sight of the dynamic woman who just happened to be in a wheelchair.

Windy set the brakes on her chair and let her wrists rest on the padded arms. "Sweating like a whore in church, but I'd take a wild guess and say I'm still better off than you."

Chris nodded. "No argument there."

Windy fanned her face. "I don't know anymore whether it's the humidity or damn hot flashes. I also don't know why I bother to take a shower every morning, it lasts no time."

"I'm fairly comfortable." Chris smiled serenely.

"Screw you!" Windy dug in her pocket for a tissue and wiped her face.

Chris reached down and flicked the bits of tissue from Windy's cheek.

"Thank you. People see anything out of place on me and think 'poor old crippled woman and mentally challenged, too.'" Windy adjusted her body in the chair by lifting herself up slightly with her arms. "So how are you really? I take it you've heard that Molly entered a plea of not guilty and told Spencer to put his plea bargain offer where the sun doesn't shine. This must be playing hell with your investigative acuity."

"If you're implying I'm bitchier than usual, just say so. My role in the Sampson investigation is purposely minor." Chris angled her head. "You and I both know that Molly's not guilty, don't we?"

"Honey, if anyone had justification to kill Jack, it was Molly. Of course, she'd be standing in a long line. Was I on the list of suspects?" Windy asked.

Chris looked momentarily confused.

"Goddamn it. I knew it. Do you think just because I'm here," she slapped the armrests of her wheelchair, "I can't kill anyone?" Windy popped the brakes off and rushed Chris, knocking her sideways. Chris just happened to be standing so that she sat down abruptly, smacking her tailbone against stone, rather than falling and hitting her head. Windy was up against Chris with hands around her throat before Chris reacted. Her grip had Chris pinned. "How do I fit the profile now?" Windy released Chris and backed up, not the least out of breath with the mild exertion.

Chris turned slightly on the bench, grimacing as she moved her butt. She rubbed her throat. "Damn, I didn't see that coming."

"Don't tell me to kiss your ass even if for medicinal purposes." Windy stared out across the panoramic view of downtown at the century-old buildings intermixed with modern steel and glass fiascos, of neat blocks laid out with a surveyor's precision, of trees and shrubs adding color to the asphalt and concrete. "I get so tired of people assuming that I'm someone to be pitied just because I happen to be in this chair. In here," she tapped her temple, "I'm still the teenage jock who loved school and swimming and Dave. I have hot flashes and orgasms just like any woman my age. I've learned to analyze topography before I find myself rolling backward or stuck in a grate. I know how to use my upper body strength to make transfers and take care of myself. I don't think about losing that strength or losing Dave. I'm like the people who are illiterate yet smart enough to teach themselves ways to compensate so that no one knows. I've always worked twice as hard as my counterparts—first to *make up* for being female, then because I was *disabled*. No one takes advantage of me."

"How about Jack?" Chris asked softly.

"I hated that son of a bitch. Anyone who had contact with him had motive to kill him. I despised the way he manipulated the system. I abhorred the way he relied on the old boys' network. I detested the way he preyed on any woman with the slightest crack in her self-esteem." Windy looked Chris straight in the eye. "There were far too many occasions when I would have liked to kill Jack Sampson. I'm surprised he lived the way he did as long as he did. This was way overdue."

"But you're a practicing attorney." Chris didn't believe what she was hearing.

"And a realist. Anyone working in city hall should be a suspect. Molly could have done it, Chris. I know it's not her nature. I don't believe it was her reason for going to his office. I think she simply defended herself. Hell, I could have struck him a blow to the head given the right set of circumstances. I happen to feel a great empathy for those subject to such adversity. Jack brought his death on himself, plain and simple. My logic will not allow me to draw conclusions without all the evidence, and we're missing something. My legal sense tells me there has to be a trial and judgment for a moral and ethical wrongdoing, but there's also a part of me that says 'yes.'" Windy made a fist, then pumped her arm. "I almost don't care who did it. Who could honestly blame Molly if she did?"

"It's not my job or training to be jury or judge," Chris said. "Due process of the law must prevail. I know that if I do my job, if the department does its job, Molly will be found innocent."

"Don't put that load on yourself or the system. You know better, dear. Gibson was an excellent choice, by the way. Has Molly thanked you?" Windy glanced at her watch. "Just keep in mind one thing—all disabilities aren't as obvious as mine." She pivoted and rolled to the push pad to open the door to the building. She turned and looked over her shoulder. "You do recognize that Molly is the one worth saving out of all of this, whatever it takes, even if it comes down to compromising that staunch integrity of hers?"

Chris stared. Windy had just made Chris's impartiality that much more precarious.

CHAPTER FORTY-THREE

Chris hated this kind of duty but figured why not kill the proverbial two birds. The chief encouraged all officers, regardless of assigned duty, to mingle with the city's neighborhoods and be a presence in the community. Her motive was to observe Eric Blackstone somewhere other than city hall—a Saturday afternoon block party was perfect.

The subdivision was definitely upper middle class and seemingly all white from the faces Chris observed as she drove along the narrow street—so much for diversity. The houses were mostly brick and mostly story-and-a-half; she would estimate the price range somewhere between starter and retirement home. The lots were narrow and long with the houses constructed near the street and close to one another. She imagined it was hard not to know intimate details about immediate neighbors. Neighborhood watch groups were a natural outgrowth, summer block parties the main activity of such groups.

A dead end street in the middle of the subdivision was barricaded at its intersection with the through street. Eighties music blared from an assortment of speakers. Grills were rolled around to the street from back decks. Most couples were in their mid- to late thirties with preteen children. An equal number of young families with babies and retired couples balanced the mix.

Chris parked and walked past the barricade. She tolerated the greeting by the neighborhood watch president who asked her first name, wrote it in neat block printing on a festive label, and stuck it to Chris's knit shirt. Chris hated that. She found a diet soda in with the tub of iced beer and popped the top. The drink would last longer than her patience for socializing.

Chris eased through the crowd and spotted Eric. He stood on the concrete curb to be taller than the woman Chris assumed to be Eric's wife who was standing on the street. He had a baby blanket wrapped around his head as though Lawrence of Arabia and wore wide-framed sunglasses. He moved slightly with the rhythm of the music as though unfamiliar with the lyrics as his wife rocked the stroller slightly. Tiny fists punched and legs kicked with better rhythm to the music than Eric was managing.

Chris moved closer. "Hey, Eric, how are you?"

Eric jumped, then recovered and smiled at her. He peered at her through the dark glasses. He spoke quickly as his wife stared. "Detective Miller." He squinted at the name tag. "Chris, this is my wife, Robin, and daughter Erin." He pointed his can of Miller Lite in the direction of his wife. To Robin, he said, "She's on Jack's case."

Robin Blackstone appeared to be several years younger than her husband but twice as socially adept. She immediately extended her hand. "So nice to meet you."

Chris nodded.

"Why don't you get me another wine cooler, honey, and take Erin with you? It's too hot out here for her. You've had enough beer, by the way." She watched her husband walk away. "Men are so useless unless you tell them every little thing to do."

Chris looked around, her wacko radar sounding loudly in her head. "So what do you do, Robin?"

"I'm strictly a stay-at-home mom. I didn't mind giving up working in advertising at all. After a year, I was fed up with the gopher job I was stuck in. At least it wasn't as fake as what Eric has to put up with." She caught his eye and motioned him to keep moving past the beer tub.

Chris studied the young woman. Robin was shorter than Chris and at least four dress sizes larger. She wore the latest uneven hairstyle hanging across her cheeks that Chris had no idea the name of. Chris also suspected that Robin's jet black hair was not her natural color. Robin had not bothered to exercise off the weight gain of childbearing and had a spare tire more suited to middle age.

"Fake how?" Chris sipped at her soft drink.

"The way the older workers just ride it out to retirement, knowing they can't be fired. The way department heads take the credit for the work of anyone under them." Robin had lost sight of Eric and scanned the faces until she found him. "You need to take her in and change her." She looked at Chris as though surprised the police officer was still standing before her.

"City government…fake…" Chris prompted Robin's train of thought.

"Well, yeah. It's like that downtown award." Robin waved at a neighbor who was clearly more important to her than Chris. "I'll be there in a second."

"How so?"

Robin frowned and closely resembled her fussy daughter. "Eric worked crazy hours to put all of that downtown information together, then turned it in to Jack Sampson for review. The next thing he heard, the city had won the award. Do you think Jack shared with city council that Eric had done the work?"

Chris didn't have a chance to answer.

"Then he worked all those hours in an 'acting' position. You know what that means. They think he can do the work but aren't quite sure they want to give him the job. 'Acting' means they can pay him a portion of the actual raise he should be earning and have him do all the work without the real title or status of the position. They can also watch for any applicants they'd rather have in the job. It sucks."

"But didn't it also give Eric a chance to try the job and make sure he really wanted to be a director?" Chris asked. To hear Molly tell it, a director's job was no prize.

"Oh, he wanted it. He has to make that kind of money so I don't have to go back to work. The five percent 'acting' bonus barely covered the new suits he bought. Two years in the director's job here would have had us ready to pull out equity and move on to a bigger city and a higher paying job. But Jack set him up to blow his chance. Now he's being moved back into his old job and we're stuck until we start over somewhere else."

Chris thought it sounded like the use of the royal we. "It sounds as though you have his career all planned out for him."

"I have to. He has no ambition other than to drink and watch sports. His job barely got me into the Junior League. I really want to become involved with the Young Republicans. I've been trying different churches to see which has the best social contacts for us. Too many of the churches around here are too homo tolerant." She shivered. "I won't have that around Erin. One man and one woman is the way life is meant to be. That woman who worked with Eric is one. I keep telling him not to have anything to do with her. Those women are too mannish and overbearing."

"Did you ever meet Molly Hamilton?" Chris's grip of the aluminum can tightened.

"Of course not. I don't want to be around any of those people. The city ought to fire her, not suspend her until the trial is over. She's made it to pretrial, she's guilty. Why doesn't she just give it up and admit she killed Jack? I read the newspaper."

"That's funny because most workers at city hall seem to think Molly's the one who should have had Jack's job and that she carried your husband until Eric stabbed her in the back." Chris leaned closer. "She also happens to be my girlfriend."

Eric had made the circuit of the neighbors and changed Erin's diaper and outfit. He stood beside his wife, listening. "Isn't she something?" He grinned and hugged Robin as he asked the question.

"She certainly is." Chris smiled. Living with Robin would drive Chris to tune out the rest of the world, too. She studied Eric, watching for how genuine he was and wishing she could see his eyes better. She had the feeling that Robin and Eric used each other equally. Eric needed a wife and child to fit the white-collar mold; Robin needed direct deposit. What a twisted way to live. Chris thought that the two deserved each other and felt sorry for the baby.

"I'll be back in a minute." Robin hurried off to the neighbor she had just waved at.

Chris looked at Eric. "Are you doing okay with Jack and Molly both gone?"

"Special project management is the perfect job for me." He eased a can of beer out of Erin's stroller pouch. "I can set my own pace and find grants and awards to go after."

Chris nodded. "Molly believed in you."

Eric took a long drink. "I liked batting clean-up for her."

"How was your relationship with Jack Sampson?"

"He hired me to be his deputy but wanted everyone to get used to me before he put me in a new position." Eric made it sound so simple and matter-of-fact. "He also set me up to fail, just for the entertainment of it."

"So you pretty much carried Jack's workload as a way of earning a promotion, then got shafted?" Chris remembered how upset Molly had been with Eric's air of effortless entitlement.

Eric slid his glasses halfway down his nose. "It's only a temporary setback. I'll make myself indispensable to the new director, then move up again. I'm a natural born leader."

Chris watched Eric's eyes. He truly believed he was capable of the director's job and that he was a hard worker. "No hard feelings about Jack?"

"None worth mentioning." Eric looked over his shoulder toward the food being served. "He taught me a lesson I needed to know and will use in the future when I hire support staff." Eric flashed an empty smile.

Chris caught herself again wondering how Molly had survived as long as she had.

CHAPTER FORTY-FOUR

Chris eased through the side door of the auditorium. This was one of the *related* duties of her job that she truly enjoyed—the D.A.R.E. program. The community was so into the program to prevent drug abuse and violence that special workshops had been organized in the summer to bring together staff and parents from all of the city's schools to brainstorm new programs for student involvement. Chris wholeheartedly agreed with the concept of police officers having face time with kids and parents. If they didn't reach out to kids, the community was lost; if parents didn't buy into the programs, there was no point in trying to recruit the kids. She had actually enjoyed the eighty hours of training.

Chris arrived just in time to vote in favor of a welcome back dance in September at the middle schools that were already involved with the D.A.R.E. after-school dance program. Thank goodness they found professional dance instructors willing to donate their time instead of the officers trying to teach the kids; of course, a comedy workshop might not be a bad idea. Discussion began about activities at the elementary schools.

Chris glanced about the room. She was impressed to see all the other officers who worked with the program present. As much as they all grumbled about being overworked and stressed out, they knew how important this was. Besides, the kids' take on things made spending time with them worth it. Chris thought of it as her reality check.

Chris stood along the side wall rather than disturb half a row to find an empty seat. Why was it no one ever left an aisle seat vacant? It was her fault for being late; she shouldn't have answered her phone that last time.

"Psst, Chris," the voice carried the whisper only a short distance.

Chris looked around and saw a head of frosted curls—Donna Brooks.

Donna pointed to the empty seat beside her. Chris only had to apologize to four people as she sidled past them.

Donna leaned over once Chris was settled in the narrow seat. "This is my husband, Tim."

Tim grinned at her. He was dressed in work clothes—matching dark blue pants and shirt lightly dusted with drywall compound with a wide belt holding his cell phone and knife cases. A baseball cap was balanced on his knee. "I wouldn't miss this for anything."

"Isn't this incredible? All the schools have come together instead of making a rivalry out of it." Donna shook her head.

"Absolutely. Your boys have been through the program?" Chris asked. She knew about Tim Jr. and Zachery from her case file.

"Just the K-4 Visitation," Donna said.

"We bought them T-shirts and they know it means to say 'no' to any pills or look out for each other around groups of boys," Tim said. "They can't wait to sign up for the dance program. My boys dancing." Tim rolled his eyes.

"Mr. Two-Left-Feet, No-Rhythm, *All-White* Real Man." Donna elbowed him good-naturedly.

Chris smiled. She could see the attraction between the two, clearly friends, as well as lovers, and completely comfortable with each other.

"How are things at work?" Chris asked Donna.

"Better without Jack, empty without Molly. They'll never find someone as good as she was. That damn Jack. And Eric keeps his original job." Donna made no attempt to hide her hatred. Tim squeezed her hand. "He knows about my spying and Jack. We're working our way through it." She nodded toward Tim. "I'm so worried about Molly."

"Molly is too honest," Tim said.

"You both sound as though you think Molly is guilty and gone for good," Chris said.

Donna leaned back and raised her eyebrows. She lowered her voice so that only Chris could hear her. "Molly carried a heavy load. Even as much as we finally talked—about what I did with Jack years ago, about Project Hugger, and about Eric being our *acting boss*—she wouldn't discuss it. Molly has something deep inside her that no one can help her with, as all of us do. If I have learned one thing in this life, it's that nothing is more important than family, whatever form family takes. I'll do whatever I have to in order to protect mine. Molly is no different. If Jack pushed her over the edge, and I said if, it was over family, not work." Donna reached for Tim's hand. "I don't back down when it comes to all three of my boys, whatever it takes to keep us together."

"Molly's not backing down, either," Chris said. "She's made the pretrial officer work for her background information. She wouldn't discuss past relationships or her family in Michigan. I hope it's to her advantage to have a bench trial."

"A judge decides?" Donna asked.

Chris nodded. "Molly refused a jury, said they'd be too easily swayed by an attorney's theatrics. She knows she's innocent and she's counting on the judge seeing it that way also."

Tim finally spoke. "Sometimes you have to do what you have to do."

Chris had more than she wanted to think about as she turned away from the couple as her chief came to the podium.

"In closing, and on behalf of the department, I'd like to recognize the parents who joined us on nightly walks through our worst neighborhoods, putting the drug dealers and gangs on notice of our zero tolerance when it comes to the community's children."

Chris was amazed as the seemingly innocuous parents stood one by one. Chris had been on a few of the walks; her department rotated participation. There had been incidents of shots fired in the air and bottles thrown from buildings—these had been no casual evening strolls.

Donna stood when her name was called. She raised her arms and cheered with the others as the audience clapped for them—the parents with the determination to actually do something about a bad situation.

CHAPTER FORTY-FIVE

It never failed to freak Chris out that she had to go to the outpatient cancer center at the hospital for her breast sonogram. She had been through the scare of a cyst found in breasts deemed "large and dense" during her mammogram two years earlier. She didn't know whether to be flattered or worried; it depended on how she was using her breasts. Chris chuckled, realizing her silliness was her equivalent of whistling past the graveyard. This was her second year of having an uneventful sonogram that she was relieved and thankful for after what she had seen Ruth go through.

"Detective Miller." A man called to her from across the lobby.

Chris turned and looked to the opposite side of the outpatient waiting room and saw Campbell Chamberlain. She winced as she watched the effort it took for him to rise from the chair. He hobbled across the room and extended his hand.

"All is well with you?" he asked.

Chris sensed that he was genuine. "Yes, just an annual screening that always makes me hold my breath."

He nodded and touched a spot on his cheek. "A small skin cancer."

"Coffee or soda?" Chris nodded toward the machines in the corner.

"I've accumulated a pocketful of change. Help me get rid of some of it before I go home. My wife hates hearing me walk around the house jingling." He smiled.

Chris understood why this man had meant so much to Molly—a calm reassurance generated from him. It was as though it went unspoken that since Campbell handled everything life dealt him, he could help others also.

They stood before the vending machines. Chris opted for a ginger ale enhanced with green tea. She didn't know if she believed all the benefits listed on the can but figured she couldn't go wrong with no caffeine and the redeeming ingredient of tea. Chris smiled as Campbell selected a classic Coke.

"My dad wouldn't drink anything but those, either," she said, pointing to the familiar red and white can.

"It's the only sugar I consume—keeps me from snacking. Also helps keep my stomach settled." He shrugged.

They turned and went to the large plate glass windows that overlooked a small garden.

"How are you doing, having to manage utilities and community development?" Chris asked.

Campbell frowned. "Tolerable. I don't intend to do but so good of a job or council will make it permanent." He cut his eyes at Chris. "I hate the way Molly and I left things."

"Do you blame her?" Chris concentrated on the light taste of the drink.

Campbell turned to her, clearly puzzled.

"You gave her up to Jack because of me," Chris said softly.

It was as though Campbell saw the sun rise in the west. "Is that what she thinks?"

"She overheard the conversation between you and Jack when Jack outed her."

Campbell shook his head. "She misunderstood."

Chris was perplexed. "She heard Jack tell you about us, then she heard you agree to pull her from a critical project because you were disappointed in her. How could you let her sexuality make any difference to you? Molly adored you. She counted on you to survive the rest that goes on in city hall."

"Are you done?" Campbell asked.

"For the moment." Chris mentally slapped herself for crossing the line and allowing this to become a personal conversation.

"I didn't care about Molly's proclivities away from work. That's always been the beauty of our relationship. We keep ourselves focused on work and don't let *feelings* clutter it up. Neither of us is any good with emotions. I first liked working with Molly because she didn't come into the office crying half the time, she came to work. She's like me in that respect. We have to stay focused on work to keep all the rest at bay."

"But that day…"

"I was disgusted that Jack had found leverage and was calling in that card. Molly deserved so much better. I didn't know if the others on executive staff and council were ready to know about her. Tom and I were so close to having Jack out of city hall and being able to give Molly the job she had earned."

"Why didn't you let her in on what was being set up?" Chris asked. "She thought she was the one being betrayed. She thought all the white-collar males had turned on her."

Campbell drained the can. "Jack was a bastard to everyone. He didn't deserve to breathe the same air as Molly. I looked in his eyes and knew what he was going to do with the photograph of you and Molly. He was finally going to be able to ruin her in the community. It was up to me to stop him." Campbell crushed the can and looked at the mangled aluminum in amazement. "I didn't know I could still do that."

"So your strength surprises you sometimes?" Chris asked.

"It's always a pleasant surprise when anything on me works as it's supposed to," Campbell said.

"Tell me again where you were the night that Jack Sampson died."

Campbell studied Chris; Chris had the distinct feeling she was no match for this man.

"I was driving alone on the Blue Ridge Parkway. I wanted to see if the fish were jumping."

"No gas or meal receipts?" Chris asked.

"I don't keep receipts and there's nowhere open on the parkway that early in the spring."

"No one else saw you?"

"It's the parkway. Maybe a few deer saw me pass."

"How do you feel about Molly now?" Chris didn't know where that question came from.

Campbell didn't hesitate. "I respect her more than anyone else I know. I've never witnessed a keener mind. I hope she puts the next few years behind her and starts fresh somewhere."

"So you think her guilty?" Chris felt oddly disappointed.

"I shouldn't have allowed her to be the final solution to Jack. There was more Jack was trying to tell me that day—something about

Molly's family that he had discovered. I cut him off." He looked at the angle of the sun. "I need to get back to the office." He started to walk away. "I'm glad you had a good report today." He hesitated. "She'll be in my prayers when the trial starts."

"Every day feels like Halloween, even though it's a week away."

"And it's going to last a long time this year." Campbell raised his hand as he walked away.

Chris watched him. She thought of his military training and the action he had experienced in Vietnam. Jack Sampson had been a fool to think he could manipulate Campbell Chamberlain, and Eric had better hope a new community development director was hired. He would not advance working for Campbell.

CHAPTER FORTY-SIX

Chris frowned at her cell phone as though a harsh look would silence the ringing. She really didn't want to talk to anyone. Thanksgiving was a week away, and she didn't feel particularly thankful this year.

"No message means no obligation to call anyone back," Chris said to Dolly. The cat was lying on Chris's lower legs and kneading the afghan Chris had pulled over her when she stretched out on her bed. "I refuse to look at the missed call list."

Dolly closed her eyes and settled on her haunches for a nap.

Five minutes later, the cell phone rang again.

"Goddamn it." Chris snatched the phone off the bedside table. It was 5:30. She had come home long enough to catch a nap before going back to the office to work uninterrupted through the night. She intended to pull the file on Jack Sampson and go through it one more time now that it had been several weeks since she had looked at the crime scene information.

"Yes!" Chris barked into the cell phone. She didn't recognize the number; it wasn't one of her saved contacts.

"I can't believe it actually happened." A woman spoke between sobs.

Chris closed her eyes. "Who is this?"

"It's Donna Brooks. I just watched the early evening news."

"You thought she was guilty!" Chris rubbed Dolly's head to reassure her after forgetting how sensitive the cat was to tone of voice.

"But I didn't think she would be convicted of voluntary manslaughter. She can't be punished for this. It will ruin her life and career. It wasn't her fault." Donna was near hysterics.

"I'm not hearing anything new here, Donna." Chris eased Dolly onto the bed, piling the afghan around her in a nest. "I don't have time for this."

"Why wasn't the truth enough? Why didn't Molly's attorney convince the judge to dismiss the charges?"

Chris stood and gathered her shoes and sweater from the floor. "Donna, it doesn't work that way. Molly admitted all along to a struggle and leaving Jack hurt in his office. What she said she left and what we found didn't reconcile. We failed for not finding all of the evidence. We needed the murder weapon and never found it. We never identified the trace evidence found around the impact site of the blunt force trauma." Chris felt close to tears.

"I should have done it. I was the spy—for Jack and Tom. I sold out to get my job and benefits back. I traded Jack sex with me years ago. I finally told Tim. If Jack hadn't already been dead, Tim would've killed him—my mild-mannered, henpecked husband. I should be the one in jail," Donna said.

"Should've, could've, would've." Chris remembered the refrain her father used about needing excuses. "I can't help you make peace with all that."

"You don't understand." Donna's voice dropped. "Molly could take anything Jack dished out. I used to tease her about always being so calm, at least on the surface. She didn't allow him to get to her. She'd spout off like the rest of us afterward, but he didn't get to her until just before he died."

"That much is obvious," Chris said as she pulled her sweater over her head.

"Damn it, you're not listening to me!"

Chris sat on the edge of the mattress. "You have my full attention for the next five minutes before I go back to work."

"Jack found out something early this year, something that had to do with Michigan and Molly's childhood, something that Molly never talked to me about, something that finally rattled her. How much about that time in Molly's life do you know?"

"I know that Molly's parents split when she was little, not that unheard of in the eighties. Molly's mother died. Molly reconciled with her father. I know that was a struggle for her." Chris stared at the far wall as she concentrated.

"But what details did she ever tell you?"

"Not many." Chris frowned. She hated that Donna was beginning to make sense.

"There's more you're not saying."

"Molly had nightmares about her childhood that she would never explain. She always said she didn't remember much when I woke her up." Chris fought the doubt creeping into her consciousness.

"But?" Donna pushed Chris.

"But the way she would cry out scared the shit out of me because of the terror in her voice."

There was more that Chris wouldn't say aloud. There was Molly's easy understanding about spending last Christmas separately, which Chris later realized equated to Molly's reluctance for Chris to meet her family. Molly had claimed it was because it made no sense for Chris to use all of her vacation leave for such a long trip. Molly wanted Chris to wait and meet Syd and Jimmy when they came for a summer visit.

"Thanks, Donna." Chris's voice dripped with sarcasm as she pressed the end button.

Dolly rubbed against Chris's back as though nudging her toward the door.

"I get it," Chris said. "I have to know, don't I? I know Molly's innocent, but I also have to know the rest." Chris looked at Dolly. "There was no way Jack could have caused her to kill him."

Dolly stared without blinking.

Chris went into her home office and booted her computer.

CHAPTER FORTY-SEVEN

Chris had stared out the small window of the airplane until her neck hurt. She gritted her teeth and held her breath as the wheels bumped down onto the runway's thick layers of asphalt and concrete.

She had packed light, filling one small duffel as a carry-on, preferring not to check a bag. She thanked the man who had sat next to her and respected her silence throughout the flight, yet took her bag down from the overhead compartment for her.

Chris slipped the long strap over her head. She had never managed a shoulder bag even when it had been no more than a purse.

Chris followed the deplaning line. It felt good to walk after five hours of travel, including a layover in Chicago. Once inside the terminal of Capital Region International Airport, she glanced at the sign boards of what Lansing, Michigan, had to offer. The blonde in the bikini promising a nonstop flight to Cancun was tempting.

The blond woman waving to Chris from the café was equally attractive. Chris had a flashback to Ruth, her first lover and partner who happened to be a decade older than Chris. "Syd?"

The woman hugged her. "Welcome to Michigan, sweetie." She motioned Chris to a table in the corner.

Strangely enough, Chris was tired enough to welcome sitting again. She had left Virginia mid-morning, and it was now mid-afternoon, already a long day factoring in how early she arrived at her home airport. The days prior to her taking a long weekend to travel had been packed. More like them waited for her when she returned to work and played catch-up. Vacation days always seemed that way—time off at a price.

"Thank you for driving in to meet me," Chris said.

Syd glanced down at her hands. "Thank you for understanding why we shouldn't have this conversation at my home." She sighed and brushed her hair back from her face. "How is Molly?"

"I haven't seen her in a month. She became tired of my lectures and asked me to wait to see her again after the trial was over."

"Jimmy is pitching a fit to go to Virginia. Ham just won't discuss any of it." Syd reached for her glass of beer. "May I get you one of these?"

"Please." Chris eased out of her jacket as Syd went to the bar. "Thank you." Chris welcomed the beer, not caring what brand it was.

"There's no sense beating about the bush, is there?" Syd asked.

Chris shook her head. "Molly's parents split when she was a kid. Her mom died. Molly reconciled with her father. What am I missing?"

"And you think Jack Sampson found out something that set Molly off?" Syd referred to the first telephone call she had from Chris.

"If—and I'm still saying a remote *if*—Molly killed him, it had to be to protect something or someone very dear to her."

Syd nodded. "That can be only one person—Helen."

Chris waited.

"Molly should have explained this to you." Syd looked away. "I'm sorry. I just couldn't do this over the telephone. I had to look into your eyes first."

Chris reached across the table for Syd's hand. "I understand. I wouldn't have pushed you to talk to me if I had any other choice. I'm beating myself up for having doubts about Molly and trying hard not to accept that the system has failed Molly."

Tears came to Syd's eyes. "There are records of Helen's hospital stays and Ham's jail time."

"The two are related?"

Syd nodded. She took a deep breath. "Molly's parents were never married. Ham drank and smoked as hard as he worked. He hit Helen and couldn't remember afterward what set him off or what he had done, except to know that when he awoke in jail, Helen was in a hospital room and Molly in foster care. It happened three times. Ham walked out on them so he wouldn't do it again. Helen never wanted it known that Molly was illegitimate. Helen was born in 1940. In her mind, a single woman raising a child was still a big taboo. She died from lung cancer when she was fifty-five and never touched a cigarette other than to clean up behind Ham's smoking. I met Ham after he had bached it for a year and stopped drinking. He only tried to strike me once and I put him in the hospital. After that, he was a model husband and father. He's so ashamed of what he did to his first family that he barely tolerates the sight of Molly."

Chris processed all of this carefully. "Why did Molly ever want to see him again?"

Syd drained her glass before she spoke. She waved the waitress away. "Molly told me that she promised herself to come back to Michigan once a year to visit Helen's grave. She heard about Jimmy and wanted to make sure Ham wasn't doing to us what he did to them. She hadn't seen her father in fifteen years when she met him for the first time as an adult when he was sixty years old."

"He never hit Molly?"

Syd shook her head. "No, but it was worse for her being a witness to what he did to her mother, then taken from her home until Helen was well."

It all made sense to Chris. Whatever caused that final confrontation between Molly and Jack Sampson was triggered by what Molly experienced as a child. "You have to explain this to Molly's attorney. The judge found her guilty but is still deliberating her sentence. This would at least give mitigating circumstances, regardless whether the verdict is right or wrong." The pain of saying this showed on Chris's face.

Syd took a deep breath. "What makes you think I haven't already?"

Chris felt her eyebrows shoot upward.

"Molly will never forgive me." Tears ran down Syd's cheeks. "Molly refuses to let any of this be brought up and discredit all her mother did to protect her. She told her attorney that her innocence would prove itself. She will not allow any hint of this to go on record."

Chris was stunned. "That's crazy."

"That's Molly, and it's her choice." Syd stood to leave. "You won't change her mind. I've tried for seven months. Accept that she is going to prison and decide if you can wait for her." Syd kissed Chris's cheek and was gone.

Chris had little detailed memory of the hotel she had booked or her return flight.

Chris was at Gibson Frost's offices when the security guard made morning rounds unlocking the doors from the parking deck to the elevator lobbies. She sat on the carpeted concrete outside of the entrance to the suite and waited. Gibson was among the first group to emerge from the elevator. Chris stood to greet him. He gave her one long encompassing glance.

"You went to Michigan?" he asked as he shook her hand.

Chris nodded, then followed him to his office. He closed the door behind her.

"I take it you talked to Sydney Hamilton." Gibson settled into his executive chair and leaned back.

Chris nodded again.

"Molly gave me two instructions when we started this case—she would tell the truth, and she would not allow her past to be used as any kind of argument because it had no bearing."

"And you agreed?" Chris sat on the edge of the side chair.

"I agreed and so must you. Molly will not destroy her mother's reputation on the off-chance it might lessen her sentence. She relied on police investigation and forensics to support her testimony and free her."

"So I failed her." Chris hung her head as she walked to the door of Gibson's office. "Do you think Molly killed Jack accidentally?"

"No. Her only hope is for you to find who came in that office after her." Gibson walked across his office and opened the door for Chris. "I'll help you any way that I'm able, but according to what is on record now, she is guilty and will be sentenced to a prison term."

Chris had never felt so focused in her life—Molly's future depended on her.

CHAPTER FORTY-EIGHT

Chris tried to remember how many times since she became a member of the detective unit that her boss had asked her for a *ride*. She didn't need more than one hand to count on. She knew what this meant—there was a need for a strong, off-the-record conversation. Chris sighed.

"So how's everything going?" Ray asked.

Chris glanced toward the passenger seat. "Okay."

Ray Oulds nodded.

"How's everything going with you?" Chris knew they had to play the game of professional conversation—stilted because it was forced, not their usual updates or jokes in passing.

"Not bad." Ray rolled the window down. "I'm tired of heated air. Can you believe it's in the upper fifties in January?"

"I know what you mean." Chris opened her window also. "We've had just enough winter to complain about it. Of course, our guys can always find something to complain about."

Ray barked a laugh. He filled more than his half of the front of the car, spilling over toward Chris unintentionally. Chris would not want to come up against him in a brawl; she knew all the training in the world would make her no match for the sheer bulk of the man.

"Are you okay with the sentencing?" Ray's tone was too casual.

"As okay as I can be," Chris said. "Six years is a long time to be in limbo with your life. The verdict is what I'm struggling with."

"Why don't you take some time off? I know this case has been hard on you. Take a few days to do what you need to for Molly. Do something for yourself besides a quick trip to Michigan." He stuck his elbow out the window.

"Can we really discuss this case now that we've been excused by the judge?" Chris glanced at Ray.

"Sure."

Chris sighed. "A very small part of me can see Jack pushing Molly's buttons enough for her to strike him a blow hard enough to kill but not the carnage that was in that office. That was someone hitting a man after he was down. Molly would have helped Jack up, given him a defensive weapon, then hit him again."

Ray nodded. "I hear what you're saying."

"I just don't buy that Molly was capable of killing someone, even Jack, and walking away leaving a body to be found. She wouldn't have done that to the custodians." Chris signaled a turn.

Ray chuckled.

Chris continued. "It could be any one of four or five people as best I can tell."

"What's really bothering you?" Ray corrected the steering wheel before they hit the curb.

"Sorry." Chris kept her eyes forward and tightened her grip of the wheel. "Molly would throw herself in the way of violence but not cause it. I've failed her, the system has failed her."

Ray pointed. He was directing her driving, making a circuit of the downtown area and outlying subdivisions where he made a point of showing himself daily. "I almost kept you off the case."

"Really?"

"Yeah. I saw the photograph that made the rounds of the guys. Did I ever tell you that I met Molly not too long after she came to work for the city? She's a straight arrow, you know what I mean."

"I do."

"I knew when I met her that she didn't have much use for men. You can just tell sometimes, you know?"

"Yeah."

"Then to have to work with that bunch in city hall. When you have a strong sense of ethics, I don't know that that's the best place to be even without a Jack Sampson."

"You knew him?"

"I knew he was a piece of shit." Ray didn't say it vindictively, just matter-of-fact.

"Cap, you amaze me."

"Ain't I something?" He said it so dryly that Chris had to laugh. "Miller, it's none of my business who you sleep with. I thought you and Molly a good match. I knew you had to be involved in the investigation, no matter how it turned out. I also knew I could count on you to do your job."

"This investigation is killing me," Chris finally admitted.

"Sucks digging into the details of people you know, doesn't it?"

"Hell, yes."

Ray drummed his fingers on the dash. "I want to be upfront with you. I left you on this case because you had an inside track to city hall. I knew I could count on you to put personal feelings aside." He leaned out the window and pointed to his head as they passed a bicyclist with no helmet. "You're going to stay on this investigation, aren't you?"

Chris debated her response, but she had to go with instinct and duty. "Yes, sir, with or without your sanction."

Ray turned his head stiffly and studied her. "I figured as much."

She understood what he needed to hear. "Active cases absolutely come first, but when I have the opportunity, I'm staying on city hall. The hard part, Cap, is that I like those women. I can identify with them easily enough since I worked there a while when I finished college. I need to find out the truth about Sampson's death to be with the woman I want in the rest of my life. We've missed something."

Ray waved to his counterpart as they drove through the women's college campus. "Let's head back downtown."

Chris took the next day off. It was time to pick up the last of Molly's things since she was no longer suspended but terminated from her job. Like Molly, her career played a huge part in Chris's self-esteem and sense of purpose. Chris honestly did not understand people who were lackadaisical about their work—it was something a good forty years of your life would be spent doing, so it damn well better be work you were passionate about. She mentally climbed down from her soapbox and brought herself back into focus about city hall as she entered the building.

She rode up in the creaking elevator and thought back to her first encounter with a very different Molly. Could that really have been almost a year and a half ago? Chris could not imagine weeks without Molly, much less years, and that shocked her. She jumped slightly as the elevator door clunked open.

Chris listened as she opened the glass door leading into the administrative offices. Sometimes the dying end of a conversation was very revealing. All she heard were file cabinet drawers being opened and closed.

Chris turned the corner and almost walked into a woman who always tried not to be seen—Sharon Rogers. "Good morning."

Sharon nodded. "Hello, they're all in a meeting."

"When aren't they?" Chris grinned.

"Isn't that the truth?" Sharon rolled her eyes. "People think managing council's and Barbara's and Tom's schedules aren't enough to keep someone busy."

Chris shook her head. "Mind if I walk through? I'm still processing what happened on the far side of the building."

"Tom told us that the police have access to everything and anyone here. We're to help. I don't see that that has changed."

"Thanks, Sharon." Chris started to walk away. "Did you ever work for Jack Sampson?"

Sharon quickly shook her head. "No, thank goodness. I wasn't pretty enough for him." She didn't make it sound negative as far as she was concerned. Sharon purposely wore drab clothing as her own style of camouflage. Her shoulder-length hair had not changed style since high school twenty years ago. "I like being comfortable rather than showy."

"I heard that," Chris said. "Thanks again. I won't be here long."

Sharon returned to her filing.

"Comfortable is an understatement," a voice said wryly from the second admin cubicle.

Chris couldn't contain a chuckle.

Susan stepped around the end of her desk and looked at Chris appraisingly. "Still trying to figure out which one of us bashed old Jack's head in despite what the judge came back with?"

Chris stopped and slid her hands in her trousers pockets. She understood why Molly liked Susan and why Spencer loved her. What was not to like or love—trim body, good makeup, great taste in clothes, and a sharp mind. "Let's just say I'm trying to make peace with the first homicide case that has directly affected my life."

Susan leaned against the partition wall and eased one foot out of its shoe. "It's a damn shame the judge couldn't just say Jack got what he deserved and leave alone the poor soul who did us all a favor."

Chris faked a shiver. "That's cold."

"Maybe, but Jack was awful to everyone here in varying degrees. If there was a good project, he had a scheme attached to it. If there was a decent person, he didn't rest until he had some angle figured out to control them. If there was an attractive woman who wanted to make a trade, he took her up on it and never let her forget. My guess is that he pushed the wrong person too hard at the right moment."

"But not you?"

Susan held her hands up. "Shit, I've never been able to hide anything. He made a move on me once and I hit him hard enough for him to want to call his mama. He left me alone after that. Sheer reflex. I had brothers."

Chris laughed. "I'd like to have witnessed that."

"More should have done the same. I hate it when women don't have enough self-esteem to take up for themselves." Susan slid her foot back into her shoe.

"See you later."

"Do yourself a favor, Chris, accept that this situation sucked big-time and concentrate on being there for Molly. Call Spencer. You two need to talk. We'll get Molly through this." Susan squeezed Chris's arm, then disappeared into her cube. Her voice carried. "Nancy's in the executive staff meeting as the scribe. Before you ask, she dealt with Jack because of Campbell but wasn't important enough to be on Jack's radar." Susan said it as a matter of fact with no trace of vindictiveness.

Chris approached the ninety-degree turn in the hallway. She glanced in the corner office. Frankie and Rusty were elbow to elbow with a thick pile of spreadsheets. They both looked up when she stopped in the doorway.

"Interrupt us, please." Rusty said with a grin.

"Amen." Frankie leaned back and stretched.

"Number crunching?" Chris blinked at the matching hot pink tie and sport jacket worn by Rusty. So much for somber winter colors.

"Always," Frankie said. "If we commit to one more big project, you'll be locking us up in jail for fraudulent use of city funds."

Chris raised her eyebrows.

Rusty held his left hand palm up. "Revenue from taxes and fees." He held up his right hand. "Pie in the sky projects and routine expenses." He juggled both hands, never bringing them in balance.

"New projects sound so good. They're the sexy expenditures. Maintenance and service costs are too humdrum to interest anyone, but the city would be up the proverbial creek if not mindful of them,"

Frankie explained.

"I don't envy your jobs at all," Chris said.

"No one does, that's why they leave us alone most of the time," Rusty said.

"Except when they need funding pulled out of the air to make the sexy projects work and themselves look like heroes?" Chris asked.

"Bingo. Give the lady a cigar," Rusty said. "You catch on quickly."

Chris nodded toward the back corner office that had belonged to Jack Sampson. "Any ideas about what really happened?"

Rusty deadpanned. "We do work in the haunted area of the building."

Frankie rolled her eyes.

"I'm not demeaning anyone, but those custodians are never going to come back here to clean." Rusty was mildly defensive.

Frankie explained. "The late-night guys have complained about a ghost on the second floor for several years. They never see anything, but they hear someone moving about. Before you go there, neither of us was here the night Jack was killed."

"Someone driving by would have heard us celebrating if we had been," Rusty said.

Frankie smacked his arm. "We were bored out of our minds at a conference in Williamsburg. I have the receipts to prove it."

"It rained the entire three days, nothing to do but stay inside and listen to the same war stories we hear every time a group of CPAs gathers." Rusty's tone was as dismal as the weather had been. "It could have been someone from outside waiting for all of us to leave the building. It could have been the ghost scaring Jack enough to trip and fall, hitting his head just the right way." Rusty popped the heel of his hand against his temple.

"Yeah, that should have been Molly's defense—the city hall ghost did it. Sorry to interrupt." Chris continued along the hall, passing Campbell's office on her right and Nancy's cube on her left. She heard a strange noise farther along the hallway—a rhythmic thumping.

Chris looked in the next office on her right belonging to Eric. He had thumb tacked a small basketball hoop several feet above a large recycling container. Files were open on his desk. Chris watched as he glanced at a document, balled it up, and tossed it toward the hoop.

He looked over at Chris. "Ah, Molly's *friend*. Of course, everyone is Molly's friend." He tossed another paper.

"How about you? Are you Molly's friend?" Chris leaned against the door casing.

"I was once." He held his hands palm to palm, then spread his arms. "But our paths diverged."

"Paperwork is a bitch, huh?" Chris looked at his desk deliberately.

"Only when you're trying to remove any trace of being here since it seems I contributed nothing. I'm sure you've already heard them whispering about me. I'm being demoted to my old job, if I care to stay, which means I shouldn't." He slid his palms along the sides of his head, smoothing his gelled hair. "Big *if* to wrestle with."

"Do you have another job lined up?"

"Prospects and a helluva reference if I agree to leave quietly and soon. That's the way government works."

"So you'll end up with a promotion somewhere else if you leave here before you're bumped down?" Chris didn't attempt not to sound bitter.

"Oh, yeah. Ain't it cool?" He flashed a chilling smile at her.

Chris backed away. "Good luck. Let us know where you relocate to, just in case."

"You bet. Don't want any dark clouds following me." He tossed another paper.

Donna leaned against her partition. "Next."

Chris turned and studied the woman—there was a definite challenge in her stance and eyes.

"Still think Molly's innocent? It must be nice to have that kind of relationship." Donna smiled with no humor in her eyes. "Oh, and thanks for all your help the night I called you when Molly was convicted."

Chris shook her head. "I don't know what to think about anyone anymore."

"We're a fairly easy read. Susan is the brains behind Barbara and Tom and most people know it. She also thinks Molly could do no wrong even if she killed Jack because Jack was a waste of skin."

"I never heard that one before, but it's appropriate." Chris inclined her head toward Campbell's office. "What about him?"

Donna's expression became guarded as she thought about

Campbell. "Some people think he's gruff or mean, but his mind is just always on something. He stays focused so as not to be caught up in his own pain. He doesn't pay attention to the petty things like most of us. A John Wayne type, you know? He's seen combat and barely survived. He deals with a horrible illness and barely survives. He quietly handles almost anything."

"Almost?"

Donna thought about her response. "He's God and country through and through. Openly accepting that Molly is a lesbian wasn't easy for him. He knew, but he didn't want to admit he knew. How crazy is that? Molly thought Campbell walked on water. It's all so goddamned unfair. Molly has a long six years ahead of her. So do you. I put all her books and papers together." Donna pointed to a hand truck with three neatly stacked paper boxes just to the side of Eric's door. "I was the one who cleaned out Molly and Jack's offices."

"Lucky you," Chris said.

"It amazes me the way the vultures descend as soon as it's known someone isn't coming back to an office. All the small stuff disappears," Donna said.

Chris picked up on Donna's innuendo. "What doesn't fit the pattern?"

"That damn downtown revitalization trophy. I still haven't seen whose office it's been appropriated for. Must be on one of the council member's mantels."

"I'll keep an eye out." Chris backed the cart away from the wall and started along the hallway. She glanced into the GIS room. Tamika looked up. She and Angela were shoulder to shoulder, whispering, Tamika seated, Angela on one knee.

"How's our girl doing?" Angela asked.

"She's waiting to be transferred to Goochland. I've already filled in the visitor application," Chris said.

"Don't let Molly push you away." Angela straightened up. "She needs you now more than ever. She's going to need all of us to get through the next few years. Windy's already figured out a visitation schedule for us to rotate through."

Tamika elbowed Angela.

Chris studied the women. "So you've just accepted that Molly did it and are planning visits?"

Tamika answered quickly. "I'm thinking about going back to

school for my master's."

"City government work is not quite as pleasant as you expected?" Chris asked.

"Only if you have the right boss," Angela said. "I lucked out with Windy. Who knows what the next CD director will be like. There are too many Jacks out there."

Tamika surprised herself with the bitterness in her voice. "This place is a snake pit and you know it. The ones like Molly and Windy try and are beaten down. The ones like Eric keep floating to the top."

"And the ones like Jack?" Chris asked.

"Finally get what they deserve if you can survive long enough to wait for it to happen." Angela's voice was barely audible. "I tried to tell Tamika that before she used her connection to Barbara to back up her interview."

Tamika's phone rang.

Chris glanced at her watch. "Go ahead. I need to move my car, don't want to get a ticket."

"See you." Tamika reached for the phone.

"No doubt," Chris said.

"I'll walk with you." Angela fell into step with Chris.

They stopped at Molly's former office. The work surfaces were empty.

"I don't think Tom has the heart to hire anyone right away," Angela said. "I'm betting our next engineer won't be a woman."

Chris longed for the smile and silly giggle she remembered from her first meeting with Molly. She glanced at Angela. "How bad was it, really? Could Jack have pushed Molly to murder?"

Angela didn't hesitate to answer. "He was a monster always on the prowl for a woman he could intimidate. If he wasn't after sex, he was after power. I don't know which took a greater toll. He left me alone because of Windy. Check how many women left jobs here, yet wouldn't really explain why in their exit interviews. Molly was on the trail of that. She was determined to take Jack out, but she made the mistake of thinking she could do it aboveboard."

"Did he abuse Molly?"

"The worst way possible. He messed with that terrific mind of hers." Angela squeezed Chris's hand. "Hell, I've been saying all along that any of us could have killed Jack. Molly just happened to be the last one in the room not to get out in time."

Chris left the building feeling ill at ease. Retracing Molly's workday just left nagging doubts in her about everyone. How many of the people she had just spoken with were better off with Jack dead? All of them. Who would be willing to push the baby stroller out of the path of a runaway bus? Molly.

CHAPTER FORTY-NINE

Molly actually smiled as she shelved the books in the library. She had forgotten how much she loved to read. She enjoyed working the desk and checking out books, learning the other women through their author preferences. She looked up, recognizing the purposeful footsteps along the aisle. "Morning, ma'am."

"Good morning, Molly. Busy as usual, I see." The warden made rounds as she entered the building, making her way to her office. She was in her late fifties, dressed in a crisp business suit, and ruled the facility as tightly as her hair was curled.

"Yes, ma'am."

"The consultants will be here at 2:00. You'll join us?"

"Yes, ma'am."

The warden continued. "Morning, Ingrid. You're behind already this morning." She was in the hallway by the end of her admonishment.

"Suck-up," a voice whispered from the next aisle as the other inmate worked the carpet sweeper toward the front desk.

"You bet," Molly said.

Ingrid chuckled.

In the month that Molly had been on *campus*—that analogy still cracked her up—she had signed up for every class available just for the classroom atmosphere whether on site or online. She had even volunteered for an apprenticeship as a carpenter's helper and looked forward to it with the coming warm weather. She thought of all the bad jokes and B movies about women in prison and hated to admit that the Virginia Correctional Center for Women in Goochland had recentered her.

Molly's emotions had run the full gamut. She had been

shocked upon arrival, in denial the first days, and struggled between claustrophobia and panic with the realization that prison was her new reality. She had what her mother would have called a Jesus talk with herself, forcing herself to see the light. Molly knew her choices were limited—fight the routine with everything in her and make herself miserable or adapt and make the best of an incredibly bad situation. She chose the latter.

Molly was content for the first time in a long while. She stayed busy and worked at anything she was assigned to but felt no pressure to be the best or to constantly prove herself. The VCCW readily accepted her volunteered services as a civil engineer on the open setting that blended with the surrounding community; the prison's wastewater treatment plant served the locals. Goochland reminded her of being at church camp as much as anything with grace said before family-style meals and activities to fill the day.

Molly returned to her bunk in the dorm. She opened her locker to hang up her sweater and allowed her gaze to trail down the row of photographs—Chris hiking, Windy and Dolly snuggled on the sofa under an afghan, Angela and Tamika raising glasses at dinner, Gary's softball team, and Donna wearing a hardhat at her new job as construction estimator. Everyone had stayed in touch and was supportive. Molly had begun seeing a counselor weekly and finally accepted help with her memories.

She reread the last letter from her father. He had helped her with the trial costs, wiping out his savings and ignoring Molly's promises to pay him back. Most of his letter went on about his latest fascination with the nesting habits of the black squirrels around the house. He wrote that Jimmy was finally settling down and marrying his girlfriend from high school. Molly marveled at the postscript from Syd—a blot of deep red lipstick and spot of her perfume at the bottom of the page.

Molly opened the letter on her bunk that she had saved for morning break—a note written in Chris's neat block printing. *"Will see you this weekend and bring a money order for the next batch of books you want to order. It won't be as long as it's been. Soon, sweetie. Love, Chris. P.S. Any chance of making this a conjugal visit?"*

Molly returned to the library, whistling.

Chris saw Molly as soon as she entered the common room used

by all visitors. Chris waved. Molly smiled. They stared across the table at each other like two lovesick schoolgirls.

"About damn time you *let* me come to see you," Chris said.

"I wanted to be settled. It took two months to get here and the past weeks to fit in. It's hard enough thinking about you, much less seeing you come in and leave without me," Molly whispered. "I've got peeps." She winked.

Chris nodded. "I get it. I was just impatient to make sure you're okay. Do you need anything? I brought the money order."

"A computer geek who knows security systems." Molly grinned. "I'm surprisingly okay. All the mail helps."

"I need to talk to you about something I did."

Molly sighed. "What's her name?"

Chris tried to kick Molly under the table. "Funny. It does involve another woman, though—Syd."

Molly stopped smiling.

"I went to see her before your sentencing."

"Chris, it is what it is. Accept it as I have…almost."

"I know what Jack resurrected. I know about your parents. I know what you must have seen as a child."

Molly stared down at her hands. She was very calm when she looked up. "I'm glad you know. I couldn't discuss it. Syd knows more than anyone else."

"Syd feels badly about talking to Gibson Frost, but she was only trying to help with your case."

Molly's face tightened slightly. "I know. I can't fault Syd for loving my father and me."

"You're really okay?"

"For the most part. I know who to avoid here. I don't wake up in a blind panic every night." Molly took a deep breath. "I've had plenty of time to think about the past ten months of my life, and I haven't tried to hang myself with my pants yet."

"Be serious."

Molly shrugged. "I'm a looped recording. I didn't kill Jack. I'm starting to feel like what's the point of saying it anymore. Everyone here jokes about being innocent."

Chris slammed her fist on the table, then held her hands up in apology to the guards. "Sorry." She hissed at Molly. "Don't you dare give up. I haven't."

"Calm down. It's not like any of this is going to change." Molly glanced about.

"Walk me through that night, and tell me everything this time."

Molly's eyes closed as she nodded.

"You're standing in Jack's office," Chris said. She knew the crime scene photos by heart—sofa on the left wall with coffee table before it, desk in the far right corner, conference table and chairs in the near right corner, bookcase beside the door, and wide windowsills as a continuous catch-all.

"We all avoided being alone with Jack in his office unless we absolutely had to." Molly's face was pale.

"As best we reconstructed, you went in to meet with Jack and sat on the sofa while he was at his desk. He left his desk and approached the sofa, there was a struggle, and Jack's head impacted with the corner of the coffee table."

"That's right," Molly said quietly, opening her eyes.

Chris pointed. "What happened to the award that set on Jack's windowsill?"

Molly blinked. "What?"

"The initial blow to Jack was a simple bump to the back of his head from the corner of the coffee table causing a goose egg, easily an accident. The blows that followed were from a blunt object—maybe that damn trophy. Repeated blows that caused a skull fracture and bleeding within the brain. According to Donna, the trophy's missing." Chris waited.

Molly closed her eyes, re-creating the scene. "I remember seeing the trophy on the windowsill as I looked at Jack on the floor bitching about bumping his head." She took a deep breath. "He confronted me about being a lesbian and about playing everyone in the office to like me. He told me I'd never work locally again. He couldn't wait to tell everyone about my parents. He wanted to dominate me, mentally and physically. He *touched* me. I pushed him away. He fell backward, losing his balance and hitting his head on the coffee table as he sat on the floor. He was so pissed. I looked at that damn trophy and almost picked it up, but I couldn't do it."

"Hot damn!" Chris said.

Molly was still in Jack's office on the night of his death. "Put yourself in our place, the women of the office. Every time we moved, we felt his eyes on us checking us out. Every conversation we walked up on, we knew the insinuations Jack had been making. Every time one of us wore something as simple as a skirt, we felt his eyes studying the shape of our legs and trying to position himself in meetings to see as far up as he could. Just walk down the hall in front of him and you could feel his eyes burning into your butt. Put all of that together and it was a constant, malevolent action of chipping away at our self-esteem because we wanted our jobs. He was never quite blatant enough to be caught. Every damn one of us in this office will tell you the same. It was different for the men. They endured his comments as locker room talk, but it affected them also, repulsed most of them. Ask them. Jack always had some bit of trash to talk and some item of blackmail to hold over every one of us he needed to control. It's like the projects he gave us to work on. He always withheld at least one or two pieces of critical information so we couldn't quite do the work that was needed. He could finish something up and take the credit as the boss needed by all the underlings not quite smart enough to do it all themselves."

Molly had to stop for a moment. "I managed all those years to fend him off. When he threatened to reveal what Ham did to Mom and me, I lost reason. Students still remember Mom for how she helped them. I thought no one knew that there wasn't a marriage and divorce between my parents." Molly was exasperated by the uncomprehending look on Chris's face. "Being an unwed mother was a big deal to Mom. What was important to her was important to me. I wouldn't have that come back on my mom's reputation."

"You're sure you didn't pick the trophy up, hit him, and walk out with it?" Chris managed to ask.

"He said pretty much what I just repeated. Then he landed two hard punches when I tried to get away." Molly's voice broke. "I have spent my adult life following my mother's example of denying that my father beat her. The dreams are so bad. I see Ham hitting her over and over. Jack's threats sent me back to being eight years old." Molly rested her forehead on her hands for a moment, then looked up at Chris. "I shoved Jack, but I didn't kill him. Chris, he was sitting on the floor threatening me and I walked out. All I was worried about at home that night was how soon he was going to fire me. I left Jack Sampson alive."

The miniscule doubt Chris had allowed burned out in her mind.

CHAPTER FIFTY

Chris had tried her best to find someone to run this errand for her. She just didn't have the time or inclination to go to city hall but no such luck.

"Goddamn people who work downtown and come out every two hours to move their cars, taking the on-street parking." She heard the stories from the two retired uniform cops who ran parking enforcement. Her favorite was the woman who tried to hide the chalk mark on her tire with lipstick, then actually applied same to her lips to deny what she had done.

Chris bit the bullet and pulled into an hourly lot and surrendered a dollar out of her own pocket for the convenience. She tucked her chin and concentrated on walking to the building without making eye contact with anyone.

"Focus on getting the damn map and back to your office, or you're going to screw up the case tomorrow," Chris mumbled to herself as she approached the double doors into the building. She had found that talking to herself usually cleared a path for her anywhere she went. She scurried out of the elevator and headed toward the map room. "Ray is going to fire my ass if I mess up one more testimony because I've been concentrating on Jack Sampson, and it would serve me right. Unemployment would give me more time to free Molly, though." Chris grinned to herself.

"Detective Miller, what a surprise." Eric stood in the aisle between the flat drafting table and the plat cabinets lining the wall. He raised himself by placing his hands on the surfaces and straightening his arms, then swung his body like a pendulum. "How may I help you?"

Chris stopped in the doorway and stared. Who in the hell was this punk in a suit and what had he done with the normally morose Eric? "I need a map for an exhibit in court tomorrow. I called yesterday and talked to Mark. He was to have it ready for me to pick up. I have foam board at the office."

Eric jumped while on a back swing and landed near the back of the room. He snapped his fingers and went to a pile of rolled drawings on the old wooden desk before the windows. He read the sticky notes held in place by rubber bands. "Mark did as promised." Eric picked up the three-foot-long roll. He swung the paper like a bat, stopped mid-swing, flipped the map end over end, and handed it to Chris. "I'm guessing there's no charge."

Chris couldn't stop staring. What was up with Eric that was making the hair on her neck stand on end? "Seems silly to take funds from one city pot for another." Chris shrugged. "What's with you working in the map room?"

He grinned until Chris felt her face ache. "We're taking turns covering walk-ins during lunch hour to give Mark a break, also lets us cross-train. It's all part of our new director's plan to flatten management." He mimicked a horizontal plane with his flattened hand.

"You decided to stay?" Chris couldn't stop herself from asking questions, even though she had a solid five hours of work waiting on her desk before she could clock out.

"I didn't receive a good enough offer to make it worth my while to relocate. It's also a crappy time to try to sell a house. I'm back where I started. I just love do-overs. I have another award pending for the city. It's such fun generating those creative numbers, and I'm so good at it."

"I bet." Chris felt as though she wanted to run from the room screaming. What was wrong with her?

"How's Molly?" Eric was suddenly concerned and sympathetic.

"Good. She's already made herself indispensable to the warden. Once a nerd engineer, always a nerd engineer." Chris managed to smile.

"I might have known. Be sure to tell her I thought about her when I helped our new director screen city engineer applicants. I made sure the top three candidates had site development experience."

"I'll tell her."

Eric stepped closer and lowered his voice. "You have to love this place. All we need is a solid prospect that a team of us schmooze into relocating here, turnover of council members, and Barbara's takeover from Tom. Jack Sampson will be forgotten. I may make deputy director again before I leave here." He nodded to reassure both of them.

"I'm glad for you and your family." Chris struggled to find a positive comment other than "you're crazy as hell."

"Work has actually been fun lately. Everyone finally stopped tiptoeing around how Molly left. We're finally blaming her for any mistake like you always do with the last one to leave a job. My screw-ups are all but forgotten." Eric stuck his hands in his pockets and rocked in place. "But I stick up for Molly. I bat cleanup just like always. It's all in knowing how to lay in wait for your moment and go in for the kill." He mimed swinging a bat again, sans roll of plans, then hit downward repeatedly. He locked eyes with her as though challenging her.

Chris felt as though all the breath had left her body at once. She knew she was staring. She also knew who killed Jack Sampson. She backed toward the double doors of the office. "Thanks again, Eric."

"Don't be a stranger." Eric smiled and waved.

CHAPTER FIFTY-ONE

Chris walked along the hallway not really seeing where she was going other than focusing on getting out of the building. Her professional detachment was blown. She had just looked into the eyes of a killer, and she could not tip her hand that she knew.

She pushed the employee door open into the hallway. She was almost at the elevator. She needed fresh air. She wished she could call Molly.

"Do you mind?" Windy's tone was clearly pissed off.

Chris looked down. She carried the drawing under her arm like a battering ram. She had just jabbed Windy in the side of the head.

Windy ran her fingers through her short hair. "It takes me hours to come up with this just-out-of-the-shower-and-air-dried look. It isn't easy being a natural beauty." She looked at Chris, waiting for a laugh. "What's the matter?"

Chris pointed to Angela's door.

Windy rotated the chair and headed back where she had just come from. "I guess I can wait to go to the restroom."

"I think it's already too late for me." Chris smiled feebly.

"I'll repeat my question." Windy closed the door to the hall behind her. She caught Angela's eye. "What in the hell is the matter with you?"

"How could none of us have picked up on this before?" Chris asked herself.

"Keep going." Windy directed Chris toward her office. "You too." She nodded to Angela. They closed the inner door. Chris and Angela sat on the sofa as Windy took her usual place behind her desk.

"One more time, Chris. What's the matter?" Windy asked gently.

"I'll need proof. I'll follow him. I won't tell Ray until I know for sure." Chris thought out loud.

"Girl, talk to us before she explodes." Angela placed her hand on Chris's arm and pointed to Windy with her other hand.

Windy rocked slightly back and forth in her chair, not a good sign.

Chris looked at the two women as though noticing they were in the room with her for the first time. "If he knows that I know, he'll disappear."

"Chris!" Windy clapped her hands.

"Sorry." Chris briefly closed her eyes. "I just came in to pick up a map. Eric was filling in for Mark in the map room."

"Eric killed Jack." Angela jumped ahead of Chris.

Chris nodded.

"Molly always took up for him. The rest of us thought he was an empty suit," Windy said.

"It makes a lot more sense than Molly killing Jack." Angela released Chris's arm. "Sorry, you probably have bits of my nail polish in your flesh."

"We looked at him briefly and accepted his alibi that he was at home and let it go at that," Chris said.

"Based on Robin?" Windy asked.

"Oh, boy." Angela rolled her eyes.

Windy nodded. "She's just as much a freak as he is. I've always felt sorry for that child. She's a doll baby."

"Molly always made excuses for him," Chris said.

"None of us thought he had gumption enough to do any real work, then we found out he was up Jack's butt the whole time." Windy shivered.

"Then Jack shafted Eric to lessen the trouble he got them into over leaking that announcement." Angela followed Windy's lead.

"What tipped you?" Windy asked Chris.

Chris thought carefully. "He taunted me. He mentioned Molly. He swung this like a bat." She held up the plans. "I could just see him doing it. Does that make any sense at all?"

"To us," Angela said, "because we know Molly and Eric. To anyone else, I doubt it."

"The key here is, can you prove he did it?" Windy asked.

Chris gritted her jaw. She looked at Windy and nodded.

CHAPTER FIFTY-TWO

Chris had shadowed Eric for a solid month, juggling what she ought to be doing for her job with what she needed to do for Molly. She used every spare moment to watch him. Chris had come to the conclusion that she didn't know whose life was more pitiful—his or hers.

She pushed against the floorboard to lean the back of the seat toward the rear of the car. She needed to stretch. She felt as though she spent more time in her car than her apartment and likely did. She certainly wasn't sleeping much. Even Molly had noticed the difference in Chris during the previous weekend's visit. Chris had not told Molly what she suspected about Eric, only that she was working extra hours because of her caseload. Molly had little interest in hearing about other criminal cases, so she let Chris off with the easy explanation.

Eric came out of his house looking as though he had just broken into it. He wore heavy black sweats with the hood up, bicycle gloves, and bright white athletic shoes. He trotted around the corner of the house.

Chris looked down at her nylon shorts and T-shirt. "Oh, good, I didn't overdress for tonight." She had stopped at her apartment after pulling the day shift and changed clothes.

Eric popped out of his driveway on a pale blue scooter.

"You've got to be kidding—gangsta meets Barbie." Chris started her car and waited until he was at the end of the street before she pulled out to follow him. "He shouldn't be too difficult to keep up with."

Eric puttered along the edge of the parked cars and turned onto the avenue as though heading downtown. He went four blocks, then turned at a brown and white recreation sign.

Chris glanced up. They were heading for a branch of the bike trail.

Eric had parked the scooter and flipped the brake by the time Chris pulled into a space. She watched him lope out of the parking lot and onto the eight-foot-wide trail. He headed toward the river.

Chris stretched as she locked her car, thankful that it was early enough in the evening for the trail to be fairly crowded; personally, she loved Daylight Saving Time. She matched the pace of Eric's jogging and actually enjoyed the chance to exercise. She almost zoned out enough to miss him darting down a side path.

The main trail was paved and followed the abandoned railroad bed—no grades steeper than three percent. The side paths were narrow and criss-crossed the main trail in a series of switchbacks up and down the undeveloped ravines on either side of the trail. Norfolk Southern in its heyday had established a two hundred-foot-wide right-of-way that remained in virgin timber except for the rail bed in the center.

Chris broke out in a sweat and pumped her arms to keep her legs moving as the path ascended. Her thighs and calves protested. "Dumbass is going to pass out in those heavy sweats." They crossed the paved trail, dodging a group of bicyclists, and headed down again through the woods.

Eric stopped at a cluster of deadfalls. Trail volunteers made it a practice to push downed limbs around rotten stumps to create thickets for wildlife habitats.

Eric rested his foot on a ten-foot-long section of toppled trunk and retied his shoe. Chris watched in fascination as he tenderly patted the bark of the tree before continuing along the path.

"What the hell?" Chris waited until he was around the next bend, referencing the downed tree before she advanced. She glanced ahead to make sure he hadn't doubled back. Always before, he ran at least an hour.

Chris thumped the trunk where he had patted the bark—hollow. She picked her way through the brambles to the base end of the trunk. Chris broke off a short branch before she knelt and looked up the hollow log. She poked with the stick into the dark cavity of decay, ready to jump back if anything moved. Her prodding was mushy until she finally stretched her arm full length while her shoulder was all the way up the trunk. She felt a solid mass.

Chris sat back on her heels and looked into the recess of the hollow. "Shit! Molly, you owe me big-time." She crawled into the stump until she reached the bundle, then backed out, trying to have as little contact with the soggy interior of the tree as possible.

Chris placed the bundle on the ground and used the stick to unwrap a beach towel. She stared at a deformed trophy for downtown revitalization. The cup was partially broken loose from the base, as well as dented and crushed halfway in.

Chris reached for her cell phone. First she called Ray followed by Spencer and Gibson. They would meet at the station and bring Eric in for questioning.

Chris bowed her head, stared at the Jack Sampson murder weapon, and wept.

CHAPTER FIFTY-THREE

Chris went back to her apartment and quickly showered and changed. She then returned to the station. Ray was on his way in with Eric. Eric's attorney would meet him there.

Chris paced her cubicle. She glanced about the bullpen. The usually raucous chatter was silenced. Jackson set a tall Starbucks cup on the corner of her desk, nodded, and walked away. She sipped the coffee, neither needing the caffeine nor wanting to chance a pee break later but grateful to have something to do with her hands.

She heard the murmurs of the boss on the floor. An interview room was set up.

Ray Oulds sat across the table from Eric and his attorney. Chris stood in the front row of the group in the observation room, looking over Ray's shoulder through the one-way glass.

Eric leaned back in his chair, draping one arm over the back, hooking one leg around the chair leg and extending the other. He might as well be watching two baseball teams he wasn't particularly interested in. Eric's attorney, Pete Finerman, looked as though he had come directly from a late golf game, dressed in khakis and polo shirt. Chris caught herself glancing toward the floor at Pete's shoes—New Balance, no spikes.

Ray placed a photograph of the trophy as Chris had unwrapped it on the table. He waited as Eric studied it.

"So?" Eric looked up past Ray and stared into the window.

Ray tapped the photograph with a pencil. "We've already matched your fingerprints. The rest of the lab work will be done tomorrow." Ray glanced at the clock on the wall. "Today, rather."

"It was her, wasn't it?" Eric asked. "Detective Miller?" He squinted at the glass. "The lesbian cop."

Ray did not respond.

Eric nodded. He looked about the room, showing no emotion. "She'd do anything to get her girlfriend out of prison." He pumped his hips. "Well, almost anything."

He looked as though Ray had been waiting for him outside of his shower. His skin glowed from the run, his hair was long and trying to curl without the layers of gel holding it slicked in place as usual. He wore a white T-shirt and faded blue jeans with rips in the knees.

"My client," Pete began.

"Has nothing to say. I plead the Fifth," Eric said. He crossed his arms and remained silent for the duration of the initial questioning.

Eric watched at Ray as Pete stopped scribbling notes. He waited patiently for the next attempt to get him to talk.

Ray spoke toward the video camera on the tripod in the corner of the room. "Ending the interview with Eric Blackstone regarding Jack Sampson on May 29, 2006, at 2:45 a.m."

"Damn," Eric said. "Memorial Day. I'm missing a paid holiday from work."

Chris stared.

Eric was placed under arrest, booked, and charged with first-degree murder. Two months after Eric's arrest, Pete Finerman represented Eric at the pretrial investigation. Eric entered the room with a buzz cut, sallow skin, and an assortment of bruises and abrasions. The officer assigned to Eric began the drill of background discovery. Eric was ready to talk.

"I should have thrown that trophy away," Eric said to no one in particular. "But I was sentimental about the first project Jack screwed me over on."

"Eric," Pete warned him.

"I worked so hard for that damn trophy. At least I finally got some good out of it." Eric ran his hand over his head as though tousling phantom hair. "Jack was confused that night, about me being in city hall so late. He had no idea I usually went back several nights a week to check what everyone was really working on. Robin never knew the difference when I was in the basement watching television or when I had slipped out. I wouldn't have missed seeing Molly finally deck Jack for anything. It gave me the perfect way to get even with both of them." Eric might have been rambling about sports statistics from his tone.

Pete looked on in horror as he was unable to silence his client. The night in Jack's office unfolded as Eric spoke.

Jack Sampson was confused. He was in city hall. It was dark outside the windows that dominated two walls of his corner office. He was on the terrazzo floor on his hands and knees. His comb-over was out of kilter. He looked up toward the sofa. "You hit me." His memory was slow to return. He reached for the very coffee table in front of the sofa that his head had grazed as he fell reeling backward earlier when he argued with Molly. "You ungrateful little son of a bitch." He touched his head and stared in wonder at the hand that came away red.

"Stay down," Eric challenged him.

"By damn, do you think you're going to get away with this? My head hurts like hell. I'll have you charged with assault." His hands bore down on the end of the table as he struggled to push himself upright. The forty pounds of excess weight he carried didn't help. "I'm not done with you myself yet, though." He finally stood, swaying slightly and blinking his eyes.

Jack's eyes froze wide open as he watched Eric calmly swing the downtown revitalization trophy in a wide arc that connected with Jack's shoulder when he tried to turn away. The cup of the trophy crumpled.

"I guess you think that's yours more than mine." Jack took a tentative step forward and blinked to control his vertigo.

The trophy was swung in another wide arc that impacted the heavy base against Jack's temple, opening the closed head wound and causing blood to gush down Jack's neck.

Jack glanced at the red spot growing in size on his dress shirt, tried to speak, and fell facedown on the floor, making no effort to soften his landing.

Eric dropped the trophy to the floor and stared. "Home run."

Jack didn't flinch when prodded. The pool of blood around his head spread across the terrazzo, settling into the slight wear lines around the bits of stone.

"That's going to be a bitch to clean." Eric knelt and studied his boss. Jack had lost consciousness. Eric was fascinated to watch as Jack's breathing and respiration stopped.

It was quiet in city hall that late at night. The desktop computers had been logged out of or had gone into hibernation after several hours of no activity. The telephone lines were silent; it was too late even for messages coming in to voice mail. There was no background rumble of the elevator's equipment raising and lowering its cab or the sounding of its bell each time the door opened or closed. A few of the overhead lights remained on floorwide, wired to a separate circuit for security lighting.

Eric removed the handkerchief from Jack's back trousers pocket and felt for a pulse, finding none.

"The cleaning guys will find you." Eric grinned. He enjoyed scaring them. Sometimes instead of staying late to pilfer offices, Eric came in early and played his own version of tag with the men.

The custodial crew came through each night around 4:00 a.m., emptying trashcans and vacuuming the floors. The men worked third shift in pairs to keep each other honest and awake. They were repeatedly told not to touch anything on the desks to protect themselves from accusations of theft or damage.

"I can be home and showered for a 9:00 program to watch with Robin." Eric closed his eyes and compartmentalized his thoughts. He covered his hand with his sleeve and swept everything off of Jack's desk. They had already rearranged most of the furniture. He flipped off the light switch and locked the door to Jack's office. His shoe heels clicked against the tile floor as he hurried from the department, the last employee to leave. City hall was deserted.

Eric was tried and convicted of first-degree murder and sentenced to better than three times Molly's term.

EPILOGUE

Molly leaned against the front door as soon as she was safely inside with the door closed behind her. She didn't turn the deadbolt; she was safe.

Dolly came midway down the stairs and stopped to look at her.

"Hey, girl, I've missed you." Molly walked to the steps.

Dolly leaned forward to butt heads with Molly.

"There's no place like home, sweet Dolly." Tears ran down Molly's face. She gazed about her little house. She had been so happy here and taken it for granted—never again. "I can't believe it was only two years ago that I moved in here."

Chris walked out of the kitchen. "How expensive would it be to have central air put in?" She fanned her tank top, flashing her breasts at Molly.

"I kind of like you not wearing many clothes." Molly wiped her face with her hands. "I can't believe you carried the payments."

"That's what happens when you give someone your power of attorney. The mortgage company didn't care whose money it was. It was just one less foreclosure for them to deal with. Hell, it was easier than putting everything in storage. Now you have to let me move in as co-owner."

"You don't want a bigger, newer house?" Molly sat on the tread of the steps below Dolly, her legs no longer able to support her. Dolly rubbed back and forth against her, purring as though to tell her it was all okay.

"Are you kidding? This is huge after my apartment. Besides, I want to keep us close." Chris grinned. "Want me to leave you two alone?" Chris stopped at the bottom of the stairs.

Molly stared, still not quite believing that she was free. Tom had already called and offered her a job. She'd have to think about that. She didn't have to think about Chris. "Absolutely not. How soon can you move in?"

"All it takes is a U-Haul."

Molly stood and hugged Chris as though she would never let her go. "And a second date."

About the author

Mary Jane Russell is a native Virginian—the sixth generation to be raised on the family farm. She recently retired from local government after thirty-one years of service, during which she set a series of firsts—first female draftsman, staff engineer, project manager, and first female director of economic development.

Her lifelong love has been books and reading; her dream since a teenager was to be a published writer. This made her second career an easy choice. She is encouraged by her Cardigan Corgi, Winnie, and ignored by her cats. She lives with her partner in Roanoke, Virginia, and is discovering the joys of being an honorary grandmother.

She is also the author of *The Arcanum of Beth* from Intaglio Publications.

You may also enjoy...

**The Arcanum of Beth
by Mary Jane Russell**
ISBN: 978-1-935216-01-8
Price: $16.95

Beth Candler's life is good. She finally realizes there is more to living than working all her waking hours as an accountant. She finds a new love, Louise Stephens, and moves into a home in the country. The death of Beth's mother brings her brother and sister-in-law back into her life. Beth has it all, and her sister-in-law wants it. Lou is only too willing to oblige. When Beth dies in a tragic accident, her best friend Janet Evans takes charge.

**Of Course It's Murder
by Kate Sweeney**
ISBN: 978-1-935216-11-7
Price: $16.95

Kate Ryan is sent to New England on a photo assignment. Seems her editor's ex-cousin, the hapless flamboyant Simon Merriweather needs photos of his new Inn for the local travel guide. It was to be a nice quiet week of reflection for Kate. What could go wrong?

Enter Kit Parker, Emily Masterson and Rebecca Townsend. Newport, Rhode Island's old, very old money... The irresistibly delightful elderly friends of Simon arrive for the grand opening. All hell breaks loose one stormy night and what happens?

Of course... It's murder!

Echo's Crusade
by JM Dragon
ISBN: 978-1-935216-02-5
Price: $16.95

Echo Radar is outgoing and happy, working as an advertising executive in a reputable firm with a bright future for promotion. Karen Thompson, from a poor unstable background, works at the same advertising firm as Echo. Where Echo prefers a relaxing environment in her free time, Karen helps others through the Greystoke Project, which caters to the very people she had once been—destitute and down on her luck.

Two women form a bond and look forward to the prospect of a romantic relationship when the disturbing events of a Thanksgiving holiday bring the walls tumbling down around them.

Echo is now on a quest, and with the help of Detective Roan Keating, searching for justice becomes *Echo's crusade*.

Picking Up The Pace
by Kimberly LaFontaine
ISBN: 1-933113-41-3
Price: $16.95

Who would have thought a 25-year-old budding journalist could stumble across a story worth dying for in quiet Fort Worth, Texas? Angie Mitchell certainly doesn't and neither do her bosses. While following an investigative lead for the Tribune, she heads into the seediest part of the city to discover why homeless people are showing up dead with no suspects for the police to chase.

Her reporting yields a front-page story and a bloody lip—going undercover is not exactly encouraged of rookie writers. But she is quickly thrust into a world of breaking news and police politics, hate mail, and death threats. Angie can only hope that her reporting will aid police in putting dangerous men behind bars before they harm those she's trying to help.

You can purchase other Intaglio Publications books online at www.bellabooks.com or at your local bookstore.

Published by
Intaglio Publications
Walker, La.

Visit us on the web
www.intagliopub.com